CW01511471

PAST REDEMPTION

PAST REDEMPTION

David Mark

SEVERN
HOUSE

First world edition published in Great Britain and the USA in 2024
by Severn House, an imprint of Canongate Books Ltd,
14 High Street, Edinburgh EH1 1TE.

severnhouse.com

British Library Cataloguing-in-Publication Data
A CIP catalogue record for this title is available from the British Library.

ISBN-13: 978-1-4483-1201-6 (cased)
ISBN-13: 978-1-4483-1202-3 (e-book)

All Severn House titles are printed on acid-free paper.

MIX
Paper | Supporting
responsible forestry
FSC
www.fsc.org   FSC® C013056

Typeset by Palimpsest Book Production Ltd.,
Falkirk, Stirlingshire, Scotland.
Printed and bound in Great Britain by
TJ Books, Padstow, Cornwall.

Praise for the DS McAvoy novels

"An irresistibly charming detective cracks another colorful case"
Kirkus Reviews on *The Burning Time*

"An involving, nail-biting police procedural from a masterful
storyteller"
Kirkus Reviews on *Flesh and Blood*

"[Delivers] the kind of grisly torture and murder scenes that have
rightly linked his work with that of Val McDermid"
Booklist on *Blind Justice*

"Polished prose, lovable recurring characters, and a stunning
revelation make this a mystery to savor"
Kirkus Reviews Starred Review of *Past Life*

"A fine police procedural . . . Ian Rankin fans will be pleased"
Publishers Weekly on *Past Life*

"[Mark is] on the level of Scottish and English contemporaries
such as Denise Mina, Val McDermid, and Peter Robinson"
Library Journal Starred Review of *Cruel Mercy*

"To call Mark's novels police procedurals is like calling the
Mona Lisa a pretty painting"
Kirkus Reviews Starred Review of *Cruel Mercy*

About the author

David Mark spent seven years as crime reporter for the *Yorkshire Post* and now writes full-time. A former Richard & Judy pick, and a *Sunday Times* bestseller, he is the author of the DS Aector McAvoy series and a number of standalone thrillers. He lives in Northumberland with his family.

www.davidmarkwriter.co.uk

For Eli and Arte, again.

'And I – my head oppressed by horror – said:
"Master, what is it that I hear? Who are
those people so defeated by their pain?"
And he to me: "This miserable way
is taken by the sorry souls of those
who lived without disgrace and without praise.
They now commingle with the coward angels,
the company of those who were not rebels
nor faithful to their God, but stood apart.
The heavens, that their beauty not be lessened,
have cast them out, nor will deep Hell receive them –
even the wicked cannot glory in them."'

— *Dante Alighieri, Inferno*

PROLOGUE

Thirteen years ago . . .

The man – the thing – lurches. Writhes. There's a clank of chains: the tearing of flesh.

'. . . please . . . sstoppp . . .'

The plea is all froth and mucus: viscose, gloopy – speech bubbles popping in a skillet.

'. . . wrong man . . . wouldn't . . . never harm a child . . .'

Pain twists the sounds into squawks; rattling, half-choked sobs. The man – the thing – gags upon the sibilant 'sss': a hanged serpent suspended from a tree. It drifts into the black, greasy air. Fills this unholy place, with its reek of seared meat. Of burnt fur. There's a fizzing metallic taste to the air: static and ash.

'I'm not . . . not what you think . . .'

The reply, when it comes, is almost tender.

'Look. Taste. Breathe. This is what awaits you. This is your Eternity.'

At his ear, gentle: 'This day was always going to come.'

There's a moment of clarity – a fresh burst of adrenaline that clears his head like a snort of smelling salts. For an instant, he sees himself. Sees himself dangling in the dark: a spider wrapped in twist upon twist of tight, biting thread. Sees himself inverted: hog-tied, suspended in a darkness thick as blood. He twists against his bonds: a primal instinct.

Bleeds. Weeps. *Seeps.*

'Name them,' comes the voice. 'Name your sins.'

The man coils again: an escapologist strait-jacketed beneath a burning rope. Upon the dripping walls, mouths leer and drip in an orgy of voyeuristic delight. From below, the scorching kiss of rising fire.

'There can be no Heaven. Not for you. But you can still choose your Hell. There is suffering so much worse than this. There are eternities beyond comprehension. They wait for you. Wait now, beyond the flame. Name them. Tell me where to find them.'

His head is full of blood. He can't feel his lower half any more. At his wrists, a sensation of familiarity: the gristle of entrails, tied in knots. He thinks of Loki. Of Sisyphus. Prometheus. Of Brutus. Chewed to mulch and acid in the belly of the Great Beast.

'Unburden yourself. There can be no deceptions here.'

A sensation at his belly. The touch of soft feathers. The sound of shrieking gulls. Then he feels himself being opened up. Feels the bird's beak and talons rip into his sinful flesh.

'Name them, and this can come to an end.'

He shrieks. Twists. A shoulder dislocates then pops back into place. Blood drips into the stagnant water below.

'This will begin again tomorrow. That which I take will grow back. And tomorrow, it will feed again.'

'Please . . .' he begs. 'I'll tell . . . I'll tell . . .'

Something disturbs the water. A light flares. For the briefest moment, he sees Hell below. Sees the small, black space where he dangles and writhes. There are loving frescoes moving upon the shimmering walls: monstrous things sliding into and over one another, a grotesque tableau of beaks and claws and curving talons. Smells burning flesh. Feathers. Sees his own reflection on the black bile of the stinking water. Sees himself. Knows himself.

His name is Decland Parfitt. He has slaked his appetites in ways for which there can be no redemption.

A fist within his guts now. His mind fills with pictures of white feathers stained red. He gasps, bloody-lipped, stitches tearing, as he feels itself being disentangled. Feels his innards spill like a bag of snakes. Hears viscera slip-slap into the dark water as his nostrils fill with the reek of scorched iron, burnt resin: cooked flesh.

'Say their names. Say what you did.'

A burning sensation at his cheek: a blade moving deftly over the greasy, porcine fat. He feels pieces of himself being cut away. Hears the shrieks from the creatures that swirl, ravenous, in the filth of his mind.

He starts to speak.

'Good,' whispers the voice at his ear. 'Free yourself. Empty yourself . . .'

The fist in his guts twists again. There's the sound of flapping wings. A sudden desperate banging: metal upon metal, fists upon wood.

He feels himself come apart. Gulps down a breath of methane. Ethanol. Flame . . .

And then he is burning. The room fills with liquid fire. The dank nothingness beneath him becomes a river of flame, reaching upwards like the souls of the damned. He wriggles. Squeals, as the fire wraps itself around him like a burning shroud.

There's a moment when he watches the frescoes dance in the flickering light of his own burning flesh. He sees red eyes and hooked claws; monsters of feather and fur. Sees the doorway – a little rectangle of garish light. Sees the outline of an intruder. A woman. Small. Dark. For an instant, he believes in salvation. Believes that the Holy Mother has come to Hell to intercede. He does not deserve this. Nobody deserves this.

'Put it down. Put it fucking down!'

He knows the voice. Knows the woman who wades through the burning lake and rips at the sodden material about his burning flesh.

He feels his bonds burn through. Smells burnt offal. Rotten eggs.

Feels himself falling. Falling and rising, his world inverted: blood and inhuman utterances sloshing out of his ears and nose and mouth.

He hears a scream that is not his own. Hears huge feathered wings beating against the walls. He opens an eye, and watches the angel burn.

And then there is only the darkness, and the pain, as Hell reaches up to claim one of its own.

'Lizard King' Caged Over Sick Fantasies

By Alison Willison, PA North
03.06.2011

A 'wicked' and 'calculating' paedophile jailed for abusing scores of unconscious girls is to be questioned in connection with several unsolved child abductions.

Decland Parfitt, 49, showed no emotion as the Recorder of Hull, Judge Valerie Dudgeon, jailed the children's entertainer for fourteen years.

Outside court, Detective Chief Superintendent Patricia Pharaoh told reporters that Parfitt was 'pure evil' and would now be grilled over numerous unsolved abductions – including the disappearance of eleven-year-old Carmel Barry, who was snatched from her aunt's caravan at Skipsea in 2010. Her body has never been found.

At Hull Crown Court, Parfitt pleaded guilty to 114 counts of indecent assault, child abduction, and indecency with a child, administering noxious substances and taking indecent photos.

Parfitt, a registered foster carer, ran a mobile petting zoo packed with exotic creatures, and criss-crossed the country visiting schools and holiday parks with his wild birds, arachnids and reptiles. He was known as the Lizard King and wore a clownish safari suit and pith helmet while performing demonstrations with poisonous spiders and snakes.

Parfitt's hearing was repeatedly delayed due to the defendant's ill health. This newspaper understands that Parfitt attempted to take his own life after being questioned in connection with the disappearance of eleven-year-old Carmel Barry from a Skipsea holiday park last March. He appeared in court via video link. Police have refused to confirm or deny rumours of an alleged vigilante attack on Parfitt prior to his arrest.

Although no charges were brought in connection with the

disappearance, evidence uncovered during the investigation revealed Parfitt's sick and twisted fantasies.

The judge ordered Parfitt to sign the Sex Offenders' Register and banned him from working with children for life.

Earlier, the court heard how Parfitt used his two foster daughters as 'bait' to lure children back to his house where they were sedated before being photographed in sickening poses.

The court heard how police discovered nearly 10,000 indecent photos, involving countless victims. On undeveloped rolls another 15,000 images were found, featuring hundreds of girls.

Earlier this week, the court heard how Parfitt gave the girls tablets, which he claimed were vitamins, shortly before they went to bed.

Once unconscious, Parfitt photographed them and placed placards on their bodies with lurid descriptions of how he wanted to kill them. The court heard he painted their necks and faces with red paint to simulate blood and held knives and daggers to their throats. In some of the images, exotic animals were also used as props.

Authorities are conducting a serious case review to examine how Parfitt was approved as a foster parent.

In mitigation, Parfitt's lawyer, Cillian Dodds QC, said there was no evidence that Parfitt had distributed any of the photos to other paedophiles. He also argued that because the children had been drugged during the abuse, most had grown up unaware of what had happened until police showed them the disturbing footage.

In court, a statement from one of his foster children described Parfitt as a 'kind, loving and thoughtful' guardian, who always made her feel safe and loved. She claimed Parfitt was the victim of a conspiracy.

Transcript of voice note, received April 26, 2024, 11.06pm

'. . . it's Trish, like you don't know . . . I saw him again, Aector. Saw that place. Under the ground, in the dark. It wasn't a dream, I swear . . . Please . . . (*Laboured breathing. Laughter.*) Christ, would you listen to me – all snot and shivers. Shouldn't have called this late – I just needed . . . I'm sorry. I'll put the cork back in the bottle. Roisin will be glaring, I'll bet. I'm sorry – I know you're worrying already but . . . bad dream, you're right. Glass of water and bed . . . I can't, Aector. I can't close my eyes. It's like he's just waiting for me with his arms outstretched. The fucking Lizard King. Decland Parfitt. All the evil I've swam through – all the horrors I've seen. He's the one who scared me. I don't like being scared. I don't . . .'

Transcript of voice note received April 26, 2024, 11.51pm

'. . . They're going to let him out, Aector. That thing. That monster! He's only drawing breath because I put the fire out . . . scooped up enough of him for the doctors to stitch him back together. (*Sobs. Laughter.*) They're going to approve his release, Aector. Next parole hearing, he's going to walk. Walk out with a decade's worth of hate and hunger all fizzing around inside him. I can't . . . shit I've spilled it . . .'

Transcript of voice note received April 27, 2024, 00.23am

'It was real. I can't pretend it wasn't. For that moment when I stood in the doorway – watched him dangle there, flesh cut into feathers, burning on the end of a barbed-wire noose . . . It was the walls, Aector. Wriggling. Moving where the light touched them. The stench of it . . . bad eggs and burnt offal and . . . The pictures – like they were alive. Great big collages – dancing demons and devils, and . . . I swear I smelled sulphur, Aector. And I swear there was somebody else there. The person who'd taken him – who did all of those things to him . . . they were in that room with me. (*Pause. Sound of liquid sloshing.*) Had the choice of catching them, or saving Parfitt's life. I put the fire out, and it let him get away, Aector. I don't know which bit I regret more . . . in fact no, fuck that, I know exactly what I regret. I regret not catching that evil bastard before he could do what he did . . . I hope he walks out right into the arms of whoever took him last time. Hope that Virgil . . . that vigilante . . . hope he's waiting. Let them take him right down through the circles . . . make him say what he fecking did . . .'

David Mark

Transcript of voice note received April 27, 2024, 00.25am

'. . . The foster daughters . . . Gaynor. Ruby. What he did . . . what he didn't . . . those little . . . little girls . . . (*inaudible*).

Transcript of voice note received April 27, 2024, 01.14am

'. . . he's the worst fucking person in the world . . .'

PART ONE

ONE

A country road near Cherry Burton, East Yorkshire
Sunday, 22 September, 2024, 11.03pm

' . . . Said you'd be here, and it's me that has to deal with the fall-out, you selfish prick. She just needs to know where she stands. Is that too much to bloody ask?'

Joe can't quite make out the words – not over the screech of the wipers across the dirty glass and the pneumatic hiss of bald tyres on the rutted surface of the darkly sparkling road.

'. . . ducking out . . . just think you can call in sick as a bloody parent!'

Can't see out of the windscreen either. The wipers need replacing, and the rain's hanging in the air like dust. He isn't sure he knows this road. There are trees to his left and a farm somewhere yonder but it's all just dark smudges and blurry lights.

'What emotional cripple are you slithering your way into tonight, Joe? Who's listening to your sob stories and telling you your ex sounds like a cold-hearted bitch? Are they listening? Are they fucking there right now . . .?'

Joe doesn't drink any more. It'll be three years in January since he last allowed the sweet, smoky burn of a half-decent whisky slip down his gullet: each sip a coin tossed into a wishing well. He'd be back on it already if it wasn't for smoking weed. Smoking weed and eating junk and shoveling down daily handfuls of prescription medication. He's been on antidepressants for two decades. Takes antacids and proton pump inhibitors for gastro esophageal reflux. Two different meds for his blood pressure. He can't remember if it's too high or too low, but the doctor had jabbed him with needles and made him bring her twenty-four hours' worth of urine samples, and had seemed quite pleased with the readouts when she finally got the dosage right, so he'll keep taking them just so she's not disappointed in him. He can't handle people being upset. Doesn't like letting people down. Would kill to avoid repercussions. Would gladly commit murder to avoid an uncomfortable confrontation.

'If you'd seen her face when she came out and saw it was me . . . you can't do that to her. You don't get to duck out just because you're having a wobble!'

There's pure contempt in her voice. It's comforting, in its way. Familiar, even. For a moment he can imagine they are still together and he's sitting in his armchair in their living room and she's listing all the ways he's let her down and done things wrong and failed to measure up to her impervious standards of what it takes to be a husband and father and functioning member of society.

'I thought it was best,' he says, gripping the wheel tighter. 'I had a fever. They told me to . . .'

'*They told me to, they told me to,*' she mimics, dripping scorn. 'Christ, Joe, isn't that one of your things? Isn't that what you said over and over – that you don't do what people say? That you deserve special treatment because "you're different"? That there are people who do what they're told and people who forge new paths? I've got it written in my journal. I've underlined it.'

He swallows. Feels tears building up behind his eyes: tightness at his throat. He snatches a glance at the speedometer. He's doing 55mph. He's pretty sure it's a 60 zone but wouldn't be able to swear to it. Can't remember turning down this road, with its procession of tall, spindle-limbed trees and its glimpsed squares of chocolate-dark soil. He thinks he may have driven up here before, back in the early days – back when she was hot for him and never needed much of an opportunity to slip from the front seat into the back. They'd been interrupted by a horse, once: nostrils huffing steam on to the glass. He'd thought that was what he was getting – a life of heat and passion and doing things their own way, and at their own pace. Thought their sweaty couplings would be routinely interrupted by equestrian perverts. He grips the wheel tighter as he remembers – heart clenching as if dropped on a hot skillet. Thinks of *her.* Feels the flood of golden light that always swamps his veins when he pictures the way she used to look at him. His eyes blur. He feels a pain in his gums, in his jawbone, skin fizzing with the sheer agony of being in the fricking wrong again.

He glances up. Listens to the silence. Thinks about speaking and realizes that if he opens his mouth, he'll either cry or throw up. He hears his counsellor's voice, all earnestness and 'sixty-an-hour's worth of forced compassion and profound insight. '*It sounds like you don't like yourself very much, Joe . . .*'

He snatches a look at the black road. Watches the wipers squeak across the dirty glass. There was a vehicle a little way ahead of him back at the roundabout but the driver's put their foot down since passing into the total blackness of the farmlands that quilt this swathe of East Yorkshire. Memories rise. He remembers collecting conkers here with the older kids. Came to collect brambles a year or two ago, he's sure of it. Took them all for hot chocolate afterwards and got pizza on the way home so they wouldn't have to go through the agony of fighting about who was going to eat what at tea-time. She'd dressed the part: fingerless gloves and riding boots, autumn hues and a bobble hat. She'd looked spectacular. She always looks spectacular. Always makes him feel like an arthritic blobfish, bimbling along in the wake of a shimmering mermaid.

'I can come back,' he says. 'Come get her . . .'

'It's nearly midnight! God, are you simple? Either you're well enough or you're not. I don't believe a word of this anyway . . .'

He lets her shout at him, voice bleeding out of the speakers. He glances to his right and locks eyes with his own reflection. Middle-aged. Unremarkable. Short hair, round face: patchy beard, wet eyes. Sees himself and hates himself and wishes that, for just one moment, he could decide whether he's got everything right or everything wrong. He'd thought he was on the right path. Fiancée, step-children; a little smasher of their own; a house with roses around the door; cats and a dog and a car in the drive and him a bantam cock strutting around their village like a gentleman farmer. In every direction he had seen vindication. Seen legitimacy. He must be OK, mustn't he? Must be a half-decent person if he had these emblems around him. No matter the fights. No matter the volleys of savage, targeted abuse. It was worth it for the moments of holding hands and kicking through the leaves and watching the sun setting burgundy and gold above the tree line beyond the river. And then the argument that ended things; the one that wasn't like all those that came before. She didn't love him. Wasn't sure she ever had. He was a non-person. He was a construct. He was a toxic narcissist and a control freak and she couldn't find even a scrap of respect for him. He had to leave. They could be co-parents. They could make it work . . .

'I can't do this,' he says, desperately. He says it every day. Mutters it, between whimpers, as he totters from room to room in the rural granny flat where he's dumped his meagre possessions and where he tries to make good memories with his little girl three nights each week. 'I don't know why this is happening. Don't know what you want . . .'

'I just want you to be where you say you are! Do what you say you'll do!'

He wants to roar down the line. Wants to unleash the beast inside him. She used to say this shit every day. Used to tell him how he'd let her down or failed to measure up every time he forgot an appointment or didn't get round to one of the umpteen items on his daily to-do list. No credit for the stuff he achieved, of course. Not a word of thanks or appreciation for all the good stuff. Just criticism, barbed and brutal, jabbed again and again into the fleshy, vulnerable places that she'd spent years persuading him he was safe to expose. He wishes to Christ he was the person she thinks he is. The lads at the Talking Club all see things his way. God how he misses their company. They were just getting somewhere. Making some progress, in that little bare room above the café. Roscoe had got them seeing things differently. They weren't bad men – just humans, stumbling along. Nobody has their shit together – that had been the message. He'd felt fucking wonderful when he heard it spoken aloud by such an educated, intelligent man. For a while there, he'd felt as though he was starting to feel like he could make this work. And then the club closed. No warning, no message – just locked doors and a bunch of sad-eyed men kicking their heels on the pavement and feeling rejected one more time. They'd gone to the pub, of course. Turned their tears into silly stories. Bitched about their exes and their kids. Found their old grooves. He can't climb out on his own. Can't be better than this.

'I just needed to see her. See you. Breathe her in. Do you know what I'm feeling? I've got a fever. I can't even breathe. I felt so guilty bowing out and now you're telling me that I should, yeah, and that I've broken my daughter's heart and made everything worse . . .'

He hears himself start to sob. Despises himself. Snatches his hand across his face. Snot bubbles in his nose. He lurches as the car thuds into a pothole, wincing as the chassis scrapes the jagged rim of the tarmac. Jerks the gear stick into second and the engine screeches in protest. He snatches his hand across the windscreen, smearing the steam into brushstrokes of dirty water. He can't see a bloody thing . . .

'Oh for God's sake, Joe, I can't take the amateur dramatics any more. This is shit for your therapist, not for me. You tell me you'll have her, and then you're too poorly, and then you turn up with presents and these big sad eyes . . . I don't want her around you when you're like this.'

'Don't,' he sobs, and the windscreen wipers screech across the glass, smearing raindrops and dirt and leaves. He winces through the porthole. The insides of the windows are misting up. He starts to fiddle with the blowers, unsure whether to blast them with hot or cold. It's not his car. She's got that. Got the house and the furniture and the pets. He can't even tell people she left him. Threw him out. Made him leave. Got shot of the loser. He wishes she'd at least had an affair. Could have handled her trading him in for something better. He's been replaced by an absence. What she yearned for was his removal. She needed space, and the space was the exact size, shape and weight dimensions of him.

'Joe, where are you? Are you driving?'

'Just out,' he mutters. 'Don't know where to go.'

'Well that's bullshit for a start, 'cause when you were at the house you said you were on your way to talk to somebody about some work, so either that's a lie, or this is a lie. Your lips are moving, so you're lying, but I don't know which direction you're lying in, or what you're even trying to get out of it or . . .'

He screws his eyes shut. Sifts through her words for anything with which he can sustain himself. Bella's sad that she's not with her Daddy. That has to mean something, right? He doesn't want her to be unhappy, but unhappiness is part of life, and if she gets glum because Daddy isn't there, then maybe that means he's worth something. And the accusation. The unspoken suggestion that he's cancelled date night with his youngest in favour of some hot shenanigans with whatever floozy has fallen for his bullshit. Maybe, given time, he can mould all that into something that can keep him going. God, she could save his life with a single kind line, doesn't she know that? He thinks of birds pecking at bloodied skin. Thinks of curved beaks sliding under splintered ribs. Thinks of the way she used to look at him, back when he still believed his own bullshit and thought that he still had time to catch up with his lies . . . and . . .

There's a shape in the road. There's no time to react but for an instant he sees shiny blackness. Thinks of molten tar and burnt skin.

Sees his headlights cut the shape in two just as he wrenches the wheel to the left, then the right, and—

A thud. A sickening crunch and then he's bouncing off the window, stamping on the brakes, tyres skidding over the wet, black road.

'Fuck . . . shit, fuck, somebody in the road!'

Her voice, again. 'Fucking amateur dramatics, Joe. I don't believe . . .'

He glances in the rearview mirror. His brake lights cast a red glow on to the dark country road. The light from his exhaust adds a shimmering fog to the wet night air.

He winds down the window. Pokes his head out and feels the rain on his brow. Starts to cough and feels it burn in his lungs. Hacks up something vile and spits it in a tatty hanky pulled from his shirt pocket.

He looks at the thing again. It lies across the road like a chrysalis. It's wrapped in black. There's an indentation where his wheels crunched it into the tarmac. Had it been that shape when he hit it? Had it been laid out or standing up? He can't work out which of the things he can see is a memory and which an act of imagination. His counsellor would tell him that this is half his problem.

'Joe? Joe, don't give me the silent treatment. You really would do anything to avoid consequences, wouldn't you? Even faking a bloody crash . . .'

He flicks his thumb over the paddle behind the steering wheel. Turns the volume down. Listens to his heart thud in his chest. Hears himself wheeze. Breathes in a lungful of the damp air within the boxy little car. Smells old takeaways and coffee cups; mouldy clothes and spilled windscreen wash. Smells weed, too. Smells it on his clothes. On his fingers.

He fiddles with the sat nav on the car console. Glances up. No vehicles ahead. None behind. Makes sense of where he is. Makes some calculations. There are no cameras. Probably no cameras since the big roundabout. He's in the back of beyond. Miles from home. No reason to be here. No reason to be connected. He could ring it in. Anonymous call. Do phone boxes still exist? Maybe he could pop into a supermarket and buy a disposable phone. Did they call them 'burners'? He seems to think so. But by the time he's done that, somebody else will have found them.

Slowly, he breathes out. Slips the car back into first. Glances again at the shape behind him and tells himself that this is one thing too many. He can't deal with this. Can't be expected to. He's poorly. He's depressed. He's got real shit going on.

As he pulls away, he looks back one more time.

By the time he's home in bed, he'll have convinced himself that the bag didn't wriggle as he drove away.

TWO

Davenport Avenue, Hessle
11.46pm

There's a whisper of winter in the air. The blackness shimmers as if dusted with ground glass. Tiger stripes and helixes coil greyly upwards from the smouldering fire pits, the cast iron chimenea. Frost rimes the branches of tall, rain-blackened trees, towering over the high hedges and big gates; dead and dying leaves billowing across the spacious, well-kept garden in artful, crinkle-edged flurries. Above, the moon is almost full: a hooded eye – black clouds scudding across its ivory-coloured lens.

It's Mabon – the celebration of the autumn equinox. Tonight, those who believe in the old ways gather to give thanks for the second harvest. On this sacred sabbat, day and night are equal. All things are in balance. It's a time of equality and harmony: a time to let go of the past, and to welcome in the new.

A celebration is taking place at the back of number six. A dozen men, women and children stand in a clumsy circle, looking embarrassed and shuffling their feet. Some hold hands. Others jam their fists in the pockets of thick winter coats, turtle-necked inside pashminas and bobble hats. They've eaten well. Tabitha served up spiced pumpkin soup and home-baked bread, apple tarts and rosehip cordial. She wants to get things right. The visitors are very much going along with this. They're showing willing. Tabitha has had a hard year and if this witchy nonsense is what she needs to stay off the gin, they'll play along. But they'd like to get back inside.

A fire burns in a wrought-iron pit: flames jabbing upwards like

the beaks of hungry chicks. Fairy lights have been strung in a lazy
spiderweb around the patio: their colours reflecting back from the
necks of beer bottles, wine bottles, all bobbing in the frigid water
that half fills the old Victorian bathtub, propped up on its golden
bird claws. There's an altar at the end of the patio: flames flickering
red and gold amid the pumpkins and candles and imitation skulls.

> *Equal hours of light and darkness*
> *we celebrate the balance of Mabon,*
> *and ask the gods to bless us.*
> *For all that is bad, there is good.*
> *For that which is despair, there is hope.*
> *For the moments of pain, there are moments of love.*
> *For all that falls, there is the chance to rise again.*
> *May we find balance in our lives*
> *as we find it in our hearts . . .*

Detective Inspector Aector McAvoy smiles as he hears his wife's
words. Her voice is both a lullaby and a prayer, an incantation and
a song. At moments like this he feels so astonishingly proud of her
that he fears it will lead to an aneurism – that he'll be found, bleeding
from the ear beneath the big sycamore, hedgehogs and squirrels
nosing at his pockets and a big dead smile on his face.

McAvoy isn't on the guest list. Shouldn't be here. It's Roisin's
night – she's the one being paid to lead the celebrations and bless
Tabitha's sacred space. He should be at home, or at work, or out
the back of their little cottage on the waterfront, sitting in the
moonlight and letting his big brain unfurl like a map. He's spent
most of today hunched at the wheel of the family car: three and a
half hours down to Chatteris, Cambridgeshire, then back again,
interrupted by forty minutes holding the fragile remains of Helen
Shah, withered beyond her years, as she sobbed against his chest
and told him that she still believed in him; still believed he would
bring her justice; still believed that Declan Parfitt, the Lizard King,
abducted and killed her daughter sixteen years ago. Still believed
she would be reunited with her remains, and that Parfitt would die
behind bars. He'd been able to offer nothing more than another
promise – he'd keep going. Whatever happened, he would do
everything within the law to ensure justice. She'd smiled at that: a
slash of crimson lip and yellow teeth, all snot and salty tears. Justice.

That's what he'd received in the sulphur-reeking darkness, deep in the nuclear catacombs beneath the old wireless station at Bempton Cliffs. McAvoy hadn't asked her how she'd known. Couldn't bring himself to interrogate her as she sat there, in her living room, rigid on the clear plastic covering of the high-backed sofa, tea growing cold in the pot on the table, glancing up through her fog of tears to lock eyes with the photograph above the fireplace; the smiling, dimpled face of her daughter, Kaylani Shah: nine years old when she was taken. She's never been returned.

He'd wept on the drive back. Wept the way he always does when there's nobody watching and his head sloshes with the tears of those left behind. Had to pull in at Doncaster Services and get himself together. Drove here. Drove to Roisin. He fears the darkness that creeps into his thoughts when she's out of his sight.

He stands a little way off from the rest of the group, giving off the air of a toddler struggling with the rules of hide-and-seek: adamant that if he closes his eyes hard enough, he'll become invisible. He's not really here. Wasn't invited. He's sort of a 'plus-one', if anything, but McAvoy is 6 feet 5 inches and eighteen stone: all muscles and hair and scars. He's very much a plus-three. He'd been sincere in his protestations when Tabitha scurried into his solitude and insisted he come and join the party. She couldn't possibly have him loitering at the end of the road – not in a neighbourhood like this. Every curtain for half a mile had twitched in the few minutes he'd been permitted to linger in the cone of yellow light, enjoying the feel of the autumn air as it blew patterns in the red-grey tangle of his beard. This is an area where members of the Neighbourhood Watch take the role seriously: an area where people use words like 'ruffians' and 'yobbos' and 'short, sharp, shock' without embarrassment. They know the market value of their property to within five pounds and live in mortal terror of the local old folks' home being sold to a private developer with a yen for social housing. Seeing a well-dressed Viking leaning against a lamppost at the end of the road was enough to set the local WhatsApp group ablaze. It wasn't long before Tabitha Arnold, the owner of the great mercantile palace at number six, had taken his elbow and escorted him through the gates, placed a mug of soup in his hand, and told him he was more than welcome to join in. It was, she confided, going to be very special.

He hears a little giggle from one of the women at the far side of the group. There's a titter from one of the teens. Tabitha shoots an angry glance at the girl. They'd promised they'd take this seriously. Promised they'd behave.

McAvoy can't read his book in this light so contents himself with his phone. He's got reports to read. Reports to write. Needs to cross-check a witness statement with the timestamp on a security video. He double-checks his email. Too late to hear back from the prison, he knows that, but he checks all the same. Nothing yet, same as thirty seconds ago. He permits himself a frown. All he needs is a response from Parfitt's psychologist or the Governor at HMP Ovenden. He's never known such difficulty in gaining access to a prisoner. He understands that Parfitt is fragile with a complex set of physical and psychological needs, but the authorities seem to be deliberately obtuse. He doesn't know whether it's a territorial issue or a genuine concern for the prisoner's welfare. McAvoy isn't quite sure how else to appeal to their better nature. They'll be gentle with Parfitt, he's made that plain. Won't push him. Won't lean on him too hard. They'll treat him like a vulnerable adult, and not the monster who they believe was responsible for abductions, assaults – and at least two murders. The weight of responsibility stoops him. Unless McAvoy's Cold Case Unit can prove he was responsible for one of the other crimes of which he's suspected, he will be out by Christmas. McAvoy knows what he's asking Santa for this year.

He sends a quick message to his son: *All good?*

The reply comes back seconds later: *She won't do what she's told! Tried briebery and threats and she's just looking at me like I'm simple.*

Another message pings through a moment later: an asterisk, and the correct spelling of 'bribery'.

McAvoy folds his mouth around a smile, unsure which of his children to feel most delighted by. They're perfect replicas of their mum and dad, and their relationship has very much the same power dynamic. Fin is a teenager now and a shade over 6 feet tall, but his little sister Lilah is very much in charge. She's not yet into double digits but has the cast-iron self-belief of somebody who has lived a dozen lives and been right in all of them. Fin spends most of his time trying to do the right thing, believing in people's better nature and the benefits of keeping one's temper and using a soft, soothing voice. Lilah, like her mum, doesn't trouble herself with such matters.

She says and does what she wants to say and do. She's never met a consequence she hasn't been able to kick in the nuts.

In his hand, his phone buzzes. It's Lilah.

Fin's a little upset. Am I allowed to make him a mug cake in the microwave? I would ask Mam, but she'd say no. xxx

McAvoy sends back a thumbs-up. Sends a trio of kisses too, in case the thumbs-up feels too impersonal.

A moment later, the phone buzzes again: *Love you. You're the best xxx*

His chest seems to swell as he thinks upon his little girl. He doesn't know whether he believes in blessings and curses, angels and demons, Heaven and Hell . . . but he knows Lilah is every bit as other-worldly, as majestic, as absolutely-fricking-awesome, as his wife.

McAvoy looks again at the group. Tabitha is the only one taking things seriously, despite the best efforts of those around her. She'd told him as much as she'd led him into the large, well-kept garden. Tabitha and the girls had been stringing rowan berries all day. Boiling rosehips. They hadn't been able to forage any blackberries but there'd been some big plump ones in Waitrose, and that was really rather like foraging, wasn't it? They were all so keen to get things right. To do things properly. She'd been away on a Sacred Feminine retreat that had been so empowering and her friends and family were very much on board with her new preoccupation. They'd worried about her after she quit work, but she was really becoming the person she felt she was always meant to be. She was embracing nature. Embracing the old ways. Roisin was an absolute godsend. McAvoy hadn't asked which god. He'd just muttered and smiled and blushed and then he'd taken his soup and his soda bread and retreated to a spot where he wouldn't get in anybody's way. The soup's dreadful. He can't help hoping that he'll trip over a tree root and spill it before he's forced to do the polite thing and swallow it down.

McAvoy glances over to where Roisin is finishing her incantation. She hasn't dressed up for Tabitha. She looks like she's about to head out for a night at a casino rather than lead a scared ritual. She's in her mid-thirties but looks younger: dark hair, dark eyes, slim waist and sparkling costume jewellery. She wears tight black

trousers, a strappy little top and a burgundy leather jacket: her hair
tied up with a silk scarf. She can't see him, he's sure of it, but
there's a half smile on her fine features when she shoots a look into
the patch of darkness at the edge of the patio.

'You're a big squirrel.'

It takes McAvoy a moment to locate the source of the unexpected
voice. The little girl has sneaked up on him, moving over the wet
grass in zebra-striped slippers. She's wearing a onesie, hood pulled
up in a way that twists her ears and plasters strands of wavy brown
hair across her face.

'Hello,' he says, in the low, neutral voice he uses on small children, hungry women and heroin users threatening to stab him with
a needle. 'I'm Aector. Have you just got out of bed?'

'School night,' says the girl. She's got a fluffy owl zipped into
the front of her onesie, head poking out through the zip. 'This is
Bert,' she explains. 'He's an owl. His head doesn't turn though. I've
tried. Mummy had to get the sewing kit out.'

McAvoy moves away from the trunk of the tree. Glances over at
the circle. Roisin has her eyes closed, her palms raised to the fire.
Only Tabitha is paying attention to the words she softly speaks into
the flame. Tabitha has embraced the Pagan lifestyle. She'd like to be
a witch. She's spent a small fortune on Roisin's lotions and potions,
charms, spells and protective amulets. Roisin had already made the
decision not to sell her anything else, uncomfortable at the idea of
feeding somebody's addiction to a way of life that Roisin was born
into, and from which she has never strayed. She doesn't mind charging
a few quid for the occasional smudging stick or a bouquet-garni of
medicinal herbs, but had never considered hiring herself out as a
witch-for-hire until Tabitha suggested it. She and her friends – she
and her girls – they were so desperate to get it right. It had been such
a difficult year. They wanted to welcome in the new season and let
go of the past. They wanted to know they were honouring the spirits
correctly. *It would be*, she suggested, *so much easier if you just showed
us what to do. And we could pay you for your time, of course. . .*

'You're a Rozzer, aren't you?'

McAvoy finds himself smiling. He hasn't been called a Rozzer
in years.

'That's a word I don't hear very often. Where did you hear that?'

'You're Scottish,' she says, ignoring the question. 'And massive.
And your wife's a witch.'

McAvoy runs the words back in his head, checking for insults. Decides that she's factually accurate.

'I'm Daisy,' she says. 'I'm six.'

'I'm Aector. I'm a lot older than that.'

'Daddy says Rozzers are agents of the state. You're here to keep people scared. He says if you spent more time catching real criminals instead of punishing motorists, the world would be a better place.'

McAvoy nods, thoughtfully, as if giving it consideration. 'And what do you think?'

She stops for a moment, seemingly pleased to be asked. 'I think baddies shouldn't get away with it.'

McAvoy gives a little nod. 'My boss thinks the same.'

'What do you think?' she asks, learning quickly.

McAvoy can't bring himself to offer a glib answer, to talk to her like she's inconsequential. He searches for the right words. 'I think it would be nice if we all just got along.'

She wrinkles her nose, disappointed. He feels his spirits sink. Wonders what it says about him that even a six-year-old thinks of his ideologies as unspeakably naïve.

'You bothering my man, are you?'

They both jerk their heads up at the sound of Roisin's approach. She's pretending to glare at the little girl, who giggles and half hides behind McAvoy's leg.

'Go OK, did it?' he asks. 'Sounded brilliant from here.'

Roisin shrugs. It doesn't matter to her either way. She's spent Mabon the way she always does: foraging, baking, letting go of the old and welcoming in the new. She conducted her own rituals for the safety of the family before she took the call from Tabitha. She's shown them what to do and how to do it and she's been paid damn well for her time. The fact that they didn't take it particularly seriously doesn't matter one way or another. She's done her bit.

'This is Daisy,' says McAvoy.

'We've met,' says Roisin. 'This is the best one. Her sisters are fecking halfwits, but this one . . . she's awesome.'

Daisy smiles as if she's come downstairs on Christmas morning and found a unicorn under the tree. 'Say that when they're listening please.'

'Let me look at you,' says Roisin, squatting down and staring into the girl's eyes. 'Thought so,' she says, earnestly. 'Touched by the spirits, I'd say. You've the makings of a powerful witch, so you do. I gave your mammy a book for one of your sisters, but I doubt they've read it. Get your reading up a level and then see if you can nab it. You'll be leading a coven in no time.'

'I know the book you mean,' she says, excitedly. 'I could, couldn't I?'

'Wouldn't be the worst thing on earth if you turned one sister into a frog and the other into a bluebottle, would it? Let them fight it out among themselves.'

Daisy giggles again, then stops suddenly, eyes wide. She looks up to where a light has just come on, somewhere on the third floor.

'Busted,' says Roisin, apologetically. 'Pretend you've been sleep-walking. Look tired. Do a drowsy face. Get back into bed without a word. You might get away with it.'

'Really?'

'Or say you couldn't sleep for the noise. Make her feel guilty. That'll work too.'

'Roisin, I don't think . . .'

Roisin and Daisy both shoot disapproving glances at McAvoy, the message clear: stay out of things you don't understand.

Daisy hurries off. Roisin waits until she's gone before she reaches up and grabs her husband by the beard, pulling his face down and kissing his mouth. She tastes of rosehips. Of pumpkins. Her fingers are sticky with apple juice. Her warm hands snake under his jumper and nip at his sides. She chews his lip, grinning up at him. She loves Mabon. Feels most like herself at this time of year. He feels her bag bang against his hip. It still contains her shoes. She's bare-foot, soles planted in the wet ground.

'You kept your temper,' says McAvoy, when she lets him go.

'People get embarrassed,' she shrugs. 'They hold themselves back. Their choice, their loss. Are the kids pretending to be in bed?'

'Lilah's making him a mug cake to say sorry. If we get back and the microwave's in the garden, I never gave permission.'

Roisin smiles. Slips her bare feet into her shoes. It's a mile walk back to their cottage on the foreshore. They'll have each other all to themselves. They could walk through the country park if they really wanted some alone time, but Roisin doesn't suggest it. Bad memories linger in those dark woods.

'Did the prison call?'

McAvoy shakes his head. Roisin squeezes his arm. She takes the
mug of cold soup from his unresisting hand and pours it on to the
ground without a word.

'Oh, I'm fizzing in every cell,' gushes Tabitha, hurrying over.
'Ro . . . that was . . . transcendent.'

Roisin smiles. 'That's the vibe I was going for. I am one
transcendent mother-fecker.'

'You're OK making your own way, are you?' she asks, nervously.
'One of my friends – she's having such a hard time with her ex and
we're sort of all at battle stations. He was supposed to have their
daughter tonight but then he was too poorly but he still turned up
with a bag of treats and toys . . . I think we're in for a late night.
I'm lucky with my Bryan, really. Made the split really easy. I think
he would have given me whichever half of his body I asked for if
it meant the other half could wriggle away.'

Roisin slips her hand into McAvoy's. He feels her drawing something on his palm with her index finger. Doesn't question it. She
keeps him safe. He may have scars, but without her, he knows he'd
have perished years ago.

Roisin smiles, and gives Tabitha a quick, one-armed hug. 'We'll
leave you to it, anyway. Blessed Mabon.'

McAvoy weighs two-and-a-half times as much as his wife but
she still manages to pull him away from the darkness beneath the
tree. He mumbles a goodbye and some words of thanks and then
they're moving over the wet grass and on to the black road and
through the big gates.

'Go on then,' says Roisin, when they're back on the big wide
street and heading downhill towards the water. 'How was Helen?'

McAvoy tries to think of the best way to describe her. Comes up
short. 'Broken,' he says. 'Just broken.'

Roisin stops and puts her hand on his face. Peers into him.
'There's more, isn't there? Something bothering you that you wish
you weren't bothered by. What's Trish asked you to do?'

He stares up, trying to make out a pattern in the stars. Screws
up his forehead. He knows that his new rank comes with more
responsibility, but he feels horribly ill-suited to the new task that
Trish Pharaoh has dumped in his lap. He needs to convince a documentary crew to drop the programme they're intent on making – a
show in which he knows he will be considerably more than a foot-
note – and instead focus on the Cold Case Unit's re-investigation

of Parfitt. They need the publicity. Need for Parfitt's name to be on people's mind. His victims, too.

'I'm meeting the documentary crew in the morning,' he says, once he's stumbled his way through an explanation. 'I think they'll go for it. God knows what we'll do if they don't.'

Roisin squeezes his hand. 'You'll stop him,' she says, with a certainty that makes him feel like he's falling. 'He won't get out. He won't hurt anybody else.'

McAvoy holds her. Kisses the top of her head. For a moment, he sees Declan Parfitt in his mind's eye. Sees the ruination of his flesh; the deformities carved into and out of him. He thinks of Trish Pharaoh, silent in the dark catacombs beneath the building on the clifftop: the copper who saved a multiple murderer from an unknown vigilante. Thinks of the crime scene photos: empty beds and pulled-back bedclothes, the whiff of ether and blood. He wants to shake it away. Wants to give the responsibility to somebody else. If they can't prove what he did . . . Parfitt could be free by his next parole hearing. Could be back out in the world – his flesh cruelly deformed but his hunger unsated. He could come back here. Could start again. Could be loose on the same streets where his daughter rides her bike; where Daisy sleeps in the cool air of a big sash window. He can't stand it. Can't face it. Can't allow it.

'She should have let him die,' says Roisin, gently. 'Should have stood back and let him burn.'

McAvoy swallows. Licks his lips. Nods. 'If she had the chance again . . .' he begins.

'She'd warm her hands on the flames,' says Roisin. 'She'd let the demons take him.'

'Yes,' says McAvoy. 'Yes, she would.'

Roisin angles her head. 'You wouldn't though, would you? You'd save his life, just like she did. It's who you are. You don't believe anybody's past redemption.'

McAvoy feels his shoulders slump. Lets the words rush up like bile. 'What he did . . . the lives he took, the agony he put them through . . . I have this picture in my head – he's burning and I'm just watching . . . revelling in it. He's the closest thing to evil I've ever come across.'

'And he'll be out by Christmas if you don't prove what he did,' says Roisin. 'So . . . you'd best do what you do best.'

'Bumble along and hope I get lucky?' asks McAvoy, uncertainly.

Roisin pulls him closer and grabs a handful of his hair. Kisses him, soft and deep and fierce. 'The right thing,' she whispers, into his mouth.

THREE

Pearson Park, Hull
Monday, 23 September 2024, 12.56am

Trish Pharaoh sits on the swing at the edge of the play park. The toes of her biker boots don't quite reach the pitted rubber surface beneath. She'd made a half-hearted attempt to get a little momentum going, but she's given birth to four daughters and can never be sure which new and exciting experiences are going to make her wet herself, so she's settled for dangling: a monkey in a tyre.

She looks around, checking the darkness for any note of wrongness. She's not afraid. Isn't scared of very much, truth be told. Her application for the role of Head of Crime may have painted her as a 'motivated, dynamic and creative individual' but she'd got the job because she isn't scared of doing what must be done – and because in some cases, she knows where the bodies are buried. Her superiors know she'll do whatever it takes to get a result. When she crosses the line, they trust her to make sure it doesn't come back to haunt them. They owe her. She's given them thirty years. She's been a copper longer than she was a person.

She reaches down. Rummages in the depths of her handbag. Her scarf unwraps itself and she makes a grab for it as it slithers free, landing in a perfect coil upon the damp rubber.

'Bastard,' mutters Pharaoh. 'You did that on fucking purpose.'

She sits and broods for a while. She's been here for more than half an hour. Her apartment is only a few hundred yards away but she's in no hurry to go back. She's spent her entire life surrounded by people and still hasn't got used to living alone. Her daughters are all spreading their wings. She's a grandma now – a thought that makes her smile and shudder at once. She's brought the nipper to play here a handful of times. It's pleasant during the day. Downright lovely in the summer, with the ice cream parlour and the duck pond and the Hot House.

She scowls. Stops fighting it. Raises her head and glares through the hanging rain – past the climbing frame and the darkly shimmering trees to where the Hot House looms, like a grounded ship, against the lip of the pond. Parfitt used to bring his foster daughters here. Had a key and used to let himself in after hours. In her suicide note, Gaynor Chessman detailed the things that happened here, in the heat and the dark, amid the green leaves and the greasy glass; the spiders and the lizards and the birds. Pharaoh could recite the note from memory. Had to be physically restrained when the smug bastard from the Crown Prosecution Service told her it wasn't enough to bring any further charges against Parfitt as the victim wasn't alive to be cross-examined.

Pharaoh rests her head against the cold metal of the swings. Thinks upon the girls. Of what they endured, both in Parfitt's care and in the years before they were handed over to him like presents waiting to be unwrapped. They were eight and nine years old when they were placed with him, up at his funny little farm by the cliff edge at Skipsea. He was single, and childless, and he wanted to provide a safe haven for those in need. He'd never married. Never been in a long-term relationship. But kids loved him. There were always squeals of delight when he turned up at campsites and schools and birthday parties with his mobile menagerie, looking studiedly ridiculous in his comedy safari suit and pith helmet. Nobody in Social Services objected to his becoming a foster father. Nobody said a word when two damaged, emotionally vulnerable young girls were placed in his care. They'd struck lucky, according to some. Landed on their feet. Been plucked from lives of neglect and abuse and given a stable environment and a father figure just aching to love them.

Pharaoh doesn't know when the abuse started. But she knows that it did. Knows that it kept Parfitt's hunger at bay for a time. Gaynor, the older of the pair, was his favourite. Pharaoh has half an idea that she made herself a sacrificial lamb. Accepted Parfitt's attentions to spare her sister. Said as much in her suicide note: two pages of scribbled text that spoke in maddeningly oblique terms about what Parfitt did to her. She'd been on heroin for nearly a decade by the time she took her own life. Had resorted to trying to sell her story to the newspapers, just to raise enough money to fund her next high. She spent her last years in hostels and shop doorways. Pharaoh's seen video footage of her hunkered down with the unhoused crowds in Manchester and Glasgow. Seen her being moved on by store security and community support officers in Sheffield and Leeds. But she came back to East Yorkshire to kill herself. Came back to the place where he hurt her and put a rope around her neck. Gave herself to the darkness – to whatever it was that woke her screaming on the nights she couldn't score.

Ruby remains adamant that it was all lies. He never touched her. He was a good dad and Gaynor was sick in the head. She'd been through so much before they were placed with Daddy. She projected her memories of the bad men she used to know – got herself all confused. The photographs were forgeries. He was the victim of a hate campaign. Daddy simply wasn't capable of the things they accused him of. He could come and stay with her when the parole board gave the nod. She would care for him. Give him a safe place to begin again. Just her, and her boyfriend, and Aramis – her seven-year-old stepson. She has a picture in her head that has sustained her for more than a decade. Wants to play happy families with Daddy.

There's a sudden clang as the metal gate hits the fence. Pharaoh squints and makes out the outline of a familiar shape. She closes her eyes. Says a word of quiet thanks.

Pharaoh stuffs her scarf back into her bag and rearranges her leather jacket. She watches as Ruby makes her way between the roundabouts and slides. She's late-thirties now. Red-haired and blue-eyed. She's wearing a black roll-neck jumper and velour jogging trousers tucked into hiking socks and steel toe-capped boots. She smells of cigarettes, white wine and chip spice.

'For God's sake, Trish, you don't need to keep doing this,' says Ruby, in her Hull accent, with a half-hearted scowl. 'I've told you it won't make any difference.'

Pharaoh shrugs. 'I live up the road. I don't sleep unless I'm properly stoned and I don't get to smoke weed in case it somehow . . . what's the phrase they say in the rulebook . . . "doesn't look good during a public inquiry". I've nowhere else to be. I'd rather be here. With you.'

Ruby plonks herself on the swing beside Pharaoh. She can't quite reach the ground either. They look at each other and something like affection passes between them. They've known each other a long time. Watched each other age at different speeds.

'Here,' says Pharaoh, and hands Ruby a bag of Edinburgh tablet. 'Weren't easy to find.'

'Seriously?' Ruby's eyes widen as she tears into the bag. 'How did you . . . like, I told you that years ago . . .'

'Lady Grey tea, too,' says Pharaoh, pulling a tartan thermos from her bag. 'Slice of lemon, isn't it?'

Ruby makes noises of pleasure as she munches on the powdery, crumbly fudge. 'You didn't make it, did you? I mean, that's going too far.'

'Baking?' muses Pharaoh. 'That's the thing you use the hot box in the kitchen for, yes? I use it to reheat takeaways, love. If I'd made that, it would taste of a veggie pizza, with extra ham.'

Ruby laughs. 'Extra ham?'

'Here,' says Pharaoh, and passes Ruby a white plastic cup. 'Keep yourself warm.'

They sit together in silence for a while. Pharaoh doesn't push. She's felt Ruby begin to thaw the last few times. She's felt herself making headway. Getting through. Even as every voice in her head is screaming, she keeps her manner soft. She knows there's a way to disentangle Ruby's memories; to make her think again about the caged demon she's intent on releasing back into the wild. She also knows that time is running out.

'I don't think I even feel her any more,' says Ruby, quietly. There's a far-away quality to her voice; an unhealthy white pallor to her skin. 'Gaynor, I mean.' She rests her head against the chain of the swing. 'For a while, I felt her here. Just the whiff of her. Like an echo, or something. Same down at the foreshore. On the bridge. Now it's just habit, I think. I don't hear her. But I go through the motions in case it comes back. In case she does.'

Pharaoh puts her hand on Ruby's. She's cold to the touch. There are flecks of paint on the backs of her knuckles. Her nails are chipped. Pharaoh stares at the side of her face. There are burst capillaries in her cheeks. A bruise behind her ear. Her lips look sore, seamed with the tideline of red wine. Is she shaking? Pharaoh can't be sure.

'Is he behaving himself? Your Greek god.'

Ruby seems to get smaller. Pharaoh sees again the moody teen she once was, all pout and attitude, glaring at her as she dictated the statement that provided an alibi for her foster father. Sees the shadow of that girl in the young woman before her: loyal to the hand that feeds her.

'He's been lovely,' says Ruby, with a sniff. 'Should see him with Aramis. Proper doting dad.' She rustles the bag of sweets. Rubs the heels of her hands under her eyes. She fumbles for a cigarette and her fingers shake as she lights it.

'With him now, is he?' asks Pharaoh. 'The nipper?'

Ruby nods. Looks away, to the place where she and her foster father spent their 'special times'. Pharaoh suspects he used to bring the other girls here too. She thinks he was playing make-believe. They were avatars for Ruby – the girl he didn't allow himself to touch. Touched her sister though. Took her to a hell beyond enduring. She killed herself the same day she'd received a phone call from Parfitt's psychologist, Dr Munroe Durrant. Would she consider giving evidence at her foster father's parole hearing? Perhaps, given the passing of the years, she might have come to a different conclusion about what truly happened when she was young . . .

Her suicide note was accompanied by an old photograph. It had shown the white building by the pond. The Hot House. Had shown Decland Parfitt's arm around the shoulders of two dark-haired sisters: football tops and white shorts, bare legs and flip-flops. Parfitt had looked a little off-guard, as if the camera had flashed before he'd been able to compose himself. There'd been something unsettling captured in the candid snap: a look in his eyes and a set to the twist of his mouth that had suited his nickname perfectly: the Lizard King. In that moment, he'd looked like a monster masquerading as a man.

'You've been to see him, then,' says Pharaoh, quietly. 'Twice this year.'

Ruby wipes her nose. 'He hasn't got anybody else.'

'And Mem's OK with all this, yeah? Having a paedophile near his son? Giving him a place to stay?'

Ruby flashes angry eyes. Bares her teeth. 'Don't. Don't use that word . . .'

'For fuck's sake, Ruby . . .'

She stands up suddenly, stuffing the plastic packet into the pocket of her jeans. She grimaces as she swallows as if her throat is full of pins. 'It's too late,' she hisses. 'Maybe once . . . maybe.'

'It's not too late, Ruby. Now's the perfect time.'

'Even if I wanted to – Mem would never let me help you.'

'Let you?' demands Pharaoh. 'Jesus, Ruby, we can protect you. And why the fuck would he not want to keep a child abuser behind bars?'

'Mem's been fitted up before,' says Ruby, twisting the chains of the swing. She drops her cigarette. Sparks dance. 'He knows what you do. And Daddy's written to him. Explained.'

Pharaoh wants to spit into the darkness between them. She's read the letters exchanged between Parfitt and his foster daughter's partner. She can still taste the bile.

'Ruby, even if I'm wrong about the girls he took – he's admitted to his other crimes. He's a convicted sex offender. He's in group therapy, working with men just like him, reconciling himself to what he's done. I know how much you want to help people – what a big heart you've got. That club you started, for men who need to talk – I know it did some good for people. You've got a sense of right and wrong – that's never been in doubt. But look, even if you don't believe the rest of it, you saw the photographs. What he did. To so many girls, girls you knew. And to Gaynor . . .'

Ruby pulls at the material of her bobble hat. Her hands shake. Pharaoh sighs. Lights a cigarette and hands it to Ruby. She takes it and sucks on it as if drinking a milkshake.

'This is the last time,' she says. 'I don't think I can do this any more. Be here. Think these thoughts. It's too much.'

'Ruby, there are things you don't know. The man who took your father, who did those things to him . . .'

'You let him do that!' spits Ruby. 'He's told me. He knows you gave him to that . . . that fucking animal! You don't think I understand it, but I do. You couldn't prove he did what you thought he did, so you gave him to this monster – the one they're all afraid of; the one who comes to show you what waits in the darkness for those who don't change their ways. The one they all talk about.'

Pharaoh feels a sudden chill in her guts. *Don't say the name*, she thinks. *Don't admit you know the name, because if you do, I've got to ask you some difficult questions and you're never going to trust me again . . .*

'Mem knows the truth,' says Ruby, eyes shining. 'Knows how far you'd go. Daddy didn't do these things. You're just bitter. Bitter and angry because you got it wrong – because you made a prat of yourself when we did the party for your daughter. This whole thing is just you trying to save face and you know it!'

Pharaoh can't speak. For a moment, she's back in her house on the Scratho estate in Grimsby and a silly man in a safari suit is showing her daughter and her friends a glass case containing a tarantula while a red snake winds its way around his forearm. Her daughters are making faces and giggling and he's loving making them laugh. He makes balloon animals. Lets them hold the friendlier of the lizards. And Pharaoh's standing in the corner of the room, pickled in red wine, trying to keep herself upright and to hold the camera straight. She's heard good things about the friendly eccentric from Skipsea, and her girls deserve a treat. They've lost a lot recently. Lost their big house and their expensive cars. Lost their dad too – an aneurism robbing him of most of his speech and movement. She's having the garage converted to cater for his needs. Not all of their friends from the old school, from the old neighbourhood, bothered to reply to the invitation. But Sophia and her sisters are enjoying themselves. And the silly man in the safari suit is funny and engaging. His daughters too, though they're quiet and don't smile much: just stand there in their branded overalls, handing him his props, putting the animals back in their cages and terrariums. She wouldn't have seen it if she'd had one drink more. Wouldn't have seen him snap the photograph of Sophia Pharaoh, cross-legged on the floor in front of him, staring up, wide-eyed and beautiful, all dark hair and red cheeks and carrying the sadness of a girl who knows her dad will never be the man he used to be and isn't sure whether to rejoice or come apart. Pharaoh sees the expression on his face. Sees something that speaks to a part of herself that is all primal instinct and fight-or-flight intuition. She sees a bad man. And he's taking pictures of her daughter.

'You know you were wrong about him, Trish. You had to justify how you behaved that day – had to prove you were right or else what would be, eh? Just another paranoid mum who thinks everybody's trying to screw their darling girls.'

Pharaoh grips the chains. She hears the echo of somebody else's voice in Ruby's words. She's repeating what she's been told.

'Ruby, all I've ever . . .'

Pharaoh stops short. She senses a movement in the darkness by the climbing frame. She squints into the black air.

'Fuck,' stammers Ruby. 'Fuck, he can't . . . he followed me . . .'

Pharaoh reaches out, trying to take a hold of the young woman. Tears are spilling from her eyes.

'Ruby, come with me. The officer I told you about – he can help you, give you a safe place to work through this; come to the right decision . . .'

'To do what you say instead of Mem?' spits Ruby. She shakes her head. 'I'm sorry,' she mutters, though whether it's to Pharaoh or whoever she fears in the darkness, Pharaoh can't say.

'Ruby, there's nobody there. You're in freefall. Mem isn't protecting you, he's controlling you. And Decland Parfitt is the devil. A devil I pulled out of Hell . . .'

And then Ruby's pushing past her, flinging the butt of the cigarette, knocking over the Thermos, stumbling and slipping for the park exit.

'Ruby, don't . . .'

And she's gone. A moment later, Pharaoh hears the gate squeak. Glares to where the trees turn black.

Pharaoh stays where she is. Shivers.

'Should have let him keep you,' she whispers, and in her head she pictures Decland Parfitt, burned and mutilated, gasping for breath in her arms. 'Should have given you to the one you all fear.'

For an instant, her mind is full of McAvoy. Shame rises in her gut. She's told so many lies.

Under her breath, barely there: 'I'm sorry, Aector. I had no choice.'

FOUR

4.26am

A blue tent, on a black country road. Figures in white suits. Everywhere: red.

Detective Sergeant Ben Neilsen swallows hard as he looks again at the figure on the ground. He's seen a lot of bodies in his eighteen years as a copper. Hasn't seen one like this.

'Bloody hell.'

'Indeed.'

'That's, well . . . yes.'

'I said much the same myself. Call came in at twelve oh six am through 999, requesting ambulance and police, although she did suggest that there might not be any need to hurry.'

'And he was just laying there?'

'He was lying there, Sergeant. He wasn't laying anything. He's not a chicken. Chickens lay, Neilsen. Chickens.'

Neilsen turns away, covering his grimace with his gloved hand. *Chickens lay, Neilsen. Chickens.* He hopes he can remember it perfectly so he can recreate it for the rest of the team.

'Call made by one Lorraine Whitley-Beal. Mrs Uniforms sent her home, but she would have been willing to wait. Driving back from an engagement, saw the shape in the road and stopped to investigate. Found *him*.'

Neilsen ducks under the flap of the forensics tent and back out into the cold morning air. He feels his DCI next to him. Smells him too. His breath is a fiery menthol. There's a nasty rattly noise as he swallows a crunched-up cough sweet. Unwraps another and pops it into his mouth.

'Initial thoughts, Sergeant?'

'Ben'll do, Guv. I've said before . . .'

'Initial thoughts, Sergeant.'

The DCI crunches another cough sweet. Looks left and right down the desolate road. Neilsen's yet to learn very much about DCI Jeremy Wolsingham but his mates in the Criminal Investigation Department have already perfected some of his mannerisms and habits, hands forever coupled at the wrist behind his back – rising himself up and down on the toes of his tatty brown Oxfords as if waiting for some recalcitrant student to disgorge a Latin verb. Wolsingham gives off the air of a headmaster at a private prep school – somebody whose earnest thirst for the betterment of others has proven more exasperating than they'd imagined. He has a tendency to correct people's grammar and use of language – hungering for an exactitude and a sense of personal pride that seems conspicuously absent from his own appearance. His grey hair pokes out in tufts from the matted fur of his fleecy hill-walking hat and the lines from his lower lip to his jaw are dug so deep he might be mistaken for a ventriloquist's dummy. Nobody in Humberside CID has been able to find out much about him, but he's in his early fifties, with gaps in his service record that suggest large chunks of time on projects so classified, the files can't be accessed without permission of the Chief Constable, bearing a signed photograph of the King. Neilsen's team had been expecting the mysterious new appointee to be some suave action man: a Hollywood homicide cop with a square jaw and a determination to do things his own way or not at all. Instead they got a scrawny, half-starved specimen in cord trousers that were shiny at the knees. The sleeves of his charity shop raincoat are patterned with a Jackson Pollock of smears and stains: his gaunt face reduced to a supporting player by the eye-catching bristles of nostril and ear hair that stick out of his orifices like thistle heads. Neilsen, who dresses in designer labels and spends a fortune on gym memberships and branded clothes, keeps wanting to reach out and tidy him up.

'Can you conceive of a good reason to dump a body here, Sergeant?'

Neilsen looks around him, feeling mildly put upon. The landscape is flat and unremarkable: fields chopped up into squares and oblongs by old hedgerows and the occasional stand of trees. 'You're suggesting he wasn't killed here?'

'He's in a bag, Sergeant. I don't like to get ahead of myself, but it seems highly unlikely that this was an elaborate suicide. The location must be significant.'

Neilsen doesn't feel at his best. Doesn't quite know how he's got lumbered with this. 'Maybe whoever dumped him hoped he'd be squashed under a farm vehicle,' he muses. 'Disguise what really happened. Of course, you'd take him out of the bag, wouldn't you? I would, anyway, but then I'm not high on adrenaline and fear. Toxicology should be interesting. I mean, we can't discount the whole autoerotic aspect either. I've read about people who get turned on by climbing into enclosed spaces. Lots of avenues to consider.'

'All a tad unlikely, Sergeant. Fanciful, even.'

'Just because something's fanciful, doesn't mean it isn't possible,' says Neilsen, parroting a phrase that his real boss, Trish Pharaoh, has beaten into her team over the years.

'You should have that written down and framed. You could hang it next to your Live, Laugh, Love poster.'

Neilsen licks his lips. Thinks of home. Of his bed. Of his partner, Chrissie, and her kids and the pancakes he was planning on making them all for breakfast. It had half killed him to wrench himself out from under the blankets, muttering and fumbling around in the dark as he wrestled himself into suit, two-tone leather shoes and the knock-off Dolce and Gabbana overcoat that Roisin McAvoy had sorted out for him on a strict 'don't-tell-Aector' understanding. He was still digesting his cereal bar when DCI Wolsingham ushered him inside the tent and showed him the figure in the big leather holdall. They haven't been allowed to touch him yet, but the science officer's preliminary assessment has given them the basics. White male, aged anywhere between 55 and 75, wearing dark clothing and unlaced trainers. There's a gash in his throat: a slash that reaches almost to the bone. The black T-shirt he's wearing is stained with blood, but it's the mess beneath that causes Neilsen's gorge to rise. One of the science officers had lifted the dead man's shirt to reveal a grotesque labyrinth of ropy scar tissue – whorls and sigils and letters carved into the man's pale white flesh and imperfectly healed.

'No ID,' muses Neilsen. 'No wallet. No phone. Too cold to be out without a coat.'

'They may have been tossed nearby. Fingertip search as soon as we get the numbers up, if you please.'

'Fingers crossed for fingerprints, then,' says Neilsen, wincing at the repetition. 'I don't want to make snap judgements, but a man with old wounds like that – I reckon he'll be known to us.'

Beside him, Wolsingham sucks on his throat sweet, lips pursed. He looks as though he's listening to a particularly sublime symphony. Neilsen can't decide whether he's going to find him endearingly eccentric or a pain in the arse.

'What are you busy with at present?' asks Wolsingham. 'And don't say you're here with me, I won't find it funny.'

Neilsen feels his stomach clench. He can sense he's going to be landed with this. Landed with an unknown dead man on a country road. He's been a Detective Sergeant for a couple of years and has his heart set on making DI within Humberside Police. He's a local lad and has already turned down offers of transfers to other forces. He's the son of a trawling family, a proud descendant of Hessle Road's glory days. He became a police officer so he could help the people he knew – even if that invariably meant locking up a lot of his friends. He's happy in the Cold Case Unit. Happy to be doing something that matters.

'I've been working with DI McAvoy – due diligence on Parfitt.'

Wolsingham wrinkles his nose, as if he's just confessed to getting up to no good behind the crash mats in the gym hall with a prefect.

According to the rumour mill, which often takes the form of
Detective Constable Andy Daniells, Wolsingham thinks McAvoy
gets special treatment because he's the Chief Superintendent's
favourite. The Scotsman's spared rotation into general CID and sits
at the head of a small task force looking into Humberside Police's
cold cases. It's a relatively new unit, and Neilsen's proud of the
work they're doing, however painstaking and frustrating the results
have so far proven to be. They're all focused on one job. Keeping
Decland Parfitt in prison has taken on the importance of defusing
an atomic bomb. It feels like there's a velociraptor in a cage and
only a handful of police officers, in a dingy unit west of Hull, are
holding the door shut.

'Man like McAvoy doesn't need his hand holding, Sergeant. Big
lad like him, he can do the work of the pair of you. No, you're with
me. I'll let you take the lead on this one. Keep me up to date so I
don't get any nasty surprises. You can do the press interviews if
there happen to be any. You have the right look.'

Neilsen runs the conversation back in his head. Listens again to
the slightly nasal accent as it does battle with the gathering wind
and the distant swish of tyres on tarmac. Wonders whether he's
pleased to be given an opportunity, or pissed off at being pulled
away from the unit where he knows he's doing something that
matters. Immediately he chides himself. Knows what McAvoy would
say, were he to confide in him. *We all deserve justice, Ben. Even
the bad people. Sometimes, especially the bad people . . .*

'Thanks, Guv,' says Neilsen, with a nod. 'Will you tell the
Boss . . .?'

'I'm the Boss, unless I'm much mistaken,' says Wolsingham. 'I
do believe the letters *DCI* feature quite heavily on my warrant card.'

'Detective Chief Superintendent Pharaoh,' says Neilsen, without
rancor. 'The Parfitt case – it's something she's treating as top priority.
We all are.'

Wolsingham points at the blue tent, and the scarred body in the
bag. 'That seems rather pressing, Sergeant. I'd ask you to furnish
me with an identity at your earliest convenience. You have my
number.'

Neilsen doesn't get a chance to reply. Watches him turn and stalk
away to where the police tape flaps and twists on the gale.

'Aye,' says Neilsen, out loud. 'Aye, I do.'

FIVE

Pharaoh slams the door behind her. She'd woken from sleep into a swirl of nightmare – taken a walk in a futile bid to clear her head. Stamps her way up the swirly carpet to her flat on the first floor. Drops her keys and spits the word 'bastard' like a bullet. Falls into her flat as if carried on a wave.

She stops, one hand clutching the little sideboard in the hallway. She looks at herself in the mirror. There's darkness under her eyes unlike any she's seen before. She's starting to look like her dad: hard lines in her face and lips turned down at the corners. *Resting bitch face*, according to her late husband. *Face like a slapped arse*, according to the neighbor who she briefly dated when she got back from Sicily. *Scary Granny*, according to her two-year-old granddaughter, who'd heard her on the phone telling a senior colleague how many ways she was going to insert him inside himself if he didn't stop talking; the imagery complex, but robustly delivered.

'Breathe,' she tells herself. She fumbles in her jacket. Finds her cigarettes: the black ones she used to smoke daily but which she now keeps in reserve for nights like this. There have been more nights like this, lately. Nights beset by visions and bad dreams. Nights where she's woken bathed in icy sweat, bedsheets whipped into meringue nests – nights when being alone has terrified her the way it did when she was a child.

She unzips her boots. She's barefoot beneath. Bare-legged too: just a jacket over her wet nightie. She'd already been out the door and on to the cold, dark street before she'd asked herself what she was running from.

'Sort yourself out,' she hisses at herself, baring her teeth. 'Do your fucking job.'

She makes her way into the kitchen. Finds the rosé at the back of the fridge. Takes a swig straight from the bottle. It's ice cold and delicious. She's glad there's no mirrors in here. Isn't sure she could bear to see herself, fifty-something and falling to bits, swigging zinfandel without a glass at this bloody hour.

She puts the wine back. Makes herself a coffee in the fancy machine. Squeezes the granite tops of the counters and screws up her eyes. Makes herself remember the dream.

She'd been back in Hell. Had been in the dark, in that terrible place. Had been breathing in the reek of burning flesh. She concentrates hard, focusing in as if turning the dial on a wireless. She sees herself, climbing down; cold, wet metal under her hands. Sees the light of her torch drawing panicked zig-zags in the pitch darkness. A shriek of pain as she stumbles forward, banging her knee on something metal. And then the sound. The static and screams, muffled behind the closed metal door at the end of the hallway.

Pharaoh gives herself to the memory; to the nightmare that woke her and sent her running into the street as if fleeing a blaze. Tries to recall the words. Tries to separate the language from the unintelligible screams.

'Name them. Name your sins.'

She remembers the feeling of absolute terror; the certainty that beyond the door lay something too terrible to imagine. She doesn't want to see. Doesn't think she can let Parfitt walk out alive if she catches him in the act. Bites down on her cheek and tastes blood. Tells herself there's a child in there; a child being used for a monster's pleasure.

From her jacket, she pulls her extendable baton. Slides it out to its full length. She checks her phone. No signal, but it's recording. Whatever happens, she's going to make sure everybody knows what he is; what he's done . . .

'Police!' she shouts, and puts her shoulder to the door. It crashes inwards and Pharaoh stumbles into the dark space. Sees the man, dangling, in the barbed-wire web. Sees figures writhe and fuck and fight in rippling frescoes upon the damp walls. Candles, on the floor; intertwined triangles of salt; candles at their points, flames guttering fatly in puddles of pig-fat stinking wax.

And then movement at her side. The smell of gunpowder and oil. Leathery skin against her face; a voice, wet, at her ear . . .

'You will burn for this . . .'

And then there is the whoosh of flame: a sudden wall of fire rising in torrents of liquid gold; heat beating her back, singeing her hair . . .

Pharaoh rubs her hand under her nose. Tastes blood. She takes a sip of her scalding coffee. Pads into the living room and kicks the pizza box off the coffee table so she can sink into her battered armchair and put her bare feet on it. She reaches down and rummages around among the books and case files on the floor. Reaches out with her leg and uses her toes to pull the cord on the standard lamp by the sofa. Sits in the soft yellow light and gathers her thoughts. She hadn't been able to watch the whole video. Only made it through a few frames before she'd retreated to bed. She'd only succeeded in giving herself nightmares. Lesson learned. Should have finished the job. Should have womanned the fuck up and done the job properly.

She glares at the laptop. Opens the lid and presses play, picking up where she left off an hour ago, stomach in knots after her meeting with Ruby. God, she's so close she can feel it. Can feel him. Can feel the nearness of the man that hid in the shadows and tortured Decland Parfitt into madness and Hell.

On the screen, Parfitt is standing in the custody suite at Queen's Gardens Police Station. It's February 8, 2011. Less than forty-eight hours from this moment, Pharaoh will save Parfitt's life, deep in the hidden tunnels beneath the old RAF station on the cliffs at Bempton. But here, now, in the footage that unspools greyly on the dirty screen, she's having to free a prisoner that she knows is guilty of taking, abusing and murdering a child. The CPS say they haven't got enough. Yes, he knew the girl. Yes, he was friendly with them, but he was friendly with everybody. He was a kids' entertainer, for goodness' sake, and the only witness was a child. All the youngsters loved him, with his big wide smile and friendly eyes; his silly safari suit and his green pick-up truck full of exotic creatures and caged beasts. He'd co-operated fully. He'd been friendly and understanding and only too happy to help. Pharaoh had pushed so hard in the interview room that she'd felt herself getting a stitch beneath her ribs. God she needed to lock this bastard up. She knew what he was; what he'd done . . . had known ever since she booked the oily prick for her second daughter's birthday party and found him in her eldest's bedroom, breathing hard. It was only Ruby and Gaynor's presence that had stopped her from beating him to jelly. That, and the fact she was so drunk she couldn't trust herself to stand up straight, let alone call it in. Ruby had told her she'd got it wrong. Gaynor, too, had said that Daddy wouldn't do something like that.

So she'd kicked him out. Cuddled her children. Promised herself she would look into him properly. She'd done just that. Saw the truth of him. Saw what he was.

Pharaoh watches herself on the screen. Sees Parfitt and his lawyer: three-piece pinstripe suit and an Italian calfskin briefcase. Sees Parfitt putting his big safari jacket back on, his face all humble – apparently apologizing for their child getting too worked up at a birthday party. He's pleased to be putting this all behind them.

On the screen, Parfitt spots Pharaoh, lurking in the corner of the frame. She's younger. Thinner. Darker. Still married and a mum to four girls. Pharaoh pities the poor cow on the screen. Back then, she'd thought she'd been through the worst of it.

Parfitt approaches her. Extends a hand.

'Hit him, you silly bitch,' hisses Pharaoh, at the screen. 'Rip his fucking throat out.'

She remembers his voice: refined; exact. He has the manner of a particularly earnest C of E vicar, oily hands and arse-clenching piety.

'No hard feelings, Detective Chief Inspector. I know you were just doing your job. I truly hope you find whoever did this terrible thing.'

Pharaoh watches herself. Sees her own face sour: sick in her throat, hands in fists at her sides.

'We'll have you, Parfitt. We'll fucking have you.'

She watches the custody sergeant reach down and subtly put his hand over the microphone beneath the desk. The rest of the recording is muffled. She sees Parfitt's solicitor clip-clop his shiny shoes towards her. Can recall the heat on her cheeks as he told her that they were considering suing for harassment. Remembers the little smile that flashed across Parfitt's face: a snake moving through the bulrushes.

He'd extended his hand again. Pharaoh had grasped it, planning to pull him close and whisper another 'fuck you' in his ear. Instead he tugged at her arm, his strength extraordinary. She falls against him and for a second his mouth is at her ear: 'Tell Sophia to wear the black knickers – they make her look older . . .'

And then he's walking away from her, across the custody suite, and she's standing there, gasping for breath, before her every instinct is consumed by a primal, protective rage. She sees herself run towards him, raising her hands, ready to beat his brains out on the custody sergeant's neat, shiny floor . . . and then a big sergeant is holding her back, tugging her back into the frame of the picture; the custody sergeant knocking over his chair, yanking at the wire under his desk . . .

The screen goes black. There's no more.

She sits back in her chair, staring up at the ceiling rose. Traces the cracks through the artexed ceiling. Slows her heartbeat. For a while she just sits in the dark. She knows her own mind. Knows already what she's going to have to do. The knowledge hides in the dark places in her consciousness, skulking, sly. She needs to tease it out. To look it full in the face and see if she can stand it.

She holds her phone in her hand, hoping for some indication that Sophia is awake. She wants to ask her, again, what she remembers. She can already picture the exasperated look on her face – the big hand gestures and extravagant eye-rolls. She shared half a dozen messages with the older girl who'd come to the party. She'd been a little bit thrilled to have made friends with a proper teenager; one who smoked and drank and only went to school when they felt like it. Sophia had been a little in awe of her. The two sisters ran away from every foster family and care home where they tried to separate them. They spent as much of their lives on the streets as they did under any kind of supervision. They experienced every kind of abuse and indignity before washing up with the strange, twinkly-eyed man who promised them they would be safe if they just let themselves trust him. It had been the animals that sealed the deal. Gaynor loved birds. Ruby had been drawn to the spiders. They gave him a chance. And he showed them what he was.

She thinks, inevitably, of McAvoy. She's been holding him in reserve, coming up with excuses to keep him from meeting Ruby until she's ready. He's Pharaoh's trump card, but to play it right, she's going to have to put him in danger. She's going to have to use his own nature against him; to place him where she needs him, and to do what she needs him to do. Ruby's ripe for flipping but she won't do a damn thing that Mem hasn't condoned. She needs Mem in custody. And Mem despises coppers. He's got convictions for violence against the police. He'll go berserk the second he sees a big copper on his patch, talking to his girl. And then, well . . . Pharaoh has to hope that Ruby gets the message.

Idly, she flips through pictures on her phone. Lingers for a while on her holiday in Sicily. Remembers blue skies and crystal waters

and a chauffer who'd made her every Godfather fantasy come true.
She'd gone away to think about retirement. Thirty years in and a
decent pension; a chance to go and do some other kind of good in
the world; to spend time with the grandbairn; write a book, find a
bloke she could tolerate.

Parfitt was what stopped her. Parfitt, free. Parfitt, and the opportunity to take up the position of Humberside Police's Head of Crime.
To lead CID and apply resources as she saw fit. A chance to keep
McAvoy out of harm's way and give him the job he deserved,
tackling cases nobody else gave a damn about. A chance to make
up for the worst mistake of her life – whatever the cost.

She closes her eyes again. Feels sleep drifting in like oil.

Her last thought before the darkness takes her is of Decland
Parfitt, dead in her arms; skin in bubbles and smears, staring sight-
lessly; dancing flames on his black irises. Sees herself sliding him
into the heart of the blackened pentagram. Sees herself put her hands
together, and begin to pound upon his chest.

Sees herself bring a devil back from Hell.

SIX

Humberside Police Station, Hessle Road, Hull

M cAvoy considers himself unspeakably rude if he arrives
for a meeting anything less than ten minutes early. He was
here for 8.43am, which wasn't bad at all, considering the
school run and the epic melee that had broken out between mums,
commuters, two cyclists and a frazzled delivery driver who'd blocked
the narrow road by the shops on The Weir. He'd been quite pleased
with himself. Even had time to let Roisin shape his beard and snip
a couple of inches off his increasingly unruly hair. He's never been
able to work out where his parting should go. As with most things
in his life, the lines seem increasingly blurred.

He's in one of the bland little meeting rooms on the first floor.
He's got an office downstairs but he fears that inviting his guests
on to his own territory might appear combative, or worse, an attempt

to assert control. McAvoy spends a lot of time worrying about such things.

He glances at his watch. It's wooden and varnished a deep red. It was a gift from Roisin. He doesn't wear his father's watch any more. Doesn't wear the old school tie either. He's been wearing a black tie at work for months now. Black suit, white shirt. In his long woollen coat, he could be mistaken for a Gangland heavy, though the sadness in his eyes and the mildness to his smile spoil the illusion.

9.32am.

9.41am.

He swivels in the chair. Reads a report on his phone. Texts Roisin. Just kisses, this time. There's nothing else he wants to say.

His phone rings in his pocket, tucked in with his bundle of keys and some of Lilah's broken toys. He spills a miniature surfboard, sand shoe and an orange Lhasa Apso puppy on to the grey carpet and permits himself a curse. He disentangles his phone on the fifth ring, just before it goes to voicemail.

'McAvoy,' he manages, and begins to apologise, instinctively.

'They've said no,' spits DC Andy Daniells, genuine anger in his voice. 'Not well enough. No more details. We've got to go to the bloody Prisons Minister if we want to challenge it.'

McAvoy lets out a soft snarl of frustration. His gums tingle. There's a creeping, crawling feeling on his palms.

'Thanks, Andy. I'll be back up in a while.'

DC Daniells hangs up without a goodbye. McAvoy knows the other members of the Cold Case Unit will be taking it just as hard. They're already pissed off to have lost Neilsen, seconded to work as bagman for Wolsingham on a suspicious death out Walkington way. McAvoy hasn't had a chance to read the morning briefing. He's focused entirely on Parfitt. They all are. They all know what Parfitt is. They can't prove it – not yet – but for the Governor to be actively denying them access for interview seems deliberate and obtuse. He wonders what they have to hide. Wonders whether the Governor understands the full gravity of the situation; whether he knows what lurks beneath the burned, scarred shell of Decland Parfitt. He wonders if he should tell Pharaoh. Decides she'll already know.

The door opens at 9.53am. Gemma Tang stumbles into the stale little room like an explosion in a glitter factory. She's full of apologies;

hair tangled in her cat-eye glasses, her satchel and record bag thrown over one shoulder and dragging an awkward, hard-plastic suitcase with her other hand.

He smiles, rising from the chair and extending a hand. 'Gemma,' he says. 'You look well.'

'Oh stop, stop,' grins Gemma, as she starts stripping out of her green duffle coat and smoothing down the crinkles on her bright, floral dress. She's got glitzy slides in her dark hair. Costume jewellery, similar to that worn by Lilah when she plays dress-up, sparkle on her fingers, at her ears, at her throat.

'Hang on!'

Gemma makes a face and pokes her head out into the corridor. Her hair bounces sleekly, as if she were shooting a shampoo commercial, as she spins to give her undivided, bright-eyed attention back to McAvoy. 'We got separated. It's a maze! Much preferred Queen's Gardens, didn't you? Had character. Anyway, sorry to have kept you . . . this is Halle. You've had emails, I gather . . .'

Halle is tall and athletic. Bumble-bee dungarees tucked into Doc Martens: orange bobble-hat and twin plaits of bottle-black hair. She's wearing little round eyeglasses and fingerless gloves. She looks about McAvoy's age. Younger maybe. He can't tell any more. Doesn't know whether she's styling herself after an eco-warrior, a hipster barista or a lumberjack. Her energy is less frothy than Gemma's. She looks like she hasn't hit enough people yet today, and is glad it's still early.

'Halle Spence,' she says, extending a hand and giving McAvoy's a squeeze. The scratchy wool of her gloves very nearly causes him to shudder. He can't stand the feeling of wool on his bare skin. Goes to pieces when he sees Roisin pulling on a rough sweater over naked flesh.

'Aector,' he says, and indicates they should take a seat. He'd fetched the water jug and glasses himself. There'd been a pot of coffee, too, an hour ago. He's hidden it behind his own chair and bag, along with the cups and saucers, in case they pour themselves a cup of stewed, tepid coffee and mistake it for an act of psychological manipulation. He doesn't want to seem like he's trying to assert his dominance. He can almost hear Pharaoh slapping herself on the forehead and telling him to stop being such a wet lettuce. Can hear his dad, too. Bloody Jessie, he called him, sometimes, though he'd said it with that smile of his – the one that said he wasn't sure where his boy had come from, but he was glad he was his.

'Good to see some of the old faces again,' smiles Gemma, pulling out a folder, laptop and a recording device from the depths of one bag, and a double Mars bar from another. She grimaces. 'No buffet car,' she explains. 'Had to ask the lovely cabbie to stop for this on the way or I would have died, and then the blasted phone rang and well . . . my stomach feels like my throat's been cut. Not the triumphant return I'd planned, if I'm honest. The trains! I mean, it's a lottery. But here we are.'

McAvoy rolls his sleeves down. Rolls them up again. Wonders if she's done. She's not.

'It's going well enough, as you can see. You understand the project, yes? I mean, true crime is mainstream now, which makes it so exciting for us to try and put our own stamp on an established art form. We're going for the human story – the emotional carnage of losing your loved one to a serial killer. We've earmarked Hull for the third episode in the series, if we can make it work . . . which is . . .' she takes a bite of Mars bar and rolls her eyes in fake ecstasy. '. . . rather up to you.'

McAvoy sees a chance to jump in. To steer things in the direction he'd like them to go. Can't quite force himself to barge in. He can already picture them getting annoyed; feeling misled, bamboozled. God he hates people being upset. Hates them being upset with him most of all. He gives his attention to Halle. She's not even listening to her associate. She's just staring at McAvoy as if reading the small print on the side of his face.

'Your Chief Constable already gave us the nod,' she says, pulling a battered notepad from the pocket of her dungarees. McAvoy's oddly pleased to see her remove a stub of pencil from behind her ear. 'We know how this goes, Aector. You're going to try and get us to change our minds. And Trish has served you up because she thinks we're going to fall for the whole sad-eyed giant shtick. Well, you're going to have to work pretty damn hard, Buster.'

McAvoy can't hold back the little laugh that erupts at the back of his throat. He's never been called Buster before. Never had his name so horribly mispronounced.

Halle drums her fingers on the desk. She gives McAvoy another hard stare. 'Better be bloody good, is all I'm saying,' she mutters, ruefully. Beside her, Gemma makes a face.

'Halle's very committed to making the show we pitched, Aector,' says Gemma, her face full of theatrical apology. 'I mean, I was there. I was a part of it, in my own small way. We know what happened, and the only thing that's stopped us from going ahead is the fact that I knew you would have reservations. Must be the old police press officer in me, eh? Still got a bit of conscience—'

'Which isn't necessarily suited to running a production company,' finishes Halle. She clenches her jaw whenever she's not talking. 'So . . . out of deference to my partner here, and in part because I thought it might be the only way to actually find out whether you were real or make-believe, we've dragged ourselves over from Manchester. So, come on . . . give us whatever it is you're offering and we'll see.'

McAvoy allows himself a moment. He's glugging with water already but permits himself a small sip to wet his lips. He really does hate confrontation. Doesn't argue if he can help it and never raises his voice. But he does understand the impulse.

'Detective Chief Superintendent Pharaoh has asked me to brief you on a current cold case investigation. I'm happy to do that, provided we stick to the terms agreed. As for "deals" and "hard sells", those are words I'll be thinking about after you've gone. I'm going to talk to you about a missing child. Whether you think I'm serving him up to you as a bribe is really between you and your conscience.'

There's silence in the room for a moment. Halle gives a small, knowing smile. Thaws a little. 'Oh, you were right about him,' she says. 'He's not making this easy for himself, is he?'

'We're sorry, Aector,' says Gemma, adopting the manner of a remorseful preschooler. He remembers her fondly from her time in the press office and always felt she brought a competence and compassion to the job, despite her slightly scatty approach. He's glad the production company is doing well. Is glad they're illuminating successful prosecutions and the convictions of some very bad people. He knows that with confidence in policing at an all-time low, his job is getting harder by the day. The new Chief Constable is doing his damnedest to change perceptions. Chief among his strategies is permitting a documentary crew to work alongside the murder squad in real time. It's McAvoy who's drawn the short straw.

'Can I presume you've done some initial googling,' says McAvoy. 'And I do apologise for using that as a verb.'

'Not a lot to get the mouth-watering,' says Halle, wrinkling her nose. She glances at her notes. 'Decland Parfitt. Lots of child porn convictions – nasty stuff, but nothing jaw-dropping. Reading between the lines . . . questioned in connection with one Carmel Barry, aged eleven. Disappeared from a caravan park out near . . .'

'Skipsea,' finishes McAvoy. 'Saturday, September second, 2010. Last seen at 11.05pm by her aunt, Paulene Haiz, who had a home nearby and who had previously worked as a cleaner at the caravan park. Paulene reported her missing when she came to check on her and wish her good night. Carmel's never been found. She'd be pushing twenty-five, now. Her auntie has accepted that she's never coming home, but, well – the chance to lay her to rest, to give some kind of justice . . . We believe Decland Parfitt is the key to giving her that. Giving it to others, too.'

Halle wrinkles her nose. 'She was alone in the caravan? At eleven?'

'There'd been an argument,' says McAvoy, diplomatically, and pictures Paulene folding up into herself, wet-faced, as she told him, as she'd told so many other coppers, that she will never forgive herself for taking the easy option that chilly, wind-blown autumn night. 'We'll come to that.'

'No sign, no note,' mutters Halle, reading from her pad. 'Reported missing, couple of appeals, some local stories, a couple of nationals, wee bit here and there on some missing person charity websites . . .' She makes a display of glancing at her notes. 'Nothing much recently, save for one rather self-congratulatory puff-piece in the Hull Mail last year. A new "cold case" unit undertaking major reviews of unsolved murders, abductions and violent assaults. I read the interview with Auntie Paulene. Skimmed it, anyway . . . seems like the police didn't have much interest, what with her history. What's the phrase . . . chaotic lifestyle?'

McAvoy wishes Pharaoh were beside him. Winces inwardly as he realizes he'll have to recount this entire exchange verbatim for her pleasure.

He takes a breath. Releases the line he's been practising. 'Significant new intelligence has emerged that links Carmel's disappearance with other missing persons cases and unsolved sexual offences currently under review.'

Gemma and Halle have the sense to say nothing. They give him an encouraging glance. This is better.

'As you know, a decision has been made by the Police Authority to permit a small documentary team to witness aspects of an ongoing investigation . . .'

Halle scowls. 'Well, we put in a bid nearly a year ago, but we heard it went to Wagtail TV . . .'

'We've yet to reach an agreement with any production company,' says McAvoy, parroting the line Pharaoh had insisted he use. 'But given Trish's respect for Gemma, she's minded to give the green light to you. On this cold case.'

Halle takes a moment. 'And she made this decision just after Gemma got in touch and said we were doing a series on serial killers and were going to feature Simeon Gibbons . . .'

McAvoy flinches at the name. Swallows, hard. It's been a decade or more, but he can still feel the flames upon his skin; the blaze at his neck. Can remember sinking into the forest floor, blood at his face, his neck; upon his hands. . .

'Perhaps you should watch the video,' says McAvoy, reaching down and picking up his laptop off the floor. He opens it, swivels the screen away from him, and stops, finger hovering over the keys, momentarily reluctant to press play. It's Pharaoh's call, but he fancies it's one that will come back to haunt them. He's had such feelings before.

He takes a breath. Gathers himself. When he speaks, his voice is soft, his manner still. To talk of Carmel pains him. To know that he has yet to bring peace to her aunt is a lash he strikes himself with daily.

'I've been looking into Carmel's life,' he begins, blinking slowly. 'Getting to know her. Understanding her, or trying to. It's a privilege. I try and treat her secrets with respect. I've read her diaries and her letters and the things she posted in chat rooms. I know Carmel. And I grieve for what was taken out of the world. There was a loveliness to Carmel. She was kind. Sweet. A bit odd, according to her family. Always had her head in the clouds; always away with the fairies. Amazing imagination, though. And friendly. Would talk to anyone. Never afraid to ask questions. She liked to read. Liked wildlife programmes. She was a member of a junior animal welfare club. Got a letter every month updating her on the penguin and the gibbon she sponsored with her own pocket money . . .'

He pauses. Gathers himself.

'Somebody snuffed that light out one night in September 2010.

They opened the window to the caravan, slithered inside. Drugged her. Rolled her up in her own bedsheet. Dragged her out through the open window. Loaded her into a vehicle.'

'And she hasn't been seen since,' finishes Halle, nodding, with due solemnity.

McAvoy directs his words at her, holding her gaze. 'I call her auntie once a week to update her on the progress of the investigation and every week I hear the pain and the loss in her voice. She knows Carmel's dead. She's always known.' He shakes his head and fears for a moment that his eyes will turn glassy. Swallows, hard. 'Carmel deserves to be able to rest. To come home. So do the others.'

'We're sorry, Aector,' says Gemma, sitting forward. She seems to mean it. Seems cross with herself. 'Please, what's on the video?'

McAvoy rolls his head from side to side, hearing something creak then crack. 'Decland Parfitt,' he says. 'We've identified a suspect. Carmel's abduction and three other open investigations from neighbouring forces.'

'We've identified a suspect. Carmel's abduction and three other open investigations from neighbouring forces. In 2011, Detective Chief Superintendent Pharaoh – at that time a DS based in Grimsby – was involved in the apprehension of one Decland Parfitt, lately of Withernwick Lane, Great Cowden. That's not far from Skipsea, Gemma – as you no doubt recall. Parfitt was at that time a suspect in the attempted abduction of a nine-year-old girl called Kaylani from a holiday home in Skipsea . . .'

Gemma and Halle exchange a look. McAvoy wonders what they're saying to each other; what hidden communication is passing from one to the other. Wonders what they know.

Halle shakes her head, as if the world just got a shade too ugly. 'And Pharaoh nabbed this Parfitt for it, right? And now you're linking him to Carmel's disappearance too.'

'Among others,' says McAvoy, feeling things slipping out of his control. 'There's a briefing document being prepared. You're bound to have questions. We can't provide all the answers but, if you're amenable, it might be the kind of unfolding, live-action project that you've been petitioning to make. And it's new. Fresh. Nobody's heard of this one.'

'There may be a reason for that,' says Gemma, apologetically. 'He might be a nasty sex offender with one hell of a taste in pre-teens but, let's be honest, they're ten a penny. It would need to be something really significant. And he's inside, yes? Which makes access to him very difficult for us. And for you, no doubt.'

McAvoy decides to press on as if he hadn't been derailed. 'A witness came forward. Somebody saw him climbing out of the window, bag over his shoulder, like Santa Claus gone bad. She recognised him as the same man who'd been entertaining the children earlier in the day. He wasn't wearing his safari suit but she recognised his face.'

'Did she raise the alarm?'

McAvoy swallows. 'The witness was a child. She wasn't initially believed.'

'But you got him in the end?'

'He was identified five days after the abduction.'

'I don't remember much of a drama about a missing child,' frowns Gemma.

'There was a different news agenda at that time,' says McAvoy. 'There was local interest but because she'd had a history of running away, well . . .'

Gemma nods. 'The optics didn't appeal?' She turns to her partner. 'Any more than two surnames in one family and the national press have a tendency to write people off. There used to be a shorthand on the top of some police reports – SOS. Stood for "Scum on Scum".'

McAvoy swallows. Wonders whether it's too late to pick another career. 'Trish interviewed Parfitt. Pillar of the community, loveable eccentric, foster dad to two darling daughters. Nobody thought he'd done it except for Trish. She's always said the same – she looked in his eyes and just knew what he was into. She says she's looked into eyes like that only a handful of times in her career. Nobody's ever burned with that hunger the way Parfitt's did.'

He stops, unsure if he's sharing too much. He wonders whether Pharaoh would approve of him sharing her words.

'She spent hours with him,' he continues. 'Hour upon hour in the interview rooms, trying to get inside his head. He didn't budge. Didn't give an inch. He was with his youngest foster daughter at the time she was taken. They were walking on the headland, just the two of them. We could ask her and she'd confirm it. She did, too. Not so much as a flicker. Yep, he was with her, and she was with him. There were no forensics, no DNA to link him to the scene. All we had was a shaky witness statement and Pharaoh's gut. But he held firm. Ran down the clock. He was released on the grounds of insufficient evidence.' He pauses, unsure how to phrase things. 'So somebody took matters into their own hands.'

Halle smiles. She's liking this. 'At some point after leaving Grimsby Police Station at 11.25am, Decland Parfitt was abducted by persons unknown.' He pauses. Breathes. 'And this is what they did to him.'

McAvoy presses play. The screen fills with a slow flick-pad of images. They look like postcards from Hell. Parfitt is bound in barbed wire, dangling upside down in the centre of a crow-black room. The image is illuminated by the camera flash: a burst of strobing light which casts an eerie yellow glow across the wounds upon Parfitt's back. The screen flickers. Close-ups now. Close-ups of the pieces sliced away. Of the savage artistry perpetrated upon every part of him. Another flicker and the visitors sit back a little in their chairs. Parfitt is aflame. He writhes and twists as if trying to emerge from a chrysalis. Another flicker and the screen fills with flame.

'Whoever took him – they fled the scene when Trish – Detective Chief Superintendent Pharaoh – entered the premises. But they set him alight as they went. Trish saved his life.'

Halle looks aghast. 'He survived all that?'

'Some of him did, yes. He was treated for sixty per cent burns and required numerous other skin grafts to cover what was done to him, but . . . it was what they did to his mind that took the time to heal. He'd been drugged – the exact cocktail of drugs still being a matter of discussion and conjecture. What's clear is that he'd seen terrible things. Been places nobody should go. He kept speaking of Hell. Of damnation. He couldn't be tried. While healing, an extraordinary stash of home-made pornography, of simulated child murders, was found on his laptop. Hard copies – polaroids – were concealed within the various magazines and animal welfare files that he kept in his little animal sanctuary in the cellar of the family home, hidden among the spiders and the lizards and the birds. That's where he liked to go. To sit under the red light and look at his trophies. He got fourteen years. Real prison.'

'And now you're linking him to the abduction of Carmel?' asks Gemma, eyes bright. 'Gosh, what sort of resources are you throwing at this? I mean, this could really be something, don't you think, Halle?'

'You mentioned a video,' says Halle, thoughtfully. 'They're just stills. Where are they from, anyway?'

'Trish had to use the flash of her phone to illuminate the scene as she entered the building. There are other stills but they're too blurry to be of use. What we do have is the video shot by the forensics team after Parfitt had been airlifted to hospital. It's rather . . . harrowing.'

Halle gives him a look that says she's seen it all. Gemma winces. Looks down at the floor.

McAvoy presses play.

Twenty minutes later, McAvoy phones Pharaoh.

'They went for it, didn't they?' She doesn't sound pleased – just satisfied that another arduous task has been ticked off the mountainous to-do list. 'I knew they bloody would. You owe me, my lad. You bloody owe me big time.'

'Happy to leave Gibbons for another day, provided Auntie Paulene is "willing to play ball".'

'She will,' says Pharaoh. 'God, when they see her up on the headland with her spade . . . it's got Netflix all over it.'

'It feels wrong.'

'You always feel wrong, Aector. It's your defining characteristic.'

McAvoy makes himself chuckle so she doesn't think he's annoyed with her. It rings hollow. He feels like he's done something wrong. Sold out Carmel just to spare himself embarrassment.

Pharaoh sighs, as if hearing his thoughts spoken aloud. 'Sainsbury's, twenty minutes. Tall Americano, extra shot. And a Bakewell . . .'

'You've got the briefing . . .'

Pharaoh takes a breath. Were she to have a family coat of arms, she fancies this would be the motto: 'Fuck it, I'm hungry.'

McAvoy smiles. This time, it's real.

SEVEN

Gemma hunches into her coat. Stuffs her hands in her pockets. Breathes in the city she used to call home. Still the same smell: sea salt and diesel; warm bread and damp oats.

'What's the smell?' asks Halle, sucking on a cherry menthol flavoured vape and flaring her nostrils.

'The docks,' says Gemma, warmly. She steps away from the kerb as a blue van hisses through a puddle. Halle swears as a spray of dirty water spatters her dungarees. 'Other side of the city smells of cocoa, from the factory. Always made my mouth water.'

Halle glares up and down the long road: neat terraced houses facing a deserted park. The streetlights haven't been turned off yet: soft yellow flares amid the hanging swirls of grey. Gemma watches as a little flurry of leaves tumbles through the halo of light.

'He's all you said and more,' says Halle, nodding back towards the brick frontage of the police building. 'If I turn up dead, he's who I'd want investigating.'

Gemma sticks out her lower lip. 'Don't talk like that. I don't like that.'

Halle sucks her lips together, biting back on whatever it is she'd like to say. Gemma feels her stomach clench. Stupid girl. Stupid! Why had she said that? Why had she said it in that way? God, Gemma, won't you ever bloody learn? Softens her body language. Plays the little girl.

'I'm sorry,' she says, fluttering her eyelashes: a toddler keen to make amends. 'I got over excited.'

Halle gives her a nudge with her arm. Looks awkward. 'It's got legs, definitely. I mean, whatever it is he's not telling us is going to be the story, but even with what we've got . . .'

'And the Gibbons documentary wasn't really going anywhere,' confirms Gemma, relieved that nobody's cross with her. She makes a mental note to tell her therapist at their next session. She's still doing it. Still trying to please authority figures by acting like a naughty child.

Gemma's phone pings in her pocket. She grabs it from the warm cocoon of her duffle coat and gives a nod of appreciation.

'Good as his word, too,' she says, looking up and down the road. Gemma realizes she's looking for a passing taxi. She'll be waiting a while.

'He's sent the file?'

Halle sucks on her cheek as she reads, fingers moving swiftly over the keys. Her eyes widen. Gemma's content to wait. Halle's got experience. Got good contacts. She's got a track record. She's done this before. Gemma knows she's the junior partner. She's got no ambition to be anything else. Her ex-husband robbed her of any sense of worth. Now she just wants to hitch her wagon to somebody who at least looks like they know where they're going.

'Here,' says Halle, and hands the phone over. The screen is paused on an image of a middle-aged man in a comedy safari suit and an over-sized white helmet. He's smiling: capped teeth in a pleasant face.

'. . . this is Molly,' he says, to the camera. He raises his hand. There's a huge spider on his forearm, all hair and eyes. 'I try not to let the children stroke her as it really isn't good for her. They can develop bald spots, which might sound funny but isn't great news for poor Molly. And I don't want to be sitting making tiny spider wigs at my age.'

He grins reflexively as he delivers his often-used joke. Beckons the camera to follow him as he ducks under a wooden door frame and into a dark space lined with cages and glass. 'This is The Arc,' he says, proudly, as the camera jerkily moves across vivariums and tanks: lizards and snakes static in their hot, humid cells. There's a terrible scratching and snapping sound from a cage at the rear of the room. A reddish snout noses through the bars, teeth chewing on the steel.

'Still fighting it then, eh, Missy?' asks the man, sadly, hands on his hips. 'I'm trying to help you, you silly goose.'

He addresses the camera directly. 'Rescued from a hunt,' he explains. 'Terrified half to death. Half-mad and terrible wounds at her throat. She's recovering but the madness has got her, you can see it when you look in her eyes. She needs a little tenderness but she just won't trust that I know what's good for her. But she won't get what she wants until she earns it. Until she learns to accept love. She could have such a life here. She would mean so much to so many. Or she could go back out to where it's cold and dark and scary and everything's trying to hurt her. She'll see the wisdom, eventually. Or she'll go mad in there and I'll have the sad job of putting her down.'

The little video clip comes to an end. Gemma looks at Halle, who's got a smile on her face as she taps away at her iPad, teeth chattering. Above, seagulls whirl and shriek, turning in lazy circles in the relentless grey.

'I think it's called a pith helmet,' says Gemma, absently. She can't shake the feeling that the man in the video was looking directly at her as he spoke. Can't forget the intensity, the perfect stillness, in his gaze. The phone buzzes in her hand. She performs an awkward swap with Halle, switching gadgets. Halle takes the call as Gemma looks at the address and phone number of Carmel Barry's aunt.

Behind Halle, she notices the bulky silhouette, collar up, big shoulders loose, stray licks of red hair curling in the wind. Halle follows her gaze.

'So yes, really, the sooner the better,' says Halle, into the phone. 'I know it's short notice but given that we're here and it's becoming such an important project for us, well . . . yes, that is more apt. Excellent. Well you'll love Gemma, and I'm sure she'll be able to allay any misgivings you may have . . . yes, he is a lovely man. Wouldn't want to meet him down a dark alley, of course. And he did give us his personal reassurances that you'd participate, so . . . thank, you. OK. Bye.'

Halle ends the call. 'Paulene's expecting you. Just use cabs and keep the receipts – we've got a bit of a leeway on the budget. Get as many guide shots as you can. Think cinematography, yeah? Think visually. Don't lose sight of the medium. Get the camera on her from the off so if she suddenly tells you everything it's raw – not the diluted shit we end up having to use when they've already had their cry on the way to the bloody studio.'

She follows Gemma's gaze. Gemma feels the hairs on her arms rise as an eerie, prickly sensation crawls across her, spider-like. She doesn't like the look on her colleague's face.

'He's the story,' she says, pointing at the disappearing figure. 'You don't get scars like that unless you've been through something life-altering . . .'

'But I told you how he caught Gibbons,' protests Gemma, and the feeling continues its rise up her neck. She can feel tiny, hairless legs moving purposefully towards her face. 'There was a confrontation. He was hurt.'

Halle shakes her head. 'You go and sweet talk the auntie, yeah? She's not like the picture he painted – not on the phone at least. Said she would help because Aector's such a lovely lad and she'd promised Trish, but she doesn't sound like she can blub on cue, so you might have to give her emotions a bit of a poke. You're good at that.'

Gemma feels herself getting smaller. Feels her eyes prickle. Wills herself not to cry. That's what her ex used to hate the most about her – the way she could turn on the waterworks; make him feel bad for shouting at her by giving in to tears when all it got too much. She doesn't want to be that person any more. Knows that to ensure people really like her, she has to make sure they never find out what she's really like.

'You're following him?' she says, as Halle turns away, bag banging against her. 'Halle, he's giving us an open invitation . . . I mean, do you think it screams like, y'know, "mutual trust", if you're tailing him? Oh God, I feel so silly even saying that.'

'I'll get a hire car,' says Halle, ignoring her. 'You think drop-offs have reached this end of the M62, yet? No bloody cabs.'

'Halle, seriously . . . I worked with police officers for years – if Trish finds out . . .'

'Doesn't scare me,' says Halle, brushing some dirt off her shoulder. She stalks off without a goodbye.

Gemma holds herself closer. Wonders if she's got the stomach for this. She feels homesick for Humberside Police. Wishes she could turn back the clock. Make different decisions. Be better. Do it all differently.

She sniffs back tears.

Turns her back.

Walks away from the big brick building and into the grey.

EIGHT

Gardham Road, Etton
10.17am

'Plenty more where that came from. Glad to be rid of it. Can't stand the ruddy stuff myself but I'm good at making it, and it seems a shame to let the apples go to waste . . .'

Neilsen takes another scoop of apple crumble, muddled with home-made custard. He hasn't had anything this sharp and tart and warm delicious since his second-to-last fiancée.

'More coffee in the pot, if you need to unclog your mouth a bit.'

Neilsen swills an inch of strong, black coffee around his mouth.

The caffeine makes his blood feel fizzy and awake, but the great bowlful of home-made pudding is making him want to fall asleep in front of the fire.

'That was wonderful, Lorraine,' says Neilsen, pushing the bowl away. He'd like to undo his belt a little, but he fancies he's already overstepped the mark. He's only been in her kitchen for twenty minutes and already Lorraine Whitley-Beal has fed him two desserts and given him a bag of scones to take home. She seems thrilled to have a handsome young police officer in her kitchen, and set about feeding him up the second he entered the warm, low-ceilinged kitchen at the back of the cluttered little cottage on the outskirts of Cherry Burton.

'I always used to tell the kids that the secret ingredient was love,' she says, with a big grin. 'It's not, of course. It's sugar.'

She takes his bowl and washes it up in the deep ceramic sink, staring out across a dreary vastness of scrub and fallow land. She settles herself in the floral, high-backed sofa and sips her tea, regarding him over the floral lip of her china cup. It's the first time she's been still. She gives off the energy of a wasp trapped between two panes of glass.

'So,' says Neilsen, pulling his notebook from the inside pocket of his suit. He feels as though he's lost the right to talk about the urgency of the situation, having paused proceedings long enough to polish off a mid-morning dessert. 'It's a road you know well, I gather. Would you mind telling me a little about . . .'

Lorraine eases herself forward in her chair, plucking a feather from her tights. She's wearing a mid-length pleated skirt and a cardigan over a matching, baby-blue sweater. Her stocking feet are crammed into plum-coloured slippers that bulge around her bunions. Her face is round and pleasant – brownish hair shot through with grey. She's pleased to be able to help the police. Wishes she could do more.

'You just do the scribbling and I'll tell you what happened,' says Lorraine, with a look of apology. 'I've been on me own nigh-on eight years now and I've sort of lost the art of conversation, if you'll forgive me. I ping-pong all over the place when I'm answering questions – just ask our Louise. Lovely girl, once you get past the squint.' She takes a moment for herself, perhaps considering the absent Louise's future prospects. 'Heart of gold, mind.'

Neilsen sits back, getting comfortable at the pine two-seater table.

There's a little black telly in the corner of the kitchen, though the big iron cooking range opposite gives off so much heat that he's amazed the set hasn't melted.

'Our Auntie Beryl has chickens,' says Lorraine, absently, in an accent that seems to hail from considerably further north-east. 'Bloody pests, the lot of them. Forever escaping and take more looking after than a Royal baby. They're her pride and joy, which is a dispiriting thing to say out loud. Anyway, Beryl's laid up with two broken wrists – silly sausage wears three pairs of insoles and still can't get her posh shoes to fit; took a tumble that sounded like she was snapping firewood, I tell you – so muggins here has the delight of feeding the birds and settling them down for the night. That's where I'd been, as I explained when I called it in. When I found, well . . . him.'

Neilsen nods. Looks up from his notes and sees her staring at him. Seems to be checking that he's keeping up.

'I'm not one to shock easy,' she says pointedly, and leaves a pause for Neilsen to write this down. She seems like somebody whose refusal to go to pieces in a crisis forms the bedrock of her sense of self. 'Gave me a start, though. I mean, I didn't look more than I had to. Wasn't even sure I should get out of the car. But I think I knew what it was as soon as I saw it. Saw him, I mean.'

She's looking at a memory. Neilsen lets her fill the silence.

'Bad road of late, that one. I get no help with the Council Tax so I feel well within my rights to say that the local authority could do with a rocket up its backside. Some of the puddles and potholes on the back roads – they need a bloody lifeguard. I head down there slow. Lesson learned the hard way . . .'

'You drive a Suzuki Jimny, is that right?'

'Yep – the nippers call it the Cricket. Jiminy Cricket, get it? Powerful little thing. Nippy too. But hit one of those divots at anything over forty and you're likely to bend the chassis.'

Neilsen sits forward. 'Do you remember seeing any other vehicles ahead of you, Lorraine? Even in the distance? Even the lights?'

Lorraine plucks at the pleats in her skirt, looking pained. 'I knew you'd ask me that,' she says, a little troubled. 'I've been thinking about it since I woke up. Trouble is, I don't know what's a memory and what I'm just picturing because I want to help. I mean, I know there must have been other cars on the road because there always are, but how can I tell whether what I see in my mind is from last night? Do you see the problem? I mean, I so want to help, I truly do . . . Do you know who he is, yet? What the poor man was doing there?'

Neilsen fancies that DCI Wolsingham will be asking him the same question before lunch – preferably wrapped up with a ribbon and bow. He doubts he'll give him a double helping of crumble and custard first.

'Enquiries are at an early stage,' says Neilsen. The words seem to fall short of the actuality. He doesn't know anything. Won't until they get fingerprints and blood samples back, and that could take a bloody age. He feels distinctly put upon.

'The bag he was in . . .' muses Lorraine, sipping her tea. 'I've seen them at airports. Huge great things you can fit the kit of an entire football team inside. Can't be that many people have access to a bag like that. And those scars – he'll be in your system somewhere, you mark my words.'

Neilsen glances at the flat-topped magazine rack beside the sofa. There are two crime novels sitting atop a stack of copies of the East Riding Mail. She knows her stuff, it seems. Could teach Neilsen a thing or two about investigating.

'I'm going to feel a right apeth if I can't give you anything useful.' Lorraine frowns. 'But he was just there. Just a shape in the road, and so I got out to see, like anybody would. There he was. Just a body in a bag, there in the middle of the road. I knew it was a 999 situation but ambulance seemed wrong, given he was cold as the grave.'

'You touched him?'

'Oh yes. Neck. Wrist. Felt inside the shirt for a heartbeat. How do you think I felt the scars?'

Neilsen smiles his most reassuring smile. 'Would you be able to give me the clothes you were wearing, please, Lorraine? Procedure, I'm afraid . . .'

'Say no more,' says Lorraine, hauling herself to her feet and looking thoroughly delighted to have the opportunity to secrete yesterday's clothes in a real police evidence bag. 'You'll be wanting the thingummybob too, yes?'

Neilsen is glancing at his phone and doesn't hear the question at first. Wolsingham's insisting he lean on Forensics. Wants an ID before close of play today. He's harassing the CCTV unit. Pecking away like a hungry bird.

'Thingummybob?'

'The wotsit that my Louise fitted to the dash after I had the little accident in June. Records everything. Not sure who'd want to watch it but it means that if you have a little fender-bender, at least you all know what happened. Didn't give it a thought until just now. I can send a message to our Louise. She might even have watched it by now – it all goes through her phone. She'll be flapping like a one-winged hen when she hears about all this. Thinks I'm simple, sometimes, though I'm the one with a handsome young man in my kitchen and she's the one working an early shift at Lidl, so I don't know which of us is winning. Anyway, will that be a help? Come in handy?'

Neilsen stares through the rain-speckled glass at a sky the colour of wet sand. Feels a sunrise inside him. Wonders whether he might be permitted to celebrate with custard. He knows McAvoy would. Knows Pharaoh would already have her head in the bowl.

'Very handy indeed, Lorraine. Very handy indeed.'

NINE

Cold Harbour Road, Bishop Burton
11.23am

Joe sprays a blast of anti-perspirant into the drifting cloud of cannabis smoke. Wafts his hand around in the air. Screws his eyes shut and holds on to the drug as long as his lungs will allow. Blows out a ghost of hopes and dreams and bad air. Sparks dance in his eyes.

They won't come yet. Might not come at all. Nowt to do with you, Joe, nowt at all . . .

He's slumped at the foot of his bed, lopsided, wet-faced. He's wearing a dressing gown over yesterday's jeans. There's mud on the shins. Mud on his boots too. He smoked himself insensible when he got home last night. Dropped off around 3am. He knows he left her some voicemails. Sent a couple of texts, too. He doesn't think he told her about the thing on the road. He might have. Doesn't trust himself. Doesn't know himself.

Loser!

The voice inside his head is hers. *You're a fucking loser, Joe. What you see and what the world sees – they're a million miles apart.*

He flops back on the bed. Wishes he were the smoke, dissipating into the hanging mist. He would love to turn to vapour. Can imagine drifting through her. Knowing, for one perfect moment, what it is to be her; to know what she wants.

He'll call the police this morning. Definitely. He'll have a shower and brush his teeth. Shave his head. Put on a shirt that doesn't look like it should be wrapped around the end of a ladder on the back of a van. He'll do the right thing. He'll prove himself to her. That's what she wants, isn't it? The kind of man who knows when his Direct Debits are due; the sort who pays his parking fines within seven days and hasn't been using a fictional tax code on his invoices for the last twelve years. The sort of man who does the decent thing and informs the authorities of things they really ought to know about, like a body on the road; a body in a bag, wriggling on the sparkling road . . .

He tries to cry. Gives a few sobs and pulls the right faces but he can't do tears the way other people seem able to and just ends up feeling like a tit. He bites the fat of his thumb instead, clamping down until he's on the verge of breaking skin. He rarely leaves a mark these days. He can hurt himself the way he needs to and nobody will think any less of him for it. He might actually be permitted to indulge in his new addiction in peace.

He pulls himself up. Sees his own reflection staring back from the window. Sees his own translucent self: a stained-glass cut into squares by the patchwork fields beyond the window; patterned with hay bales and huddled sheep. Sees the beauty in his misery, even as it drowns him.

That bloody noise again. Is it the pipes? Christ, that's not a job he can afford. So many things to sort; so many plates to keep spinning. Why can't anything just work? Why is it always fucking him!

No mistaking it now. Three hard bangs on the front door. He rolls backwards on the bed and grabs the door handle, yanking it open. There are three closed doors between himself and the front door. They must have been banging hard for him to hear. He feels panic begin to rise. Coppers, definitely. Coppers or bailiffs or a delivery driver . . . fuck . . . fuck!

He stumbles to the window and looks out across the damp grey cement of the farmyard. His own car's down there. His friend's fancy Jag. A little further away, by the wood store, in the U-shaped forecourt by the old milking pens: a Volvo XC60. Not a bailiff, then. Not a delivery driver . . .

A handsome man in a smart grey suit steps back from Joe's front door, craning his neck and looking up at the granny flat. He's taking a good lungful of the midday air, too. He's smiling. Smiling to himself!

Joe feels himself coming apart. Wonders if this is how an aneurysm feels. He's always rather liked the idea of being genuinely catatonic. He'd like to really lean into mental illness; to be looked after. He'd like oblivion of any kind. Would like it more than prison, and he knows that's where he's going if he answers the door stinking of weed. Even if he can sweet talk the bastard – somehow summon up an echo of charm – it'll get back to her, and she'll look at him in that way and his heart will fucking splinter, and . . .

He's got one leg out of the window before he knows what he's doing. Sits there in his dressing gown, balls crushed against the ledge. It's only a few feet. *You're young. It'll hurt, but you can handle pain. Get yourself down to the river and have a little think. Come back, sort yourself out . . .*

'I know you're in there, mate. Ben Neilsen, Humberside Police. I really do need you to answer the door . . .'

He's doing this for his little girl, he tells himself. She doesn't need to know the truth about who he is. Not yet.

He leans out. Watches as the cop squats down in front of his car. Cranes his head and considers the tyres. Pulls out his phone and starts taking pictures.

Now, he tells himself. Now, when your ears are buzzing and your heart's thudding and the world's full of fibreglass and sparkledust and . . .

'Here, fuck! Don't be fucking daft, mate . . . Joe, seriously, you'll . . .'

He topples from the windowsill.

For a moment, there's the sensation of flying. It's nearly a rush. *You'll crush this, Joe. You've got this.*

From below: 'Oh, you silly bastard!'
His tibias snap like light tubes.
And then there's just so much fucking pain.

TEN

Pharaoh presses her thumb between her eyebrows. She looks like she's pushing in a drawing pin. She's got her eyes shut behind her sunglasses. She's got a mouthful of half-decent Bakewell tart on the go, but her expression is of somebody who's just discovered a room-temperature oyster under their tongue. She's squeezing her head against her phone, grinding it into her shoulder. If it were a sponge, she'd have wrung it dry. She mutters something unintelligible, and hangs up with a grunt.

She takes a moment. Composes herself. Fixes McAvoy with a manic smile.

'So, Ben's day isn't going swimmingly . . .'

McAvoy has his head in his palm, fingers in his hair, scratching at his scalp. He's hot and uncomfortable. Everything's small and crowded and loud. He's scalded his top lip on his hot chocolate, knocked over the salt cellar twice and spilled half a cup of water on his thigh. He has to lean in to hear Pharaoh. He can smell last night's wine on her breath. Her cigarettes and coffee, served thick and black as pitch. He jiggles his legs under the Formica-topped table. Listens as Pharaoh gives him the lowdown on Neilsen's day so far.

'Off his tits, according to Ben. Jesus, he's out of my sight for five bloody minutes! Both legs are broken and one of his wrists is facing the wrong way. Ben's got a bruise the size of a watermelon, right down his back and shoulder. Provided quite an effective crash mat, apparently.'

'And how is DCI Wolsingham responding to this news?' asks McAvoy.

'We're alone, Aector – you can call him Wolsingham if you want. Or "wanker" is good too.'

'Wolsingham, then,' says McAvoy, pushing up the sleeves of his shirt. He glances over to where an elderly woman in a red coat is trying to manoeuvre her trolley between two tables. There are a group of workmen in hi-vis jackets tucking into breakfasts and debating, at high volume, whether the new lass at the office is into Les, or Dave. The old woman's muttering apologies. Saying 'excuse me' as if it were a prayer and generally apologising for being a pest. McAvoy can't bear it. He leans over and closes his fist around the edge of the nearest table leg. Drags it three feet to the left. One of the workmen emits a 'whatthefuck' as his breakfast disappears sideways. He glares at McAvoy. Clocks the size of him, and the Humberside Police lanyard around his neck.

'Thanks so much,' says the elderly woman as she makes her way to her seat.

'Is there any chance you could concentrate, Aector?' asks Pharaoh, moving the condiments around on the table. 'Are you even listening?'

'Ben's hurt, and the driver is on his way to hospital,' says McAvoy, feeling the tips of his ears go pink. He feels like he's been caught daydreaming in class.

'On the plus side, the fall seems to have knocked some sense into him.'

'Ben?'

'No, don't talk soft. The driver. Joeseph Hayder, forty-one. He's babbling away to Ben faster than the poor lad can write it down. Seems he was out for a drive and having an argument with his ex and the next thing he'd gone over an obstacle in the middle of the road. Didn't get out of the car, didn't look inside it . . .'

'He said that?' asks McAvoy. 'He knew it was a holdall?'

'Driver behind him had a dash cam, thank goodness. Ben's going gentle with him,' says Pharaoh, wiping a crumb from her lip. 'Seems Hayder's biggest fear is this getting back to his ex. Won't name her, but his Facebook profile shows him with one Alesha Babb. She posted a rant just after midnight – stupid ex cancelled his night with their daughter then showed up anyway with a bag of presents. Claiming to have bronchitis or the plague or something. They were having a barney when he saw the "obstacle". Went home and smoked enough weed to put Snoop Dogg in a coma, so we'll have to get him cleaned up a bit before we can interview him properly. Anyway, upshot is, there was a vehicle ahead of him at the roundabout. Said it was either a four-by-four or a small pick-up truck but wasn't really paying attention, what with his eyes being full of tears. Can't wait for his witness statement. Going to be pure poetry.'

'He was seeing somebody else, then?' asks McAvoy. 'That's where he'd been, or where he was going . . .'

'Makes for a better story than "having a drive to clear my head", which is what he's sticking to.'

'Any previous?'

'Caution for shoplifting in 2008.'

'Job?'

'Freelance stage and set designer, if you can believe that's a thing.'

McAvoy pulls on his lower lip. Shakes his head. He's got nothing more to contribute. Can't find the space in his mind for the anonymous body on the road. His skull is overflowing with Decland Parfitt.

'Ruby's ripe,' says Pharaoh quietly, taking off her sunglasses and fixing McAvoy with her intense blue eyes. There's an apology in her gaze. He's not going to like what she needs him to do. 'Should have seen her last night, Aector – just this cloak of hopelessness around her. I think that bastard's had his hands on her again. There were bruises, though she's had so many over the years I doubt she even notices any more. I thought I had her, Aector. Really bloody did. But she won't let go. Not Parfitt, not Mem. She thinks she's going to get to play happy families with a domestic abuser and a child killer.'

She pushes her tongue against her teeth, anger squeezing her features. She starts playing with the salt cellar, knocking it nervously from hand to hand. Her bangles clank in the spilled salt, the soggy crumbs.

'Showed up later than she usually does,' she says, and she doesn't need McAvoy to reply. Carries on, half to herself. 'She's definitely starting to thaw but there's something in her that won't let her see the truth. It's like she knows that if she accepts she was wrong, she's not mentally strong enough to deal with the fall-out. I mean, imagine, Aector . . . you've alibied the guy who's been abducting kids. You've covered for him. You've freed the monster who raped your sister . . .'

McAvoy drums his fingers on the tabletop. Does as he's told. Imagines it. Feels it: great waves of misery and shame. He almost can't bring himself to put her through it, no matter what the cost.

'I'm going to tackle the prison myself,' says Pharaoh, pushing her sunglasses back on and shooting a look at the workmen as they pull on sodden coats and finish up their last slurps of coffee and tea. One of them looks as though he's considering putting the table back where it belongs. Sees Pharaoh's expression, and leaves it be. 'This Dr Durrant who's been giving you the runaround – he's not there any more. Checked one of the trade journals and he's gone back into academia, whatever the hell that means. Some scatty soul is in post now. We might get a bit more with this one. Chaplain's neither use nor ornament. We'll get in, though. Even if I have to scale the bastard wall.'

'I've pushed as much as I can,' says McAvoy, a little hurt. 'I've made it absolutely plain. They're not budging. Doctor's orders. He's not well enough.'

'And what does that mean?'

'It means we can't talk to him. Which, in turn, means we're stuck with what we've got.'

'Which is fuck all,' snaps Pharaoh. It flies in the face of all that she's told the team, the Chief Constable, the Parole Board and the press. For all the resources she's quietly funnelled into the investigation, they've got no more on Parfitt now than they did when she first brought him in: all helpful and puzzled and ridiculous in his safari suit and pith helmet, long socks and shimmering pin badges. Back when he was a school governor, a foster parent, a children's entertainer and a dealer in exotic pets. Back when he was getting his kicks drugging children and simulating their murders; red paint at their throats, hair braided into pigtails.

McAvoy drops his head. She's right. She's always bloody right. They haven't got enough. Nowhere near. They know where Parfitt was during great chunks of the Nineties and Noughties but they haven't got the evidence to guarantee a conviction – despite what he told Gemma. All they really have is Pharaoh's cast-iron belief that he snatched at least two prepubescent girls. None made it home. They're still listed as missing. Their families carry the weight of their absence like Sisyphus.

'So you're the big gun, my boy,' says Pharaoh, brightening. 'You're my ace in the hole. She'll warm to you. Every bugger does.'

'You've been making progress though,' says McAvoy. 'You said . . .'

'Aye, I did, but if Mem has started putting the boot in, she might need to get herself another protector.' She flashes him a grin. 'The little boy's a sweetie. *Aramis*, if you can credit it. Dotes on him, for all the thanks she gets. Mum's not on the scene. She's only putting up with that nasty bastard because she wants to keep the lad safe – you mark my words.'

Pharaoh softens her voice. Stares past McAvoy at some memory she doesn't seem inclined to share.

'He was the only man who was ever good to her,' she says, and her words carry an echo, as if she's said all this before. 'Gave her a home. An education. Kept her safe and warm and loved. Abused her sister right under her nose. Drove her to take her own life. But Ruby, she's loyal as they come. Won't hear a word against him, even now. Still goes to visit like the dutiful daughter.'

McAvoy rubs his big hands together, kneading his broken knuckles with his pinkish, freckled thumbs. 'Mem,' he says at last. 'He doesn't like the police, I gather.'

Pharaoh snorts a laugh. 'He'd watch us all burn, my boy. He's a bad man.'

McAvoy thinks of the little he knows about Ruby's partner, Agamemnon Ricci. He goes by 'Mem'. Has four convictions for violence and another two for conspiracy to supply. He's a formidable specimen – as tall as McAvoy, and with a steroid-fuelled, bodybuilder physique. With his prison tattoos and bleach-blond hair, his gold chains and lurid designer loungewear, he revels in his reputation as the hardman of Wincolmlee.

'If you go now, you might catch her on her own,' says Pharaoh, as if the idea has just occurred to her. 'Mem and his little acolytes go to the gym at this sort of time. Just go and introduce yourself. Let her know there are other decent people in the world.'

McAvoy breathes out, long and slow. 'Do I say you've sent me?'

'I don't send you anywhere, Aector, you're a grown man and the head of the Cold Case Unit. You're popping in because you've heard she might have had some trouble and wanted her to know there were people who could help. And yes, you say I sent you.'

McAvoy chews his lip. Thinks of Decland Parfitt, comfortable in his specially adapted jail cell. Thinks of him sitting there, with a smug smile on his mangled face. For a moment, he can visualise the window sliding open at the rear of a drafty caravan. Can see a shape, silent and purposeful, slithering in through the blackness: a hand clamping down upon the face of a sleeping child. Can see an empty bed, all tangled blankets and piss. He swallows, hard. Thinks of Lilah, and a sudden feeling of powerlessness fills him. Parfitt can't be allowed out. Whatever it takes, he can't be allowed to slither away from justice. He knows where the bodies are buried. Only he can provide closure for the families who don't even have the mercy of a headstone for their lost girls.

'We'll stop him,' says Pharaoh, her expression hard. 'I've been trying to get this evil bastard for more than twenty years, Aector. I swear to you, if they let him out, I'll be waiting at the gates with a fucking sawn-off. No pressure, but I want you to keep that in your head when you're talking to Ruby. What is it the Yanks call this – a Hail Mary? I think it means a last throw of the dice. Well, you're a big fucking dice, Aector.'

'I think it's a die when it's singular,' says McAvoy, and winces when he realizes he's spoken aloud. 'Not that it matters, of course, but . . .'

'Go and show her the world has some good people in it,' says Pharaoh, ignoring him.

'How do I do that?' he asks, feeling prickly and sick.

Pharaoh reaches across the table and takes his hand. She pushes her sunglasses down her nose and holds his gaze. Whatever it is that passes between them, it helps.

'Just be you, Aector. Just be you.'

ELEVEN

Wincolmlee, Hull
12.55pm

McAvoy parks a couple of hundred yards away from Ruby's place, tucking in between a works van and a battered Peugeot. The road curves here and he has a good view of the big brick warehouse with its faded livery, standing guardian over the smaller, white-painted premises to its right. Wincolmlee has the feel of a dystopian videogame: a crowded wasteland of disused warehouses and abandoned factories, clinging to the banks of the muddy River Hull. He brought the kids down here for a walk, once. Pointed out some of the interesting things he'd read about in the guidebook produced by the local history unit. Fin said it felt like there were zombies around every corner. Lilah said it smelled of cat wee and hot chocolate.

He pulls his collar up as he climbs out of the people carrier. He's never been worried about how he looks but his collar carries a faint whiff of Roisin's perfume and he likes having it near enough to breathe in.

He checks his phone, rather hoping that Pharaoh will have sent him a message telling him to leave it for another day. Instead, there's a message from DC Daniells. There's been a communication from the private forensic science service that Pharaoh has brought in to examine the blood samples taken from Parfitt in the wake of his rescue from the darkness out at Bempton all those years before. Daniells doesn't offer any more, but the presence of the shock-face emoji gives McAvoy enough adrenaline to get himself moving towards Ruby's premises.

A light rain is falling and he enjoys the feeling of it on his face. Takes a deep breath, and finds himself agreeing with Lilah's assessment – the old tannery does indeed give off an ammonia whiff strong enough to make the eyes water. He finds himself imagining what Wincolmlee was like in its heyday: the bustling wharves and warehouses, the barges and cargo ships cutting channels in the chocolate-coloured sludge of the waterway. Developers have ploughed some money into the area, hoping that the area will be earmarked for regeneration and gentrification. Judging from the number of weatherbeaten For Sale signs, they would have been better off buying magic beans.

McAvoy quickly runs through what he knows about Ruby and her crooked little building. Until a few years ago, Ruby ran a café at number 260. It had no airs nor graces – if it was in London, it would have been called 'The Caff'. It did big breakfasts and mugs of strong tea. Ruby and an older woman wore striped tabards and served up ham rolls at lunchtimes and three types of pie, with chips or mash, on the occasional Sunday. It didn't make much money but it ticked over. Gave her a safe place to host the little meeting group for men struggling with their mental health. Did some good.

McAvoy gives a polite knock on the wooden door. Through the dirty windows he can see the space that used to serve cholesterol

and caffeine to big men in fluorescent jackets. It's deserted now.
There are still tables laid out and he can make out the shape of a
till and a serving hatch at the back of the rectangular space, but it
looks thoroughly abandoned.

He steps back from the door and gazes up. Pharaoh's adamant
that Ruby's spending her days here, burrowed into the building that
used to house her dream. She sleeps at Mem's place off Beverley
High Road, but if he's going to get her on her own, in a place where
she's strong enough to listen, this is his best shot.

He tries again. Knocks harder this time. It seems to echo off the
big brick walls of the narrow road. There's no sound save the gusting
of the autumn wind and the occasional clatter from the nearby timber
yard. McAvoy finds himself conflicted. He doesn't want to be here,
but he can't leave until he's exhausted all options. Pharaoh will give
him hell if he doesn't.

The old brewery next door looks as though it's only being held
up by wishful thinking and bloody-mindedness. To the other side
is the forecourt of an empty car-parts specialist: the kind of place
McAvoy could lose himself for an hour, browsing batteries and
alternators and random ranks of automotive whimsy. It's closed now.
Abandoned, like everywhere else. Steel railings line the perimeter;
tops splintered into jagged spikes and garlanded with barbed wire.
McAvoy finds the chain-link gate and tries the handle. It opens
without a squeak and he steps on to the forecourt, ducking under a
dangling coil of wire. He glances up. There's a security camera on
the wall. Another across the way, mounted to the signage of the
showroom. He takes a couple of pictures on his phone. Stares up
at the side of Ruby's place, hoping he'll see somebody peeking out
from behind a curtain. He feels a sudden urge to shiver as he stares
up at the damp brick and dirty glass. He's read Ruby's file so many
times, he fancies he could choose her as his specialist subject on
Mastermind, but to stand here, clothed in the shabby sadness of this
bleak wasteland . . . he feels like he understands her. Understands,
too, why she would be so keen to provide a safe space for broken
men. He believes ninety per cent of her statements. Believes, truly,
that Parfitt never touched her. He was, as she claims, 'a brilliant
dad'. He was also a paedophile, child abductor, rapist and murderer
who drove her sister to suicide with a campaign of ceaseless abuse.
He drugged their school friends and acted out his depraved fantasies
as they slept. He stole children from their beds and took his pleasures

from their agony. McAvoy knows this to his bones. According to Trish, Ruby knows it too. He just has to get her to let go of the one certainty she has held on to her entire life.

He turns around, growling to himself. Should have called first. He'll put a business card through the door. Might have to try her boyfriend's address anyway. Maybe Pharaoh's friendly patrol car can swing by again tonight and see if the lights are on. Until then, there are other avenues to explore, calls to be made, work to do . . .

He turns at the sound of a screech of tyres and brakes. A blue Volkswagen Frontera slams to a halt against the kerb. All four doors open in unison, engine still running. Four big men climb out. The chassis of the vehicle lifts by half a foot as they spew on to the pavement.

McAvoy recognises Agamemnon Ricci from his mugshot. He was sitting in the front passenger seat. His driver is a smaller, younger man. Lank black hair and near-ghostly pallor, wearing a faded camouflage jacket and blue jeans. The two men from the back seat are even bigger than Mem. One is olive-skinned: stubbled and mono-browed; white muscle vest under a loud Hawaiian shirt. The other is every inch ex-Forces; black boots, pressed jeans and a Help for Heroes hoodie. He's holding a length of pipe: smudgy rose-petal tattoos on the backs of his hands; knuckles white around its length.

'Fucking told you, you prick. Fucking told you what would happen . . .'

It's Mem who's speaking. Mem in the lead, ducking under the coil of barbed wire and stamping towards McAvoy like a Rottweiler who's just caught a lap dog pissing in his water bowl. His accent is North London. So's his temper.

'Never fucking learn, will you? I don't care how fucking big you are, I'm putting you on your arse and stomping a fucking hole in you . . .'

McAvoy reaches inside his coat for his ID. 'Mem, isn't it?' he begins, using his gentle voice. 'Detective Insp—'

The man in the Help for Heroes hoodie throws the pipe the instant he sees McAvoy reaching into his coat. McAvoy sees it just in time, lurching to his right. It catches him on the top of the shoulder with an impact he feels all the way to the tips of his fingers, and then Mem is rushing him, shoulder-barging him up against the wet brick wall. McAvoy's off balance and can't disentangle his feet. He thuds against the wall and feels all the air go out of him. Mem's palm is against his face now, pushing him against the brick. He can hear the others telling him to do him, to fucking kill him, to put him down and keep him down . . .

McAvoy hisses in pain as the brick punches angry perforations in his cheek. His attacker is extraordinarily strong; muscles like tarred rope beneath his tracksuit. McAvoy squirms, trying to find a space to throw a punch, but his arms are pinned at his sides and he can't find any leverage. He tries to speak but gets a mouthful of dust and rain. Mem's eyes bulge: pupils huge and black, and McAvoy gets a whiff of something sour on his breath as he lurches forward, mouth open, teeth bared, strung with ribbons of yellowish spit.

Adrenaline floods him as he suddenly realizes that Mem is intent on biting a chunk out of him. Sets his feet against the brick and pushes off from the wall with all the strength he has left. Mem stumbles back and McAvoy finds the space to throw a hard right hand. He keeps his hand open and the sound of palm on cheek sounds like a gunshot. Mem staggers back and the two other heavies surge forward.

'Copper,' gasps McAvoy, raising his fists. 'I'm a copper . . .'

Mem raises a hand, telling the others to hold back. There's a huge palm print on his cheek and utter hatred in his eyes.

'You fucking slapped me! Slapped me like a pissing girl!'

McAvoy blinks the sweat and brickdust out of his eyes. He's still got his fists up. If Mem takes a step forward, he'll throw more than an open hand.

'You threw a pipe!' protests McAvoy, eyes darting around the loose semi-circle of men. 'I was trying to show you my warrant card!'

'I never threw fuck all!' shouts Mem rubbing his cheek with his knuckles. 'You can't come wondering around here all gangstered up and not expect a beating.'

McAvoy glances down at himself, as if checking whether somebody has put him into fancy-dress without his permission. 'Gangstered up?'

'Long coat, designer shoes . . . look at the fucking size of you!'

McAvoy grits his teeth and rubs his own bruised face. There's a smudge of blood on his hand. He'll be picking grit out of his face with tweezers for the rest of the bloody day. He lets his anger show in his face.

'I'm Detective Inspector McAvoy,' he says, and his accent is much more Scottish than it was a moment before. 'I'm here to talk to Ruby. And you lot are going to stand still while I straighten my clothes and sort myself out. Then I want names. I think I might also want an apology. Either way, you're going to learn a lesson here today.'

Mem has recovered a little of his swagger. He laughs and looks at his mates. 'Learn a lesson? I had you against the wall, mate. Only let you go so you didn't wet your pants.'

McAvoy shakes his head. 'Ruby,' he says, trying to stay on track. 'That's all. I just need to see her . . .'

Mem steps forward, raising his hands again. McAvoy hears a scraping sound from nearby. Somebody's picked up the pipe.

'You don't want to do this,' says McAvoy. 'You really don't.'

'I do,' says Mem. 'You're on private property. I'm responding to a security breach. You haven't identified yourself and I've got four witnesses to that effect. We can put you down and act all surprised when we find out you're a copper. I reckon we've got a few minutes.'

McAvoy looks at the four men. The two bigger guys look delighted at the turn of events. The driver hangs back, holding the metal pipe. He's not looking at McAvoy – keeps glancing back towards the car. McAvoy follows his gaze. Sees a flash of dark hair. Sees a face he knows from files and photographs and countless interviews. Sees Ruby, staring back, watching as her protector takes on the copper who's supposed to show her that there are people in the world who can keep the bad men away.

'Aye,' says McAvoy, quietly. 'Aye, I reckon we've got a few minutes.'

Mem grins. Charges.

This time, when McAvoy throws a right hand, he closes his fist.

TWELVE

'Ten seconds,' hisses Pharaoh, into her mobile. 'She needs to see—'

'Can't, Trish – they're fucking hyenas!'

'I said wait!'

Pharaoh squeezes the leather of the steering wheel, spilling cigarette ash on the back of her hand. She glares through the dirt of the windscreen. Watches as McAvoy kicks Military Man's legs out from under him and drops him in a puddle of dirty water and spilled diesel.

'Trish, we're going—'

'Wait!'

McAvoy has Mem up against the wall, trying to stop him from scraping his cheek against the brick. Even from here, 100 yards away behind the old paper mill, she gets a sense of the madness in Mem's eyes; visualizes his irises seamed with lightning strikes of red. She can hear him, too. Hear him roaring, screaming, telling his lads to 'kill him'.

She raises the phone. Zooms in.

'Go on, Ruby . . . see him for what he is. Believe in yourself, you poor cow.'

The big man's hauling at McAvoy's back, trying to drag him off. McAvoy doesn't budge. Lets go of his grip on Mem for just long enough to clatter his attacker with an open-handed slap to the ear. Pharaoh watches him lose his senses from the feet up: knees buckling, grasping for balance in empty air.

'The skinny one,' she mutters. 'Where did the skinny one go?'

She looks back to the car. Sees Ruby slide across from the rear of the back seat. Sees her climb out on to the damp pavement. Sees her make eye contact with the man who can protect her from the bad men, gasping for breath on his knees, blood trickling from his nostril, wet patch spreading across his joggers . . .

'Go!' shouts Pharaoh, into the phone. 'Now!'

There's a sudden explosion of sound: the blare and whoop of two diphthong police sirens: officers slamming right boots to the floor of the two patrol cars, bursting out from their waiting position at the end of the far block. They screech down the abandoned road like toy cars hurled by a child and slam to a dead stop beside Mem's car. Ruby covers her face as if expecting a blow.

Pharaoh looks back to McAvoy. Sees the skinny lad appear as if materializing from the bare brick to McAvoy's right. Sees something glint in his hand.

'Aector, knife!'

There's nobody else in the car but she says it out loud. Feels her throat constrict. Feels her cheeks fill with acid and saliva as her heart falls into her guts. She's done this. Caused this. He's going to take a blade to the ribs and it's *her fault, her fault* . . .

Through blurry eyes she sees the four uniformed officers sprint into the forecourt, ducking through the chain link; voices bouncing off the walls of the warehouses and wharves.

McAvoy slams Mem back against the wall. Turns just in time to see the skinny lad trying to ram something hard and sharp into his chest. Throws himself sideways, pushing Mem the other way. The blade strikes brick. McAvoy clatters to the wet ground. Takes a stamp to the knee. Another to the ribs.

'Get her away!' screams Mem, to Military Man. 'Get her—'

And then he's on the ground, two fluoro-uniforms on his back and Skinny Man is dodging between the others, jigging left and right like a tricky winger searching for a gap by the corner flag.

Pharaoh puts her foot to the floor. Her little two-seater shoots forward, a sleek greyhound freed from the traps. Heads turn and she watches, teeth bared, as Skinny Man skips between the two uniforms and clambers over the chain-link fence like a monkey, hauling himself on to the dirty red slates of the showroom. Pharaoh screams to a stop beside Mem's car; the doors open, Ruby holding the bonnet with one hand and her chest with the other. There are fresh bruises on her cheek. Scabs on her knuckles. When she pulls in a shuddering breath, Pharaoh sees the gap in her lower row of teeth. She's taken a true pasting; the kind Pharaoh can still feel in the cold, empty moments when alcohol leaves her system.

'In,' shouts Pharaoh, reaching across and throwing open the door. 'Ruby, get the fuck in!'

She turns to look at Mem, scrabbling on the ground beneath the weight of a big, tattooed police constable. McAvoy's hauling himself up, still dazed. He looks confused when he spots Pharaoh beyond the chaos of the wriggling bodies. Screws up his features. Rubs at his ribs.

Pharaoh sees him making sense of it. She's used him. Kept things from him. Held back, and used him as little more than bait. She feels the impact of it like a punch to the lungs.

'Ruby . . . he's going down. We can protect you!'

Behind her, McAvoy glares up at the distant figure of the skinny man: moving over the rooftops. Hears one of the uniforms yelling into their radios, calling for urgent assistance. Hears somebody say 'officer down' and makes sure they don't mean him.

'Ruby!'

She stumbles towards Pharaoh's car. Sags into the driving seat. Up close, Pharaoh can make out the imprint of a bootprint on her neck.

'He can't hurt you any more,' whispers Pharaoh, shoving the gear stick into second and tearing away down the still-abandoned road. Out of the corner of her eye she sees movement from an upstairs window of a warehouse: a flicker of colour from behind the broken panes of glass. Clocks the vehicles parked up in ones and twos along the length of the road. Spots the hire car and scowls. Files it away for later.

'He was protecting me,' sniffles Ruby. 'He thought your officer was . . . thought he was somebody else . . . another . . . he thought . . .' She dissolves in on herself.

Pharaoh doesn't speak. Twitches her eyebrows so her sunglasses fall from her brow to their proper place. Tosses the nub of her black cigarette out of the window. Floors it.

For a moment, she sees McAvoy; shoulder slumped, hand at his ribs, watching them go.

Under her breath: *I'm sorry.*

THIRTEEN

Castle Hill Hospital, Cottingham
1.23pm

Neilsen lets out a grunt of pain as he slides his left arm into the green plastic coverall. He's only just put himself through a similar agony, grunting and wheezing in a cubicle at Next as he wrestled his injured arms and bruised chest into a half-decent grey suit and acceptable shirt. He'd refused the offer to go home. Would work on with a bruised clavicle and sprained wrist and wouldn't make a fuss about any of it. But he'd be damned if he would go through the rest of the day wearing a suit covered in footprints and mud.

'Nearly there? Let me help you.'

Neilsen smiles his thanks as Denise, one of the lab technicians, helps him sort himself out. He feels a bit like a kid being smartened up for school. He half expects her to lick her palm and wipe a smudge from her cheek.

'He's very excitable today,' says Denise, conversationally. She's a jolly, enthusiastic woman in her mid-forties. She's got kids and a husband and a caravan at Withernsea. And she spends her days up to her elbows in the dead.

'Excitable?'

'Dr Vergette. Told me to tell him the moment you got here. I saw him recording a video diary entry in his car so he's obviously already got his eye on his memoirs.'

Neilsen pulls on the thick blue wellingtons. Snaps on the blue nitrile gloves.

'You were hurt, I hear,' says Denise, peeling herself out of her own protective gear and shaking out her scruffy brown hair. She wipes her spectacles on the hem of her sweatshirt, pops them back on and smiles, brightly. 'A chap fell on you?'

'Good news travels fast,' grumbles Neilsen. He's taken two paracetamol and the same number of ibuprofen and the cocktail is sitting uneasily in the protein shake and superfood smoothie he forced himself to devour at lunch. He'd thought himself safe to be alone; to feel sorry for himself and phone his partner and tell her about the horrible bloody job they've got him working on when he should be helping McAvoy. He'd barely lifted the phone to his ear when Denise had called him from the mortuary. Dr Vergette had begun the post-mortem examination on their unidentified body and thought Neilsen would want to see the results for himself. DCI Wolsingham had called a moment later, telling him that he was busy pursuing other leads and that it was Neilsen's job to attend – even with his cuts and bruises. So he's here, sore and pissed off, in the visitors' room at Hull Mortuary, Castle Hill Hospital. Here, in the visitors' changing room, with its rows of lockers, racks of blue wellington boots, and boxes of gloves; its posters offering bereavement support services and good local undertakers.

'Well, you look well on it, whatever happened.' Denise smiles, sitting down on one of the plastic chairs and pulling out a thermos flask from a cupboard. 'I like bruises on a man.'

'You'd get on with my girlfriend,' says Neilsen, the way he's been trained.

'Ah, good – I feared I'd get lumbered with Wolsingham. Knowledgeable chap but ever such a pedant, don't you find? Makes one feel unpleasantly scrutinized.'

Dr Reese Vergette is standing in the doorway in his overalls and gown, holding the door open with one hand and beckoning Neilsen in with the other. The door at the end opened on an aisle between two sets of refrigeration units – big rectangles of stainless steel, each one covered in a grid of metal hatches. Neilsen breathes in the tang of the big sterile space that he can't help but call the Cutting Room. Six metal tables laid out at even distances: sinks and pipes and silver tubes; overhead lights bouncing off hosed-down floor and gutters swirling in pink and chemical vortexes. Neilsen smells bleach and blood, shit and burned flesh. Crunches a clove between his back teeth, the way Pharaoh showed him. Concentrates on the bitterness at his tongue, mouth slowly numbing, nostrils filling with sour, barky fumes.

Neilsen glances up. CCTV cameras dangle from the white-painted ceiling, their black bulging eyes ready to record the most intimate and personal of violations.

Someone in green scrubs had followed him in, taking photos – the flash turning everything monochrome for a moment, before the colour floods back in.

Down at the far end of the room, a dark body lies beneath a set of industrial extractor fans. Neilsen looks upon the body that he had glimpsed, briefly, in the early hours of this morning, dead in a bag on a no-name road near Cherry Burton. Neilsen concentrates on the fiery taste of the clove. Forces himself to consider the naked body on the slab: a Y-shaped incision carved into his chest; a line where his skin was flensed from the skull to enable Dr Vergette access to his brain.

'Quite remarkable,' says Dr Vergette, cheerily, to Neilsen's left. 'I mean, the scarring alone would be worth a lecture series, but if you throw in the mutilation, well . . .'

Neilsen allows himself to look properly. Sees what, at first glance, he'd been unwilling to believe.

'Somebody cut his balls off,' says Neilsen, aghast.

'Quite,' says Dr Vergette. 'A long time ago, it would seem. At least ten years, possibly more. A rather bodged repair job, too. The scarring suggests cauterisation. There's a how-to guide on the internet, if you're interested. Some people can't afford gender reassignment surgery. Go to extreme lengths.'

Neilsen looks at the injuries to the man's chest. His chest is sunken where the car ran over him but it had been brutalised long before he found himself on that country road. He looks like a waxwork left near a fire. There are mangled letters entwined in the swirls and rinds of melted flesh. Neilsen thinks of hardened cheese on leftover pizza. Feels his gorge rise.

'Single stab wound, in just below the left ear and dragged across to the right,' says Dr Vergette, pulling down the overhead light and encouraging Neilsen to look at the dark trench. 'Considerable force. A sawing motion, if you will. Quite a small blade – perhaps four inches. And if you take a look here,' says Dr Vergette, lifting the body's hand and encouraging Neilsen to stare at the nails, 'what looks like the same fibres we're recovering from the interior of the holdall.'

'So he was alive when the vehicle went over him?'

'It's not within my gift to say yet – but I'd keep it in mind as an option.' He looks up at the ceiling, wistfully. 'I've been cycling out at that spot, you know. Saw three deer in that little field. One of those rather lovely moments that one files away.'

Neilsen wonders what to do with Dr Vergette's whimsy. Gives an encouraging nod. Wonders whether that might be something to think about – could the adjacent field be a significant spot for somebody? Could the dead man have been dumped at the site for some obscure personal reason? Had there been any accidents? He makes a mental note to delegate to one of the two DCs Wolsingham has nominally shunted his way. Wonders what he missed at the lunchtime briefing, and how much of Neilsen's own, swiftly compiled progress report the lazy bastard had shown off as his own sterling work when tasked with updating the upper ranks.

'You'll be wanting an ID, I shouldn't wonder,' says Dr Vergette, his eyes crinkling as he smiles beneath his mask.

Neilsen tries to keep his patience. 'You have an ID?'

'Took a bit of initiative, as it were,' announces Dr Vergette, proudly. He pushes his spectacles up his nose and rises up on his tiptoes, pleased with himself. 'Old university chum is on the board of the lab where your samples were labouring among the hoi polloi. I called in a boon.'

Neilsen's getting a headache. 'A boon? Have you got a fricking ID?'

Dr Vergette looks affronted, fanning his masked face with gloved hand. 'My dear boy, I wouldn't drag you over here just to look at some rather interesting mutilations! No, we've struck lucky, as it were. Fingerprints and dental, though we'll get to that in a moment. He's known to us. Or rather, known to you. The police. I just chop them up and rummage around – do my bit, as it were.'

Neilsen waits for more. Glances around, hoping somebody will put him out of his misery. Lets Dr Vergette heap some more on.

'Meet John Dennic,' says Dr Vergette, with an incongruous flourish. 'Date of birth, December twelfth, 1968. Not much of an age, was he?'

Neilsen looks at the man's face. Burns upon his neck: one pockmarked cheek hidden in a neat, blood-flecked beard.

'Can't get a sense of him,' mumbles Neilsen. 'Doesn't look like a person.'

'This'll help,' says Denise, brightly, and encourages him to look at the tablet she's holding out in a gloved hand. 'That's him when he was arrested in 2012. Tattoo on his inner left bicep is still legible though the rest – well, we'll be running them through the system, trying to disentangle it, but it looks like this has been done over a period of years. And if you look at the chest . . .'

Dr Vergette points to a pattern of ugly ridged flesh: a series of vaguely overlapping circles. It seems to shimmer as the light passes over it.

'Perhaps an orbital sander, studded with pins,' he muses. 'I saw something similar – S and M play date gone horribly wrong. Made a bolognese of him, she really did. All I can say is that there's a callous on his right thumb – repeated burns, the kind you get from a hot surface. I couldn't swear to it, but he might have done this to himself. That's some deep self-loathing, though I'm not a psychologist.'

'Slow down,' says Neilsen, looking into the plain, pale face of a middle-aged man. His head's shaved down to a dirty brown halo – the smudge taking on the look of a monk's tonsure in the glare of the flash. He's not familiar. Unremarkable, save the tear-shaped imperfection in the pupil of his left eye, stamped on the blue iris like a red tadpole. 'John Dennic,' he repeats, with a soft, Scandinavian-sounding 'ch'. 'Previous?'

'Attempted murder of a police officer, September fourth, 2012. Admitted the offence and took nine years. I could send you the file but I don't want you to think I'm taking over.'

'Heaven forbid . . .'

'Nearly took the victim's eyes. Broad daylight too. Uniformed officer, no provocation.'

Neilsen looks again at the ruined body on the slab. He can't reconcile the corpse and the picture on the screen. It makes him feel giddy; the world off-balance.

'And this is our man, here. Dead in a bag on a country road? What's he doing anywhere near here?'

Dr Vergette waits patiently for him to stop asking questions. He looks like an end-of-the pier magician with one last trick up his sleeve.

'Haven't shown you the best bit yet,' he says, and squeaks across the wet floor to a workbench where a series of internal organs have just been bagged and weighed. Neilsen begins to regret his choice of lunch.

'I'm not in the habit of giving "ta-dah" moments in the workplace but I do rather feel this might end up in one of those wonderful true-life cop shows, so I'm going to rather enjoy this moment.' He reaches under a silver lid and pulls out a clear plastic pouch. Neilsen peers at what looks like empty air. Then he spots it, down in the right-hand corner of the bag.

'A sim card,' says Dr Vergette, rubbing his hands. 'Nearly missed it. False tooth cap, right at the back on the left-hand side. Slightly different colour to the others. So it warranted a little poking. Sort of thing one sees in a war film, don't you think, though I didn't detect a cyanide capsule. No, just this beguiling little fellow.' He holds up the bag: a goldfish brought home from the fair. 'I rather think that might be of use to your digital forensics people. Of course, it wouldn't hurt to take a look yourself first, just to, you know, satisfy a chap's curiosity . . .'

'You've looked?' asks Neilsen. Somewhere nearby, Denise shuffles and coughs.

'In the interest of expedience, of course,' says Dr Vergette, sounding like a politician caught in a lie. 'Anyway, you'll be pleased I did. Take a look.'

Neilsen knows he needs to report in to Wolsingham. Needs to prove that there's sense and reason behind his every decision. Has to always have the potential public inquiry at the back of his mind, no matter how big or small the case. He knows what he's supposed to do.

'Last known address?' asks Neilsen, going back over his notes. Dr Vergette laughs, delighted to be asked. 'You'll love this, Ben, you really will . . .'

FOURTEEN

'Y ou did this,' sniffles Ruby, glaring at the side of Pharaoh's face. 'You've made all this happen!'

Pharaoh throws her a look, all nostrils and vape smoke. 'I'm the one who's helping you, Ruby. We can turn around right now, no problem. I can drop you back at the kerb and you get arrested for affray – or accessory to the attempted murder of a police officer – depending on how I see fit to instruct. Or you can talk to me. Properly. Like the first time.'

Ruby turns away. They're passing along one of the side roads leading up to Hedon Road and the east of the city. They'll pass the prison, soon. Past the prison and the graveyard to the docks and the wide grey waters.

'This is all to get me to change my mind,' says Ruby. 'All the time you've spent trying to be nice to me – to be the mum I never had. It's all because you want one thing. You want to prove my dad is a monster. Well maybe he is! But he wasn't to me. And I will never, ever change my mind on that. Do you understand? You can lock Mem up, and I'll still . . .' The weight of it all is too much. She dissolves in on herself, holding out her cupped hands to catch the tears as if stemming a nosebleed.

'You don't need to change your mind about him,' says Pharaoh, quietly, as the underside of the convertible grazes a speedbump. 'You just have to withdraw your offer to give him a place to live. That's a start. He's a convicted sex offender. The sheer weight of evidence . . .'

'You fitted him up. He always said you would do whatever it took to take him away from me.'

Pharaoh can't keep her temper any longer. 'He raped your sister, Ruby! She killed herself rather than go on. And you just turn your back on that? Just ignore it, because he bought you ice creams and read you bedtime stories?'

Pharaoh hasn't noticed her passenger push the cigarette lighter in. Only notices when it pops and Ruby snatches it up. She presses the glowing tip to the skin of her neck, just behind her ear. Gives a hiss that borders on ecstasy as the car fills with the smell of burnt hair and sizzling meat.

'Ruby, what are you . . .'

Pharaoh swerves over to the kerb and grabs for the lighter, burning her finger, scorching the palm of her hand.

'Give me that, you silly fucking cow!'

Pharaoh yanks it free of Ruby's grip and shoves it back in the hole. She winces and reaches past Ruby to open the glovebox. She rummages among sunglasses and flavoured vapes, bills and sweet wrappers. Finds a little glass vial and pulls it free. Twists the lid and applies a dollop of what looks like wasabi to her blistered skin. She notices Ruby looking at her. Feels the vehicle shudder as a heavy-goods vehicle thunders past with a blare of a horn.

'The police officer who just resisted the urge to kill your boyfriend – his wife makes this. It's all hedgerow gypsy shit. Could be horse-radish and food colouring for all I know, but it does wonders if you let it.'

Ruby's hair hangs in front of her face. She reaches out, hand trembling. 'I don't do that any more, OK. Please tell him I don't do that.'

'You mean hurt yourself?'

'Yes. When you see him, tell him I won't do it again.'

Pharaoh sits back. After a moment she finds a gap in the traffic and scoots half a mile down to the iron gates of the cemetery. She reverses into a gap between a council van and a Mondeo and only hits the kerb twice – hands slipping off the wheel thanks to the paste. She opens the door and grunts her way out. Stomps to the passenger side of the vehicle and opens Ruby's door for her. 'Come on,' she says, briskly. 'Fresh air. Nobody listening. Let's take a walk.'

Pharaoh takes her mobile from the pocket of her leather jacket and puts it in the glovebox. Steps back and allows Ruby to clamber out.

'You look like a moody teenager,' says Pharaoh, frowning. 'You're a bloody grown woman and you're going through a hard time. Now, let's talk about it.'

Ruby slouches into step beside her, passing through the black lacquered gates. The grass is slick with the hazy rain and the marble headstones glint among the row upon row of crumbling grey granite; here and there the splendor of some family tomb – eagle wings and golden lettering, remembrance memorials to men and women long forgotten.

'I'm not going to try and persuade you that he did it,' says Pharaoh, eventually. She stops at the crossroads between two footpaths. Looks at fallen leaves and dead flowers; sodden teddy bears and lopsided urns. Feels the weight of her job – the weight of her sin. She softens her voice a little. 'We'll never make a case against him for all of the crimes we think he's committed. There'll be people who never learn the truth about what happened to their lost child in the hours before they were put out of their misery. I've made my peace with that. But one? We can prove one, Ruby. The only thing that stopped the CPS going ahead with the prosecution was because you said he was home with you the entire night. You watched a film together, then you had a bath and he helped you dry your hair. He put you to bed – warming the pyjamas on the radiator like usual, I remember from the statement – and then he read to you. Fell asleep on the floor beside you, like he often did when you thought you might have nightmares. You held his hand to know he was there. And he was still there when you woke up the next morning. You know he didn't leave because you're a light sleeper. And we know he didn't drug you because you consented to a blood test and it came back negative. And there's no evidence to place him at the scene of the abduction, or the place where he hurt her. All you have to acknowledge, here and now, is that there's a chance he left that night. If he's threatened you all these years – if that's what's stopping you seeing what's so blindingly clear – we can protect you properly. Me. Aector – the man who just took a beating because he'd come to see if you were OK . . .'

Ruby whips her head up. 'What do you mean, "OK"? What have you heard?'

Pharaoh frowns. Considers the end of her cigarette and wonders whether she should stub it out on her palm. It might show her level of determination. Then again, it would really fucking hurt . . .

'Why was he there?' asks Ruby, face flushing. 'Mem and me were, well . . . we were out and then the lads were there and saying there was somebody at the tea room – I still think of it like that, even though it's not mine any more – and so we came tearing up here and then it just all got messy and now . . .'

Pharaoh takes her elbow. Leads them over to a bench and wipes the raindrops off with her sleeve. She sits them both down. Watches a thrush grab a worm from a patch of damp earth and gobble it down. She amuses herself for a moment with mental pictures of worm detectives, gathering around the scene of the abduction and considering means, motive and opportunity.

She shakes the idea out of her head. Runs back everything Ruby has said and all that she hasn't.

'Aramis,' she says, suddenly. 'Who's got the boy?'

Ruby looks down at the ground. 'Friends,' she says, breathlessly. 'I'll keep him safe, don't worry. He's such a good boy. Such a darling.'

Pharaoh feels like shaking her. She's not going to budge. It wouldn't matter if she had footage of Parfitt raping his victims, Ruby would never permit herself to think of the one good man in her life as the demon Pharaoh knows him to be.

'I had a bad dream last night,' says Pharaoh, her voice tired. 'After we met. After we spoke. After I saw your bruises. I was back in that place where your dad was left to die. I was in that barbed-wire web, looking at the mess that somebody had made of him. And I was screaming at myself in the dream – screaming not to save him. To let him die. To look for the person who did it and give them a fucking medal. But I didn't do that, did I? I put the fire out and re-started his heart. I brought him back. And I can live with that if he's locked away. I can't live with that if he's free. And he'll only get free if you don't tell the truth.'

Ruby doesn't look like she's listening. She's gripping fistfuls of her jogging trousers, rocking back and forth. Pharaoh feels all the temper rush out of herself, replaced with a flood of desperate compassion. She puts a hand on Ruby's back. Rubs in circles: a friend helping another be sick in a pub toilet.

'Mem has a child, Ruby,' says Pharaoh, softly. 'How can he possibly be OK with you having Parfitt in the house? I don't care how much he hates coppers – nobody likes nonces. Least of all big lumps of testosterone and violence like Mem. How many lies have you told him?'

Ruby shakes her head again. She rubs her hand over her face, smearing snot and tears. She gives a sudden manic grin, blue irises flashing, ice-white teeth carved in a rictus grin. 'Mem loves me,' she says, repeating something learned by rote. 'Mem wants me to be happy. Mem will make sure everybody's looked after.'

Pharaoh sits back against the wet bench. Stares out across the smouldering bonfire of red-gold leaves; smoke leeching into a grey sky. Hears a horn blast from near the docks. Thinks her way into Ruby's head. Mem's.

'Ruby, whatever it is that he's got on you – whatever hold he has over Mem . . .'

'He has no hold over Mem,' stammers Ruby. She sniffs; a disgusting, rattly sound. Looks like she wants to spit. Swallows and grimaces.

'Aramis,' she says, and seems to anchor herself to his name. 'I'll have to . . . I'm sorry, Trish, I really am . . .'

She stands suddenly. Wipes her face with a handful of hair. Pharaoh spots white lines where her neck emerges from her hoodie: a gleam of old scar tissue. Thinks of feathers. Of angels.

'Ruby, look, whatever I said, I'll make sure there's no comeback on you for what happened. I want you to know you can trust me – that it's about protecting people, not harming, and . . .'

'Don't contact me again, please, Trish,' says Ruby, eyes glassy, forcing herself to meet Pharaoh's own. 'I'm begging you. Leave things be. I can make it right – just . . . not now!'

'Ruby, look . . .'

And then she's turning and running through the graves, tearing through the billowing leaves and the hazy rain, past the bank of old tombs and on to the footpath that leads to the distant gate beyond the chapel.

'Fuck it,' grumbles Pharaoh, who doesn't have the lungs for the chase. She stamps back to the car, mulling Ruby's words over. What had she said, right at the beginning? The way she'd reacted about Aramis, too. And Mem. For a horrible moment, Pharaoh wonders if she might just be wrong about everything. Not Parfitt – she recognizes that evil in her bones – but perhaps he really didn't leave Ruby home alone to go out and abduct a twelve-year-old girl from a chalet near Cleethorpes. Perhaps somebody else did that.

'No,' she says, aloud, as she throws herself back into the car. 'No, fuck that. You did it, Parfitt. You know you did.'

God how she wants to talk to him. Wants to look into the ruined features and say *I may have saved your life, but I've regretted it every day since.*

She reaches back to the glovebox and pulls out the phone. Six missed calls, all from Ben Neilsen.

She calls him back at once. 'Ben?'

'Thank Christ, Boss. I've been doing my nut trying to get a hold of you. I think you're going to want to get back to the ranch, Boss. We've got an ID.'

'An ID? Oh, your body on the road? Sorry, I meant to phone Wolsingham for an update but figured he'd just ask me to call you, so I haven't quite . . .'

'In the tooth, Boss,' says Neilsen, interrupting Pharaoh in a way that would usually have led to an ear bashing that could perforate the drum. He swallows, trying to find the right words. 'I really think you need to see . . .'

FIFTEEN

Southfield Lane, Ulrome
2.25pm

She carries the spade like a scythe. Looks like Death, in her black leather coat with its damp hood, clinging to cheekbones that seem to fray her pale, papery skin.

'It's such an extraordinary gesture,' prattles Gemma, stumbling, as she holds the iPhone and keeps pace with the slim figure, stalking along the clifftop. Seabirds whirling and wheeling against the damp grey sky.

Paulene shrugs. The spade rises. She trudges on, as instructed. She nods. 'Yonder,' she says, pointing to an area of hard-standing and ruptured tarmac, shielded by a chain-link fence. Tussocks of long grass and wildflowers poke between the cracks. A long-abandoned brick building sags, splay-roofed, at the edge of the concrete space: two or three feet from the edge of the disappearing road. There are warning signs pushed in to the rocky ground. When they were first put in place, the beach was a hundred yards away. It's within kissing distance now.

'Feels bloody stupid,' mutters Paulene, and Gemma has to cock her ear to hear. 'You think I want to be known as the batty lady? The one who's up on the hillside with a spade at all hours, looking for a skeleton? All because they couldn't catch him properly the first time. On me, now. That's how it's always been, I see that now. I mean, you're a nice lass and I'll give you what you're after – Lord knows I've been interviewed enough.'

Gemma doesn't know what to say. She's already drunk Paulene's tea. Gone through her albums. Sat in the cigarette smoke and three-bar heater fug of her living room: family pictures smiling down from every wall. Carmel, pride of place, on the boxed-in chimney breast. Carmel, as she was: blonde and snub-nosed, blue-eyed and dimpled, sparkly pink cardigan over a swirly blue dress. Gemma hadn't been able to look at her. Just sat and watched Paulene smoke her fags and shake her head and *umm* and *aah* about whether or not any of this was a good idea.

'All these bloody years,' says Paulene, picking a random sod and plunging the spade down into the wet grass. She barely punctures the surface. She's wheezing from the walk. Doesn't look strong enough to push a spoon into a yogurt, let alone scour this remote, wind-blasted headland for the remains of her niece.

'Not here, is she,' says Paulene, and her voice breaks. She snatches her hand across her nose. Hocks back something vile. Glares back inland.

'Had him, didn't they?' says Paulene, sucking her gums. 'Can nearly see it from here. The building above the tunnels. Been down there twice – far as a body can go. I thought . . . well . . . I don't know what I thought. Maybe that whoever took Parfitt had taken him to that place because it was where he'd stashed our Carmel. Nothing there. Still stinks of smoke. You breathe in, you can still smell his skin cooking.'

Gemma swallows, drily. She feels the sweet tea sloshing in her stomach. Her arms aching from holding the phone. She's cold and sharp darts of wind keep slashing at her cheekbones.

'What's enough, you reckon?' asks Paulene, giving Gemma her full attention. 'You seem a clever lass, so you tell me. How much punishment is enough for killing a child, do you think? Is there a way back from that, do you think? I mean, how deep into Hell do you have to go – how long do you spend there? I mean, I've tried to find my faith these last years but what's come back – it's not like I felt at Sunday school. I mean, God's there, but He doesn't give a shit, does he? Not really. I believe in Him, but I can't help thinking He's a bastard. But Carmel – if she's up there forever, yeah? In Heaven on a cloud? He'll get there eventually, won't he? Parfitt. If he spends enough time being tortured and tormented, I like that bit . . . that's great, but . . . what if there's a catch, y'know. Or a loophole. I don't want him just walking in like he owns the place . . .'

Gemma puts the phone away. She can't stand this. She crosses the space between them and takes the spade from Paulene's hand. There's no resistance.

'Here, you think?' asks Gemma, as cold tears leak from her eyes. 'Have you tried here?'

Paulene screws up her face. 'All those years, looking in the wrong bloody place. The sods I've turned, the mornings I've woken up too stiff to move and I still came up here to look for her. Such a waste of time.' She closes her eyes. Seems to be reciting a prayer inside her head. Her lips give a tiny, hushed Amen. 'Rest, Carmel. You rest, girl. I'm so bloody sorry.'

Gemma doesn't know what to say. Doesn't know who to be. 'Trish will make sure he doesn't get out,' says Gemma, and means it. 'He'll pay for what he did.'

Paulene stares into her. Softens her eyes. 'Wish you'd been here a few years back, love. I might still have had a chance at a life. Too late now, isn't it? All well and good knowing but . . .' She stops herself. Stretches her back. 'I can do it properly, if we go ahead. I'll get myself together. It's for Carmel, isn't it? And I promised. I did promise.'

Gemma digs for a while. She doesn't know if she's doing it right, but she works up a sweat and her hands start to hurt as she chops the blade into patches of snarled-up grass and rocky earth.

'That one,' says Paulene, pointing at an empty space. 'Was a nice little wagon, that one. I know how it looks – how it sounds, but she weren't banished. She wasn't there as a punishment. She'd asked. She didn't like too much noise and all the other bairns, well, they were proper boisterous and she was . . . well, we always called her our little princess because she was that little bit refined. Always seemed a bit splendid, even when she was little, and it was all tea parties and dolls with frilly dresses while my own bairns were stuffing breadknives in the DVD player and biting the head off Barbie. True story. She liked the idea of having a place to herself for the night – and you've seen, it's no distance, is it? And it's a family place. Friendly. I mean, that's what I got it for, isn't it? Somewhere for people to stay when they come to visit. And when I think of her sitting up in bed all pleased with herself, reading her book by lamplight, listening to the birds and the sea, feeling all grown-up, and then . . .' She trails off.

Gemma shudders. In her mind's eye, a bedroom window slides open; a window at the back of a cosy, half-dark caravan. She sees a figure, one leg upon the sill. Feels acid rise as the picture in her head shifts. Sees a giant spider leg: bristly hairs and bald patches. Sees a shadow fall.

'She'd been so excited when she met him,' says Paulene, and she bites back the impulse to weep. She shakes her head free of her hood. Long white hair streams out behind her: a flag of surrender waved against the dark.

'Met Parfitt?'

She nods. 'She'd paid attention to everything he'd said. Told him loads of her animal facts. He'd been so good with her, too. She could be a lot, you know? Didn't always know when to shut up. But he listened and talked and listened and talked and made her feel special. Gave her one of his pin badges. And we didn't think it was weird, because why would we? He was in character. He was an entertainer. The kids loved him. And he had those girls with him, so there was never any reason to think it wasn't right. When we found out what he was – when Trish said they wouldn't be able to get him, that there wasn't the evidence, that she'd have to find another way . . .'

Gemma gets her phone out and turns it on again. Starts recording. She so wants to be good at this. Wants to please Halle so very much. And this is the job, isn't it? This is what she's signed up for. There's a market for this stuff and all she's doing is feeding the machine. And Halle wasn't perfect, was she? Must have stuck in her throat to admit that Pharaoh had spotted her in her hire car at Wincolmlee. She's on her way up to the coast now, having already recorded some sub-standard, fuzzy footage of McAvoy brawling with a group of thuggish types outside an empty warehouse. She hopes he's all right. Wonders who the woman was who'd climbed into Pharaoh's sports car. What the Boss was playing at.

She swallows back hot bile as she fumbles in her pocket and exposes the microphone.

'Do you think you'll ever find her?' asks Gemma, grunting, as the spade sinks into the earth.

Paulene turns and stares at the horizon; at the whirling birds and the empty air where half the old caravan park has crumbled into the sea.

'Paulene?'

'She's at peace,' says Paulene, at length. 'He gave us that when nobody else did.'

Gemma can't work out what to say. Keeps digging, until Paulene tells her to stop.

'She's not here, love,' says Paulene, with a hand on her shoulder. Up close, she smells of damp clothes and gin. Gemma realizes it wasn't tea she'd poured into her own china cup.

'Paulene?'

Then, distantly: 'She never were.'

PART TWO

SIXTEEN

Mem is sitting on the kerb, hands cuffed behind his back. His nose has stopped bleeding but there's no disguising the rising bruise where his jaw meets his neck. He looks like a child on the naughty step, scowling into the rain and exuding an air of unjust persecution.

McAvoy leaves him be. He'll talk to him when they get him processed. With any luck, a search of his vehicle will find something illegal and they can get him out of Ruby's hair for a few months; perhaps even long enough for a fresh start. If she also changes her statement and can no longer offer Parfitt a place to call home, so much the better.

He moves away from the chaos behind the metal railings. Three more patrol cars have arrived, along with two vans, sirens blaring. It all feels a little unnecessary. He can't bring himself to blame Mem and his mates for attacking him. He was on their property. And he did look as if he were going for a weapon. Of course, he'd identified himself, but maybe they'd thought he was kidding. He likes to give people the benefit of the doubt.

'You're looking a bit bedraggled, Sarge,' says DC Andy Daniells, pale blue shirt nosing through the crumpled curtains of his dark blue suit. He hands over a hot chocolate, which McAvoy takes with a smile of true pleasure.

'Means a lot, Andy,' says McAvoy, scalding his lip and anointing his moustache with marshmallows.

'Being bedraggled?'

'Pardon . . . oh, right. I mean . . . forget it.'

They stand in silence for a moment. It's not been a bad day's work, all told. They've got IDs for two of Mem's associates and they each have outstanding warrants. They haven't uncovered the name of the skinny man who escaped across the tiles, but they'll get to that. Mem might give it up. He's the one with the most to lose.

'You really might want to sort yourself out, Sarge. Seriously, you look like you've been covered in glue and rolled through a charity shop.'

McAvoy considers himself. His trousers are torn and he's lost a boot, exposing a sock that declares it to be Tuesday. His shirt hangs loose and his braces are twisted up almost as far as his sleeve.

'It's a right bloody rigmarole,' mutters McAvoy, taking another sip. He wonders if Pharaoh's getting anywhere with Ruby. He knows what she's done, of course. Almost admires it. It hurts, but he admires it nonetheless.

'Here, away from prying eyes,' says Daniells, with a smile. 'I'll sort you out.'

McAvoy allows himself to be ushered around to the side of the building. Daniells helps him out of his jacket and waistcoat and starts trying to untangle his braces. McAvoy feels his cheeks burn.

'I feel like I'm decorating a Christmas tree,' laughs Daniells, and McAvoy's suddenly grateful to have him as both friend and colleague.

McAvoy raises his eye skywards, staring up at where a watery sun is trying to push through a dusty pelmet of grey cloud. Looks over to the abandoned warehouse across the way. Sees movement, just for a moment: a face at a broken window, third floor.

'Am I done, Andy?' asks McAvoy.

'I'm not a ruddy tailor, Sarge,' says Daniells, who will continue to call McAvoy 'Sarge' long after he's been promoted beyond his present Inspector rank.

'Just pop with me, will you, please? Just a quick welfare check . . .'

McAvoy walks quickly across the damp road, gazing up at the dirty red-brick building, all smashed panes and rusted, paint-flaked iron. There's a metal grid over the old double doors, spray-painted with illegible tags. McAvoy carries on to the end, directly opposite Ruby's café and the melee in the car yard. There's a gap between the warehouse and the next building: a broken metal fence sagging in to a tangle of litters and thorns. McAvoy squints into the under-growth and makes out the barely there desired path: a patch of disturbed earth and broken branches. Steps into the cluttered alleyway and ducks under a coil of brambles. Behind him, he hears Daniells groan.

'You really need a boot, Sarge. You'll need another tetanus.'

McAvoy looks down and realizes his bare shin is exposed through the gap in his trousers. Notices too that on the boot front, he's sorely under-represented.

McAvoy moves as lightly as he can, stepping over broken bottles and fallen bricks. There's a window a few yards ahead; the shutters torn far enough away from the crumbling brickwork to allow a body to pass through.

'Why are we doing this, Sarge?' asks Daniells. 'Is this like an opus dei thing? Is it like mortification of the flesh? Because I don't think I've done anything that bad, not really, and . . .'

McAvoy puts his hands on the cold metal of the shutter. Pulls it out a little further from the wall.

'I'm not giving you a bunk-up,' grumbles Daniells, as a bramble branch twangs him in the face. 'Sarge. I said . . .'

McAvoy pushes himself into the gap. Puts his hands on the concrete sill and hauls himself up and into the gap. Drops down lightly into long, dark space; broken floorboards and rubble; refuse sacks and smashed furniture. It's dark, but he can see enough to pick his way through the murk. He feels wetness with his socked foot. Makes a face as he runs through the possibilities. Smells ammonia. Cats. Smoke. Damp . . .

'Hello!' shouts McAvoy, and his voice echoes back from the distant walls. He shivers, and watches as his breath rises to mix with the thick dust in the air. 'Hello, my name's Aector. I just wanted to see if you were OK . . .'

'Who are you talking to?' hisses Daniells, and his head emerges at the sill. 'Sarge, a hand . . .'

McAvoy makes his way back to the sill. Steps on something sharp and curses. Looks down. Shines the light from his phone on the offending sliver of metal. It's a pin badge, missing its back. McAvoy picks it up. Sharp point on one side, and a green lizard on the other.

'Sarge!'

McAvoy drops the pin in his pocket. Grabs Daniells and hauls him in through the gap, helping him down as if lowering a bride on her wedding night.

'Now what the chuff are we actually doing?' he asks, brushing himself down.

'There's somebody in the building,' says McAvoy. 'I saw a face. Nobody should be staying here . . . and it might be worth a statement, don't you think? They may have seen—'

McAvoy jumps at the sound of a sudden clattering nearby: a
bottle kicked with a clumsy foot.

'No need to be alarmed,' says McAvoy, his voice loud but his
manner soft. 'Just checking you're OK. Getting cold of an evening.
Night's drawing in. I'd be glad to help you find somewhere warmer,
if . . .'

'I never saw nothing!'

It's a male voice. Not local. Not old. It bounces back off the
sagging walls and rotten beams.

'I don't need to talk to you about that,' shouts McAvoy. 'Just
checking you're OK.'

There's a pause, then: 'Why?'

McAvoy stops, unsure how to reply. 'Why what, sir?'

'Why do you want to know I'm OK?'

McAvoy takes a moment. 'Character flaw,' he replies. Then: 'Can
we continue this over a cup of tea? My treat. Or, if you're brewing
up, I'd be glad to sit down with you, Mr . . .'

There's another clatter, and then a figure emerges from the gloom.
He's wrapped in a big coat with a dirty fleece trim: hood up, framing
a face that might be handsome if the acne disappeared and he took
a sandstone to the blackheads. He's somewhere in his twenties. He's
wearing black jeans and a pair of too-big black trainers that flap as
he makes his way through the debris.

'I'm Kes,' he says, guardedly. 'You said you were an actor?'

'Aector. Scottish for Hector.'

'Oh right. My dad always said the Scots are a fine people.'

'I like him already.'

'He hated the darkies though.'

'I've just gone off him.'

Kes laughs: a high, startling sound. Up in the rafters, something
flaps its wings. Dust and feathers float down like nuclear snowflakes
above a dead town.

'Got my rig there. Enough in the kettle for another brew, if you're
staying. I hope I've got a clean cup . . .'

McAvoy follows him into the darkness. Stops. 'You don't have
a spare shoe, do you?'

Kes grins. Reaches down, pulls off a trainer and lobs it to McAvoy.
From inside his coat he pulls out a grimy trainer, and hauls it on.
'Better fit anyway,' he says, and McAvoy places his accent.

'Lithuania?' he asks.

Kes turns back. His face, in this light, becomes almost ethereal. 'Just from here, Aector,' he says, and sweeps an arm around his lodgings. 'I'm just from here.'

McAvoy ignores Daniells' persistent tugs at his sleeve as he makes his way towards a little patch of darkness beneath a high, broken window. There's a sudden flare of red light as Kes illuminates a big old-fashioned torch with a white, hard-plastic handle.

'I'll brew up, then,' says Kes, repeating a phrase he's clearly proud to know. 'I know you're a policeman, by the way. You don't have to pretend. I saw you. With those men. You are very strong.'

'Just a squabble,' says McAvoy, looking among the piles of bin liners and towers of paperback books, hoping for a place to sit.

Kes unearths a small camping stove and lights the burner. He throws a sleeping roll down into the closest thing he has to a clear floor. 'You may have to squat,' he says, with a wry laugh. 'I don't have many guests.'

McAvoy folds himself into an uncomfortable cross-legged position. Daniells opts to lean against a sagging wall: cables and wires around his head like snakes.

'She deserves better,' says Kes, rummaging inside a big red rucksack for a tin mug. 'The lady.'

'Ruby. You're familiar with her?'

'Not familiar, in the way people say when they raise their eyebrows. Why do you do that, by the way. My dad said smut was very English. He said the English were a fine people.'

McAvoy waits for him to finish. In the red light, he's noticed that one side of Kes's face seems to twitch; the mouth a little slack when his face is briefly in repose.

'But you're friends?'

'She's given me a few cups of tea – the odd sandwich now and again.'

'She knows you're in here?'

'Perhaps. I only ever saw her when I was outside, and I don't go out much. Sometimes . . . when it gets too lonely . . . when you start hearing the birds talking in your dad's voice . . .'

McAvoy watches the change come over him. Sees his face contort and twist, sucking in spit through his teeth, upper lip twisting. In a moment it's gone: a pike taking a duckling from a flat pond.

'Kes? Are you happy here? There are people who can help . . .'

'Who's looking after the boy?' asks Kes, suddenly. 'Little fellow in the designer tracksuits and flat cap. Looks like a little Tyson Fury, I swear. That Mem, he's a piece of shit, but he loves that boy – you see it the way they are together.'

'You see a lot from here, Kes?' asks Daniells, paying attention.

'Upstairs, yes. Here, no.'

'And what have you seen from upstairs, Kes?' asks Daniells, as McAvoy reaches up to accept the cup of lukewarm tea and coffee creamer.

'There's cameras anyway,' says Kes, pushing back into the red bag. He looks like a miner following a seam. McAvoy half expects him to disappear – to have tunnelled out of the room and into a subterranean world. He scowls at himself. Hates it when his thoughts go loopy on their own.

'Is it about the man?' asks Kes, suddenly. He rocks back on his heels, hugging his knees. He looks younger. Looks cold and sick.

'The man?' asks McAvoy.

'Short man, in a raincoat. Old-style one, like from the movies. Looked in the windows like you did. Wandered around to the side and stood in front of the security cameras, just like you did.'

McAvoy sips his tea. Suppresses a shudder. Remembers leaving his hot chocolate by the kerb. Grieves.

'When was this, Kes?' asks Daniells, kindly now.

'Yesterday,' he says, immediately. 'Teatime. That's how I say it, right? Perhaps six? I heard the knock. Went for a look.'

'You always do that, Kes?'

'Not much to do,' he says. 'I read. I think. I go for my medication. I get by. And anyway, you know . . .'

'You like watching over her,' finishes McAvoy. 'Ruby. You care for her.'

'She's kind. We've barely spoken, but you can see it. Good eyes. Blue eyes. Bright as lights. Dad always said you could see somebody's soul in their eyes.' He lunges forward. McAvoy suppresses a flinch. 'Brown eyes,' declares Kes, grinning, gleeful. 'Like a big sad cow! Like Buttercup!'

Daniells clears his throat. 'What happened to the man, Kes?'

'You'll have to ask Mem. Is that his name? What's it short for? I've often wondered.'

'Agamemnon,' says McAvoy, absently. 'Mem arrived, did he? Same as today?'

'No,' says Kes, and looks down at the sodden silk of his bedroll.

Crouches back into the shadow, hugging his knees again. 'She wouldn't hurt anybody. She's a good person.'

'Ruby?'

'She let him in,' he says. 'Opened the doors and he followed her in.'

'She was already inside?'

Kes nods. Looks for a moment as if admitting it is a source of pain.

'How long were they in there?' asks McAvoy, not sure what connection he's supposed to be making.

'I didn't see him come out,' shrugs Kes. 'Not Ruby, neither. Must have been a bit later. I lose track of time.'

Daniells lets out a sigh, suddenly aware that the case he's investigating is not going to be helped one iota by his current preoccupation.

'Sorry, Kes – you're a step ahead of me,' says McAvoy, as kindly as he can be. 'I'm not the brightest spark in the box, as they say. Tell me what's bothering you . . .'

'The clothes,' says Kes, and his face twists again. His eyes are suddenly full of angry tears and he tugs at his clothes as if aflame.

'Kes, it's OK . . . please . . .'

'Dad said not to steal . . . Dad said people who steal go to prison and get raped and then they die and go to Hell, but it wasn't anybody's . . . just rubbish . . .'

McAvoy moves closer to Kes. Puts a gentle hand on his arm. 'Whatever's wrong, Kes, I can help.'

'The big bin at the end of the road. Sometimes there's something worth re— What's the word . . . repurposing?'

'That's OK, Kes. You've done nothing wrong, OK.'

'And your dad sounds like an arsehole,' says Daniells, trying to help.

'You took something from the big bin, yes?'

Kes nods. Sobs. 'I was cold. It didn't fit anyway. Not all of it.'

McAvoy looks down at his left shoe, clad in a too-tight trainer.

'There were some clothes in a bag, were there, Kes? And you took them to stay warm? That's not a crime, Kes. That should be compulsory . . .'

'Here,' says Kes, and jerks suddenly to his left, head deep in the filthy rucksack. He pulls out a black bin liner.

'She wouldn't hurt him,' he says, again. 'Dad said . . . Dad said . . .'

McAvoy reaches across and takes the bag. Looks inside and gently eases out the distinctive shape of a cream mac, chequered lining.

'Could you turn off the red light please, Kes?' asks McAvoy softly. 'Thanks.'

In the sudden gloom, McAvoy takes his phone out and illuminates the torch. Runs it over the surface of the material, taking care not to touch the interior or the fabric. He spots the bloom of blood: a red flower, blotting the lapel.

'And you didn't see him leave?' asks McAvoy, carefully.

'Could you give us a full description?' asks Daniells, peering into the bag. 'Would you recognise him if you saw him again?'

Kes folds in on himself. Shakes his head. 'I didn't see anything. I didn't see anything important. You can have the clothes. Here, have his other shoe.'

McAvoy catches the trainer as Kes flings it. Looks down at his own mismatched feet. Raises his leg and contorts himself to examine the sole; the stitching around the fabric. He knows that if he were to smell the stain, he'd catch the faintest trace of iron; of spilled blood.

'I'm wearing one of the trainers, aren't I?'

SEVENTEEN

A n hour later, and McAvoy's standing at the kerb at the rear of the old warehouse. He's reclaimed his boot but his trouser leg still flaps wildly in the breeze. A fine rain hangs in the air and when he runs his hand over his beard it comes away sodden. He's trying to process life's endless vagaries. He's just had a text from the PC keeping a watchful eye over the witness's bed. Joe, who's day has gone from bad to worse to downright silly. Things are looking up, apparently. He's currently sobbing into the neck of his ex and she's telling him it's okay, she loves him, they're going to make another go of it. He wonders if it constitutes a happy ending. Thinks: *you'll be the death of me.*

He lets himself enjoy a moment's quiet contemplation. Wonders if this is what he secretly wanted. These past months, working databases and juggling spreadsheets; deep-diving into intelligence reports and cross-referencing forensic results from crime scenes – perhaps he's been fooling himself to think it's what he's good at. Maybe it's this: the sudden thrill of the chase; the blood and thunder of scuffling in the gutter with people who wish him harm – perhaps it's where he truly feels alive. He wonders what it says about him. Wonders whether, deep down, he's no more than a big lump who can take a punch.

He pulls out his phone and thinks about calling Roisin. It's mid-afternoon and he knows she'll be sitting in their living room, barefoot and clad in velour, surrounded by her hand-woven baskets, filling them up with potions and soaps and crystals; anointing each with protection spells and tying witch knots into the bows. He doesn't want to bother her. Isn't sure how to comfort himself if he doesn't.

'Aector! You look like a postbox.'

McAvoy looks up. Pharaoh's pulled in a hundred yards away. She's wound down the window and is leaning across, sunglasses on her nose, cigarette at her lip. If she feels guilty for leaving him at the mercy of Mem and his cronies, she doesn't show it.

McAvoy walks quickly to the car. Takes a breath before hauling the door open and lowering himself down into the cramped confines of the little two-seater, knees against the dashboard, arms folded in at his sides. Pharaoh pulls away before he's even closed the door.

'If we hit a speedbump, there'll be sparks,' grumbles Pharaoh. The vehicle drives a couple of inches lower whenever McAvoy's in its embrace.

'I'm fine,' says McAvoy, with a touch of petulance. 'No harm done.'

Pharaoh glances over. 'You're going to get arrested for indecency,' she observes. 'It's OK, we can swing by home and you can sort yourself out.'

McAvoy tries to pull the material over his exposed skin; all white flesh, red hair and freckles. 'Swing by home on our way to where?' he asks.

'Ben has something to show us,' she says.

'Home's the other way,' observes McAvoy, as Pharaoh noses out on to North Bridge and turns right past the casino. The city's half deserted – the streetlamps already casting a greasy yellow light on to the hanging curtains of grey air.

'I know, Aector,' snaps Pharaoh, throwing the butt of her cigarette out of the window. She leans down as she pushes a CD into the player. It's Curtis Mayfield. She grunts, appreciatively. 'Just don't worry your pretty little head for a moment, OK? I've got a couple of things to tell you.'

McAvoy frowns. 'My car,' he says, suddenly panicked. 'Will you drop me back, or . . .'

Pharaoh slaps the wheel. 'Will you please shush?' She lets out a long, slow exhalation. 'Ruby did a runner,' she says, tiredly. 'She's not going to change her mind. I think we have to accept that. You gave it your damnedest, and if nothing else, we've got her away from him. We also get a chance to talk to him properly, when he's not full of energy drinks and bravado. So it was worth it.'

McAvoy rubs his aching ribs. 'Well, that's good, then.'

'Oh, stop looking like that,' says Pharaoh, shaking her head at him. 'If I'd told you to go and give Mem a pasting, you'd have had a heart attack. I told you to be you, and you were.' She eyes him over the top of her sunglasses. 'Did he know what he was doing, then? Fight wise? Is he the real deal?'

McAvoy considers it. Tugs at the patch of hair below his lip. Shakes his head. 'He was good at the shouting and the posturing. Didn't fight like somebody who's had to do much of it. I think he's more the sort to put the boot in when somebody else has put you down.'

Pharaoh nods, thoughtfully. 'Ben's body,' she says, as if reaching a decision. 'In the bag.'

'Yes?'

'John Dennic. Was residing at HMP Ovenden,' she says, without emotion. 'Serving a sentence for attacking a police officer, didn't return from his day out.'

McAvoy narrows his eyes. 'It wasn't me, was it?'

Pharaoh gives a snort of laughter. 'No, Aector, you don't know him.'

McAvoy's eyes widen. 'Parfitt,' he says, suddenly. 'That's a bit, well . . .'

'Yes,' says Pharaoh. 'Yes, it fucking is.'

McAvoy chews on his thoughts. Cocks his head. 'Ruby and Mem have a kid, don't they?'

Pharaoh nods. 'Aramis. Mem's child.'

'Is he with family?'

'Let's hope so, eh?'

'Kes – the chap who lives in the warehouse . . .'

'I got your voice note,' says Pharaoh, cutting him off. 'Seriously? His shoe?'

McAvoy screws up his eyes. 'We're going to have to change tack with Ruby,' he says, quietly. 'I really thought she'd see it. See him for what he is.'

'Mem or Parfitt?'

Pharaoh presses on. 'Ben says that Dennic has been the victim of horrific mutilation. Burns, incisions. Castration.'

McAvoy swallows. 'Was he on Parfitt's wing?'

Pharaoh smiles, pleased with the question. 'Aye, Vulnerable Prisoners Unit. Same as our man. For admitting an attraction to children.'

'For attacking a police officer? Thought he'd be King of the Wing.'

'That's one of the questions we'll be asking when we get there,' says Pharaoh, spotting a gap between a lorry and an HGV and zipping out into the outside lane. To their left, the vast, featureless expanse of the Humber: hammered tin beneath a wet-sand sky.

'So we've essentially got an escaped prisoner – killed and dumped in the middle of nowhere . . .'

Pharaoh shakes her head. 'An escaped prisoner who's been horribly mutilated,' finishes Pharaoh. 'Like Parfitt.'

McAvoy takes a moment. 'Just like Parfitt?'

Pharaoh shakes her head. She snatches off her sunglasses. There's darkness under her eyes: red veins on the damp parchment of her irises. 'Not like Parfitt,' she says. 'But not unlike the others.'

'The others?'

Pharaoh looks away. The moment stretches out. McAvoy doesn't step in. Whatever it is she wants to tell him, he knows she has to find the right words. He feels a thrilling sensation at his pulse points: wrists, neck, behind his knees. He imagines being the kind of man who can speak his mind and damn the consequences. Wonders how it would feel to simply slam his hand against the dashboard and say: *Jesus, please, Trish – if you can't tell me, who the hell can you tell?*

She lets out a long, low sigh. Glares through the glass.

'I might not have been entirely honest with you when I suggested we look again at the Kaylani Shah abduction,' she says, and the hinge of her jaw flexes like a bicep. 'Same with Carmel Barry. Look . . . there's a simultaneous operation in play. You might want to take a little look under your seat. And check my phone – see if Andy's messaged back. He's got your Kes looking at the image of Ben's dead man.'

McAvoy feels gooseflesh rise on his exposed skin. There's damp at the nape of his neck. Cautiously, he squeezes his arm into the space beneath the seat and his fingers close around a damp, crumpled manila folder.

'Operation Lapwing,' he reads. Opens the cover and starts to read. After a moment, he looks up and stares at the side of Pharaoh's cheek. He bites down, hard. 'We're not chasing Declan Parfitt,' he says, reading between the lines. 'We're chasing the man who took him – Virgil.'

Pharaoh nods. 'The one they're all afraid of. The one who might just have dumped a fresh body on our patch.'

McAvoy leafs through the document. Starts to jiggle his right leg. He's interrupted by a text from Andy Daniells.

'Kes says he's pretty sure,' reads McAvoy.

Pharaoh grunts. 'Pretty sure won't fucking cut it.'

'He's killing them,' he reads. 'Takes them, tortures them, dumps them. Some dead, some alive – all sex offenders . . .'

Pharaoh sings along to a line of Superfly, tapping her fingers on the wheel. She looks a little manic. Looks like there's too much in her head. 'Same technique, same patterns of injury; similarities between the things that were said; the cuts that were made; the inversion; barbed wire and rope . . .'

'But that isn't what's happened to our body on the road,' says McAvoy. A thought occurs. 'What was he wearing?'

'Black sweats, black hoodie, black trainers,' she says.

'Perhaps whoever took him . . . maybe they were taking him somewhere to, well – to put him through the wringer . . . escaped en route . . .'

'Hard to make a break for it when you're inside a bag, my boy.'

'What kind of bag?'

'One hundred and eighty litre double-stitched waterproof storage bag,' she recites. 'Our victim was five feet nine. Eleven stone eight pounds. A medium. Size ten trainer.' She waits a beat. McAvoy catches up.

'The man Kes saw . . .' he says, slowly.

'Something tells me the forensics are going to match,' says Pharaoh.

'Parfitt sent him?'

'Let's ask him.'

McAvoy swallows. Tastes bile. 'They've repeatedly refused our request for interview,' he says, not even glancing up as Pharaoh passes through the big houses and the high, golden-leafed trees that lead down towards the foreshore and home. 'The mental health services all seem to go through the chaplain, but she just keeps pushing me towards the Prisons Minister, and . . .'

'We're investigating a murder,' says Pharaoh. 'That trumps anything else. Let them say no to our faces.'

McAvoy stays seated as Pharaoh pulls in halfway along the row of white-painted fishermen cottages. Above, the Humber Bridge glares down at a landscape of muddled trees and gleaming train tracks; at the black windmill and the sodden, leaf-blown play area where a killer once lay in wait for his children.

McAvoy tugs at the patch of hair beneath his lip. Forces himself to look directly at Pharaoh. She snatches a glance at him. Scowls when she meets his eyes.

'Why didn't you tell me what we were doing?' he asks, sounding hurt. 'If somebody's killing paedophiles and sex offenders, we don't turn a blind eye. Did you think I wouldn't be on board?'

Pharaoh looks briefly pained. 'I'm Head of Crime, Aector. I'm a Detective Chief Superintendent. I get paid to take responsibility. I don't have to share every operational decision with my DI, no matter how much it makes his bottom lip quiver.'

McAvoy bites the offending lip. 'We're stopping Parfitt getting out, yes? That's the number one priority? Above all?'

'Of course,' she says. 'Finding the man who took him in 2011 – who did those things to him in the dark . . . that's secondary.'

McAvoy looks again at the names on the folder: the list of recipients. It's ultra-classified, only to be seen by the six senior officers from across four police forces who've been given responsibility for the operation. McAvoy finds his own name on page six: a detailed breakdown of the work undertaken to bring a case against Parfitt for the abductions of Carmel Barry and Kaylani Shah.

'If we fail – if he gets out . . .'

'There was talk of using him as bait,' says Pharaoh. 'I put my foot down.'

'You came back to stop Parfitt,' he says.

'I'd sooner turn a blind eye to ground glass in his porridge than risk having that monster walking free. Whatever happens, he has to stay where he is.'

McAvoy scratches at his shaggy hair. Glances up and sees Roisin, at the window. She's waving. Smiling. He wants to run to her and slam the door behind him. Wants to make a raft of their bed and sail away to some tranquil shore. Instead, he has a meeting with a monster.

'Wear the blue,' says Pharaoh, waving at Roisin and giving her a gloriously incongruous thumbs-up.

EIGHTEEN

DCI Wolsingham is already sitting in the little meeting room when Neilsen grunts his way through the door, a box of files under his left arm and two coffees in his right hand.

'Inspirational,' says Wolsingham, drily. 'If the good people of Humberside could only see you in action, they could sleep easily in their beds.'

Neilsen gets a whiff of cough sweets and poorly aired clothes. Wrinkles his nose as he sets down his burdens on the hard plastic table.

'Black, I presume,' says Neilsen, proffering one of the takeaway cups.

Wolsingham frowns, as if checking the sentence for something he can slap him with. Sucks at his top lip. Gives a begrudging nod of thanks.

'You OK with the blinds closed?' asks Neilsen, nodding at the grey fabric that hides the view of Clough Road and the warehouses and wharves of nearby Wincolmlee.

'Triggering experience for you, I should imagine,' says Wolsingham, taking a slurp of coffee. He crunches through his cough sweet. Swallows the pieces in a back-coffee swirl.

Neilsen thinks of a giant grinding bones. 'Triggering, sir?'

'I've no doubt you'd far rather be over yonder – picking up the pieces after your sainted Scotsman.'

Neilsen has spent the past half an hour telling himself to keep calm with Wolsingham, whatever the provocation. He's not sure he can keep his promise.

'Three men in custody, Sir. Intelligence that's given us a lead of John Dennic . . .'

Wolsingham pats at the air. 'We'll see about that. All sounds somewhat fanciful.'

'We specialise in fanciful, sir,' says Neilsen, playing with his cuffs and tidying himself up as he sits down. 'Our unit has caught all manner of fanciful killers.'

'Perhaps,' concedes Wolsingham. 'Seems more luck and stumble than by virtue of sparkling insight or procedural correctness.'

'Have you had a difficult day, sir?' asks Neilsen. 'Because I can pop back to the machine and buy you a Curly Wurly if you need a pick-me-up.'

The corners of Wolsingham's lips twitch in an approximation of a smile. 'Haven't had a Curly Wurly since I was in table tennis club. Could take me right back. Might start taking a bat to a ball.'

Neilsen gets the distinct impression he's being politely threatened. It's unsettling; anachronistic, as though he's being challenged to a dual. He half expects a slap across the face with a driving glove.

'John Dennic,' says Neilsen, opening his files. 'Identity confirmed. The doc is running tox as we speak and doing his best to fast-track the DNA against the database – see what else he might have been up to. I've been reading his file—'

'You eager beaver you,' says Wolsingham, sitting back.

'My working theory being that Dennic has clearly been the victim of a vendetta attack at some point in the last twenty years. Somebody hated him enough to take his balls. And he's been in the same unit, at the same wing, as Decland Parfitt, for the past eight months . . .'

'There will be a precis of events, I trust, Sergeant,' sighs Wolsingham. 'It feels like you're drawing constellations in spilled sugar.'

Neilsen pauses, scanning the metaphor. Shakes his head. 'Constellations?'

'Just get on with it.'

'Decland Parfitt has been the subject of an investigation being conducted by the Cold Case Unit,' continues Neilsen, taking a sip of soya-milk latte. 'At least two child abductions, bodies never found. Parfitt was a children's entertainer, and . . .'

'And Queen Nefertiti saved his life when he was abducted just moments after leaving her custody,' finishes Wolsingham, his eyes flashing triumph. 'I'm familiar with the case. Carmel Barry and Kaylani Shah. Both prepubescent girls taken from caravan parks. Pharaoh's ongoing quest for righteousness and redemption. An inspiring tale, Sergeant. A fool's errand, but an inspiring tale.'

Neilsen realizes he's changed his grip on his pen. He holds it like a dagger. Clicks the nib in and out as he counts backwards from ten.

'The only person who can alibi Parfitt is his former foster daughter, Ruby,' he says, keeping his smile steady as he tries not to imagine the joy of slapping Wolsingham across the face with a ring-binder. 'And Inspector McAvoy has good intelligence that a man matching the description of our John Dennic was seen at the premises yesterday. The Boss has made the decision to bring the Unit on board – alongside your own investigation, naturally, sir. I've got a call booked with a sergeant at Notts Police – they got the call about Dennic's failure to return. Jesus, it's like a revolving door! If the public knew how they just waltz in and out . . .'

'Let's change the world some other time, Sergeant,' broods Wolsingham, with distaste. He drums his fingers on the tabletop. Neilsen lets him wait.

'If Parfitt has sent Dennic to see his daughter, there's a chance that he's been sent to silence her,' continues Neilsen, outlining the theory that he's been ruminating upon since ending his call with Pharaoh. He starts speaking more quickly, his mannerisms animated. 'The Boss has been building a relationship with her – gently getting her on side, trying to help her get past the wall of lies she's built up around her dad. Her sister killed herself after she saw the videos of what Parfitt did to her, but Ruby still won't see the truth. Her partner, Mem Ricci – he's a bad lad. The sort who wouldn't stand idly by while some little nobody threatened his girl. And a stab in the back? That's pure Mem.'

'A tragedy that the Classics were ever allowed into the hands of the poor,' muses Wolsingham. 'Agamemnon. I mean, really . . .'

'We have Mem in custody, sir,' explains Neilsen. 'The Boss and McAvoy are en route to the prison.'

'I'm sure that will be delightful,' says Wolsingham, unwrapping a cough sweet and popping it into his mouth. Neilsen notices that his tongue is the colour of caramel. Wonders where he keeps them.

'At present, the working theory doesn't explain how the body ended up where it did, but given Mem's attack on the Sarge – on Detective Inspector McAvoy – we've enough for a warrant to search the café and the upstairs rooms. I'm guessing we'll see a bloodbath.'

Wolsingham takes a deep breath. The air rattles in and out through his nostrils. He pauses for a moment as a timber wagon rattles past the big gaudy frontage of Humberside Police HQ: day-glo yellow panels making the whole edifice look like its built from a mixed bag of Lego bricks.

'I do believe I'm the Senior Investigating Officer, Sergeant,' says Wolsingham. 'I do rather think that you're here to feed the machine.'

'Feed the machine, sir?'

'The dog-whistle stuff, Sergeant Neilsen. The running about and the toing and froing and the getting squashed by falling gentlemen. That's very much your area of expertise.'

'And yours is, sir?' asks Neilsen, eyes hard.

'Making sense of the chatter,' explains Wolsingham, with a sudden burst of energy.

He stands up and walks to the window, arms coupled behind his back. He angles himself so he can see past the blind and out across the rain-spattered landscape with its brickyards and tanneries; out and down to the shit-bobbing waterway.

'If they killed him at the café, they'd have thrown him in the river,' says Wolsingham, conversationally. 'It's a good half an hour out to where your Dennic was found, Sergeant. Why risk it? Unless they have a certain fondness for the alternative location.'

'It's an avenue to explore, sir,' says Neilsen, twisting in his seat to keep Wolsingham in his sights. From here, he notices that the senior officer's head is the same width as his neck. It's vaguely unsettling.

'You said you had more,' mutters Wolsingham. 'From the post-mortem examination. Your voice note was rather garbled. You mentioned a capped tooth?'

Neilsen takes another slurp of his coffee. He feels far too caffein-ated already. He's fizzy inside his skin; all jittery and wired.

'A false tooth, sir,' says Neilsen, leafing through the documents for a paper copy of the preliminary report. 'Right at the back. Detachable. You can push it out with a finger or tongue but it stays anchored in place if you don't mess about with it. That's what the doc said. Often used for sneaking contraband inside.'

'Mess about with it? The doc?' Wolsingham turns from the window and shakes his head at the dim-witted schoolboy in the plastic chair. 'I can barely get far enough down the food chain to communicate with you.'

Neilsen jerks his head away from his DCI. For a moment, he'd seen himself leaping across the divide and throwing the conde-scending prick through the window and into the parking garage. He doubts many of his fellow officers would even swerve to go around him, let alone point the finger at a suspect.

'There's a sim card inside the false tooth, sir,' says Neilsen, and there's a slight tremor to his breathing. 'Very interesting footage.'

'There's a recording on a memory card, Sergeant?' asks Wolsingham, looking at him as if he's just claimed to have seen a mermaid in Hornsea Mere. 'That's a thoroughly normal thing to say out loud, isn't it?' He shakes his head. Starts muttering to himself: 'Move to Hull, they said. Really interesting area, they said. City of Culture 2017, they said . . .'

'You're going to want to see it, sir,' says Neilsen, forcing himself to look again at the scrawny DCI. 'And we're going to need more bodies.'

'Dead ones or live ones?' asks Wolsingham, scornfully.

'Sir, when you see—'

'Have you even considered that Dennic might have been the victim of a revenge attack by the family of his original victim? Didn't I read that his initial arrest was for a violent assault on a police officer. Wouldn't be difficult to know when his release days were coming up. Finish the job, so to speak.'

Neilsen stops himself from blurting out an expletive. 'I've got the case file here, sir,' he says, patting the stack of folders. He hadn't actually turned his thoughts in that direction yet. 'Victim was one Detective Constable Richard Beresford, thirty-one at the time of the incident. Retired on a disability pension after the attack.'

He flicks through the documents in front of him. Scans the contents of his personnel file and spots the detail he hadn't yet had time to properly absorb. Shit! When the hell had Wolsingham spotted that?

'Permanent nerve damage to his neck,' Neilsen reads aloud. Coughs, before adding: 'He's working with a charity now, according to his note on the file. Helping re-house offenders. Getting them ready for life on the outside.'

'And living?'

Neilsen looks at the electoral roll, scanning the hastily prepared briefing note he'd requested from the specialist officers in Intelligence. 'Brigg, North Lincolnshire. About half an hour away.'

'How very exact of you, Sergeant Neilsen,' says Wolsingham, returning to his seat. He leans back, smugly: a pound-store Rees-Mogg.

'Could you just watch the video and stop trying to make me feel like a knobhead, sir,' says Neilsen, pissed off at himself but taken aback by Wolsingham's sudden insight. He really wants to know more about him. Wants to know how much of the ludicrous facade goes to the bone.

'A fine choice of word, Ben,' says Wolsingham, with an incongruous note of warmth. 'And yes, I really think that would be best.'

Wolsingham raises his coffee cup to his lips. Swallows empty air, for the look of the thing. He finds himself thoroughly unnerved by the arachnoid specimen in the greasy suit. He pulls the sleek black plastic tablet from inside the cardboard box.

'When you've seen it, you'll ask why I didn't show you this first,' says Neilsen. 'Coud you just pretend you've already done it and we can skip to the part where I'm feeling shitty and a bit pissed off?'

Neilsen blinks, slowly.

Presses play.

Wolsingham smiles – a genuine one this time. 'Let's see, shall we?'

NINETEEN

HP exhibit 00013B
Run time eight minutes, 13 seconds

A square space with a low ceiling. Wooden floors, long windows: cream-painted bars.

A semi-circle of battered broken chairs. Eight men, pasty and bloated; whey-faced in grey sweatshirts, blue jeans.

They're all staring at the two men who writhe on the floor at their feet. At the squawking, squirming figure, face turning purple, eyes bulging, spit frothing at his lips; at the slim, bearded, crumple-suited man who has him by the throat.

'Feel it,' he's spitting, into the other man's ear. 'Feel the fear. The disgust. The revulsion she must have felt. Let it into you. Guilt is a wasted emotion. An indulgence. Look out through her eyes, Zak. You're little Aimee. You're in your bed in your pyjamas, dreaming, safe, hair smelling of bubble bath, and then there's Uncle Zak – the funny, silly one who makes her laugh and tickles her and takes her for little treats. But he doesn't seem like Uncle Zak now, does he? He feels wrong. Feels scary. He smells funny . . .'

'Stop!' screeches the desperate, fitting man in grey. Two of the seated figures begin to rise.

'Stay in your seats,' snaps the man in the blazer and cords, face pressed up against the man in his arms. 'You face what you did. This is the process. You trust the process or you are off the course, and if you're off the course, you're not going anywhere. We've built a bond, here. We have a circle of trust. I need to know that you are willing to do whatever it takes to be free of your demons.'

He releases the hold. Rolls over backwards like a cage fighter and springs to his feet. He's wearing Converse. Cords. Grey shirt, thin red tie. There are tattoos on the backs of his hands; more on the exposed triangle of fake skin between his gaudily striped socks and his ragged turn-ups. He retakes his seat, facing the semi-circle. Puts his marker pen back into his shirt pocket. He'd pressed it in good and hard. Shown Zak how that invasive, unwanted protuberance had truly felt to the little girl when he woke her and helped himself. He has the look of a man who is teaching a hard lesson: somebody who's doling out tough love in a spirit of benevolence. He drapes his lanyard back around his neck. It reads Dr Munroe Durrant, Prison Psychiatrist, HMP Ovenden. When he speaks, he's not out of breath. His voice is pleasant, refined. Scottish-sounding. Perhaps Midlothian. He looks at each of the group in turn. The men don't want to meet his eye. A self-satisfied smile twitches the corner of his mouth.

'Until you feel what she experienced – until you truly look out through her eyes and identify with her feelings – until then we're all just sitting here feeling sorry for ourselves. Zak here has shown extraordinary courage today. He's committed to something. He's trying to get well, no matter what it takes.'

The man on the floor doesn't move. Just hugs himself. He has one arm over his head. He's not making any noise but his body is jerking as he sobs, silently. Three years ago, Zachary Lovett was jailed for sexually assaulting his niece. It had happened years before, when she had thought him the best grown-up she knew. He'd been good-looking, then. Prison has put years on him. He's all waxy and sun-starved; spots in a great rash around his temples.

Dr Durrant leans forward in his chair, elbows on his knees. He looks down the row of men. White men, save for a short, plump Asian man, hugging his legs, feet off the floor as if rats are swarming at his feet. The figure to his right leans in. Whispers in his ear. Rubs his back.

'All good, John?'

John Dennic is wiry. Fifty-ish. There's an air of quiet about him. Gentleness. He presses his lips together tightly. Manages a smile and a brisk nod of his head.

'You're not backing out on me, are you, John?' asks Dr Durrant. 'You're rather pivotal, after all.' He gives a little chuckle. A couple of the other men join in, but there's no warmth in it. They look scared. Look genuinely frightened. These sex offenders and child molesters, abusers and rapists: they huddle in on themselves, wet-eyed, snot-streaked, picking at the scabs around their thumbnails and scratching at their scalps like animals.

'This is what the vigilante did,' says another figure, seated in the centre. 'We didn't know it would be like . . .'

'Like what, Tim?'

The broad, round-faced man who had spoken shoots a look at the sad spectre seated at the far end of the row. 'This is what he did!' he hisses. 'To Dec. To my mate. This is what he does, like . . .'

There's a rumble of agreement from the others. They have a haunted look about them, wild-eyed and hyper alert. They jump at shadows. Twitch at every unexpected sound.

Dr Durrant sits back. Rubs his palms together. Looks at the hunched figure – one flame-mottled hand gripping the handle of his walking cane: tennis balls on its base to stop the sound of scraping on the prison floors. He's got his hood up, one half of his face completely in shadow. He takes his time. Doesn't reply for several seconds. Then he raises his head. His voice is raspy: two chisels rubbed against one another in the fire-scorched darkness of his throat.

'Don't know what he did,' he says, pressing one pink, ointment-smeared finger to his throat and swallowing, painfully. 'Don't remember much beyond the shock. There was pain. Fire. Then I was waking up in hospital. Never breathed fresh air since. But I've stayed on the path.'

The other men look at him with something like pity. He has authority in this room. Could tell them all to stop their treatment and they'd do it without question. He's no physical threat, but there's an air about him that seems to keep the usual predators at bay. It's as if he gives off the faintest whiff of some unsettling odour: an earthy, wet-fur kind of emanation that speaks of hidden toxicity. There are those in the main population of the prison who swear they would do him harm if given the opportunity, but nobody has ever made good on the threats. Something in their primal brain recognizes the poison in him. Fears being too close. He seems to ooze with malignancy, sitting there with his hooked back and crippled knees, his glistening skin and missing fingers; the hole where his eye used to be, padded with gauze and concealed beneath a skin-coloured mask. He keeps his hood across his face more often than not: a friar in a grimy habit.

'It's a collective delusion,' says Dr Durrant, with the air of a man who's said this several times already. 'It's a fantasy that takes on a power over you every time you repeat it. There's no bogeyman out there, you have to understand that. Nobody waiting to give you a second chance. To show you Hell and give you the opportunity to become different men. One person told the story and another picked it up, and . . .'

'My mate remembers every fucking detail,' says Tim, suddenly animated. 'And he was in Woodhall with a bloke who fathered a kid with his own daughter and was putting her through the same shit. Somebody took him. Showed him hell. Gave him another chance. Never went near her again.'

'And that's a success story, is it?' asks Dr Durrant, irritated. 'You're seeing that as a positive outcome? You like the idea that at some point, an angel or a demon or a vigilante is going to make you face your crimes . . .'

'At least we might understand why we did it,' protests Tim. 'This role play – this sticking your pen in his arse cheek and telling him he's a little girl. It's not going to work. I'm just me, no matter how many times you say I'm not. I don't know why I done that lass. I was scared and thought she would tell. That was it. I'll never make amends for that. Not ever. I don't want to be let out – I'm here

because I want to stop feeling like I do. Wanting to do the things
that have . . . led me here. Led us all here.'

Dr Durrant takes a breath. Glances at the quiet, bearded figure.
'John,' he says, smoothly. 'You've got what I need?'

Dennic nods. Stands up. He's nimble. Silent. Crosses to the
cupboard where the chaplain used to keep tea and biscuits. Returns
with a bulbous Bellarmine jug: a thick-lipped, bearded face carved
into its earthy, centuries-old clay.

The men look apprehensive. Glance at the scarred, hooded figure
for confirmation. He shrugs. It pains him. Everything pains him.

'I need your trust, gentlemen. I need you to put your faith in me.
In this process. We are pushing boundaries here. We are taking you
deep into your own natures, your own subconscious; the very caul-
dron of your being. We are going to share our truths. Bind our
consciences. We are going to see ourselves for what we truly are.'

Dennic hands the bottle to Dr Durrant, who gives him a squeeze
on the arm in thanks. Dennic glances at the hooded man as he
returns to his seat. Gets a nod of appreciation. Of approval. This is
going to be OK . . .

Dr Durrant is the first to take a sip. He passes it to the rapist on
his right. 'Drink,' he urges. 'If the Devil exists, we'll see him
together.'

There's a *click*, and the screen turns black.

TWENTY

HMP Ovenden
4.16pm

'Jesus wept!' sputters Pharaoh. 'That's . . .'

McAvoy blinks repeatedly. Raises his hand to his mouth and
smells the lingering residue of Roisin's perfume on his wrist.
'I think my nostril hairs just caught on fire.'

Pharaoh begins to giggle. 'I mean, that's got to be cruel and
unusual, hasn't it?'

McAvoy finds himself laughing too. It's little more than a snuffle, but it still sounds incongruous here, in this little office-cum-consulting room, with its tattered textbooks, outdated posters, ragged 1970s armchairs and studiedly neutral walls. They've been waiting here ten minutes. Here, on the first floor of B-block: a great grey slab of brutally functional architecture, enlivened here and there by rain-spattered sports areas and moss-slicked education buildings. There's a library, somewhere: only open one day a week now. The last librarian had a breakdown and hasn't been replaced. Pharaoh learned all of this on the hurried walk through an interminable number of white-painted gates, watched over by chicken wire and razor-blade walls. The guard who walked them over – a bubbly bleached blonde with neck tattoos who had taken an instant liking to McAvoy – had been remarkably forthcoming. She knows Parfitt, she said. Knew John Dennic too. The wing governor was doing his nut. McAvoy had taken extra care to underline her choice of phrase. He hopes to relay it to the self-same bureaucrat who had repeatedly blocked his attempts to interview him.

'Keep that door closed,' says Pharaoh, sipping from a can of Fanta and twiddling her bangles the way she does when she wants a cigarette and can't have one. 'What was the source, do you think?'

'I'm no sommelier, but I'm thinking somebody may have defecated in a kettle.'

Pharaoh gives a snort of laughter. 'I really must ask you more questions about your time at public school, Aector.'

'You're buzzing,' says McAvoy, pointing at Pharaoh's jacket, slung across the orange-and-aubergine chair. She snatches it up. Gives a grunt of annoyance, then switches into character: delighted to have the chance to catch up.

'Gemma,' she says. 'However did you manage to find the perfect time to call?'

McAvoy listens as Pharaoh makes a series of 'umms' and 'aahs', inspecting the backs of her hands with a distinct coolness. He takes in the room again. There are certificates on the wall, dangling at an angle, made out in the name of Doctor Emma-Jane Nelson. A coat hangs on the back of the white-painted door: a long black number with a hood. He's been promised she's on her way. Would linger in the corridor and ask one of the passing warders to remind them of the urgency of the matter if it wasn't for the smell of ammonia, disinfectant and par-boiled shite that wafted down the lurid green corridors.

'That's not making any sense, love,' says Pharaoh, and McAvoy watches as the groove of concentration appears between her eyes. 'She's been game from the start. I wouldn't mess you about, you know me well enough. We've got to play straight with each other, haven't we? I mean, I'm not going to ask you about the car that followed one of my officers this morning, am I? Not going to check who rented the hire car I passed off Clough Road. Because then this conversation could take a turn.'

McAvoy watches in something approaching awe as she gives a curt 'bye-bye now, bye-bye' and ends the call. She takes a swig of Fanta.

'Paulene Haiz has gone cool on talking to the documentary crew,' she explains. 'Does that sound right to you?'

McAvoy shakes his head. 'She'd do anything to find what happened to Carmel. It's all she's alive for. Same as Kaylani's mum.'

'There wasn't anything unusual in her voice when you last spoke, was there?' asks Pharaoh, tinking the ring-pull against her teeth.

'Paulene?' He considers their last interaction: Paulene standing at the window of her bungalow and gazing out at the expanse where there used to be a caravan park. All gone, now. Fallen into the sea. Wires and cables stick out from the crumbling cliff face like severed organs and unspooled guts. She can't move, though. Can't leave this place in case Carmel comes back. Carmel – the girl abducted through an open window by the man who'd made her laugh with his silly safari suit and ill-fitting helmet. The man with the spiders and the birds. She'd still been in the fight, hadn't she? Still committed to stopping Parfitt's release, and supporting the Cold Case Unit in their quest to lay a case at the door of the man who got away with her murder. 'She was tired,' he muses. 'Said she was struggling – especially after writing the victim impact statement for the parole board. But she still had the sparkle, you know? The defiance.'

'And now she's saying to Gemma that she's reconciled to the fact her niece isn't coming back?' Pharaoh shakes her head. 'Smells like bullshit in a kettle.'

McAvoy's about to respond when the door opens and a harassed-looking woman apologises her way into the room, catching her voluminous sleeve on the handle of the door and letting out a comedic 'whoop' as she tugs herself back on the world's smallest bungee cord.

'Dr Emma-Jane Nelson,' she says, brightly, trying to disentangle her long red hair from the collar of her jacket and succeeding in catching her crystal bracelets on her dangly earrings. She wears glasses on a chain around her neck. McAvoy will tell Roisin later that she was Rubenesque: milky white and flame-haired and very much the sort to be painted naked in a bathtub under strategically placed petals. Pharaoh will confide that the prison psychologist was 'a big jolly sort'. They'll agree that they liked her at once.

'That smell,' says Dr Nelson dropping a big satchel on her desk and plonking herself down in the swivel chair behind the desk. She's not much more than 5 feet tall. Mid-forties, perhaps. Her smile is endearing; her energy pure benevolent cheer. Pharaoh wonders whether she drinks. Smokes crack.

'The smell, yes,' says Pharaoh, standing so she can introduce herself properly. 'It's been life-changing.'

'It's not representative, I can assure you,' grins Dr Nelson. 'We only get that three or four days out of every seven so there's a bright side to be looked upon, if you find the right angle. I do believe the poor warder will be forgoing his tuna curry this evening. He was warned.'

Pharaoh looks as though she has more questions, but gets a hold of herself before they can emerge. 'I'm Pharaoh. Big lump over there is McAvoy. And you, Dr Nelson, have been deliberately keeping us from chatting with one of your inmates.'

Dr Nelson sticks out her lower lip. 'That doesn't seem particularly likely,' she says, though she says it with the air of somebody whose filing system is at best sub-optimal, and at worst a roaring bin fire. 'It's Decland Parfitt you're here to see, did I get that right? The lady on the front desk – sorry, I must stop calling her that – she said you became rather insistent. I'm doing my best to accommodate you but we do rather have a lot on today, so if we're a little all-over-the-place, well . . .'

'It's not representative,' finishes McAvoy. He smiles. Tries to put her at ease.

'John Dennic,' Pharaoh says. 'He didn't come back from a work placement, I'm guessing. Not an unusual state of affairs, alas.'

Dr Nelson nods. Smiles brightly at McAvoy, as if something interesting has just occurred to her. 'He's on my list,' she says, rummaging around madly in the detritus of papers in her bottom drawer. She picks out a wicker basket full of handmade gift items and puts it on the floor beside her so she can see into the depths of the drawer.

'Bellamy . . . Bridges . . . Condell . . . Dennic, yes. Haven't officially had the pleasure, yet. Apparently very well-liked. Not much on his file. No visits, no letters. A glowing reputation though.'

Pharaoh shakes her head, refusing to countenance the suggestion. 'On the VP wing? Well-liked?'

'John Dennic wasn't spending much time among the prison population, from what I understand,' says Dr Nelson, with a shrug. She has little arms: puffy palms and small fingers corseted with silver rings. 'He and a few of the more trusted inmates are participating in a study instituted by my predecessor. Part of a preparation-for-release programme.'

Pharaoh shoots McAvoy a glance. He gets the cue.

'Your predecessor? You're new in post?'

'Matter of weeks,' she says. 'Still finding my feet. All a bit different from my last job, but it's a real opportunity.'

'For them or for you?' asks Pharaoh, sitting back down.

'For everybody, silly,' smiles Dr Nelson. There's something a little eccentric about her mannerisms, her wide smile and bright blue eyes. She seems manic. McAvoy hears the words 'perimenopause' bubble up from his subconscious and immediately pushes it back down, ashamed of himself. 'Dr Durrant did things a different way, and before that it was, well . . . something of a different regime.'

'Are we going to be able to talk to Decland Parfitt?' asks McAvoy, and the use of the man's first name feels foul upon his tongue. He turns away and glares through the window. Two warders are escorting a dreadlocked man between two glowering structures, splendid in their blue uniforms and shiny boots, all military haircuts and straight backs.

'I do hope you realize, I'm still stewing on that "deliberately" accusation from before,' she says, giving Pharaoh a hurt look. 'Decland Parfitt and I have only spoken on one occasion. I'm simply honouring what my predecessor indicated was the preferred methodology for helping him on his journey.'

'On his journey?' asks McAvoy.

'Getting. well. Going home.'

'He's never going home,' says Pharaoh, her face hard. 'You know what he is, don't you? What he's done? Don't let the scars fool you. For as long as that bastard's heart is beating, he'll be a danger to children.'

Dr Nelson takes a tress of her long red hair and starts to plait it, her actions swift and practised. She unplaits it again, looking between Pharaoh and McAvoy to the storage unit and the bookshelves. 'I've been privy to some of the details of his convictions,' she says. 'I'm also aware of the investigation into other crimes he may have been involved in. All I can tell you is what Dr Durrant wrote in his last report. He's a model patient. He accepts his culpability for the wrongdoing and simply wants to put the past behind him and start again. I understand he has a daughter who is willing to give him a place to stay?'

'Foster daughter,' says McAvoy, softly. 'Maintains he's innocent. Her sister killed herself over what he did to her, but Ruby is sticking to her story.'

'So you need Parfitt to suddenly break down and confess all, do you?' Dr Nelson laughs and reaches down to pick up the gift basket. McAvoy watches as she plays with the handful of objects within: neat little pots and vials containing different oils and lotions.

'Birthday present?' asks McAvoy, trying to lighten the mood and finding himself immediately unsuited to the task.

'Our errant Mr Dennic,' explains Dr Nelson. 'One of his wheezes to keep his mind busy. It's rather touching – these dangerous men picking plants and berries and making something rather lovely. Honestly, you wouldn't have expected it of the man in the file. I wouldn't be surprised if there wasn't somebody waiting for him. Some people have long memories, though I did rather think that we had managed to maintain confidentiality about his group sessions.'

Pharaoh stands up, growing impatient. She reaches into her handbag and pulls out her perfume. Gives herself a squirt of Issey Miyake. She sighs theatrically, intimating bone weariness; defeat. 'Is Parfitt going to be allowed to come out to play, Dr Nelson? And are you going to tell me what you're so obviously trying to hide?'

'I'm not trying to hide anything,' exclaims Dr Nelson, one hand at her chest. She looks to McAvoy. He softens his gaze and Dr Nelson looks away, ears turning pink. She rummages in the mess of paperwork. Reads Dennic's file again. Makes a face. After a brief pause, she holds up a finger and raises the phone on her desk. She has a brief, bright, high-pitched chat with a gruff male voice on the other end of the line. Finishes with 'brought up at once' and ends the call looking a little self-satisfied.

'I'm not giving out rosettes, sweetheart,' says Pharaoh. 'We could have sorted this palaver out months ago. And if Dennic has been up in our neck of the woods at Parfitt's bidding, I reckon your wing governor is going to have some explaining to do. I want no more prattling on about lotions and potions and dangerous men showing they're sweeties underneath. I want Parfitt.'

'He's on his way up,' says Dr Nelson, quietly. 'He's not very mobile. Certain protocols have to be observed.'

'We'll need to see all of Dennic's visitor records. All his correspondence.'

'Isn't it Notts Police that are investigating? As a missing person?'

'He's dead on our patch,' says Pharaoh, coldly. 'We get dibs.'

Dr Nelson falls silent. McAvoy feels for her. She's new to the job; clearly harassed beyond enduring. He wouldn't want to be responsible for plumbing the depths of a sex offender's mind. Wouldn't want the responsibility of deciding who's fit to be released back into the wild.

'I can rustle up a coffee,' says Dr Nelson, looking hurt but keeping her smile fixed in place. 'Dr Durrant may have left some bourbons.'

McAvoy winces in advance as Pharaoh takes a deep breath. Wonders what stream of filthy irritation will erupt from her mouth. She deflates before she has the chance to erupt.

'Aye, go on. Please.'

Dr Nelson smiles, delighted to be given a task. She hurries out of the room, pausing to grab a set of keys from her bag. 'Shan't be a tick.'

Pharaoh sits and shakes her head, enjoying the sudden silence.

'You doing OK?' asks McAvoy, quietly. 'You didn't say much on the drive down. Your eyes look tired, Trish . . .'

'Give your head a bang, Aector,' grunts Pharaoh. She rubs her face with her palms. Takes a breath and holds it.

'The video,' says McAvoy, ignoring the slight. 'Are you going to hold on to that or hit him with it straight away?'

Pharaoh looks up. Stares into him, hard. 'I've been fantasizing about seeing this moment for years, Aector. A chance to look him in the eye and tell him that I know. I know who it is they all fear.'

McAvoy doesn't say anything. Waits for more. He isn't sure what he's supposed to be thinking. Feels like she's keeping something back.

'The name on the video,' he says softly, rolling the thought around like stale gum. 'That's the one, isn't it? That's who you believe took him down into the dark.'

Pharaoh glares. Nods.

McAvoy cracks his jaw. 'What aren't you telling me?'

'Check your phone,' says Pharaoh, tiredly. 'Ben's sent you something.'

TWENTY-ONE

Wincolmlee, Hull
5.15pm

'No bloody dignity,' mutters Andy Daniells, feeling like a
toddler trying to traverse a row of Stickle Bricks. 'None
at all.'

He's chuntering into the sweaty confines of his face covering and
his words come back in a mist that smells of his lunch. He's beginning to regret the scotch egg and tikka masala pasty. He feels all
twisted up and turned around – like the time he put his onesie on
back to front and his husband was too busy laughing to do the zip
and help him out. He's wearing white hooded coveralls – ludicrously
tight at the crotch – which he's matched with blue gloves – two
fingers in one finger-hole on both hands – crinkled yellow bootees
and wide, thumb-smudged eye protectors. He keeps scaring himself
as he picks his way across the metal tiles. There are mirrors along
one wall and the harsh glare of the nearby halogen lamps make his
reflection seem oddly spectral. He keeps thinking he's being stalked
by Casper the friendly ghost.

'Say something, Andy. And by goodness, what size did they give
you? You look like a parsnip.'

Vas Dhand is squatting down in a circle of light at the far end
of the rectangular space. They're on the first floor of Ruby's former
café: a box with dirty windows and a linoleum floor. There are dusty
chairs stacked up against one wall and a couple of tables on top of
one another. A lumpy Caramac-coloured sofa is pushed back to the
wall, leaving a bare space in the middle of the floor. There's a tiny
bar just inside the doorway: two empty optics and a lifeless mini
fridge. An empty bottle of Stag's Breath liqueur standing beside

two crystal tumblers and an overflowing ashtray. Daniells sniffs the air. Even through the mask, he can detect the ammonia, the damp, the brick dust. The bleach.

'I hate wearing these bloody things,' grumbles Daniells, who's feeling vaguely put-upon. 'A gentleman shouldn't crinkle when he walks.'

'You having a bad one, mate?' asks Dhand, who's leading the preliminary examination of the premises. He's a short, dark-haired man with glasses and an unsettling cheeriness. He had a decent career as a solicitor before he turned his back on the law to give policing a go instead. He's a crime-scene technician. A good one.

'Shouldn't grumble,' says Daniells, stepping on to one of the metal tiles and feeling the floorboards creak beneath his weight. 'Windows aren't much of a size, are they? And those stairs are a bugger, even when you're not carrying a body. It's looking unlikely, isn't it?'

Dhand's eyes crinkle, his smile hidden by his mask. 'I wouldn't be so quick to despair, my friend. Take a look. Sam, would you get the light, thanks . . .'

Another white-covered scene technician clicks off the lights and Dhand reaches into a hard plastic case. He retrieves what looks like a fluorescent tube. In front of him is an area of peeled-back linoleum, exposing bare, half-rotten boards beneath. The eerie purple light seems to hum as Dhand moves it across the floor. There are great swirls and whorls of streaky white.

'Somebody's tried to clean up but they haven't made much of a job of it,' says Dhand. 'Blood, in case you were wondering. A fair amount, I'd say. We'll have the rest of the lino up, get a second team to work the bathroom.'

'There's a bathroom?'

'Top floor,' he says. 'Well, more of a loft, really. You can see the river through the skylight. Mattress on the floor, few paperback books. It's a maze of a place.'

Daniells feels a little tingle in the pit of his stomach. He turns slowly on his metal board – a marionette with a size 38 waist. Blinks as the anonymous tech switches the light back on. Takes in some more of the details that he'd missed on first inspection. There's a velvet-effect blanket box shoved next to the sofa, its lid ajar. Dhand follows his gaze.

'You'll be waiting an age for an inventory, Andy. Here, have a

flick while we're getting busy.' He hands an expensive-looking tablet
to Daniells. Opens up a new file of images and slides his finger
over the screen. 'Left to right – uploading as we go. Pictures, mostly.
Kids' pictures. Drawings. Some photos, a scrapbook.'

Daniells starts to examine the images on the screen. Dhand's
right – there's an interminable number of images drawn in coloured
pencil and wax crayon: misshapen dinosaurs, lopsided houses;
triangle women and lantern headed men.

'Aramis,' says Daniells, remembering the name from his brief
chat with McAvoy.

'Agamemnon and Aramis – you reckon there's an inferiority
complex in that family?'

'Kes – the witness who might have placed Dennic here – he says
he never saw Mem be anything but a good dad towards the boy.
Said he was a nasty piece of work the rest of the time, but loved
his boy.'

Dhand pauses, tweezers in his hand and an open evidence bag
in the other. 'He's going to have to do that behind bars for a while,
then,' he says, and he looks down at the floor as if processing the
enormity of his responsibility. Shakes it away. 'Attacking your
McAvoy . . . what was the silly sod thinking?'

Daniells considers it. 'If he'd just stabbed somebody and dumped
the body . . . probably in a blind panic. Reacted as soon as the
Sarge went for his warrant card, though Mem's claiming he thought
he was going for a gun.'

'And Mem has had the kind of life where that's a regular occur-
rence, has he?' asks Dhand, radiating cynicism. 'He's got those kind
of enemies?'

'Seems so,' says Daniells. 'He's done some nasty things, Vas.
He's in bed with some nasty people.'

'Any word on the chap who had it away across the tiles?' asks
Dhand, standing and stretching a loud crack out of the small of his
back.

Daniells permits himself a chuckle. 'Spiderman? Not a sign. No
name either, though the description's been circulated.'

'You went all official-sounding there, Andy,' says Dhand, putting
his head to one side as if Daniells is just the cutest. 'Is that how
you talk to the grown-ups?'

'Shush, you,' laughs Daniells, who feels himself cheering up. He
continues looking through the evidence log. There are bills in ripped

envelopes, bills unopened. Magazines in neat piles: *Men's Health*, *Holistic Healing, New You*. Notebooks, too, some lined with coils of blue ink; the pen pressed so hard into the page that it leaves a deep outline on the leaf beneath. Daniells expands the size of the image. Reads a sample under his breath.

'*Dear Daddy . . . I just found myself smiling . . . I didn't mean it. I just felt the muscle twitch. It was the smell, I think. That smell you get when you walk into a pet store or a stable and it's wet hay and bonemeal and it hangs in the air so thick you can taste it. Roscoe smiled too. I felt him squeeze my hand, as if he understood what I was feeling. Perhaps he did. But he doesn't have the same memories as me, does he? Not the same associations. He's not as clever as he thinks he is. I don't think I'm as stupid as he tries to make me feel . . .*'

'Pages of it,' says Dhand, conversationally. 'All about forgiving yourself. Living with hope in your heart. Wait until you get to the bit about cell regeneration.'

'*Three hundred and thirty billion cells regenerate every day . . . not the same person . . . in jail for crimes committed by a human being who doesn't exist. The dead skin has been cast off. Every cell is a new construct . . .*'

'You think Ruby's trying to persuade herself?' asks Dhand.

'Who's this then?' asks Daniells, holding up the tablet. It shows a photograph of a framed print: a dozen men seated on padded school chairs or standing in ones and twos; men in matching fleeces, chatting, drinking tea; one or two smiles here and there. Daniells looks from the screen to the sad, lifeless room in which he now stands. In the photograph, Ruby is pouring tea from a big brown pot, a headscarf holding her hair out of her eyes,wearing a cardigan and dungarees and well-loved running trainers. She's smiling at something the man to her left has just said. He's slightly out of focus, tucked in behind the flick of her ponytail. All Daniells can discern is soft cords and suede brogues. The hair might be dark, but it's almost impossible to make out more than a curve of his jaw and the possible smudge of a roll-neck jumper.

'Any familiar faces?' asks Dhand, beckoning past Daniells to where three more technicians are filing through the gap like Chinese lanterns.

'Used to run a "Talking Club" here,' says Daniells. 'Ben's dad went to something similar, I'm sure he won't mind me saying. Lot

of the old fishermen have signed up for a bit of self-care. Talking
things out, trying to feel something and not dismiss it as weakness . . . it's important work. A lot of people were sad to see it go.
Bloke who ran it – pretty sure I've heard the name Roscoe before
now.'

'My brother goes to the one in Burnley,' confides Dhand. 'National
charity, branches everywhere. I don't see any of their paraphernalia
though. This was independent, was it?'

Daniells shrugs. He feels like he's running on a treadmill in flip-
flops and is actually rather pleased with how much he's digested,
and how quickly.

'I don't quite get the connection,' says Dhand, stepping nimbly
over the boards and helping one of his assistants to set up a step-
ladder and complex camera rig. 'You're with McAvoy's Cold Case
Unit, aren't you? So how does that—'

'Sort of right place, wrong time, or some combination of those
cliches,' says Daniells, making his way back towards the door and
trying not to trip any of the technicians, moving around him in silent
diligence. Thinks of monks, and tries not to make himself laugh.

'And this Dennic . . . he's, what . . . come to Hull on a day-pass
to threaten Parfitt's foster daughter? Mem's done him in, and . . .'

'It's not bloody Cluedo, Vas,' says Daniells, squeezing himself
through the door. He passes him the tablet and nods his thanks.
'The blood's a help. At least Wolsingham won't get to say it was
a fool's errand. I hate it when he says things like that. I barely know
the man but he makes my teeth itch.'

Dhand steps into the corridor and pulls down his mask, taking
off his goggles and pulling down his hood. He smiles, a little know-
ingly. 'You know he was a Superintendent, don't you? Got bumped
down for some naughtiness.'

'Naughtiness?'

'Cases falling apart because of bad recordkeeping or lost
evidence . . . good junior officers getting unfavourable treatment or
pulled off cases without explanation. You know, the kind of stuff
that suggests you're in somebody's debt. Heard about it at a conference. Thought he would be pensioned off.'

Daniells widens his eyes. 'And Pharaoh's got him?'

'Who the bloody hell else could handle him?' smiles Dhand.
'Anyway, least said, soonest mended.' He gives a meaningful look,
lowering his voice. 'Just tell Ben to cover his arse.'

TWENTY-TWO

There's a heavy silence in Dr Nelson's office – the kind that contains so many unspoken words that they seem to be written in the air in iridescent ink.

McAvoy hates awkwardness. Has always done whatever he can to puncture the tension in the room, even if it makes his cheeks burn to do so. He can usually be relied upon to spill his tea or stumble against a filing cabinet in the wake of one of Pharaoh's particularly vitriolic group dressing-downs. When he was still in uniform he had a reputation for defusing tense situations simply by tripping over his own size-twelve feet or knocking his hat off on the doorframe. He's never been quite sure how much of it was an act.

'Oh jings,' he mutters, as he reaches for the nearly-empty can of Tango and succeeds in spilling a dribble on the arm of the chair.

'Heffalump,' sighs Pharaoh, and the tension bleeds out of the room. 'Can't take you bloody anywhere.'

Feeling better, McAvoy readjusts his position on the chair. Watches the video of the group therapy for a second time. Shakes his head, frowning to himself.

'In his tooth,' he mutters again. 'He really wanted to keep this safe.'

'Or he wanted us to see it,' she muses, and makes her way to Dr Nelson's desk, helping herself to the pile of files. 'Best of buddies, it seems,' she reads. 'Parfitt and Dennic. I'm sure they had plenty to talk about.'

'Unlikely bedfellows,' says McAvoy, and cringes, regretting the choice of words. 'If Dennic is inside for attacking a police officer, that doesn't make him a likely confidante for a child abuser. And he's already served longer than he was sentenced, which doesn't sound right for a model prisoner.'

Pharaoh shrugs. 'When you're on the VP wing, you make whatever friends you can. And it looks as if Dennic has a temper. An appetite too. Shipped out of Franklin for attacking his pad-mate.

Time added. Same at Wakefield. Full Sutton. Seems to ping from being pillar of the prison to a fucking nutcase. And they still let him out!'

McAvoy looks up from his phone. 'How did Dennic end up in segregation with the VPs?'

Pharaoh hums to herself as she scans the pages. 'The old injury,' she says, looking up, cupping the air with her hand: a doctor waiting for a bare-arsed patient to cough. 'The old Burnley wallet, I think it's called. Sounds like the sort of thing you'd do to somebody who couldn't be trusted with their urges.'

'Or if you couldn't trust yourself.'

McAvoy hauls himself out of the chair. Runs his eyes over the images on the bland walls. There are some pleasant watercolours and some intriguing black and white sketches: wind-blown trees and wide-open skies. McAvoy inspects the signatures. Finds his eye drawn to a series of photographs, framed in a triptych. The images are of a mountain-top, haloed in exquisite gold; a sky of trumpets and coronets, cherubs laid upon sumptuous clouds as if posing upon fur.

'JD, 2021,' reads McAvoy. He peers closer at the image, trying to see past his own reflection. It's delicate. Intricate. He changes his angle to better see in the glare of the striplight. Notices a peculiarity to the way it hangs. He picks it off the hook and turns it over. The hardboard back of the frame isn't pushed down properly. Something bulges underneath.

McAvoy looks to Pharaoh, who nods her approval. He teases out the piece of card. The back of the sketch is concertinaed up at the bottom: several two-inch folds of paper. McAvoy takes the top fold and stretches it out. There's another entire half to the image. McAvoy turns it in his hands. Sees the rest of the sketch and has to stop himself from throwing the whole thing at the wall. Beneath the skyscape of celestial, ambrosial delights, lies the true subject of the image. The artist has drawn a skewed reflection of the scene above; the mountain transposed instead into the rear half of some colossal, shaggy-furred beast. Where above there are angels, here cavort demons, countless figures contorting in savagery and pain.

'Earthly delights,' muses McAvoy, laying the picture out and taking photographs from every angle.

'What's that?'

'Bosch,' he says, folding the picture back and putting it on the wall. As he does so, he notices an inscription. It's written in fine pencil. Latin. *Ipse dīxit, et facta sunt: ipse mandāvit, et creāta sunt.* McAvoy frowns, trying to remember his lessons. 'He spoke and it was done. He commanded and it held fast.' He takes another picture and recites it out loud, lest Pharaoh be hiding her gift for ancient languages under a bushel.

'I might have read that on our Sophia,' she frowns. 'Left arm, maybe. I can't keep up. What did you say about Bosch?'

'Just that it looked a bit like his depiction of Hell,' he says, and feels two parts of his brain stitch themselves together. 'I know the fire burned away most of the evidence out at Bempton, but the way you described it, it always sounded more like The Book of Hours.'

Pharaoh gives him a hard look. 'Go on, then.'

McAvoy searches for an image on his phone. He could tell her in his own words but doesn't want to seem like a show-off, or worse, that he's been holding back the same way she has.

'It was a Christian devotional book . . . Middle Ages – commissioned by the rich. Some of the copies included "illuminations". Pictures, really. The copy that belonged to Catherine of Cleves showed what we now think of as a Hellmouth – a great pink mouth masticating and gnawing at the bones of the damned. The monster's mouths gaping, ravenous. The Hellmouth, a popular image in Medieval art, was a portal between Earth and Hell surrounded by supernatural energy. Here, demonic creatures lead humans into the fiery pits of Hell . . .'

'I'm never letting you say "masticating" again.' Pharaoh sniffs, turning away.

'This Virgil,' he says. 'If the place he took Parfitt and his other victims was decorated the way you saw before the fire took it . . . there's no way that this person hasn't got a familiarity with Bosch. It's the most famous depiction of Hell. It's the art world's equivalent of Dante.'

Pharaoh goes back to the file. She glances at the clock above the door. She's getting twitchy, he can tell. Wants a cigarette. Probably wants a glass of wine and a fight too.

'I tried to get through *Inferno* once,' he admits. There are some great works of literature he's never been able to wade all the way through. Dante Alighieri's *Divine Comedy* being right up there with *The Mill on the Floss*. It had felt like a true descent into Hell – each level of suffering more brutal and hideous than the last. So had Dante.

'You'll visit me in Hell, won't you?' asks Pharaoh, and makes a slithery, serpent-like flicker of her tongue. 'From your place at the right hand of God?'

McAvoy scowls at the floor. It's the closest he gets to looking aggrieved, though he does 'hurt' with the aplomb of a damp spaniel.

'Unusual route through the system,' muses Pharaoh, considering Dennic's file. 'Ping-ponged around between prisons and wings and units.'

She finds a packet of Starburst. Helps herself to a lime and tosses a strawberry to McAvoy, who catches it in his big fist. 'You haven't been misled, y'know. You've been building a case against our prime suspect in the abductions of two girls. That's never altered.'

McAvoy makes a face. 'Which just so happens to be a way in to your real goal. Finding if Virgil exists.'

'He fucking exists,' snarls Pharaoh. 'He pushed past me in the dark. Left me there. Left Parfitt's future up to me. Put the fate of the Devil in my hands.'

'And you truly believe he's been doing this for years?'

Pharaoh shakes her head. 'And you can just imagine how popular I'd be if I let it be known I was trying to stop him. He's cutting up sex offenders and paedophiles. Even the sweetest little granny would find it hard to think he was doing anything wrong.'

'But you do.'

'Aye, and so do you,' says Pharaoh. 'I know you'd have understood if I'd told you, Aector. I know you'd have done the right thing. That's what you do. But I didn't want to put that pressure on you. Not if I didn't have to.'

McAvoy swallows his Starburst. Wonders if the world were simpler when they were still called Opal Fruits. Presumes somebody is already working on a PhD posing that very question.

'You want to talk to Parfitt because he's seen Virgil,' says McAvoy, quietly. 'You know he's never going to admit what he did but he might just be able to help you find the man who mutilated him.'

'Never been quite sure whether I want to put him in handcuffs or pin a medal to his chest.' Pharaoh scowls, crossing to the bookshelves and randomly opening textbooks stacked higgledy-piggledy on the shelves. 'I just want to look him in the eye. Find out what made him what he is.'

'It's a "he"?'

'The little we got out of Parfitt suggested a medium-sized male,' says Pharaoh. 'The rig they used to get Parfitt into the air and upside down – even with a block and tackle it would have taken some strength.'

McAvoy falls silent. From beyond the door he hears a sudden commotion: shouts and whoops and jeers. He hates prison. Knows he wouldn't survive it. He needs open spaces and big skies. Needs space to breathe. Needs Roisin.

'I spent the money on a profile,' says Pharaoh, glaring at her own reflection in the glass of a framed certificate. 'Possibly a survivor of abuse. Possibly an abuser themselves.'

McAvoy scratches at his beard, thinking hard.

'Dennic doesn't feel right,' he says at last. 'If Virgil's done this . . . if he even exists . . . it's gone wrong somehow.'

Pharaoh rummages in her handbag for her lipstick. Sorts herself out in the glass. She doesn't say anything – just waits for McAvoy to catch up.

'The earlier mutilations,' he says. 'You think Virgil got him years ago.'

'If you can bring yourself to be naughty, take a look in his file.' Pharaoh smiles, pouting as she applies the red gloss. 'Durrant paints him as a reformed character. Contributes to the group discussion, serves as a mentor for a lot of the younger prisoners – engages fully with probation services; has taken advantage of all the courses and outreach programmes available in the prison. No objections anywhere to his release, and he's been good as gold on his day passes and weekend release. Working with a picture-framer – job waiting for him when he gets out, possible role serving as a mentee with a charity based in Brigg. *Daily Mail* would go mental if they knew.'

McAvoy waits for more. He wonders if Pharaoh will insist he open the file – to watch his cheeks burn with the shame of transgression. She shakes her head at him, twitching a smile, forever amused by the battle he fights against himself. 'He's been working with a picture-framer,' explains Pharaoh. 'Two days a week. Hasn't missed a shift, hasn't come back late. That's why the authorities held off on going into full panic mode. This wasn't like him at all.'

McAvoy cracks his knuckles. Apologizes as Pharaoh winces. 'It's hard not to think that Parfitt sent him. I mean, why Hull? How did he even get there? It must be to do with Ruby.'

'I'm sure that's the way Wolsingham will steer things,' says Pharaoh, getting tired. 'And I've no doubt Ruby has a lot of questions to answer.'

'But?'

Pharaoh shrugs. McAvoy knows her mannerisms and expressions as well as Roisin's – as well as his own. She has a suspicion that she doesn't want to share. She's still holding back.

'Anything in there about the relationship between Parfitt and Dennic?' asks McAvoy.

'Both resident in the Open House,' says Pharaoh. 'Cosy, ain't it? Parfitt's mentioned a dozen times in Dennic's file. Very close, it seems.'

McAvoy hauls himself out of the chair. Crosses to the bookshelves and idly runs his fingers over the spines. They're mostly textbooks, interspersed with true-crime paperbacks and a few dusty, red-leather classics. McAvoy touches the spine of one volume, unable to make out the gold lettering on the greasy leather. He nudges Pharaoh when he makes out the title.

'Dante,' he says. He looks at Pharaoh, waiting for a comment. She looks at him blankly. 'Virgil,' he says, as gently as he can.

'Don't get all boarding school on me, Aector,' she says, and he realizes she's been teasing. 'We have libraries in Mexborough, you know. Or at least we used to.'

McAvoy breathes out, relieved. He takes the copy from the shelf. There's no signature, but the details on the fly-leaf show it was printed in 1855. McAvoy runs his fingers over the letters on the spine. Charles Bagot Cayley. He's only ever read the Longfellow translation. Hopes he never has to read another.

'You've read it?' asks Pharaoh.

'Studied it,' he confesses. 'Hideous. Beautiful, but hideous. Don't know this translation though.'

'Virgil,' muses Pharaoh. 'Our guide through Hell. Shows you the horrors, then takes your hand and leads you to safety. I've never been sure it suits him. Don't know if it's what he calls himself, or simply what they've named him.'

'They?'

'The bastards who think he's coming for them. The ones who are maybe, just maybe, rethinking their vices thanks to his . . . what's the word?'

'Torture?'

'Intercession,' finishes Pharaoh.

The door opens and McAvoy instinctively holds the book behind his back. Pharaoh takes it from him without a word – dropping it into the open depths of her bag.

In the doorway stands a stout tattooed officer in short sleeves: bulldog face glaring at the intruders. He gives something that might be a smile.

'I'm to escort you over,' he says, and his accent is pure West Midlands. 'Word's got round. You might hear some nasty language.'

Pharaoh steps in front of McAvoy. Nods, solemnly. Looks earnest and fearful. 'If it all gets too much, you will take care of me, won't you?'

The officer laughs. It's quite a nice sight. McAvoy finds himself marvelling at Pharaoh's ability to disarm people. He feels a sudden prickling sensation on his scalp. Feels his palms begins to sweat. Realizes that he's about to sit in a room with Decland Parfitt.

'Brought your own bodyguard, I see,' says the officer, whose name badge declares him to be one Paul Graves.

'Oh we get a special grant from the government for that one,' says Pharaoh dismissively, waving a hand in McAvoy's direction. 'Home Office scheme. Every department gets a massive ginger to take care of. Entitles us to the best parking spaces but he eats a lot.'

Graves laughs. McAvoy blushes.

'Shall we, then?' asks Graves, gesturing out to the foulness of the corridor. 'Bedlam today. Was it right what we heard about Dennic? Jesus, poor fucker. Sweetest bloke, he really was. Bloody garden's going to fall apart without him.' He spots the collection of little soaps and salves on the edge of Dr Nelson's desk. Picks one up and marvels at it. 'I can never say the word right . . . atho-pecary? Is that it? Tell you what though, when there was Spice on the wing and all the officers were going half loopy on the effects – he did more for us than anybody in the hospital wing. Couple of eyedrops and a glass of milk and we were right as rain. Wouldn't hurt a fly, that one.'

'He's inside for attacking a police officer,' says McAvoy, point-edly. 'And yet he was taking part in a programme for sex offenders and paedophiles. Took advantage of an opportunity to unburden his conscience, do you think?'

'Leave your prejudices at the door, eh?' says Graves, shaking his head. He looks at Pharaoh. 'Parfitt will only talk to you, by the way. Made that very plain. He's having a hard day. Him and Dennic – like I say, they were close. But he'll talk to you. Just you. He seems quite excited.'

McAvoy isn't sure what to feel. He already feels like a spare part. It all feels so unwieldy, so disconnected. He wants to be at his desk, putting names into databases and cross-checking timelines with CCTV footage. It's safe there. Safe and useful and a perfectly respectable use of his time. Something tells him that Pharaoh has other plans.

'I can argue,' says Pharaoh, looking up at McAvoy. Her expression is a little softer, her voice more gentle. 'But getting him to talk . . . that's the most important thing.'

McAvoy nods. 'I can wait . . .'

'No – I'm sorry for dragging you all this way, but you get yourself back to Hull,' she says, squeezing his arm. 'Take the car and I'll have a uniform come pick me up. Finding Ruby's the most important thing. And you'll be wanting to have your five minutes in the cell with Mem, I shouldn't wonder.'

'Mem?' asks Graves. 'Agamemnon, isn't it? Hard case? Looks a bit Greek? Caused a right fucking ruckus when he came to visit Parfitt. I've got the footage somewhere. Took three of us to hold him down. Something upset him, right enough. We'd have taken it further if Parfitt had been willing to give a statement. Not that a half-deaf, one-eyed man is much of a witness.'

'That would be very helpful,' says McAvoy.

'Of course, we've been through all this with Notts Police,' says Graves, and as he changes his position, McAvoy admires the fine line work on his chaotic, detailed tattoos. There are statues and churches, crosses and flames. 'Who he's close with, how he might have got to Hull, any indication he was planning to escape . . .' He shakes his head, as if the idea is ludicrous. 'He's due for release before Christmas. He'd have to be a fool to scupper that. And he wasn't any fool. Could talk to Dennic for hours. Kind, clever, hard-working . . .'

'Attacked a police officer, admitted to an attraction to children while inside . . .' McAvoy finishes, surprising himself.

'A place like this – you try to judge the person in front of you, not the crimes that brought them to you.'

Pharaoh gives McAvoy a little smile. McAvoy notices the slightest tremble to her hand as she pats his arm. She's nervous, he realizes. She's finally going to see him. Going to stare into the face of evil.

'Lay on, Macduff,' she says to Graves. 'You will protect me, yeah? I don't want to hear any unkind fucking words.'

And then she's gone – off to keep a date with the Devil.

TWENTY-THREE

Barton-upon-Humber
7.12pm

McAvoy checks his messages. There are updates from Neilsen and Daniells, and a reminder from Fin that it's football practice after school, so not to worry if he's in a little late. It's a group chat – just he and Roisin and their big, red-haired Highlander of a boy. He allows himself a moment of pure, big-hearted love for his son. Finds himself smiling as he pictures him: all self-conscious and studious, shy and self-effacing. He doesn't suit his body. Would be happier if he were as little and unobtrusive as his geek-squad friends. He doesn't like them to worry about him. He's so thoughtful it often renders him inert. McAvoy wishes he had some wisdom he could pass on to the boy; some hard-earned insight gained from a lifetime of fighting the same benign flaws. He sends a thumbs-up. Makes a mental note to be less hopeless tomorrow.

He's pulled Pharaoh's ridiculous little Mercedes in to fill up at the service station in Barton-upon-Humber. He can't help thinking that she's laid on this whole thing just to trick him into filling her car up. He's third in line to pay for his fuel now, clutching a packet of bonbons and an energy drink. By way of apology to the people who love him, he's also going to force himself to consume a couple of the watermelon fingers that wallow, unappetizingly, in the hard-plastic prison he holds in his left hand.

The rain begins to fall harder, streaking the dirty glass of the petrol station. The streetlamps cast gentle halos of yellow air into the grey and purple gloom; their light fading before it can illuminate the leaf-filled gutters.

'Coming down now,' mutters the large, broad-backed man in overalls who stands in front of McAvoy in the queue. 'Bloody scientists.'

McAvoy tells himself not to ask. Wills himself to keep his own counsel. 'Scientists?'

'They're the ones doing all this climate change business, aren't they? Never heard nowt about it until they started poking about and now the weather's going bloody sideways.'

McAvoy can't quite find the words to express himself. Turns his attention back to his own phone before he finds himself getting stupider through osmosis.

His phone beeps with a new message from Ben. He and Wolsingham are about to meet with the ex-cop that Dennic nearly killed. The address is in Brigg, not more than fifteen minutes away. He wonders if it would seem like he was interfering – whether Wolsingham would get sniffy and Ben would feel like he was checking up. Decides that he's over-thinking it.

He pays for the petrol. Asks for a bottle of the nice elderflower gin from behind the counter – a little present for Roisin to say sorry for not having time to cuddle when he'd hastily rushed in to change his clothes. His assertion that Pharaoh was waiting for him downstairs had hardy helped.

He's climbing back into the cramped confines of the silly two-seater when his phone buzzes again. He curses before he glances at the screen, irritated by the extra interruption. The exclamation dies on his tongue as he sees that the call is from Paulene Haiz.

'Mrs Haiz, hello, it's good to hear from you . . .'

'Aector,' she says, and there's a peculiar quality to the way she says it. For the past few months she's only spoken to him through a tongue furred with sleep and painkillers, wine and anti-depressants. Her every utterance sounds pained and breathless, as if she's got somebody sitting on her chest. She said his name with purpose.

'Would you mind if I just moved the car, Paulene. I'm in a petrol station and there's a man behind me in an Audi who looks like he's going to rupture something if I don't drive away, so . . .'

'I only need you a moment, Aector,' says Paulene, in the same emboldened voice. 'I need you to know that this thing . . . this whole thing . . . it's gone on long enough. I'll still fight to keep him locked up, don't you worry about that, but . . . those people with the cameras – it brought it home. I've given so many years to this. To finding where he put her. To learning the truth. I've made my peace with the knowledge that I do have. I'm going to lay her to rest in my head and my heart, Aector. I've got to stop living for the dead.'

McAvoy loses his eyes. There's a honk from behind him. He ignores it. Breathes out, slowly, torn between being a good detective and a good man. 'Whatever happens, I'll never stop trying to find out what happened to your niece, Paulene. I swore to you. So did Trish. And nothing will change that. Nothing.'

He hears a familiar tremble enter Paulene's voice: the prelude to tears. She coughs. Gets a hold of herself. 'I could never have stopped him,' she says quietly. 'I know that now. He took her because she was the one he wanted. He would have got her wherever she was. He'd set his sights, you see. It was a hunger. A hunger he had to feed.'

'I'm sorry, Paulene,' says McAvoy, raising his voice over the sound of the raindrops hammering down on the felt roof. 'It's taken longer than anybody wanted, but we're making progress. I wanted to talk to you . . . does the name John Dennic mean anything to you?'

Paulene takes a breath. 'I don't want to answer any more questions, Aector,' she says, and the tremble is back. 'Not from you. Not news crews. Not Trish. I know what I need to. She can rest in peace.'

McAvoy tries to interrupt. The driver behind him is now leaning on the horn. Barely catches her exit line as she ends the call. 'He's been to Hell. And he's going to go back.'

McAvoy stares at the dead phone. Had it been an unusual choice of words? He knows Pharaoh has kept the details of what happened beneath the cliffs at Bempton to herself, but the truth has a way of finding its way to those who need to hear it. Might she have let slip that the darkness was decorated with depictions of Satanic horror?

'What the fuck is wrong with you . . . fucking move!'

McAvoy looks up. There's a face at the window. For a moment, they look right through one another, each trying to delineate the features of the other through the mosaic of reflections and raindrops. The other man reacts first, kicking the door shut just as McAvoy tries to drag himself out of its embrace.

'Stop where you are,' shouts McAvoy, stumbling and slipping on to the wet tarmac, with its rainbows of spilled petrol. 'Don't you dare . . .'

McAvoy watches as the man who swung a screwdriver towards his chest skids over the bonnet of his idling Honda and hares away across the forecourt. He doesn't look back. The tails of his coat flap as he leaps the brick wall and disappears into the alleyways behind the terraced houses.

McAvoy hauls himself up. Brushes the dirt from his hands. Starts to run.

'Are you shifting this . . .?'

The angry shout fades as McAvoy's feet hammer the pavement, his knees protesting as he sprints out of the forecourt and down the side street, clattering into a wheelie-bin as he tries to keep his feet on greasy cobblestones and mulched leaves. He glimpses a shape a hundred yards ahead – a sudden flash of movement as the figure he's chasing bounds over a high wall. Something's snagged him. McAvoy feels his lungs slamming against his ribs. Squints into the haze of diagonal rain. Enjoys a moment of grim satisfaction as the figure suddenly tumbles backwards in what looks, from this distance, like a coil of white flags. He sucks in a deep lungful of air and kicks open the gate that leads into the yard where the man tumbled. Finds him flat on his back: a green washing line tangled around his chest and upper arms. He's wriggling as if trying to climb out of a spider's web.

'Fuck off, copper! I'll fucking do you!'

McAvoy doesn't say anything. Bends over, hands on his thighs. Waits for the world to stop spinning. He tries to speak, and all that emerges is a wheeze.

'I'd have got away, you Jock bastard. You didn't catch me, right?'

McAvoy wipes the sweat from his face. Looks around him. The yard is at the rear of a neat terraced house, all dreamcatchers and crystals, stained glass and macramé hammocks. There's a pink plastic doll house in one corner of the yard. He pulls his lanyard from his shirt front and waves it, generally, in the direction of the kitchen window. A plump, hippy-looking woman with tattoos and dreadlocks is bouncing a baby on her hip and watching him the way she might watch an action film – vaguely entertained but not really involved.

'Police,' he says, hoarsely. She cups a hand to her ear. He mimes a telephone. Shouts 'police' again. She nods. Plonks her baby down on the dish drainer and disappears.

McAvoy slides down the wall. Squats next to the runner.

'You're quite the athlete,' he says, as the world slows down.

'Fuck y—'

'Yes, yes, fuck you and all that stuff,' says McAvoy, tiredly. 'Get it out of your system. You might feel better.'

The skinny man makes another half-hearted attempt to free himself from the washing line. He suddenly gives a shrill, high-pitched little giggle. 'Might get a decent story out of this, eh, Jock? Make a decent yarn on the wing.'

'What's your name?' asks McAvoy, re-tying his boots and putting his head back against the bare brick.

'Like I'd tell you.' The man laughs.

McAvoy checks his pockets. Makes sure he hasn't lost anything valuable on his mad dash from the petrol station. Everything seems to be where it should. He wonders if he should handcuff the man before back-up arrives. Isn't sure he can stand the jokes that will come his way if word gets out his prisoner was bound with washing line.

'Tell me about Mem Ricci instead,' says McAvoy. 'Must be a good friend.'

The man sneers. Twists in his bonds. 'Pays the bills, innit?'

'But you were willing to do serious time for him,' says McAvoy. 'Willing to put a screwdriver in my chest.'

The man looks down at the damp floor. Chalk paintings have been daubed on the concrete and they add a colourful smear of pastel hues to the shimmering blackness.

'Wouldn't have stuck you. Just to scare you, that's what Mem said. Didn't want any more bother. She's had enough, like.'

'She?'

'Ruby. Don't see it myself but he fucking loves that lass. Gone soft for her. He was cock of the fucking walk once upon a time. Now look at him. Sitting sobbing in a circle, telling strangers all about his Daddy not loving him. Jesus.'

'You'll tell me this but you won't tell me your name?'

The man shrugs. Spits. 'What am I looking at?' he asks, as if realising the gravity of his situation. 'I never hurt you, did I? And I only ran because you chased.'

McAvoy makes a face. 'That's not true and you know it,' he says.

He realizes he should be patting his suspect down. Looking for an ID. Realizes that if he stands up, he'll probably fall down again. Stays still.

'I'm saying nowt without a brief,' says the man, almost apologetically. 'Fuck, I was almost away, weren't I? What is it – you're just the guy in the right place at the right time, are you? How did you know I'd be there?'

McAvoy keeps his own counsel. Looks up as the woman returns to the window and gives a thumbs-up. Picks up her baby, who now has a fine toupee of suds.

'Where were you heading?' asks McAvoy. 'If you'd not bumped into me?'

The man shrugs. 'Away,' he says. 'Away will always do. The lads are done, aren't they? You'll do them for what happened this morning. And Mem . . . Jesus, once you start making those kind of deals, it's over, innit?'

'Deals?'

The man mimes zipping his mouth shut. Mimes shoving the key up his backside. Smiles, gummily.

McAvoy puts his head back. When he hears the sirens, it brings no sense of relief.

TWENTY-FOUR

'**B**loody hell,' says Neilsen, moving his finger across the screen of his tablet and rewatching the grainy footage of the attack on Detective Constable Richard Beresford in September 2012.

'By our Lady Mary,' says Wolsingham, peering over the leather steering wheel of the silver 1988 BMW 325 that he uses as his work vehicle, despite the insurance premiums. They're moving slowly down Pingley Vale, reading the name plates on the brick frontages of large, splendid-looking detached homes, staring down on well-tended gardens and driveways that crunch beneath the luxurious tyres of Teslas and Porsche Cayennes.

'Sorry, sir?'

'Bloody is actually the common form of the Medieval phrase By Our Lady. Often used before the sainted Mary. So one would say By Our Lady Mary. Eventually, Mary was substituted with the word Hell. By Our Lady Hell.'

Neilsen looks up from the screen. He quickly rummages in every last recess of his mind, trying to find something he can serve up as a response. Settles on: 'That's interesting, sir.' He learned it from a barmaid, who'd schooled him in the art of talking to men of a certain vintage. *They just want you to be impressed, Ben. Just want you to show you what they know.*

'That one, sir,' says Neilsen, pointing at the big iron gates of a property called Meadow View.

'Can I presume that your lapse into the vernacular has nothing to do with McAvoy's latest misstep and everything to do with the video on your tiresome little device?'

He indicates left with a maddeningly loud tick-tocking and the metal gates slide smoothly open as they pull on to the neat white driveway that winds up towards the large, red-brick modern house on the slight rise. There are garages over by the boundary line: an arrow-straight line of conifers and leylandii. Security lights flash on as Wolsingham glides to a halt in front of the little row of steps that lead up to the central, black-lacquered front door.

'Footage came through of the attack, sir,' says Neilsen, proffering the device to Wolsingham, who takes it like a nana holding a baking tray.

'Big triangle, sir,' says Neilsen, helpfully.

Wolsingham gives him a hard stare. Presses play. Watches the footage, recorded by the security cameras in the ambulance bay at Hull Royal Infirmary. It shows Beresford, broad-shouldered, bullet-headed; short sleeves and tattoos. He's walking across the ambulance bay, looking back towards the rear door of the hospital. He doesn't see Dennic come for him. He steps out from behind an idling ambulance and kicks Beresford hard across the knee. He collapses, screaming, and Dennic mounts him. Pushes his thumbs into his eyes. Two uniformed officers come haring into shot. It takes both of them to drag him off. Beresford lies on the damp ground, leg bent grotesquely; blood pouring down his cheeks.

'That's him, sir,' says Neilsen, nodding towards the house. Beresford is standing in the doorway, leaning his weight on a sturdy cane. He's put on weight. A lot of it. There's something about him

that makes Neilsen think of a waxwork left too close to a fire. He
waves a hand in greeting.

'We don't seem like a surprise,' muses Wolsingham. He climbs
out of the car, pulling his hat down. 'Mr Beresford?'

'Dick, to my mates,' says Beresford. His blue cashmere sweater
strains at his bellies. He wears pink chinos and deck shoes. 'You're
CID?'

Neilsen appears at Wolsingham's side and they make their way
up the tasteful garden path to the warm light of the doorway. 'I'm
Ben Neilsen,' he says, and makes sure to shake Beresford's warm,
clammy palm. He gives the former uniformed sergeant a quick
up and down. He's wearing thick glasses: a special prism in the
left lens.

'I can see, if you're wondering,' smiles Beresford. 'Not brilliantly,
but better than it was. The Federation has been great. Paid for a lot
of corrective surgeries.'

'And the compensation has gone a long way,' says Wolsingham,
staring past him into a hallway tiled with red slabs. Colossal canvases
stare down from high walls: modern originals: charcoal landscapes
and Pollocky splatters of red and gold.

'I've done OK,' says Beresford, with a self-effacing shrug. 'All
told, I'd rather have my eyes.'

Neilsen purses his lips. Tries to distance himself from his
colleague. Raises his eyebrows, hoping for an invitation to come
inside. 'Any chance we can get out of the rain?'

Beresford nods. Steps back and encourages them to follow him
down the corridor and into a large, modern kitchen: Smeg appliances,
elaborate coffee-maker, copper pans dangling from a wrought-iron
grill above a central, marble-topped island. There are no photographs
on the wall. No mess, anywhere.

'Gorgeous place,' says Neilsen, hoping this can all be kept civil.
'Been here long?'

Beresford busies himself filling the kettle at the deep sink.
Wipes away the water droplets with a cloth. Throws the cloth in
a flip-top bin. Leans back against the sink, framed by the rectangular window, and gives them both a faint smile. Up closer, there
seems something grey about his energy; there's a melancholy in
the set of his jaw.

'Neilsen,' he says. 'You're one of Trish's protégés, yes?'

Beside him, Wolsingham wrinkles his nose. 'You know Trish?'

'Hell yes,' says Beresford, with a little sniff. 'She's done very well. I was sad to hear about Tom Spink.'

Neilsen gives a respectful nod. A picture flashes in his mind of Pharaoh's old mentor and boss. 'Funeral was well-attended. You weren't there?'

Beresford chews at a flap of dry skin on his lower lip. Rubs his palms together. Makes a face. 'I don't keep in touch with many of the old crowd these days. Not an easy thing, living as an ex-copper – especially when you've learned to see the opposite side of the mirror.'

Wolsingham lowers himself into a sleek, high-backed chair. Mud falls from his careworn shoes. 'You've had an epiphany, have you?'

Beresford doesn't treat it as a joke. Turns his back to the two visitors and removes a mug from a cupboard. Retrieves a neat little gift box from a high shelf: all ribbon and tissue paper. Rummages inside and finds the bag he's looking for. Throws a bag in a mug and fills it with hot water from the kettle. There's a smell of sticky sweetness, almost masking the earthier, umami scent beneath.

'John Dennic,' says Neilsen, and passes his phone to Beresford. On the screen is the prison processing shot: a nondescript man, lightly bearded; dark eyes and grey clothes. 'You've been providing him with work, I understand. Picture framing, I'm told.'

Beresford sips his herbal tea. He doesn't offer his guests anything. Sucks at his cheek, seemingly deep in thought.

'Body on the road out Cherry Burton way,' he says, at last. 'John Dennic?'

'What makes you ask that?'

'I have miraculous powers of deduction,' he says, drily. 'Notts Police phoned a few hours back. Prison did too. Got themselves in rather a panic.'

'Dangerous man on the run,' says Wolsingham, scratching at the bare, flaky skin between his ankle and his turn-up. 'Understandable.'

Beresford shakes his head. 'Dennic's not dangerous. Not really.'

'We've seen the video, Dick. Seen what he did to you.'

Beresford stares past them. Gazes back into the hallway with its works of fine and contemporary art. 'I've learned to forgive,' he says, and a strange, dreamlike quality enters his voice. 'The man I used to be, the things I used to believe . . . that man deserved everything John Dennic did to him.'

'That's a very Christian attitude,' says Wolsingham, steepling his fingers. 'Did you tire yourself out on the road to Damascus?'

Beresford rubs at the scar beneath his left eye. Raises his hand and clinks his wedding ring against the glass eyeball. 'Better to pluck it out than to look with sin,' he says, in that same thick, dreamlike tone.

'The file is a little thin,' says Neilsen, trying to keep them on track. 'No motive. No previous. Wouldn't even be on the nonce wing if he hadn't admitted to a liking for the youngsters. Almost a non-person before he went for you. What provoked the attack?'

Beresford takes a deep breath. Holds it. He seems about to unburden himself. Gives a sad little shrug instead.

'You're married, are you, Dick?' asks Wolsingham, nodding at the ring.

Beresford looks down at the floor. Clicks his tongue against the roof of his mouth. 'She didn't hang around afterwards. She's happy, though. Doing OK.'

'Children?'

Beresford gives him a hard look. Flares his nostrils. 'I know what he confessed to while he was inside, if you're wondering,' he says, with more bass in his voice. 'Before we take people on, they have to be honest about their sins. We're a big believer in restorative justice. That's what brought him and I together – he may have almost blinded me, but he also opened my eyes.'

'You've been to see him at Ovenden?' asks Neilsen.

'Not Ovenden, no. Franklin. Long Larton. I had a letter with me. I wanted to read it to him but my voice kept breaking. He took it from my hand and read it aloud. I started sobbing. He held me. Held me like a child. That's when this life started. There's before, and there's after.'

'So you would mourn his passing?'

'We should all mourn his passing,' says Beresford, with a little tremble in his voice. He reaches into a drawer and pulls out a glossy brochure. Tosses it to Wolsingham, who plucks it from the air.

'That's what we do,' he says. 'What Dennic and I were going to do. What I'm already doing.'

Wolsingham glances at the cover. Flicks through the shiny pages. 'Clean Slate,' he reads. 'A chance to begin again – free of addiction and destructive desires. People come here to detox, to get help for addiction issues, to resolve trauma, to find themselves; this is a

place to be lost then found . . . found inside the roots of the African
Tabernanthe iboga shrub, Ibogaine is a natural, psychoactive alka-
loidal substance that halts addictive patterns by neurochemically
transporting the user to a physically and mentally pre-addictive state,
what we in the business refer to as a "reset". A state many thought
they would never experience again . . . while at our Ibogaine treatment centre, the client can appraise and reappraise. Looking deep
inside, deeply into their inner self, the individual may be able to
confront their past, their traumas, their fears. They may be also
grateful to see some things, whilst being repelled by others . . .'
Wolsingham pauses. Wrinkles his nose. 'If it's all the same, I think
I'll stick with the Dordogne.'

'We have it on good authority that Dr Munroe Durrant was using
chemical compounds – psychedelics and alkaloids – on the Sex
Offender Treatment Programme at Ovenden,' says Neilsen, studying
Beresford's body language for anything written in large print. 'Do
you know Dr Durrant?'

Beresford takes a moment. Sips at his tea. He looks a little
clammy, notes Neilsen. There's sweat on his upper lip; patches on
his shirt.

'Of course,' he says, at last. 'My organisation exists to help
offenders put the past behind them and give themselves the best
possible chance at a future. There were areas of . . . convergence,
I suppose you could say. He wanted the same as I did, though our
methodologies were rather different.'

'And where is Dr Durrant now?'

Beresford finishes his drink. Places the mug in the sink. Puts his
fleshy hands on the counter top and looks from Wolsingham to
Neilsen and back again. He seems to get smaller before their eyes.
Deflates a little, as if whatever has been holding him up has turned
to ash.

'I don't think I can help you much more, gentlemen,' he says,
quietly. 'There was an idea . . . a hope. It won't work. Not without
Dennic.'

Wolsingham sucks spit through his teeth. 'I'm getting a little
tired of hearing all about the sainted John Dennic. Could you stop
writing psalms for a moment and just tell me why he went for your
eyes?'

Beresford laughs. Scratches at his chest. Makes a face, as if
something is hurting. 'I saw him,' he says, quietly. 'At the desk, at

the hospital. The man who said his name was John Dennic. I knew the name. Knew it from years ago. Took me a moment, but I felt him looking. It's taken a long time to understand it, but what choice did he have? He couldn't take the risk. Not when he had so much still to do.'

'Riddles again,' says Wolsingham. He takes a coin from his pocket. Spins it on the table top and slams his palm down. 'Heads, Ben and I take you in to the station and we do this formally. At the same time, I make a call to a couple of journalist friends and tell them that one of the head honchos at a charity for the rehabilitation of nonces is being questioned in connection with the death of the man who almost blinded him. Good story, that. Got legs, as they say.'

'And tails?' asks Beresford. He looks a little unsteady on his feet, suddenly. Looks like he wants to lie down; to fall to the ground, and straight on through.

'Tails, you stop being whatever it is you think you're being,' he says, with a tight smile. 'You know what we're here for, Dick. And you knew we were coming. So you've had time to work out what you want to say and what you don't. So serve it up and, if you're lucky, we get out of your hair.'

'Was he hurt?' asks Beresford, turning away from Wolsingham and giving his attention to Neilsen. He licks his lips. Presses them together. 'Did he suffer?'

Wolsingham clicks his fingers before Neilsen can answer. He looks like a diner demanding the waiter come and take their order. There's something different about the way he holds himself, suddenly. His accent hardens. So does his face. 'Oi, Dick. Organ grinder is this way, yeah? And I'm going to ask you to think very carefully about my job title. I'd bet in a fancy kitchen like this, there are all sorts of things with which to grind an organ, so just you—'

Beresford falls to the floor like a felled tree, knees buckling, face suddenly so many shades of purple and grey. There's a sickening thud as he cracks his head against the tiles. Jammy, dark-red blood begins to spread across the floor.

'Oh, for the love of God,' says Wolsingham, exasperated. 'Ben . . .'

Neilsen is already on the floor at his side, trying to turn him into the recovery position. Behind the thick glass of his spectacles, one eye fills with blood. Twin rivulets of red spill from his nostrils, his ears, bubbling up through his skin as if every cell in his body were coming apart.

'Fucking hell, sir. Call it in, call it in!'

Wolsingham takes his time getting out of the chair. Crosses to the sink, taking care to step over Beresford's twitching legs. He picks the mug from the sink. Sniffs it. Smiles.

'Wouldn't matter if they sent a rocket, Ben,' says Wolsingham, with a little more tenderness to his voice. 'To use the vernacular with which you are acquainted, in about fifteen seconds I surmise he will be dead as fuck.'

Neilsen presses his fingers to Beresford's neck. The bigger man is trying to speak, blood popping on his lips in crimson gouts.

'Made me . . . made me better . . .'

Neilsen grabs his phone and starts recording, even as he snatches up a towel from the front of the cooker and clamps it to the ugly wound in Beresford's head. There's red everywhere. He's coming apart like a salted slug.

'I knew who he was,' he whispers, and blood sprays Neilsen's cheeks. 'Knew who he used to be . . .'

Neilsen feels Wolsingham's strong, white fingers grip his shoulder. Feels himself shoved unceremoniously to the side. Wolsingham squats down in front of the dying man. Inserts himself into his gaze.

'What do you see, Dick?' he asks, quietly. 'Is it beautiful? Are they waiting for you? Is it all you hoped?'

'Sir, I—'

'Who was he really, eh, Dick?' Wolsingham asks, and as he presses his knee into Beresford's guts, blood spills from every pore. Neilsen can't turn away. Just watches, open-mouthed, as he oozes and sputters. 'Who was he before he became John Dennic?'

Beresford's eyes swivel madly in their sockets. Blood trickles into his ears. He chokes, tongue lolling backwards into his trachea. Wolsingham reaches into his mouth. Plucks it out as neatly as if he were fastening a tie.

'Why was he on that road, Dick? What did Parfitt send him to do?'

A sudden hiss erupts from Beresford's mouth. His lips burst: over-ripe tomatoes squeezed in a fist.

'I didn't sin,' he gasps. 'Not once. Not after . . .'

Wolsingham leans in. Puts his lips to Beresford's ear. 'I can see them, Dick. I can see them sliding in through the walls and the floor. Slinking in like shadows. They're coming for you, Dick. They know what you did. What you are . . .'

'I'm not!'

'And if we go look at your computer, that's what we'll see, is it? A man redeemed?'

Beresford chokes. Gulps down a mouthful of blood. Dies with Wolsingham's knee on his chest, his words still ringing in his ears.

'Jesus,' Neilsen mouths, taking a shuddering breath. 'Jesus, sir, what . . . what was that? Sir? Sir, what's happening?'

Wolsingham turns around. Gives Neilsen a sad little shake of the head. 'Pity,' he says, quietly.

'Sir? I don't understand. What just happened? How can it be a pity if you wouldn't let me call for help? What do you expect me to say? Jesus, he's in our custody! You threatened him before he haemorrhaged . . .'

'Pity John Dennic died where he did,' muses Wolsingham, rising and looking down at the mess on his front. 'I feel like we've lost a most enigmatic man.'

Neilsen looks down at his hand. Sees he's made a fist. Realizes just how much he wants to smash it into Wolsingham's head.

'Careers are made out of moments like these, Ben,' he says, matter-of-factly. 'It's all about the narrative. You may have just witnessed the demise of a very bad man. You may have been the officer who brought Virgil to justice. Well I never, Patricia – you were right again. *Fortes furtuna juvat.*'

Neilsen opens his mouth to speak. Closes his mouth again. There's something in the way Wolsingham is looking at him; something that reminds him of old oil paintings and leering smears of paint. Even as he moves, there's something serpentine about him.

'You think . . .?'

Wolsingham shrugs again. Reaches into his pocket and retrieves a cough sweet. Unwraps it and pops it into his mouth with bloodied fingers. 'Wrap a bow around this and you could have commendations coming out of your ears. Especially if he killed our Dennic.'

'Where did that idea suddenly come from?' demands Neilsen. He can't stop looking at Beresford's body: an ex-copper, all but exsanguinated: a puddle of fleshy red. 'Sir, we didn't do anything wrong. Whatever's happened, we just tell the truth, and . . .'

'Has that worked out well for people, in your experience?' asks

Wolsingham, arching his back. He picks up the brochure. Flicks through, absent-mindedly. 'The hottest places in Hell are reserved for those who, in times of moral crisis, maintain their neutrality.'

Neilsen feels dizzy. Sick. Feels the urge to run. 'What the fuck does that mean?'

Wolsingham nods at the dead man. 'Ask him. He's got it written in Latin in one of those paintings in the hallway. The one that looks like a mouth.'

'Sir?'

Wolsingham shakes his head, tired suddenly. 'Call it in,' he says. 'And then do exactly what I tell you.'

Neilsen knows that there will always be a 'before' and an 'after'. Knows that whatever he says next will define the rest of his career. Christ, how he wishes one of the others were here. Wishes to God that Aector McAvoy would boot the door off its hinges and drag him out of there before he gives in to temptation.

He meets Wolsingham's eyes. Feels as though barbed wire is binding him; feels as though the floor is opening up.

He gives a nod, eyes closed.

Makes a deal with the Devil without saying a word.

PART THREE

TWENTY-FIVE

McAvoy always slows down as he crosses the Humber Bridge. There's a perfect spot midway across its length where he can peer down at his own little white painted cottage, set back from the foreshore and gazing out across the water. A glimpse is all it takes to settle his stomach; just a fleeting glance at its red front door and windchimes, its neat little windows; the mobile home taking up the entirety of the backyard. Sometimes he fancies he can make out Roisin framed in the darkened glass, staring out across the shifting mud like a trawlerman's wife awaiting the return of a ship. It takes all of his strength to turn left at the roundabout beyond the tollbooth and point the nose of the Mercedes towards the city centre. All he wants to do is go home and bury himself in the great warm blanket of the people who love him. Roisin called while he was waiting for two uniformed officers to take over guarding the abandoned Honda. She was missing him, she said.

Could feel that wherever he was, some of the light was bleeding out of him. He'd walked away to the rear of the forecourt and told her everything in a rushed whisper. He was, as ever, hopelessly lost and unsure how best to make himself useful. She'd offered no advice. Just told him that she knew he would be doing the right thing, whatever the hell that thing might be. She'd shown him how to create a *putsi*, once: a hag stone and sand, stuffed in a neat drawstring bag; his name scribbled black on white. Shown him how to use Romany magic to shield himself from curses, bad luck and negative energy. He hadn't been able to get the hang of it. She'd taken over on his behalf. Guards him and their children in her every moment of wakefulness, filling their worlds with good energies and protection spells. Whenever McAvoy wakes up in hospital, he knows deep down that if not for his wife's love, it would have been much worse.

'. . . and she said that it's the only language they understand, but that's just rubbish, isn't it? Because they understand Horse. And I speak a bit of Horse and I know for a fact that they really don't like it, so I told her that, and she got all sassy about it and the next minute she was roaring her eyes out and I was the one getting told off and . . .'

McAvoy smiles as Lilah's voice bleeds from his mobile phone, tucked into the top pocket of his suit. He can't hear her particularly well over the drone of the tyres but he's got the gist of it. Lilah's in trouble at school again. She threatened Beatrice, apparently. Told her, and her little coterie of Clementines and Isabelles and Genevieves, that anybody who hit their horse deserved to have the same done to them, and then have their head shoved in a bucket of manure – preferably while detached from the rest of the body. She'd spent the last couple of hours of her school day in her usual spot outside the head teacher's office, happily reading a book and wondering what all the fuss was about, while parents in North Face puffer jackets and Dubarry yard boots trooped in for a little chat with Mrs Beesley.

'Anyway, Mammy said I should tell you myself, so I'm telling you, but I don't know why everybody is making a fuss. I mean, I didn't hit anybody. And you know that if I wanted to I could actually pull Beatrice's head clean off, but I don't get any credit for that, do I?'

McAvoy goes through the motions. Tells her that she might do well to take a breath before speaking; to count backwards from ten when she feels her hackles starting to rise. He knows it's a waste of breath. Her mother is Roisin and her godmother is Trish Pharaoh. She's never going to listen to her dad.

'Have you caught him yet?' she asks, changing the subject. 'Stopped him, I mean?'

McAvoy gazes through the rain-spattered windscreen. Stares at the distant bulk of the old Lord Line building, slowly folding in on itself at the edge of the old fishing quay. He pictures the dead carnations in their cellophane wrappers; the memorials to the thousands of trawlermen who travelled to distant waters and never returned home. Finds himself wanting to tell her something reassuring; to let her know that the world isn't quite as dangerous as it was this morning.

'We're making progress,' he explains, and hopes it's true.

'Mammy said you've been fighting,' says Lilah, accusingly. 'Brawling in the muck like a ruffian. Is that the right word? My brain gave me "muffin" but I don't think that's right either.'

'Ruffian is right,' says McAvoy. 'The right word, at least. It was nothing. Just a disagreement.'

'Like me and Beatrice, you mean? But worse?'

McAvoy laughs. Feels his heart double in size. Hangs up with an *I love you*. Slows down as the traffic starts bunching up around the Smith and Nephew flyover. Everybody slows down here to avoid the speed camera – the result being an unnatural amount of rear-end shuntings and traffic chaos. He tries to get his mind back into the investigation. Squeezes the steering wheel as he tries to make sense of things. Thinks of Trish. She's not being straight with him, he knows that. She's giving him just enough to keep him from asking too many difficult questions, but he feels as though she's keeping something from him. He feels a little cheesed off that she dismissed him at Parfitt's request.

He would probably have done the same, but it was a long old journey that's kept him from doing anything useful for the majority of the day.

He sifts through the various loose ends and unconsidered trifles that cloud his brain. He finds his thoughts drifting back to Kes. He pictures the wide eyed, ever-so-polite Lithuanian and hopes to God that providing a statement for the police will bring him a comfy place to stay and a few warm meals. Fears it will do the opposite. If there is ever a trial, the chances of getting Kes to testify seem stacked against them. He thinks again about what Kes saw. Thinks of the man who's waiting for him. Agamemnon Ricci. Mem. McAvoy has already phoned ahead to inquire of Detective Constable Sophie Kirkland whether she objects to him sitting in on the interview. She had laughed in that way of hers, perennially unbothered, and with a mouth full of jelly babies. 'You're the DI, Sarge,' she had pointed out, and made a noise that suggested her tongue was wedged between bottom teeth and lower lip.

A thought rises as he cuts left down Alfred Gelder Street, passing the golden statue and the big mirrored office building that reflects back the splendour of Holy Trinity church. Scoots through the Old Town, barely taking in his surroundings: brow furrowed as he considers all the disparate threads of the investigation.

The traffic's murder, now. He peers through the rain at the gaudy frontages of the takeaway, charity shops and Shoreditch-wannabe café bars that slice a cosmopolitan swathe through the Avenues. It's coming down hard now. To his right he sees a trio of students emerge from Planet Coffee. They take a look at the weather and wordlessly troop back in to the cosy, chocolate-scented embrace of the popular hub.

Did it matter? Had Decland Parfitt given the pin badge to John Dennic? Had the dead man spent time in the darkness, watching Ruby come and go? McAvoy grinds his teeth. Makes a note to chase up the surveillance footage from outside the empty garage beside Ruby's cafe. Hopes Daniells has struck lucky and simply not had time to inform him.

He noses the sports car forward, wedged between a timber wagon and people carrier. He doesn't know how Pharaoh ever feels comfortable driving such a fragile piece of machinery. He feels like a baked potato wrapped in tinfoil. He's not far from HQ now but the traffic is totally static. He can see blue lights flashing a little way ahead. Decides he's got time to have one last go at sorting out the Bluetooth connection to the car stereo. Pharaoh's never been able to work it out and she's had the car from new. It's very nearly a classic now, and though she spent a tidy sum on the new sound system, she tends to just use the CD player and radio – never happier than when shouting abuse at the silly sods who call the phone-in shows. He fiddles with the panel, working his way through the settings. He moves forward as the traffic starts up, glancing up and down again. Stamps on the brake as somebody runs between his car and the little pick-up truck that's forced his way in front of him. Something in the flat-bed is thrown forward, clattering against the sides of the open deck.

McAvoy jerks forward, fingers splayed against the control panel.

'. . . *William Blake drew the entwined pairs of condemned lovers endlessly circulating through what looks like an intestinal tube . . .*'

He listens. Breathes. Pictures Pharaoh at the wheel, acquainting herself with Alighieri's vision of Hell.

He flips the switch on the steering wheel and the CD changer skips to the next disc.

It takes McAvoy a moment to recognise it. *The Aeneid*. By Virgil. He clicks through the other CDs. Three are empty, and one is the best of Curtis Mayfield. McAvoy lets it play.

Something else nags at him. He looks up, spotting a gap in the traffic and managing to wiggle out past the pick-up. He finds himself thinking of the country road where John Dennic's body was found. Allows himself to wonder.

Calls Andy Daniells as he's flashing his card at the security gate leading into the car park.

'Andy . . . the CCTV from the time before the body was found – could we maybe take a look? I want to know if there was a flatbed pick-up in the area. And if there was, whether we can make out a licence plate . . .'

He hangs up before Daniells can start telling him about his day. Enjoys the feeling of pulling into the space reserved for the Detective Chief Superintendent. He's long since accepted he'll never be of a similar rank, but it's nice to make believe.

Fifteen minutes later, he's opening the door to Interview Room C. The walls are the colour of cottage cheese and the carpet is coarse and blue. So's the language emerging from Mem Ricci.

'Don't you fucking dare look at me, you Jock fuck! You big ginger bastard! You pig. You shit pig!'

'Detective Inspector McAvoy entering the room,' says DC Kirkland, looking relieved. 'The time is eight fifty-four pm.'

McAvoy sits down at the vacant chair, folding his arms on the desk. Mem doesn't have a solicitor. Said he didn't need one. He's got nowt to hide. Lounges there in his joggers and his muscle vest, steam rising from his bare arms like the air above a compost heap. He's glaring bullet holes in McAvoy.

'Hello, Mem,' says McAvoy, meeting his eye. 'I hope we've been looking after you.'

'Fuck you. Fuck you! You've fucked it all up. All of it!'

McAvoy takes a breath. Glances at Sophie, who shrugs. 'It's all been "shit pigs" and "Jock wankers" and "I'm going to fuck you in the ear" for the past hour, Aector. I'm just grateful he stopped with the "no comment."'

McAvoy interlocks his fingers. Sucks his lower lip. Gives Mem Ricci his full attention.

'Is she all right?' asks Mem, under his breath, not quite meeting McAvoy's gaze. 'Ruby, like. She sorted? She got him?'

McAvoy begins to jiggle his leg beneath the desk. 'Ruby? We're looking for her. She has questions to answer.'

'She's picking up my boy,' says Mem, scowling. 'Don't you

fucking think about asking the Social to have him. He's mine, right. You let me out and I'll go take care of him.'

'Aramis, isn't it?' McAvoy smiles at the thought of the little lad from the photograph. Feels his heart clench when he imagines not knowing where his children might be. 'I'm told he's a treasure.'

Mem jerks forward in his chair. 'What you say about my fucking kid?'

McAvoy doesn't react. Just shakes his head, looking disappointed. 'I have to be honest with you, Mem – I'm starting to think you might be your own worst enemy. This temper of yours – it's an ugly thing.'

'You're an ugly thing,' mutters Mem, sitting back. He cups his gonads inside his jogging trousers.

Scowls at Kirkland, who smiles sweetly. 'Is he all right, yeah? Aramis, like? He's with her friend, like I said, but he'll be missing me.'

'He'd better get used to that,' says Kirkland, apologetically. 'You tried to murder a police officer today, Mem.'

'Piss off.' Mem spits, dripping scorn. 'Attempted murder? Look at the big bastard – fit as a fiddle. Was just a bit of a dust-up. It's me that's got the bloody headache.'

'Your friends,' muses McAvoy, thoughtfully. 'We're still struggling to get an ID for the chap who tried to stick a screwdriver through my chest. He's being very talkative about everything else but rather tiresome about his name. Savvy enough not to carry ID. You could save us some time.'

'Fuck off,' mutters Mem, both hands in his trousers.

'I'd be happy with "no comment",' says McAvoy. He can't quite believe he drove past his own front door for this.

'That dark-haired bitch,' says Mem, sniffing the air and pulling a face. 'Farrow, is it? The one who won't leave her alone? It was her, picked her up from outside the caff, wasn't it? When your boys all came roaring in to save the day. She went off with her.'

'Detective Chief Superintendent Pharaoh has enjoyed a long relationship with Ruby,' says McAvoy, choosing his words carefully. He's very aware of the recording. 'Known her since she was a girl.'

Mem shakes his head. 'Manipulative bitch,' he spits. 'Wants her to turn on her own dad, for God's sake. Expects her to give evidence against the bloke who raised her. I mean, what sort of daughter would do that?'

'You are aware of the nature of the crimes for which Decland Parfitt was jailed, yes?' asks McAvoy, face hardening. 'You are aware that her sister, Gaynor, took her own life because of what her father did to her? You are aware that he used to drug her, and her friends, and act out his fantasies while they slept? You are aware that—'

'Bollocks,' says Mem, sweeping his hand across the table. There's nothing to knock over but he looks like he wants to break something. 'He was fitted up. It's all trick photography. CGI and that. Have you seen those deep fakes they can do now? Way I heard it, your Pharaoh would do just about anything to put him away. And Ruby would have told me if he'd touched her. Sister was a fantasist. I've been there, right. I've had lasses say all sorts about me. It's spite. It's hate. You lot prey on that.'

McAvoy closes his eyes. Tries again. 'You're happy to have him stay, are you? All happy families – you and Ruby and Aramis and a convicted paedophile, all wearing Christmas hats and pulling crackers?'

Mem's whole body fizzes with suppressed violence. He's a jack-in-the-box, concertinaed, ready to spring. McAvoy changes position. Forces Mem to look at him.

'What has he got on you, Mem?' he asks, gently. 'What has Parfitt got on you that means you have to pretend you believe him? Who did you think I was when you came racing to the rescue at lunchtime? I wasn't the first unexpected visitor, was I?'

Mem looks away. Starts to bounce his legs up and down. He looks a little smaller, shrinking in on himself. 'I'm serious, yeah. Have you checked up on Aramis? Has she got him? I need to make a call, all right?'

McAvoy glances at Kirkland. She leans in. 'Uniform are looking for Ruby. She told the Boss that Aramis was with a friend.'

'I'm a good dad,' says Mem, to himself. 'I fucking am. We're trying something, you know? Trying being a family. Aramis's mum, she was a prize fucking horror. Ruby's sweet. Kind. She adores my boy. Why can't you just leave us alone? There's always some prick trying to spoil things – always somebody trying to get in the way.'

Kirkland pulls a picture from a file on her lap. 'This man,' she says, and offers up a mugshot of John Dennic, taken at the time of his arrest. 'Is he somebody who wouldn't leave you be?'

Mem glances at the picture. Turns up his nose. 'Don't know him.'

'Your mate,' continues McAvoy. 'The one with the screwdriver. Doesn't drive a pick-up, does he?'

Mem sits back in his chair. 'This has gone as far as it's going without a solicitor. I've played along. Now I want to see my son.'

'Does he drive a pick-up, Mem?' McAvoy asks again.

Mem screws up his face. Shakes his head. 'He's not my fucking mate. I don't know what he drives. Drives me, when I tell him to. He's just a tourist, yeah?'

'A tourist?'

'Taking a walk on the wild side, y'know? Living the life. Telling himself he's a gangster 'cause he's rolling with the real thing for a while. You should be grateful he's not the real thing. I'd have put that screwdriver right through your fucking chest.'

McAvoy sits in silence. Makes Mem look him in the eyes. 'John Dennic had his throat cut with a knife. Didn't die at the café, though. Heart didn't stop until after he'd been dumped on a country road and some poor sod ran over the bag he was lying in.'

A stillness descends upon Mem Ricci. For a moment he seems entirely static, eyes not moving, expression frozen in a rictus gurn. 'You can fuck right off,' he says, at last, as the enormity of his predicament starts to dawn upon him. 'Is that what this is? You're trying to stick a murder on me? You can fuck off. You can fuck right off.'

McAvoy tries to keep his face impassive. He glances at the clock on the wall. 'We can halt there for a bit, if you like. I know you've a lot to digest. And I know I would be glad of a Toffee Crisp and a Lilt before we go much further. We've got much to talk about, Mem.'

'I'm saying nowt until you tell me where he is,' wheedles Mem, picking at the tattoos on the backs of his beefy, rope-veined fore-arms. 'He's precious, right. He doesn't trust people. Tell me who this friend was, right. Tell me who's looking after him.'

McAvoy pauses before replying. There's something decidedly authentic about the flicker of alarm that's entering Mem's body language and his tone of voice. He's really starting to worry.

'Were you together last night?' asks McAvoy.

'Me and Rubes?' he asks, looking at Kirkland and back to McAvoy. His whole demeanour is altering.

He suddenly looks every inch like a dad who doesn't know where his son has got to. 'Didn't see her most of yesterday. She had

Aramis. I had a bit of work on . . . wasn't back home 'til the small hours.'

'And Ruby was at home when you got back?' he asked. 'Aramis too?'

Mem looks away. 'Long fucking drive,' he mutters. 'He's a light sleeper. Didn't want to wake him . . .'

'And this morning?'

'She knew I had a full day – said she'd got her mate to watch him so she could spend it with me.' He closes his eyes. 'Next thing the alarm's going. So me and the boys shot round.'

'And that's where you saw me,' finishes McAvoy.

'Aye, thought you were bother, like.'

'You seemed to be expecting trouble,' says McAvoy, pointedly.

'People take advantage,' says Mem, and there's a glassiness to his eyes. 'People take the piss. Gotta show them, haven't you? Gotta show people what happens when—'

'We want to talk to Ruby about the murder of John Dennic,' interrupts McAvoy, his voice cold. 'Dennic was a padmate of Decland Parfitt's. We have a witness who places him at the café yesterday, early evening. We also know that last night, Ruby was in Pearson Park, on her own.'

Mem narrows his eyes. 'So who was looking after my boy?' He shakes his head. 'Nah, she loves him. Wouldn't leave the little bugger. No fucking way.'

'She attended the Hot House – in the park. The place where her sister took her own life. No Aramis.'

'How long have you known this?' demands Mem. 'She said he was grand. Being looked after . . .'

McAvoy feels as though a great chunk of ice is slowly melting in his belly. Something feels wrong.

Aramis is no longer a tool with which to lever through Mem's defences. He's suddenly a vulnerable child, and nobody seems to know where he is.

'Who might he be with?' asks McAvoy, changing his whole demeanour. 'Can you give us a list? Friends, family?'

'So you can find Ruby, you mean?' demands Mem. 'I know how you fuckers work . . .'

'So we can find your boy,' says McAvoy, raising his voice.

Kirkland rummages in her file, looking for a blank piece of paper. 'Here,' she says, snatching up a print-out of a photograph and pushing it across the desk. 'I'm going to give you a pen. You try and stab me and it'll go badly for you . . .'

'Shirley – the one who used to run the café with her – they're still on halfway decent terms, I suppose. And Claire, her hairdresser. She speaks to her mates online. She's always on that bloody phone. Some of the blokes from the Talking Club would do owt for her, but she'd never let one of them have him overnight. She knows I'd have gone mental. I mean, they're OK lads, but I've heard them talk. There's some demons in their heads, y'know. I mean, you have to give people a chance, like . . . but, not with my son.'

'But you'll take a chance on Parfitt?' asks McAvoy.

Mem reacts without thinking. 'You tell me what to fucking do, eh? I love her. Aramis loves her. This is what she wants. She believes in him. He says he never touched her and she says he was a brilliant dad.'

'And that's why you got into an argument in the visiting room, is it? He said something that didn't chime with her version of events?'

'Chime?' shouts Mem, throwing up his hands. 'Fuck, who speaks like that? No, we argued because he had the balls to tell me he didn't think I was good enough for her. Wasn't sure I could keep her safe. I mean, the fucking cheek! Crippled prick, sitting there with his face hanging off, shitting in a bag, and he's saying I'm not the right person for her? I don't give a fuck what he thinks he knows about me – I handle my business.'

McAvoy scratches at his beard. He suddenly doesn't know whether he's interrogating a murder suspect, or trying to find out all he can about a missing child.

'The shrink,' says Mem, and his face is darkness. 'Prick who ran the club with her. He'd do owt for her. Had to send him on his way a couple of times. She'd know better than to leave Aramis with him.' He starts cracking his knuckles. Sweat is greasing his skin. McAvoy can feel the heat of his greasy flesh from across the table. 'She wouldn't. I'd fucking kill him. I've told him I'll fucking kill him.'

'The shrink?' asks McAvoy, cautiously.

'Her Talking Club. All the sad-eyed men sharing their sob stories about how hard it is to be alive. He did a number on her, right enough. Got her half convinced she could change the world, one sad case at a time.'

'You have a name?' asks Kirkland.

'Something Jock,' mutters Mem. 'Campbell, maybe. Nesbitt?' He clicks his fingers and points at McAvoy. 'Munroe,' he says. 'Second name as a first name. We all called him Roscoe for the first few weeks. That's how Rubes introduced him, like. Seemed to like it.'

McAvoy pulls out his phone. Searches for an image. Shows it to the huge figure across the table. He glowers at the screen. 'Aye, that's the prick.' He clicks his fingers again, a tick that seems more pronounced when he's thinking. 'I've told her what'll happen if she sees him again. Slimy bastard was always trying to get in her pants. If she's with him, they're both fucking dead – you hear me.' He slams his fist down on the table. 'I want my boy!'

McAvoy nods, holding Mem's gaze. 'What does he drive?' he asks, quietly.

Mem pulls at the neck of his vest. He's looking pale. There's a green sheen to his skin. 'Proper pussy mobile,' he sneers. 'Isuzu something-or-other. Nasty sort of fudge colour. Flat-bed.'

McAvoy looks at Kirkland. She ends the interview. McAvoy stands so quickly that his chair topples over.

'That it?' asks Mem, startled. 'What you doing? I can't just sit here . . .'

McAvoy's out the door before he can finish the sentence, pulling out his phone and ringing through to the Control Room. 'Missing child,' he say. 'We need all units to look out for a seven-year-old boy by the name of Aramis Ricci. We have reason to believe . . .'

He stops himself. Thinks of the wounds to Dennic's corpse. What does he have reason to believe? What does he fear?

'Reason to believe he may have been abducted . . .'

From within the interview room comes the howl of a creature in an agony beyond enduring.

TWENTY-SIX

A ndy Daniells stands at the window of the neat terraced house. It's a little after 9pm. He wishes he were somewhere else. Watches his breath fog the glass. It's bitterly cold in this

bare space but he thanks God he's indoors. He winces in sympathy
as an elderly West African woman alights from a bus carrying a
toddler and a dozen carrier bags. Watches her scowl into the wind
and disappear into the maelstrom of swirling leaves and flashing
lights. He watches her until she evaporates into the dark. Would
rather stare at her than back into the room. It's turning his stomach.
The red glow ripples over uneven walls: egg boxes and polystyrene,
puddling in hollows and settling into the spaces between the crude
sound-proofing.

He wonders what he looks like, backlit by the soft red light.
Doubts he'd attract much business if were to try his luck in
Amsterdam.

'Makes me feel like I'm in a microwave,' says DC Kirkland,
wrinkling her nose. 'Good for migraines, apparently. Not always
just a come-on. And if it's to advertise your wares, you wouldn't
put the blind up, would you?'

Kirkland talks quickly, a tendril of her dark hair snaking into the
corner of her mouth. She doesn't leave the office much and has the
pink cheeks and bright eyes of somebody who's finally been allowed
to take the bus by themselves. She's wearing mittens and a proper
winter walking coat, box-fresh. Daniells is pleased she's here,
helping pick their way through the intricacies of Ruby's life. She's
good company, and doesn't get carried away with wild flights of
fancy. She's a diligent, caring officer but she's content to stay at
her rank, and perform the tasks she's allotted, without much in the
way of complaint. As such, she goes unnoticed. Pharaoh thinks the
world of her. The feeling is mutual.

'Some weird shit in the wardrobe in the guest bedroom,' she
continues, fully entering the bedroom. A black-out blind lies
discarded on the fake wooden floor and the small, bare room blinks
in the light from the lamppost, illuminating the grime-speckled bay
windows and the double-locked uPVC door.

'You done the nipper's bedroom?' asks Daniells, quietly. 'Putting
it off, if I'm honest.'

Kirkland joins him at the window. 'Where's your head at?' she
asks. 'So much for the Cold Case Unit, eh? All feels pretty fricking
hot to me.'

Daniells smiles, weakly. 'It's not making any sense,' he says, and
wishes he could be more specific. 'If this Dennic is due for
release . . . why not wait? I mean, what's the sudden hurry? Why

use one of your day-release perks to go and see the one person who can keep Parfitt banged up? I mean, we're thinking it's because he wants to harm her, but what possible reason do we have to believe that? For all we know he was delivering a message or bringing a gift from Parfitt.'

'He died on that empty road,' says Kirkland, turning away from the window and blinking in the eerie red light. 'You see that?'

Daniells looks at the back of the door. There are deep grooves in the paint: the wood reduced to splinters in places.

'Saw the locks, too.'

'There's no key among Mem Ricci's possessions,' says Kirkland.

'The height,' says Daniells. 'Look at the grooves.' He swallows, tasting acid. 'A kid's done that.'

Kirkland crosses the empty space. Glares at the red bulb and the reinforced ceiling rose: hefty metal hooks drilled deep into the plaster.

'It's a cell,' says Kirkland. 'It's a bloody prison.'

Kirkland makes a face. 'Why at the front, Andy? I mean, if you're going to have a room in your house where you can stick somebody until they behave . . .'

'Maybe that's the thrill,' says Daniells. 'Knowing that whatever you're up to, you're only the width of a pane of glass from all the normalcy outside.'

Kirkland considers this. Considers all of it. 'You don't know whether Ruby is a killer or a victim, do you?' she asks, as gently as she can.

Daniells feels the truth of it slide into him like a blade. 'I'm not supposed to know one way or another. Just follow the evidence and see where it goes.'

'But really,' she smiles. 'Go on.'

Daniells breathes out, trying to get his words lined up in the correct order. 'Maybe Dennic took Aramis. And now he's dead, and we don't know where he put him. I mean, he was convicted of a serious offence, he's admitted to feeling sexual attraction to children . . .'

'Those scars,' mutters Kirkland. 'Somebody punished him for something, and I've got a fair guess what that might be.'

'So maybe she's trying to find him,' says Daniells. 'That's why she won't come in. If she or somebody close to her killed Dennic, maybe it was to protect the boy. I mean, she can't be in her right mind – all she endured as a kid, all the shit with her sister; Decland Parfitt as a foster dad and then a thug like Mem asking you to be a surrogate mum to his kid . . .'

Kirkland is about to answer when there's a knock at the door. One of the techs is half in, half out of the room, glasses halfway down their nose, peering at an open laptop like the wine list in a posh restaurant.

'The search history is repugnant,' he says in a terse Geordie tongue. 'No downloads. No illegal sites. But damn near the knuckle. Lots of barely legals and extreme violence. Fetishes. Sado-masochism. But if you look at the times . . . flicking between extreme graphic imagery and social media, all but toggling between the two. They had both sites running simultaneously – too often to be a coincidence. They're getting their kicks looking at pictures on Facebook while there's extreme porn playing on the other screen.'

'McAvoy will be disappointed,' says Kirkland. 'I feel a bit strung along myself. Mem's a prick, but this . . .' She gestures at the room, with its manacles and restraints and the deep scratch marks on the wooden door.

The tech looks up, surprised. 'We have another team at Ricci's property. That laptop has been recovered separately. We found this under the mattress in the main bedroom. All very neat and tidy in there. Living room looks like something out of a catalogue, don't you think? Even the little snug for the boy, it's all done beautifully. But this . . .'

Daniells takes the laptop in his gloved hands. Starts to scroll down through the search history.

'Ibogaine,' he mutters, reading one of the web addresses. 'Pioneering psychologist experimenting with wonder drug to combat addiction and sexual disorders . . .'

He clicks the link. The screen fills with a blown-up picture of a middle-aged man. Brown beard, brown eyes, sandy hair: loud shirt collar sticking out over the cable knit of a plum-coloured sweater-vest. Daniells reads aloud.

'We've had extraordinary success. Even considering how tied our hands have been, we've had breakthroughs not just in the field of addiction, but in actively rewiring the parts of the mind that lead to – shall we call them – deviant behaviours? That Ibogaine helps addicts lose their need for drugs – that's already been proven beyond

doubt. I believe we can go further. By providing sexual offenders with the chance to actively revisit their past misdeeds, they can push themselves on to a different path – be somebody completely different. Remove that part of themselves. It has to be done carefully, but we at Clean Slate have the expertise to make it happen. At the moment we're being tied up by naysayers who are afraid of taking the next step, but believe me, this is the future and we will be at the forefront of that . . .'

'The Boss needs to see this,' says Daniells, as the clip comes to a halt. 'She's there now. With him. With Parfitt.' He narrows his eyes as a memory slaps him hard enough to make his head spin. 'That's the same bugger from the talking group!'

'Who do you mean, Andy?'

'This is that, what was his name? Roscoe? Ran the talking group with Ruby.'

Kirkland raises her eyebrows. 'That's too weird to be a coincidence.'

'Dennic wasn't sent to kill her,' says Daniells, glancing up at the hooks in the ceiling. 'He was sent to keep her safe.'

'Safe from his own psychologist?' asks Kirkland, narrowing her eyes.

Daniells stares again at the face on the screen. At the line upon line of hardcore erotica and the incongruous banalities being sought out in between. Finds his way to the music sharing platform. Plays the most recent song on the most-played playlist.

He only listens for a moment. Permits himself only a second or two of the horrifying screech and scream and drone: white noise and the screams of the suffering.

'Most played,' he whispers. He looks around again.

Suddenly, he moves to the edge of the room, just where the flooring meets the skirting board. He bends down. Tucks his fingers into the nasty plastic material, and hauls it up.

'Andy, I'm not sure . . .'

They don't speak again until he's finished. Just stand back, and take in the horror and beauty of the colossal picture carved deep into the set cement beneath: concentric circles – a spiralling descent through the layers of Hell.

Daniells takes pictures. Sends them to Pharaoh. To McAvoy.

'In this light,' says Kirkland, quietly. 'The walls like they are. The red. The screams. Jesus, do you think we've been wrong about all of it? About her? Whoever was stuffed away in here, somebody wanted them to experience Hell.'

TWENTY-SEVEN

M cAvoy's in Pharaoh's office, his back to the door. He's pulled the curtains and switched out the lights. For a moment, he permits himself to feel the weight of it. The responsibility. There's a child missing. A little boy. Aramis.

His phone buzzes in his pocket. Beads of sweat break out at his temples and brow. He answers quickly, hoping it will be Trish. Hoping that she's going to tell him he can leave – that he doesn't need to ferret around in the things she has deliberately concealed. It's not. It's Andy.

He watches the footage. Watches it again. Calls Roisin.

'Jesus, Ro,' he whispers, pressing his head against the cool of the wall. 'Dennic could have taken him before he was killed. We know so little about him – what he was doing here, why he came for Ruby . . . I mean, my head's spinning. I can't . . .'

He tugs at his tie. He feels cold, suddenly – the sweat drying on his body. He flicks the light on and winces as the glare of the strip-light hammers at his temples. He notices he's left a sweat mark on the wall. Rubs at it with the sleeve of his coat.

'You'll find him,' whispers Roisin, as he presses the phone against his face until it hurts. 'You've told me yourself how many children go missing every day. They come home, my love. Fin came home.'

McAvoy screws up his eyes. Fumbles his way to Pharaoh's desk and perches on the soft leather of the top-of-the-range ergonomic chair she had insisted upon before taking the job as head of CID. He knows better than to adjust the settings. Looms over the keyboard, knees wedged up against the desk.

'Nobody's seen Ruby since she walked off from Trish,' he says, logging in. He knows Pharaoh's username and password. Is following her instructions to the letter. Still feels bad. Still feels like a sneak.

'You don't think she's harmed a child, surely?' asks Roisin, dropping her voice. 'I know she's been through hell, but . . . if this is the same person Trish has been pinning her hopes on, and now she's maybe a suspect in a murder and an abduction, well – it's not like her to be caught out, is it? To misread people? The way she steers you around like you're pieces on a board, for feck's sake . . . Whatever's happening, it's because she wants it to happen.'

McAvoy bites his lip. Sees the flicker of yellow lights, blue lights, strobing across the closed blinds and cutting a trench in the dark blue cord of the carpet.

'It's not like that,' says McAvoy, and his fingers move silently over the keys. 'She had no idea Dennic even existed, let alone that he might be heading to the area. It makes sense if he's been sent to harm her – to stop her talking, if she's changed her mind – but, I don't know – what we saw at the prison, what it sounds like the doctor might have been doing . . .'

'Aector, my love, you're talking too fast. Just breathe.'

McAvoy feels his thoughts start to accelerate. Images collide and divide, mutate and shrink; patterns forming, dissolving; a grimace of genuine physical pain gripping his face.

He pulls up Ruby's files. Skims through the details he already knows by heart.

'She's still sitting there,' mutters McAvoy, as the reflection from the monitor casts patterns on his face. He realizes he can smell Pharaoh: that perfume-and-cigarette tang that makes his throat feel dry if he doesn't turn his head away in time. 'Sitting, waiting to talk to him. She could have done this before now, couldn't she, Ro? I mean, we're working round the clock trying to build a case against Parfitt and there's still nothing that the CPS will even take a look at. As far as they're concerned, he's just another sex offender. But Trish – she doesn't get it wrong. She always knew what he was.'

He hears Roisin give a tiny laugh. 'Pains me to say it, but aye – she's got a knack for looking into your eyes and seeing what you really are. Probably why she's in love with you.'

'She's not in love with me.'

'Jesus, Mary and Joseph,' laughs Roisin. 'You could drive a saint to smack, you really could.'

McAvoy realizes he's not feeling the tingle in his fingers any more. He's OK. He's got a hold of himself. Feels like his pulse is slowing.

'See, you're doing good, my love,' whispers Roisin, and there's a smile in her voice. 'One step at a time, yes? Don't try and do it all at once. You don't really know enough about Ruby to be able to say what she'd do. And that's because Stroppy Knickers has kept you at arm's length. Now you're hiding out in her office, accessing the files she's told you to and probably giving her a cover story for whatever game it is she's playing. Jesus, I wouldn't be surprised to find out that she hand-delivered Parfitt to that bloody madman.'

'She saved his life . . .'

'Aye, at the very last moment,' says Roisin. She softens her voice. 'She's a pain in the hole, Aector, but she's very good at what she does. And she does truly care about you. And me, even, in her way. But this idea that she's never had her suspicions that there might be a dark side to Ruby? That's absurd. She caught Delphine Hollow, for feck's sake, and she was the perfect little innocent teen who just happened to be killing her dad's conquests in her leisure time. She's seen the worst of people. If you've got your suspicions of Ruby, I can guarantee you, she's had them for years.'

McAvoy doesn't reply. He's reading the case file that Pharaoh has insisted he dig out as soon as he alerted her to the missing child. She was going to wait at the prison for Parfitt, she declared. Anything else, she trusted to him. He wishes she didn't. Wishes there was somebody else marshalling resources and ordering house-to-house enquiries: damp uniformed officers trudging around the bleak waste-land of Wincolmlee and banging on boarded-up doors.

'Aector?'

McAvoy's re-reading the original file: the report that first led to Parfitt becoming a person of interest. He'd been spotted taking pictures of a group of girls sunbathing outside a caravan a couple of miles past Cleethorpes. He was collecting samples, he said, when an older sibling had spotted him crouched down among the dunes. He hadn't even seen the girls. He was a children's entertainer; he was sorry for any misunderstanding – he was sure he could make amends, or perhaps make a donation to the charity of their choice. They might have let him go if they hadn't snatched his little digital camera from his hand and started scrolling back. He might not have been lying about collecting bugs and butterflies to feed to his menag-erie – there were no pictures to imply anything to the contrary. But when they scrolled back, they found a series of images he'd been desperately trying to delete when they grabbed him and dragged him somewhere quiet. The image showed an adolescent girl. Blue eyes, pigtails, snub nose. Red, at her throat.

'It was Ruby who cleared things up,' paraphrases McAvoy, as he silently digests the contents of the report. 'Police were called when Parfitt started getting a pasting from a couple of pissed-off older brothers. His name was already flagged as a person of interest, you see. Trish . . .'

'Trish hadn't liked the way he looked at Sophia,' finishes Roisin. 'Thought he was creepy.'

McAvoy makes a face. 'It's not strong enough, is it? This idea that she just saw him and knew? I mean, what if . . .?'

Roisin cuts him off before he can finish the disloyal thought. 'What if he didn't take those girls? What if he's inside on a copper's vendetta?'

McAvoy shakes his head. 'She said the photos were just a silly game she and her sister played. She said she was the girl in the photograph. It was just an imagination game, like storytelling or drawing pictures. She needed him home. She needed them to let Daddy go so he could come home and look after her and Gaynor, like always. There hadn't been enough to hold and God knows Trish tried. She thinks that getting away with that little incident at the beach – that's what emboldened him. Made him take Carmel. And the others.'

'Is she happy with this boyfriend, you reckon?' asks Roisin, and he hears the sizzle of paper as she sucks on one of the five cigarettes she still permits herself a day. There's a glug as she takes a sip of tea.

'Mem? He seems to think they're going to be a perfect family. Him and her, Aramis . . . and the paedophile foster father, if she has her way.' He pushes his hair out of his face. 'If she's snapped – taken Aramis to try and cling on to the idea of a happy family, at least we know she won't hurt him. But if it was Dennic . . .' He breathes deep, slowing his heartrate. Pushing out a slow lungful of air.

'What did she want you to see, do you think?' asks Roisin.

McAvoy looks again at the screen. Looks again at the name of the arresting officer. Beresford. Makes sure not to say it out loud. He always tells Roisin everything, in the end, but here, now – he simply doesn't have enough answers to open himself up to questions.

'Friends?' asks Roisin. 'Family? Who does she have in her life?'

McAvoy begins to log out. Looks again at the flashing cursor – the

log-in details of a very senior officer feeling like the keys to the
kingdom. He feels a disloyal impulse creep through his guts. Fights
it off. Stands and closes down the machine.

'It'll be a fella,' says Roisin, brightly. 'Guarantee you, she'll have
been meeting somebody for a bit of hanky-panky, the kid saw and,
well . . .'

He loosens his tie. Looks at the file number he's scribbled on
his wrist. It's in a file on the desktop, hidden away at the centre of
layer upon layer of zip files and downloads. He'd never have found
it on his own. He wonders if she's kept it as a reminder of what
she did – an albatross around her neck: a fleur-de-lis branded somewhere only she can see.

'She saw him being taken,' says McAvoy, quietly, reading the
unredacted statement. Pharaoh had served it up, high on painkillers,
while recovering from the burns sustained in her rescue of Parfitt.

'Say again, my love?'

'That's how she stopped it. She was following him. After he was
released, when she couldn't make the charges stick. She was
spending every moment keeping him under surveillance. The report
we've been working on – it claimed his disappearance came to our
attention when Gaynor phoned it in. Said he hadn't come home. In
the official version, Trish was visiting Paulene – appraising her of
developments. One of the RSPB wardens mentioned that there'd
been trouble at the radar station and she went to check it out. Pure
good fortune.'

He pinches the bridge of his nose. His tongue feels dry. Christ,
no wonder she needed to make it right. No wonder she's carried
the weight of it like Marley's chains.

'Where was Parfitt taken?' asks Roisin, and he hears something
slosh in her mug. 'I know where those things happened to him, but
where did this Virgil person snatch him?'

McAvoy scans the rest of the document. God, how he wants to
delete it. He suddenly understands why she hasn't. She needs this
to keep herself honest. She could turn herself in at any moment –
expose herself, cost herself everything. He wonders what deal she
made with herself. How many killers she has to lock up to atone
for turning a blind eye.

'There's a caravan park near Sigglesthorne,' says McAvoy. 'He
was on his way to entertain a group of children from a residential
school. Gaynor called him on his mobile to tell him that the organisers

had heard about the arrest and wanted to cancel. She'd tried to tell them he'd been released without charge, but . . .'

He reads Pharaoh's statement again. Pictures it. Sees her in an unremarkable car, trailing Parfitt in his ridiculous Lizard King tour bus.

'He pulled in for fuel at the service station nearby. It was already dark. Went in to pay for his fuel, walked back to the vehicle and that's where he took him.'

'And she saw?'

Medium build, dark clothing, appeared out of the dark and got him in the boot of a stolen Honda before she could move.

'She didn't call it in?'

'Followed instead.'

They stay silent. McAvoy watches the lights strobe upon the wall. Wishes she hadn't shown him. Doesn't know what to say to her.

'She was in the vehicle, wasn't she? Ruby? She was in the van and she didn't do anything and he spent the next few hours being cut to ribbons . . .'

McAvoy licks his lips. He realizes his eyes are stinging.

'He'd only gone in to buy her an ice cream,' says McAvoy. 'Till receipts confirm it. She just stayed in the van, like she'd been told. It wasn't until all the blue lights started roaring up the dual carriageway that she went into the garage and asked if anybody had seen her daddy.'

'She took her time, then?' asks Roisin. 'Trish? She let him have some fun before she stopped it.'

'She didn't know what he was going to do . . .'

'Yes, she did,' says Roisin, gently. 'Of course she did. Are you telling me she didn't have her suspicions about this urban legend – this Virgil? Somebody who preys on paedophiles and shows them what awaits them if they don't redeem themselves? What did she think he was doing?'

McAvoy closes the file. Feels the room spin.

'She did the right thing,' says Roisin, after a moment. 'She let him suffer, until she couldn't stomach any more. That's the only bit she got wrong. Should have let the bastard—'

'Ro?'

'You don't think she's there to finish him off, do you?'

McAvoy sees his face reflected back in the screen. Wishes to God that she had chosen a different priest for her confession.

TWENTY-EIGHT

RSPB Bempton Cliffs

Halle shrinks inside her coat. Pulls a face. She'd like to spit, but the wind is whipping in from every direction and she doubts her mood will be improved if she ends up with her own saliva in her eye.

'Glorious, isn't it?'

She forces a smile. Ken Riddle seems to be seeing something entirely different in the vista before them. She sees grey air and dark skies and seabirds that whirl in the air like loose pages of a newspaper. She smells rain and sea salt and bird shit. She can barely feel her ears but her head is full with the raucous cacophony of kittiwakes, fulmars, gannets and gulls. Ken appears to be staring at a vision of grace and beauty: a look of beatific wonder on his face.

'Luckiest man alive,' says Ken, taking a deep breath, hands on his hips. 'Not on staff any more, but they let me volunteer on the days the wife doesn't need me to drive her into Brid. Not a bad life, all told.'

Halle holds her phone in front of his face. Tries to suppress a shiver. Fails.

'You said you had some memories of Parfitt?' she says, teeth clamped together at the back. She readjusts her position. Feels her boot squash something. Decides she'd rather not know.

'Came as a shock, right enough,' says Ken, watching the flight of a drifting gannet. 'I mean, nobody knows what goes on behind closed doors, do they? But, well – we do eccentrics pretty well in this country, don't we? And that was the worst he could have been accused of before all this. Just being a bit weird. But he adored those girls. If I'm honest, I actually thought he was a bit . . . well, what do you say these days if you want to say somebody's a bit of a left-footer?'

'Gay?' suggests Halle.

'That's a bit strong,' says Ken, playing with the front of his raincoat. He's in his early seventies but has the healthy, red-faced look of somebody who spends their life in high, windswept places. 'I just didn't think he was into hanky-panky. And least of all with his own daughters. When word got out, well . . .' He puts his hands in his pockets. Stares at the sea. Suddenly his eyes brighten and he points, excitedly. 'Seal, love. See. Just there, where the kittiwake's bobbing . . .'

Halle doesn't even turn her head. She wants to get this done. Gemma is waiting somewhere nearby. They've still got to get some atmospheric shots of the wireless station, up on the hill half a mile or so away from the headland. She doubts she'll feel any happier once she's up there. Can't see what all the fuss is about. Apparently, this is a tourism hotspot. People come from miles around to see the nesting seabirds and the crashing rocks. Even Gemma spoke fondly of a rain-lashed Sunday spent watching the puffins fledge.

'Mate of mine was a copper for years,' confides Ken, moving away from Halle's proffered phone. 'Said old Dec suffered plenty before they charged him. That copper – you see her in the paper sometimes, appealing for help or saying she's grateful that the judge made the right decision . . . nice-looking lass. She was the one who pulled him out of there, you know that, don't you? Pure luck. Right place, right time. I'll be honest with you though – even if I knew my nearest and dearest were down there, I don't think I'd have gone into the tunnels in the dark.'

'You've been down there before?'

'Years back,' confides Ken. 'You know it had a reputation for Devil-worshipping, don't you? Coven used to meet there. That was the rumour, anyway. Certainly a bloody scary place, if you'll pardon the language. You said your friend was waiting for you up there?' He glances at the ink-black sky. Down at the grey seas. Makes a face. 'Wouldn't want to seem like your dad or anything, but I'm not sure that's the best idea. Tomorrow, eh?'

'Can't stay,' mutters Halle, who thinks her fingertips are going to drop off at any moment. 'Heading back to civilisation tonight.'

Ken looks a little offended. Gives her a quick look up and down and seems to decide that he's out of his depth. 'That'll be all you want from me for now, is it? I left half a tin of soup on the hob and the cat will have helped himself.'

Halle manages a tight smile. She's done well out of Ken Riddle. He'd been a neighbour of Parfitt's, as well as a warden at the cliffs where Pharaoh found what Virgil had left of him. She even managed to swing by Parfitt's old house on her way to meet the old boy. There's not much left of it now: just the burned-out shell of the little white-painted cottage and the blackened remains of the outbuildings.

'Half broke the girls' hearts, having to put those animals to sleep,' says Ken, shaking his head. 'Nobody to look after them, was there?'

'Nobody to look after the girls, either,' says Halle, hoping he'll stop soon.

'Pretty self-sufficient, those two,' smiles Ken. 'You'd see the pair of them up on the cliffs sometimes, just staring out to sea like they were waiting for a ship to come in. Ruby was the clever one, I reckon. Such an artist. You'd see her sitting with her sketch book, or her camera around her neck. Other one – offed herself in the Hot House in Hull – she just went along with what her sister did. Bit more fragile, that one.'

'They did go through rather a lot,' says Halle, as a sudden blast of icy air makes her collar slap repeatedly against her face. She stops the recording. Forces herself to shake Ken's hand.

'Yonder, if I can't talk you out of it,' says Ken, looking worried. 'And this will be on one of the satellite channels, will it? Or is it for proper telly?'

Halle doesn't reply. Turns her back and stomps off along the coastal path, hands in her pockets, the screech of the gulls in her ears. She wonders what she's actually achieved today. She's got some half-decent footage and a couple of interviews that might add some colour, but in terms of a single cohesive narrative she isn't even sure what she's trying to say. It feels wrong. It's felt wrong since McAvoy first tried to sell her and Gemma on the idea this morning.

She trudges on, head down, wincing into the teeth of the gale. The clifftop is sloping ever higher and she can feel her heart thudding against her ribs. She feels a little strange, suddenly. There's something old – no, something somehow ancient – about the air to this place. It's as if nothing from the modern world has a place here. She feels like she's walking on a mountain of fossils and dinosaur bones. Could imagine herself being led to the clifftop like a witch destined for the pyre.

'Hal!'

She turns at the unexpected sound, whipping in alongside the screeching birds. She looks this way and that, trying to find her friend.

'Gem? Gem, this is fucking horrible! I think the hire car is fucked, so . . .'

Gemma appears a little way ahead, holding her mobile phone like a torch. Her eyes are gleaming. She smiles, hugely, as she scampers down the slope.

'Magical, isn't it?' gushes Gemma, giving Halle the clumsiest of air kisses. 'I got inside. One of the metal doors is hanging on its hinges. Just a wee nudge and you're in. I think somebody's been inside recently, actually. Looks like it's been forced. I've took a few snaps but I thought I should wait for you. Y'know . . . the expert.'

Halle feels herself wishing she were the kind of person who could tell people what they want to hear. Wishes she could tell Gemma that she's done well and that this whole trip has been worthwhile: that it has the makings of a great piece of TV.

'I wish you'd told me to bring different shoes, Gem. These are knackered.'

Gemma makes a face, crestfallen. She nods back up the slope, eager. 'It's amazing,' she says, as they begin to trudge back up.

'I know,' mutters Hal. She rummages around for her phone. Glares at the screen as she reads the message. It's from one of the company freelancers. Missing child enquiry in the Humberside Police area. He has it on good authority that the kid is connected to the ongoing investigation into the death of a man named as John Dennic at the lunchtime press conference.

She lets out a low growl. Wishes she were somewhere else. They have people for this. She didn't become a producer so she could spend her days tramping about the cliffs. She's much better in an office. Better when she can have a soya milk latte and a piece of hibiscus biscotti.

'That one,' says Gemma, pointing at the squat brick building. It's fenced off, but the wire hangs loose and the fence has been stamped down. Gemma swings her light in the direction of the doorway. 'Cement's been dug away around the frame, see. Looks like somebody's been inside recently. Which got me thinking, actually – I mean, why did they bring Parfitt here in the first place? There must have been so many other locations they could have gone to torture him. It must matter, mustn't it? And that got me thinking about the Devil worship, and all this talk about what was going on down there – what the place looked like before the fire took hold . . .'

'Just hold the light still, Gemma,' snaps Halle, putting her palm against the rusted metal door and giving it a nudge. She peers inside. Clicks her fingers and lets out a sigh as Gemma fumbles passing her the phone. She turns it around and shines the light into the darkness. She can make out a spiral staircase. Can see loose wires and broken ceiling tiles. Can see the darkness where the fire caught hold. Can see . . .

She stops. Shines the light at the little item that dangles from the broken banister at the top of the stairs. She feels Gemma's nearness, her hair blowing into her open mouth.

'Jesus, Gemma, you are such a toddler . . .'

'What's that?' asks Gemma, unperturbed.

It takes them both a moment to realize what they're looking at. At the incongruity of it.

'That's a little flat cap,' says Gemma, quietly. 'Like a Peaky Blinders cap, for a kid . . .'

Halle pulls her head out of the gap. She feels wrong suddenly. Feels the kind of fear that she thought she had left behind in childhood.

'We should call him,' says Gemma, rubbing her arms. 'There's something not right about any of this. I don't feel right.'

Halle shines the light at the muddy area at her feet. There are recent footprints. A man. Perhaps another. And a child.

She pulls out her phone. Starts to dial. Winces at the screech of the seabirds overhead. Turns, slowly, at the echoing squeal from the hinges of the old door.

'I think we should go,' she says, quickly. 'You call him. Tell him there's something wrong.'

A waft of air billows out from behind the half-closed door. She smells damp. Flame. Hears something, too. Hears the cry of a child.

They don't say any more. Just turn from the door and start to walk quickly away.

Only as Gemma reaches McAvoy's number do they start to run.

TWENTY-NINE

P haraoh's had enough. She's been shunted into two different waiting areas and escorted through an interminable number of clanging, rain-speckled gates, only to be deposited in a small, drafty wooden outhouse: rough wooden table and a couple of mismatched chairs; pale blue plasterboard walls and a trio of metal filing cabinets. It smells of too-sweet perfume and hot Bovril; a combination that would be eye-watering if not for the fear of her tears freezing to her cheeks. She feels like a player on a stage, promenading around a vast amphitheatre and disporting herself in a series of increasingly irritated tableaus. She's been waiting hours. Getting colder. Getting hungrier. Getting more desperate for a proper cig. The phone reception is patchy at best and she's finding it increasingly difficult to marshal the incident room and get her head in the right space for a showdown with the Devil.

'Breathe, Trish,' she says to herself, flicking the switch on the three-bar fire and discovering, for the sixth time, that it remains broken.

She plonks herself back down in one of the uncomfortable chairs. Stares at the darkened glass, reflecting back into the shabby room. She realizes her shoulders are hurting again. There's an ache at her jaw and across her sinuses. In the corner of her vision she can see little white dots: creamy blobs, like spores upon toadstools. She suffers a sudden pang of loss. Remembers lying with her head in her husband's lap, letting his big thumbs knead the ache and pains out of her face. She can almost recall the pressure of his palms upon her forehead, fingers moving rhythmically, the ache of pleasure in her scalp. She lets herself peer at the memory. Sees Sophia sitting on the rug in front of the TV. She's reading a book – the screen set to one of its screensavers – a roaring log fire. She wonders where the other three are. What day she's remembering. How long it stayed nice before it turned to shit. She scowls, irritated with herself. Curls her lip as she remembers Anders and the mess he left her in. Hates that he's crept into her thoughts. She tries to make sense of it and realizes at once how he slithered out of his locked room in her subconscious. He'd just had the aneurism, hadn't he? Just told me how much money he'd lost and dropped half-dead on the carpet. And you got the call, didn't you? Got the tip that led you to Decland bloody Parfitt, but you couldn't do anything about it because you were so busy nursing the sentient carcass Anders had become that it was months before you followed up. And when you saw him, and you knew what he'd been doing and what he was, and you started asking yourself how many more he'd hurt because you were too busy feeling sorry for yourself and dealing with your own poxy life, and you needed a reason to get close, so you invited him to enter- tain your daughters, 'cause there's something not fucking right about him . . .

She stops herself. Bites down on her lower lip. Realizes that her hands are shaking. God, she wants a drink. Why had she sent Aector away? She needs his big, solid presence at her side. Needs to know, through his nearness, that she's still one of the good ones. She knows that by the day's end, she'll have done what must be done. Knows what's at stake and doesn't give a damn. The girls are all grown up now. She can retire when she chooses. She's already outstayed her welcome. She's going to go out on a high, and whether that comes through jailing an abuser and killer of children, or going down for killing the bastard, will all come down to what the fucker says when she's finally allowed to stare into his beady eye and demand he finally give up his ghosts.

The door clunks open and a tall, white-haired figure in a dark robe bursts in like the comic foil in an amateur stage play. They almost trip over their own feet as they turn and slam the door as if a gale were holding it open. They turn and give Pharaoh a hectic, wide-eyed smile.

'Yvonne,' they say, and clasp their hands together as if in prayer. 'Prison chaplain, as is.' Their badge advertises their pronouns: a hard-won identity dangling on a lanyard.

Pharaoh stands. Extends a hand. 'Trish,' she says, and feels her hand being squeezed. She looks up into bright, blue eyes and exqui- sitely whitened teeth. Puts them at 6 feet 2 inches in their sensible, wide-toed shoes.

'I've been given the runaround, Yvonne,' says Pharaoh, as Yvonne makes their way to the seat behind the desk. 'I mean, am I seeing him or not? I'm about five minutes away from going batshit, if I'm honest, and when I get that feeling it really is hard hats and flak jackets time. Because if I have to march in here with forty bloody squaddies and a rhinoceros, I will fucking do it, love.'

Yvonne blinks in the face of the tirade. Holds up a finger, as if asking for quiet. They reach into the bottom drawer and pull out a tasteful, lilac-coloured Thermos and two plastic cups. They pour, theatrically, raising the thermos in the manner of a French waiter pouring coffee. 'We're seeing Decland Parfitt directly, Trish,' says Yvonne, closing their big hands around the little beaker and pushing the other across to Trish. She takes it. It's thick and black and tastes of orange squash, black coffee and Bovril. She swallows, grateful.

'Sorry,' she says, tiredly. 'My head's a shed. I've been wanting to talk to this man for a long time.'

Yvonne makes a show of taking a laptop from the satchel at their feet. Starts to talk as the machine powers up, fingers moving over the keys like albino tarantulas.

'I can understand the connection between you,' they say, smiling sweetly. 'You saved his life. He speaks of you often. I believe the delay has been caused by some medical condition, no doubt exacerbated by the loss of his friend. But he'll be here soon. Willing to answer your questions. He's very broken up over Dennic.'

Pharaoh puts the cup back on the desk. Shakes her head. 'You know what Parfitt did, yes? And all the things he didn't, I'll bet. That's Dr Durrant's specialism, isn't it? Pushing boundaries? Unlocking the doors in our heads. He and John Dennic must have had so much to talk about, what with their interests in botany. Toxins. Ibogaine. Tell me – what did he find when he opened Parfitt's file? Demons and snakes and flame.'

Yvonne doesn't reply. Takes a breath, arranging their face into something earnest and ever so understanding.

'I've had many discussions with Decland Parfitt,' they say, pushing the laptop aside and steepling their fingers. 'He's made good progress. Committed to the process, if you'll excuse the rhyme. Taken every possible step to become a man that can exist in the world. A man who can trust himself not to do harm. That's why we've recommended release, Trish. I know you've badgered the poor admin staff, but Munroe – Dr Durrant, sorry – he was at such a pivotal stage in Decland Parfitt's . . . well, we hesitate to use the word "redemption" but, as a person of the cloth, well . . .'

Pharaoh stops herself before her mouth can run away with her. She feels a surge of respect for the chaplain. How many jeers must they have endured. How many threats and taunts and promises, just for the right to shave the moustache and live as their true self – all 6 feet 2 inches of them. *Good for you, love*, thinks Pharaoh, and has to remind herself to be pissed off.

'You said they're close,' she says, and takes a suck on her vape. 'Close enough that Parfitt would know if Dennic was going to do a runner?'

Yvonne wags their finger. 'A deft play, Trish. Quite the first serve. That's not what you're going to ask and you know it. That's the question South Yorkshire Police asked, but they didn't know what you do, did they?'

Pharaoh notices that she's plucking at the fabric of her tights. She's jiggling her leg, spilling storms of compacted dirt on to the nasty cord carpet. She gives a tight smile. 'Do you think Parfitt might have sent Dennic to kill his former foster child?'

Yvonne sits back, shaking their head: sleek, white-blonde hair bouncing at their neck. 'He feels nothing but love for that woman. I know that must sound insane to you, but Dr Durrant, well – he helped him put out the fire. Helped him defeat his demons.'

Pharaoh sits forward, anger gripping her features. 'Fuck that, love. Fuck that. You can tell me whatever psycho-babble you like, but that man – he took children from their beds. Two children we know about, more we're pretty damn sure about. And that's on top of drugging how many hundreds of little girls and taking pictures of himself simulating their fucking deaths. You're telling me that he's found Jesus and that's all just gone, are you? He's not the same man who told me what he was going to do to my little girl?'

She throws herself back in her seat, half cuffing herself in the face as she bats away the tears that flow, disloyally, from her eyes. She turns the sob into a wail. Shakes her head. 'This Dr Durrant – I've seen what he had them doing. That's why he's gone, isn't it? That's why he's gone from being the bright new face of pioneering psychology to yesterday's news. That's why you've got that mad baggage trying to make sense of his files. That's why I haven't been able to see him. Because he got a group of sex offenders off their tits on illegal narcotics and had them act out their crimes in front of one another.'

Yvonne's mask slips a little. They finger the cross at their neck. 'Dr Durrant left the prison at his own choosing. He's gone back into research-based academia. I understand he's planning a book. And with regards to the accusations you're flinging around, can I presume you have some kind of evidence?'

Pharaoh rolls her head on her neck. Feels tired, suddenly. Lets herself listen to the sound of the rain on the glass; the wooden building settling on its timbers; the wind whistling through the cracks around the door. She's never thought of herself as a genius, but by God she knows people. And she knows when she's touched a nerve.

'Been coaching him, have you?' she snarls. 'Making sure he doesn't let slip what's been going on out in the cosy house where the sex offenders get to play swingball and drink their Ovaltine? And use the fucking internet! Jesus, you must all be terrified of the power he's got over you. Is that how he's getting you all to sign off on his release? He's got the goods on what happened when Dr Durrant was given free rein to get a load of sex offenders off their tits and tell them to share their deepest, darkest secrets and desires? What happened? Did one of them go too far? Stoved in somebody's skull in the heat of the moment? Won't take me long to go back through the records – quick call to the Prison Ombudsman for a list of deaths at this prison, and . . .'

Yvonne makes to stand. 'Enough,' they say, testily. 'Dr Durrant came to us with the highest of recommendations and made extraordinary progress with offenders who had never before truly faced up to what they'd done. It was radical. Pioneering. Some even began to see things from the perspective of their victim for the first time. It was wonderful and agonizing all at once – as if they were being bestowed with a soul. Dr Durrant did that.'

Pharaoh shakes her head. 'If Parfitt isn't a danger any more, it's because of what was done to him that night. All the bits and pieces that were cut away and poked inside out. That's why he's not as dangerous as he was – because he's been neutered. But he'd still take a little kid in a heartbeat, love. I've seen into that man's soul, and I don't even know if I believe in the fucking things.'

Yvonne looks affronted. 'What kind of a thing is that to say?'

'The bloody truth,' snaps Pharaoh. 'Who knows? Who knows

whether God was really just a big fucking dinosaur or we're a computer game being played by an alien with sixteen heads. I can't even accept that we live on a big blue ball spinning through space and time. All I know is that Parfitt gets off on harming children. Harming them in ways you can't imagine.'

'I've read the files,' snaps Yvonne, pushing the screen of their laptop. 'I speak to these men every day, Trish. I've heard the worst things you can conceive of. Decland Parfitt is one of countless offenders with whom society has no idea how to deal. We can't kill these men. Can't lock them up forever.'

'Castration?' shrugs Pharaoh. 'Somebody did that to poor sainted John Dennic, didn't they? Quite the horticulturist, wasn't he? Tell me, is that how Dr Durrant was getting his potions? Growing them here, right under your noses?'

Yvonne takes a breath. Closes their eyes, and Pharaoh notices by the infinitesimal motions of their mouth that they're praying. Sees them mouth 'Amen'.

'Praying for the strength not to kill me?' asks Pharaoh, almost impressed at the sudden calm that descends upon the chaplain. They have the slightly manic energy of the true believer.

'I don't allow myself to become emotionally involved,' says Yvonne, all smiles. 'I . . .' They pause, irritated by a sudden buzzing from the phone in the pocket of their long, black raincoat. 'Apologies.' They check their messages. Nod.

'He's ready when you are,' says Yvonne, lowering their eyelids and looking away. 'There will be a full report into Dr Durrant, I can assure you. Nobody is pleased about what is, well . . . what has been alleged about Dr Durrant and some of his more pioneering practices. But I've been privy to some sample pages of what the research ascertained and the breakthroughs that . . .' They sag a little, deflating from the feet up. 'It didn't help everybody, I under-stand that. Men like John Dennic . . . men who'd closed down that part of their mind, who'd convinced themselves it was somebody else, that they weren't to blame – it came as an avalanche. Men like him – sensitive men, quiet men – they heard things in that room that brought back some terrible memories. The things he alleged, well . . . Of course we have procedures, and such . . .'

Pharaoh jerks forward as if she's hit the brakes. 'It was Dennic who told you what was happening? John Dennic?'

'Dennic was instrumental in facilitating the whole enterprise,' says Yvonne, lips twitching at some memory. 'The garden; the use of outdoor spaces; changing the kind of books that they had access to; encouraging them to be creative and look inside themselves. He was a quiet man but people listened to him.'

Pharaoh keeps her expression hard to read. 'And you said they were mates, yeah? Look . . . the question you know I wanted to ask you. Did Parfitt send Dennic to kill Ruby? Tell me what you think.'

Yvonne tugs at their cross again. Scratches at their hair. 'Dennic wouldn't harm anybody,' they say. 'And Parfitt wouldn't ask that of him. Not now. He's going to be released – it's been quietly guaranteed. His living arrangements, well, that's far from ideal, but the pathology is all wrong – even when he was offending, his preferred sexual partner was an adolescent female. Blonde, where possible, but he had wigs for those who didn't conform to his beauty standard. I do believe that's what saved Ruby – she could never pass for a porcelain doll, could she?'

'Partner?' spits Pharaoh. 'That's the word you're using?'

'I mean we are content he is no threat to Aramis,' continues Yvonne. 'We've met Mr Ricci and both ourselves and the agencies involved are satisfied to support his release. Of course, there will be a stipend to provide some of the modifications required to ensure he's going to be comfortable, given his condition, but . . .'

Yvonne can't continue to meet Pharaoh's eyes. Snatches their gaze away as if they've walked into a cobweb.

'You tell yourself what you like, love,' whispers Pharaoh, as she hears the door clunking open. 'You've made a deal, haven't you? You think I don't know what's happened to the rest of them? All of Dr Durrant's shining stars. Half mad in psych wards, I'm guessing. Or dead. And this Virgil they're all scared of? An invention. He probably planted it there himself. What was it, some nice cushy funding stream? Or, better yet . . .'

Yvonne shrinks further into their chair. Pharaoh feels the anger go out of herself. Feels a familiar wash of compassion for the wretched specimen who can barely hold themselves together across the desk.

'He's writing a book, isn't he? Jesus, he's writing a book on his patients. On Virgil. On all the secrets they spilled to him when they were tripping. God, how much does he know? If he has confessions; dates, times, places – do you know how much pain we could stop if he would be willing to share what he knew? We can turn a blind eye to some of it, but . . .'

'We don't know where he is,' says Yvonne, quietly. 'Can't make sense of half of what he wrote in his notes. He left some of his audio recordings in his desk and it was just gibberish: chanting, Latin, all this white noise and screams. There had always been reports of noise from some of the group sessions, so it seemed best to just . . .'

'To pretend it didn't exist and hope the fucking fairies came to make it all better?' Pharaoh shakes her head, nostrils flaring, hands palm down on the desk. 'Dante Alighieri,' she says, in note-perfect Florentine. 'Bet you a pound to a fucking penny you were listening to the *Divine Comedy*. Or maybe Aenid. Dull as shit in places but quite astute in what it has to say about human beings. Has a way of crawling under the skin – the notion of Hell. I read something recently, might just tickle you. There've been experiments. Biomedical neuro-engineers – now that's a powerful weapon on the Scrabble board, eh? They've observed that when people go to the Prado in Madrid and look at Bosch's *Garden*, they barely glance at two of the panels of the triptych. Not more than a second or two looking at paradise. Not even perdition. On average, they spend thirty-three seconds exploring the grotesque. The horrors. The suffering beyond enduring. That's what people want to look at. I think our mutual friend knew that better than anybody.'

Yvonne's resolve crumbles. They seem to puddle over the sides of the chair suddenly, to sag inside their own skin.

'He sent me the first chapters shortly after he left,' says Yvonne. 'It was going to be published anonymously, or so he said, but he wasn't ever going to go through with that. Not if he was going to be the man who helped cure sex offenders and unmasked a vigilante killer. He'd want that all to himself.'

Hot bile rises in Pharaoh's throat. 'That's what he thought he was doing? Hunting a killer hidden in the subconscious of the men he'd attacked? You realize how fucking mental that sounds, yes?'

'He got very good results,' whispers Yvonne. 'Parfitt saw things. Went back into the flame. Saw the life he could have lived if not for his terrible hunger for that which he can no longer permit himself. He rewrote himself, Trish. Truly. Those letters that Dennic read to him . . . letters from Ruby that made him weep for what could have been. Dr Durrant did that.'

Pharaoh closes her eyes. 'Dennic read them to him?'

'He's partially sighted. We have books on tape but Dennic was very good about reading to the other men who hadn't perhaps had so much schooling.'

From the doorway, the cold, damp guard gives a pointed cough.

'So he knew all about Ruby,' says Pharaoh. 'Even if Parfitt didn't tell him, he'll have known all about her.' She grinds her knuckles into the desk. 'This educated man? He's an ex-squaddie. Worked security in Saudi. I don't think I've seen so much as a GCSE to his name.'

'He spoke of finding himself when he was overseas,' says Yvonne, grasping for something they hope to be a lifeline. 'The terrible things he did to himself. The lengths he went to . . . to atone.'

Pharaoh straightens her back. There's a tingle at the back of her neck; the migraine drifting down from her skull to gather at the nub of her neck. She can feel a burning sensation in her fingers and toes. Her lips tingle.

'He castrated himself,' she says, quietly. 'Did those things to himself.'

Yvonne nods. 'We have lots of people who self-harm, Trish. Of course, not in such an elaborate manner, but . . .'

From the door, another cough.

'Get yourself a sweetie and hush-up,' snaps Pharaoh, glaring. Gives Yvonne the full force of her temper. 'This man . . . this man who despises paedophiles so much that he cuts off his own balls? He cosies up to one of the sickest bastards in here? Reads him letters, joins him on his shamanic journey into the heart of darkness, care of Dr Durrant? Hears him confess to what he's done and then can't do a damn thing about it because it was all shared in a sacred space?'

Pharaoh pictures Ruby. Pictures John Dennic standing outside the abandoned café in Wincolmlee. Had he gone to tell her the truth about the man she wanted to free? The man she wanted to invite into her home?

Yvonne fumbles at the keys, bringing up copies of the correspondence between Ruby and her foster father.

Pharaoh reads one at random. Feels her stomach clench.

'Dear Daddy,' she mutters. 'He makes me feel like I'm on fire. Takes my hand and leads me into the flames and it hurts, it hurts so much, but it's so powerful and raw . . . you know what I mean. You know how it feels to want things which you can't have. I'm so proud of you. All that you've endured – all you've put yourself through. Just a little longer and we can all be together, making up for lost time . . .'

She stops. Snatches up her phone and gives a small whoop to see there's a brief moment of signal coverage. Logs on to Facebook and searches out the photos of the talking group that found a brief home above Ruby's shop. Scrolls through the pleas for new members, the begs for extra shares, the positive memes encouraging men to come forward and share their experiences and trauma in a safe space. Scans the photographs, feeling her throat tighten.

Batters out a brief trio of messages. Aector. Neilsen. Daniells. Attaches the link to the Facebook page and tells them to have it enlarged and cleared up as humanly possible. He's there, at the far right of a blurry snap: Ruby and Shirley – her mate – Mem and a couple of body-builder dads; three older men, tracksuits and over-coats and tired, sad eyes. And him. Leaning out of shot. Even dressed up as somebody else, he's showing off; playing a role. Dark jeans, dark jacket, gold chain, buzz-cut and goatee.

The shrink who took her foster father back to Hell to face what he had done. Who bathed in his memories and fantasies, his confessions and his agonies, until it half drowned him.

Pharaoh turns to the guard at the door. 'Now we can fucking go,' she mutters. She gives a last look at Yvonne, visibly coming apart at the desk. She can't bring herself to leave it there.

'You're braver than most,' she says, as gently as she can manage. 'Try and remember that when you're lashing yourself.'

She walks out into the rain-spotted darkness.

'He's waiting for you,' says the guard. 'He's got a lot to say.'

Pharaoh grits her teeth. 'I'll bet he fucking has.'

THIRTY

10.01pm

S hirley Ralph lives in a first-floor apartment on the corner of Princes Avenue. It's an ugly building: a squatting toad, throatily bulging over the remains of the Victorian architecture that had been sacrificed in its name. Too late to call in anything other than exceptional circumstances.

'There used to be weed dealers operating out of this place,' says DC Daniells, in the passenger seat of the two-seater. 'When the Headhunters were first—'

'I remember,' says McAvoy, grunting as he pulls into a parking space and the steering wheel digs into his gut for the umpteenth time. He's trying to keep his mind focused. Doesn't want to drift into memory; to look directly at the pain he endured at the hands of bad men.

'There's going to be no dignity in getting out,' mumbles Daniells, extricating himself from the seat belt. 'I spend so much of my life looking a tit.'

'Nobody's watching,' says McAvoy, checking the mirrors and seeing the dark, rain-flecked car park deserted. 'Now.'

The two big men swear and harrumph their way out of the vehicle, which rises a few inches on its suspension and emits an audible sigh of relief.

'She's going to go on about this,' says Daniells, as they make their way down a footpath to the garish blue double door – rain slapping off overhanging leaves and aiming for the space where their necks disappear into their collars.

'She's got more on her mind,' says McAvoy, checking the address on his notepad. 'She's with him now. In there. Sitting across from him.'

'She's been in with worse,' says Daniells, ringing the buzzer. 'It's all she's got left, really. Getting him to admit what he's done. He's out if not.'

McAvoy glances over at him. He's grim-faced. Doesn't look like himself. The air around him hangs differently, somehow. He looks like he's running out of whatever it is that keeps him going.

'I haven't ordered owt.'

McAvoy jumps when the crackly voice blurts through the intercom. 'Mrs Ralph? It's the police, would you—'

'Haven't ordered owt, mate. You've got the wrong house.'

McAvoy closes his eyes. Tries again. 'My name's Aector McAvoy, Shirley. I need to talk to you about Ruby.'

There's silence for a moment, then the buzzer sounds and the door clicks open. McAvoy leads them into the garishly bright hallway and through an internal door to the narrow stairs that lead up to the floors above. The door's already opening outside flat three when McAvoy reaches the top.

'Not dead, is she? Hasn't done her in?'

McAvoy pauses. Catches his breath. Shirley's small-framed and bottle-blonde: cheekbone and jawbone, décolletage and shoulder-blades, pushing against her pale skin like hammers and chisels and nails. She's forty-something. Bright eyes and bad skin. She's wearing fluffy pyjamas, holding a hot-water bottle to her stomach.

'We were rather hoping you could tell us where we might find her,' says McAvoy, gently.

A small, brown-haired girl pokes her head out from between Shirley's legs. She glares at the intruders.

'It's story time,' she says, giving them hard eyes. '*Faraway Tree.* Chapter six.'

McAvoy gives her a smile. 'Well, you tell old Moon Face and Silky that if they can just loan us the world's best storyteller for a wee minute, I'll send him a few extra toffee shocks, OK?'

The little girl beams. 'I like Saucepan Man.'

'Horsepan Ham?' asks McAvoy, putting one finger in his ear. She giggles, delightedly, and Shirley gives McAvoy a look of sudden warmth. The girl emerges fully into the corridor: baggy pyjamas under a dressing gown and Oodie. She isn't so much dressed as mummified.

'You've got wee ones, then?'

'Not so wee, but aye,' says McAvoy, as Shirley opens the door and ushers them down a little corridor to a savagely cold living room cluttered with an explosion of children's toys. The squishy Draylon sofa houses two Disney princess castles and the tatty sheep-skin rug in front of the TV is strewn with countless plastic figures. It looks like there's been a terrible battle.

'Go on now, Gaynor – you go finish brushing your hair and I'll be in as soon as we're done.'

Gaynor looks a little put out and adopts a suitably despondent walk as she slouches into her bedroom.

'She likes you,' says Shirley, clearing a basket of laundry off a high-backed armchair and sitting down. McAvoy clears a space on the sofa.

'I'll put the kettle on, shall I?' asks Daniells, from the doorway.

'It's a pigsty, love. I'm ashamed to call it my kitchen. Just haven't got the hours, y'know?'

'You must hear a lot of traffic,' says McAvoy taking in the rest of the room. A multi-coloured storage unit leans against one wall, handles hanging off, disgorging books and blankets and snuggle socks, which dangle down the front like ivy. McAvoy notices a whole pile of charity shop children's classics piled up by the TV. Above the storage heater hang random squares of paper, patterned with squiggles and finger paints.

'Nightmare in summer, with the windows open. Nice to hear people having a good time, but not when your bairn's having a nightmare.'

McAvoy nods. Breathes out, slowly, and watches his breath sparkle in the frigid air. Shirley notices. Shrugs. 'Pay-day's Friday,' she says. 'Hot-water bottle and hot chocolates until then.'

McAvoy sits forward, wrists on his knees. 'We're not just looking for Ruby, Shirley. Her partner's lad – Aramis. He's only seven. We were rather hoping there might have been a mix-up – that he's here, playing.'

Shirley raises her hands to her mouth. McAvoy notices faded ink on the backs of her hands; chewed nails and an old gold wedding ring, worn on the wrong finger.

'He's not here, mate,' she says, and it comes out in a rush. 'She's not neither.' She starts to breathe quicker, shaking her head. She squeezes the hot-water bottle against her stomach like a child. 'He's done her in, hasn't he? I said that bastard would do her in. Not the boy, though. No, that's . . .'

McAvoy leans forward. Puts his face directly into Shirley's gaze. 'It's going to be OK, Shirley,' he says, softly. 'She's your pal, yes? You're friends?'

Shirley is fanning her face with her hands. He sees her pat the pocket of her gown. Pulls out a vape and takes a slurp. Her breath comes raggedly, tears at her eyes.

'I'm sorry, you must think I'm the sort that just goes to pieces . . . I'm not, it's just . . . that family. That poor girl.'

McAvoy takes a moment. Flicks his eyes to the door, where Daniells is coming in with three mugs of tea. He gives a minute shake of his head. Not the time.

'Your daughter,' says McAvoy, making a connection. 'Gaynor? That was Ruby's sister's name, yes?'

'My little surprise,' says Shirley, managing a smile. Her eyes are flowing freely now. She dabs at her face with her knuckles, her wrist. McAvoy sees white lines within the cover-up tattoos on her exposed forearms. Feels a great rush of hatred towards himself for being here; for doing this.

'She's your youngest?'

'Two older boys, off making mischief,' she says. 'Gaynor's seven. I found out I was pregnant after Gaynor . . . well . . . after she did what she did, y'know.'

McAvoy nods. He does know.

'You knew both women?'

Shirley shakes her head. 'Ruby was my mate. I just knew Gaynor through her. I mean, they had a difficult relationship, like. Always did have. Grew up with only each other. Split up God knows how many times, but they always managed to find their way back to one another. Ruby says they played merry hell running away from care homes and foster homes and the like. She got good at it, so she said. Gaynor was always the stick in the mud. Sounds old-fashioned, a phrase like that, but she always came out with old-lady stuff like that. Don't think I heard her swear until she got together with Mem.'

McAvoy glances at his watch. Realizes how much time he's already wasted, haring up and down the country and scrapping with petty criminals while a little boy and his stepmum were missing.

'Shirley . . . you know her well. Best friends, I'd say. You'll forgive me for saying so but it's an operational requirement that we take a look at people's social media profiles. You and Ruby, you've had some good times.'

Shirley grins, a flood of memories bringing colour to her cheeks. She sniffs, and fresh tears fall. 'All she wanted was a family,' says Shirley, looking down at her slippered feet. She makes a half-hearted attempt to pick up some crumbs from the carpet. Gives up and slumps back in her chair.

McAvoy stares through the gap in the curtain. From here, he can almost make out the entrance to Pearson Park; to the site of Gaynor's death, and Ruby's night-time pilgrimages.

'Was she pleased when you chose the name Gaynor?' he asks.

'More than my fella was,' says Shirley, with a dry laugh. 'Sounds like a pub landlady name – that's what he said. But Ruby – she was in such a mess after Gaynor's death, not talking, not leaving her flat . . . you know she was doing a degree, don't you? Art? Photography? She was going great guns. Little job in a sofa shop two days a week. Liked her country walks and her sketching. Then

Gaynor and, well . . . I suppose her dad was always there in the background, like. But it was hard to talk to her about it.' She jerks away, hiding her face with her hand, but McAvoy recognizes the sudden flash of guilt that had momentarily changed her features.

'There's no shame in wanting to know, Shirley,' says McAvoy, motioning for Daniells to bring the teas. He appears in the doorway and hands over an assortment of mugs.

'Don't know what you were warning me for – it's spotless in there,' beams Daniells, perching on the arm of the sofa. 'I'd take my hat off to you, if I wore one. Tried for a while, but my husband said it made me look like a big toe wearing a bobble hat, so I went back to *au natural.*'

Shirley makes a little snort of laughter and bites it back at once.

'You know what her father did, don't you?' continues McAvoy, scalding his lip on the stewed, strong tea. 'I've seen the pictures, Shirley – the two of you having the best time, all pink cowboy hats and prosecco – all those nights out, and you never asked her about it?'

Shirley's expression hardens – a defensive reflex. 'I'm not saying that, neither. I'm saying she didn't talk about any of that stuff. Didn't mention the crimes at all. She spoke about her dad but it was like he were a saint, or something. This decent, loving, kind bloke who came and gave her this childhood right out of Enid Blyton. I mean, I know what lies we tell ourselves, but . . .'

'But you couldn't understand it,' finishes Daniells, gently. 'Fuck, that's hot.'

'If I were as bolshy as some of the mates she's had – I'd have just said, wouldn't I? Just come right out and asked her what the fuck she was playing at, going to visit a paedo in prison? The same paedo who drugged God knows how many of her mates and photographed himself having his fun with them while they were asleep? I don't care if he did read to you and bought your first bike – you should be wanting him to burn in his cell, like any normal person.'

McAvoy takes a moment. His sides are hurting, suddenly; the bootprint on his ribs stinging with fresh pain.

'When did you last speak to Ruby?' asks Daniells.

Shirley finds her phone in the pocket of her gown. Fumbles through messages and apps. 'Got a text yesterday morning, eight fourteen am. It's not a rude hour when you've got a seven-year-old. Just sent me a picture she'd found. One of her hippy-dippy, positive affirmation things. Here.' She shows an image of a daisy releasing its seeds. 'I sent back a heart. What else do you say? She's a dreamer, for all her big brain . . . oh, she did phone this morning but I didn't pick up, so . . .' A sudden thought seems to grip her, the angles of her face narrowing further so for a moment her face is a sharp beak. 'I was asleep. I mean, that wasn't when he . . . she didn't . . .'

McAvoy takes the phone from her hand as she starts to hug herself. 'It's not like it was,' she says, picking at the hem of her gown. 'We fell out after the café closed. I didn't blame her for it going under. I mean, with the pandemic and where it was and . . . well, I got something else, so it wasn't like she'd dragged me away from a top job to go and butter rolls in her café. No, it was good fun, but it couldn't last. Not with that . . . that fucking nutter.'

McAvoy sips his tea. 'You know her partner? His son?'

Shirley glances at the door to her daughter's bedroom. There's a picture of a rocket, silver crayon and glitter on black paper.

'He did that one,' says Shirley. 'Grand little lad, that one. I'd always have him, if she asked, but she barely asked. Just back in the beginning, you know . . . and I felt so shitty about it all. I mean, she's my mate, and he was bringing her out of herself after all the sadness, but it wasn't right, was it? Not palming the lad off on me, much as my Gaynor loves him. He'd never have laid a finger on her but he's a big lad, and well . . . I didn't want to be the one who told him.'

McAvoy's about to speak when he suddenly realizes they've been talking to one another at cross-purposes, as if on a satellite link-up. He's not entirely sure they're talking about the same person.

'Agamemnon Ricci,' says McAvoy, cautiously. 'You're saying he wouldn't lay a hand on her?'

Shirley frowns. 'Not in any way she didn't like! No, they have their barneys but he'd never put a hand on her.'

McAvoy looks over at Daniells, who's staring at his notebook, flicking the pages. He, too, has read the domestic violence reports. Each briefing Pharaoh has prepared for the team has explained just how much of a hold Mem Ricci has over his partner. She'd had bruises today, hadn't she? Grazes at her face, glimpsed as she stood by the car, staring at her boyfriend as he pissed himself, ducking into Pharaoh's car without a further backwards glance.

He calls the voicemail service on Shirley's phone. Puts it on speakerphone.

'. . . no worries at all, no, it's just we've got loads on and there's somebody coming to see the upper room, and it's getting a bit of a deathtrap, so maybe if you took him, then . . . you will, oh great, you are such a diamond, Shirl, I'll be right over, no worries . . .'

There are no other voicemails. Just the high, bright voice of Ruby Chessman, faking a conversation for the benefit of her half-asleep boyfriend.

'I never spoke to her,' says Shirley, sitting back in her seat. 'What's she going on about?' She grips the hem of her gown, teeth suddenly bared. 'She used to do that, y'know. Leave me these imaginary fucking conversations, so she could squeeze a couple of hours away from him – go and do whatever it was that made her go how she's been going.'

'And how's that, Shirley?'

She sucks on her vape. 'He'll have done her in,' she says, and her bottom lip is a plucked string. 'But not that lovely boy.' She starts to cry, unable to stop the sobs. McAvoy feels a sudden draft as the door slowly opens. Gaynor is standing in the doorway, her eyes burning holes in the intruders. 'Mummy?'

Shirley dries her eyes. Manages a mad, gleaming, snot-streaked smile.

'We have Mr Ricci in custody, Shirley,' says McAvoy, managing a weak smile for Gaynor. 'But Ruby was seen after his arrest. We don't believe she's been harmed. We need to speak to Ruby in connection with another matter.' She twitches, reaching down to scratch at her shins, almost knocking over the last dregs of her tea. 'Does the name John Dennic mean anything to you?'

Shirley looks at her daughter. Puts her arms out and beckons her over. Folds her in a hug.

'I told you, he'd never hurt her,' says Shirley, kissing her daughter's head and holding her tight.

'Then whom do you mean when you refer to "he", Shirley?' he asks, wincing, the tips of his ears turning pink. He feels like he's playing Scrabble without any vowels.

'Her love doctor,' whispers Shirley, dripping scorn, mimicking her friend's mannerisms as she spells out every syllable. '*He understands, Shirl. He gets it, Shirl. He makes me feel alive, Shirl. He's all I can think about, Shirl. Can you look after Aramis so I can go and shag him, Shirl . . .?*'

From inside Shirley's robe comes an admonitory 'Mummy' from a disappointed Gaynor.

McAvoy and Daniells exchange a look. 'Shirley, this is incredibly important. Is Ruby involved with somebody? Might she have taken Aramis to be with this person?'

'She said it was over,' whispers Shirley. 'Months ago. He was . . . he was taking her to places she didn't want to go. That's how she put it. She was scaring herself. That's half the reason the club stopped – the little talking group we had going. Helped people. Mem's not half as bad as he comes across, you know. Really wanted to make a go of it for her. With her. But he was never going to swallow that. Not that saintlier-than-thou bastard.'

'Who, Shirley?'

'Roscoe,' she says, and wrinkles her nose. 'Never gave us more than that. First names only. The whole thing was his baby, though. From the off, he was in control. Poor lad from the charity never got a look in. Right know-it-all. Real cult-leader vibe. I never fell for it. But she did. And God knows, she's been through enough hell. I didn't think the universe would mind her having a little bit of something for herself, even if he was a sanctimonious prick who got his kicks raping her mind.'

She covers Gaynor's ears as she says this. Sniffs. The lines at her eyes bunch together like the footprints of tiny birds.

McAvoy takes out his phone. Googles a name. Holds it up to Shirley's face for inspection.

'He's lost weight since then; beard's a bit longer, but yeah, that's the prick.' She looks like she wants to smash the phone to pieces. 'He's killed her, hasn't he? Juiced her of all her pain . . .' She stops, mouth hanging open, taking a deep, rasping breath. She snatches up her phone. Scrolls frantically through her messages. Jabs at the screen and hands it over to McAvoy.

'. . . *he's into the taboos. Wants to push my boundaries. There's a therapy he knows about. Radical and really unconventional, but he thinks maybe if we take me back into my head – I don't know, almost like hypnotize me or something, then maybe I can relive it and change the ending. Undo it all. Put the smashed pieces back together – that's what he said. But he said he adores my fragility too. I can't help thinking what it would be like if we were a proper family. Me and Aramis and him. I know it's crazy, I mean Aramis isn't even mine, but he says he would do anything to show me what love can truly be. God, Shirl, the things he comes out with when he's touching me – I feel like I'm in a different universe.'*

'She's told him she wants to leave Mem,' says Shirley, coldly. 'Told him, and he's gone for her. All that nasty stuff they did together, all that feeling each other's anguish and joining in the sacred union . . . it's all bollocks. He liked hurting her and she liked being hurt . . .'

McAvoy hauls himself out of the chair. Gives a nod to Daniells. Pharaoh doesn't answer. Wolsingham's phone goes straight to voice-mail. He's beginning to run out of people he feels subservient to. Fears he's going to have to somehow make sense of everything.

In the cold lobby of the ugly building, he stops and rests his head against the cold wall. Calls Roisin.

'The psychologist,' he says, when she breathes his name. 'Parfitt's prison psychologist. He's been having an affair with her. Trish is with Parfitt now, but I don't know if he knows any of this. If he engineered it or if he's as clueless as everybody else. And the boy. Aramis . . . I think she has him. But I've no idea where to start looking because Trish has deliberately led me to believe she's somebody that she might not be, which means we've been looking at everything backwards from day one.'

At the other end of the phone, Roisin breathes softly. 'Just the child, my love. Everything else is noise. Find the boy.'

McAvoy scrunches up his face. He feels as though he's being squeezed inside tightening armour. His fingertips and toes are tingling with a feeling that isn't quite pain. He can't quite seem to catch his breath.

'She's gone to be with a man, has she?' asks Roisin. 'Playing happy families? It will be somewhere that means a lot to her, my love. A fantasy scene but painted on somewhere real. Where did they meet? How did they fall in love?'

McAvoy can't answer. Doesn't know. Ends the call.

Seconds later the phone buzzes in his hand. He answers without thinking, hoping to God it will be Pharaoh.

He's already answered before the name registers.

'Gemma, I'm so sorry, I know it must feel like we're giving you the runaround, but . . .'

'There's somebody here, Aector. Somebody moving . . . we can hear a little boy . . . Halle's bleeding, Aector. I don't know where she is . . .'

The sweat turns icy cold on McAvoy's skin. Gemma's voice is a terrified whisper, each syllable ghosted by an echo of the preceding word.

'Gemma, where are you? What's happening? Tell me where you are . . .'

McAvoy pushes his finger into his ear, squeezes the phone against his face. Listens to the emptiness; the aching, hollow silence.

'Aector, they're coming. They're . . .'

There's a sudden thud, then silence.

McAvoy holds his breath. The line is still live. For an instant, he hears what might have been the cry of a child.

There's a crunching sound, and then nothing but dead air.

THIRTY-ONE

Pharaoh doesn't let herself pause before she opens the door to the little potting shed at the far end of the prison garden. Doesn't take a breath. Doesn't get herself in the right head-space. Comes through the door like a local in a neighbourhood pub. She's shaking on the inside, but she'll be dammed if she shows it. She's been waiting for this for more than a decade. Waiting for the chance to look him in his eyes and . . .

He's sitting in a plastic chair. Jogging trousers, sweatshirt, a blanket around his shoulders. He looks up.

Eye, Pharaoh corrects herself. *Look him in the eye.*

She breathes in. Smells soft earth and rain, rotting vegetation and wet hay. There's a slightly medicinal tang to the air. Pharaoh stays in the doorway, letting herself drink him in. She'd known he was in bad shape, but she hadn't imagined this. Hadn't imagined herself feeling briefly sorry for him. She bites down the wave of compassion that rises up as she stares at the ugly mess of ridged, ropy skin that covers one half of his face. He wears a skin-coloured patch over the gaping hole where his eye used to be. His hair grown lank and grey on the unburned side. The other is a mess of glistening sores. Slick flesh is riddled with craters and cracks, oozing red. One of his ears is a stump of blackened gristle.

'Decland Parfitt,' says Trish, taking out her cigarettes from the inside of her jacket. Her fingers shake as she lights one, but her voice is steady: unruffled. 'You're looking well.'

The figure in the chair twitches a smile. Raises his head and focuses on her with his good eye. The neck of his sweatshirt hangs loose and she can see the tip of the deep white scars that run from his neck to his nuts. He raises his hand, slowly. There's a huge snail squatting on the back of his arm, mobbing in agonisingly slow increments across the pink, scar-shimmered flesh.

'Patricia,' says Parfitt, and his voice sounds like two metal files being rasped together. He lifts the snail to his face. Peers at it. Directs his words at the creature's slimy head. 'A Detective Chief Superintendent now. Done very well for herself. Caught a lot of bad people. Popular, too. Pride of the force, though I reckon there's no shortage of older men with white hair and cufflinks who'd love nothing more than to see her fall on her face. Don't know what to do with her, do they? Don't know if they fancy her or want her to be their mum, but they don't like how it makes them feel. Don't like giving power to somebody who really knows how to use it.'

Pharaoh leans back against the workbench, pushing a tray of seedlings out of her way. She hops up on to the bench, kicking her legs. She breathes out a cloud of smoke. Glares through it.

'Sorry about your mate,' says Pharaoh, making sure to keep on staring after he's looked away. 'I know you don't have normal feelings, but there must be some part of you that feels a bit responsible. That feeling? It's guilt, Parfitt. Shame, even. You've felt it before but you pushed it down. Told yourself lies. Told yourself you weren't doing any harm.' She shakes her head, oozing disgust. 'This is your little empire, is it?' She glances around the little wooden shed, listening as the rain and the wind rattle against the window shutters. 'How the mighty have fallen, eh?'

Parfitt eases the snail from one arm to the other. Pharaoh notices the glistening trail that the creature has left in the liniment that smothers Parfitt's exposed skin.

'Who's this, then?' asks Pharaoh, trying to keep control of her feelings. She needs him to talk. She won't get anything out of him if she tries to appeal to his better nature. No, she needs to get him talking and trust to luck that something useful dribbles out.

'Michelle,' says Parfitt, quietly. He raises the snail to face height.

'There were two, but a bird got in when the door was open. We've got the shell on a shelf but all the meat – took the lot.'

'John Dennic,' says Pharaoh, again. 'Are you going to tell me why he was at Ruby's place?'

Parfitt shuffles in his seat. 'He's dead, then. It's not just the wardens having a bit of fun with me?'

Pharaoh feels that disloyal rush of compassion. Forces herself to ignore it. 'Besties, were you? BFFs? What was it, Parfitt – he's the only one who understands you? Only one who knows what it's like to be a victim of persecution and victimization? Your letters to the Parole Board – beautifully written, Parfitt, truly. Almost brought a tear to my eye. And you spin a good yarn.'

'I've been here a long time, Patricia,' says Pharaoh. 'I've served my time.'

Pharaoh shakes her head. 'I've told you, Parfitt – I know what you are. I know what you did. We'll link you to those girls. We'll prove what you did. This fantasy of yours – playing happy families with Ruby and Aramis . . .'

Parfitt jerks his head up at the name. 'She's going to bring him to see me, if we can get permission,' he says, with a dreamy, far-away smile slashed deep into his ruined features.

'You're mad,' says Pharaoh, grinding her cigarette out in the dirt of a tray of seedlings. 'Do you think they'll permit that? Even if they ever did, it's all gone to shit now, Parfitt. Your friend, Dennic – his blood's all over the upstairs room at Ruby's café. And Ruby's done a runner. We've got Mem in custody, but . . .'

'The boy,' says Parfitt, suddenly. 'Who's got the boy?'

Pharaoh takes a breath before replying. Stares again at the wooden walls; the trays of plants; the sacks of bulbs in their dirty mesh bags. There's a pile of rotten logs and tree bark at the far end of the bench, greasy with fungus.

'We have to hope that Ruby does,' says Pharaoh. 'But Ruby is currently a suspect in the murder of John Dennic. Your mate. The lad you sent to remind her where her loyalties lie.'

Parfitt sits back in his chair a little. Rummages in the pocket of his trousers. He pulls out a small tobacco tin and levers the top off with his stump of thumb. Inside is a yellow, jelly-like substance. He dips one of his fingers in it. Begins to apply it to the scars upon his cheek.

'Goodbye present,' explains Parfitt, and there's a grotesque squelching sound as he smears the ooze upon his weeping scars. 'Knew he wasn't coming back. Didn't want me in pain. God, he had no place in here. Decent man. Good man. Saw a person in pain and decided to do something about it.'

'In pain, were you, Parfitt?' asks Pharaoh, cleaning her sunglasses with the hem of her shirt. 'Needed a friend?'

'I don't suffer the way you might hope, Patricia,' smiles Parfitt. 'I'm in pain, yes. I'm not pretty. But I have made the most of my time in prison. I've come to terms with who I am. I've made my peace with my sins. I know what I used to be, and I know the life I still want to live. I'm in control, now. I'm not the same man who walked into the fire.'

Pharaoh hides her sneer behind her hand. 'You don't need to keep up the act with me, Parfitt. I've always known what you are. What you're capable of. What you would do if given time alone with a child.'

Parfitt shakes his head. 'I've completed the SOTP scheme. Horizon, too. I've co-operated. Played along. I've let that silly man poke me with his marker pen and press my face into the ground so I can feel what my victims endured. I've built relationships. My daughter is waiting for me on the outside – the self-same daughter who has never believed a word of the allegations against me . . .'

'Foster daughter,' points out Pharaoh. 'She only had the one blood relative, but she killed herself after you raped her.'

Parfitt shakes his head. Looks away. 'Gaynor was a troubled girl. I did my best. Did my best for both of them.'

'You turned her into your accomplice,' spits Pharaoh. 'Had her bringing the pretty girls home for you for sleepovers so you could drug them and have your fun.'

'I did a lot of good in my life,' mutters Parfitt. 'My hunger – it was a medical condition. You can no more judge me for feeling my compulsions than you can blame a diabetic or an asthmatic for being made that way.'

'But you acted on it, Parfitt. You built your life around your obsession. All the bullshit with the safari suit and the animals and the silly voices – you were making yourself trustworthy and attractive to children. I've seen it so many times. And I'd have helped you stop, Parfitt. I swear, if you'd confessed . . .'

'If I confessed, I'd never have met Virgil,' says Parfitt, smoothly. 'And I'd still be a sinner.'

Pharaoh lights another cigarette. Wafts the smoke with her hand. She stares at the pitiful figure in the chair and tries to find any similarity between the wretched specimen and the nicely spoken, slightly manic entertainer who had made so many children squeal. Tries to see the Lizard King and fails.

'You put out the flames but it was Virgil who saved me,' says Parfitt, with a note of far-away reverence. 'I didn't know his name then. I don't know what he calls himself. Virgil is the name we gave him.'

'We?'

'The redeemed,' says Parfitt. 'Virgil took me to Hell. Showed me what awaited me. Punished my sinful flesh. You ensured my heart kept beating – you ensured I had a future.'

'We all make mistakes,' smiles Pharaoh, nastily. She shakes her head, pissed off at the way her day has gone. Pissed off that she might have got Ruby so wrong. 'Why was he there, Parfitt? Where has he been going on his weekend passes? What is it – you're frightened that somebody else will cast a spell on her, are you? Somebody else will turn her head and she'll stop peddling your lies? She'll finally admit that she wasn't with you those nights and that you were out abducting and murdering little girls . . .'

Parfitt shakes his head. 'All these years and you still don't understand,' he mutters. 'I've lived in your head all this time and you don't know anything about me. But I've seen what awaits, Patricia. I've been to Hell and I've changed my ways. Virgil showed me how.'

Pharaoh picks up one of the little pits and pushes her fingers into the soil. 'Where would Ruby take Aramis, do you think? If her world was caving in and she wasn't thinking straight? Places that meant something to her?'

'She's a good girl. Daddy's girl.'

'It's taking a lot of effort not to punch you, Parfitt.'

Parfitt gives his attention back to the snail. 'Dr Durrant thought he understood,' he says, quietly. 'Thought he was going to "cure" us. All ego, all self-aggrandizing rhetoric, that one. But we played along. You don't co-operate, you're a problem and you don't get parole. So we "volunteer". Let him in.' He shakes his head. 'He opened up to a room of predators, Patricia. Don't you think we saw him for what he was?'

Pharaoh lets out a breath. 'Your chaplain thinks he's the Second Coming.'

A spit bubble pops on the ruined half of Parfitt's mouth as he gives something that might be a laugh. 'John did more for us than he ever did. Gave us a real space to be free. What Dr Durrant gave us – it was John's magic. He could have grown enough 'shrooms in here to dose the full prison but he only ever used his skills to help us. Showed us the way.'

Pharaoh stops herself before she replies. There's a strange tingling feeling in her lips. She can hear her heart beating and the rushing of blood in her ears. She suddenly sees it. Sees what she hasn't allowed herself to. Allows the darkness to flood in. Takes herself back to that terrible place beneath the cliffs. Remembers the figure in the shadows. Goes deeper. That day, when Decland Parfitt first entered her world. Parfitt, with his silly costume and his multicoloured van and his two darling daughters, different as night and day. Pushes on, picking up images and discarding them, trying to find the place where she got it wrong. Thinks upon the body of John Dennic; gelded and tortured beyond enduring. Dennic, with his skills and his wisdom and a face that people trust. Dennic, who pinged around the system, always a step or two behind Parfitt, until he found himself on the same wing, and volunteered to join Dr Durrant's treatment programme. Dr Durrant, who had spoken so openly about the use of psychedelics to cure sexual deviancy. Parfitt had started the gardening programme, hadn't he? Become Dr Durrant's number two. Had his own little potting shed where he could brew up whatever potions loosened tongues and allowed a room of damaged, dangerous men to look deep inside themselves and share their deepest fantasies . . . And she sees Ruby. Ruby, sticking up for her dad. Ruby, telling her she's got it wrong, she's drunk, her dad's a good man, it was just a misunderstanding . . . sees Gaynor, cold and blue on the Hot House floor.

'You told him everything, did you?' asks Pharaoh, quietly. 'Dennic?'

Parfitt nods. Rubs the lotion into the skin around his eye patch. 'Dr Durrant didn't know what he was doing,' hisses Parfitt. 'He didn't understand. When he heard about Virgil . . . it got into his head. You could see it, the way he kept talking about him, how he came to admire him. He'd go on and on at me in our one-on-ones, trying to get every last fragment of it out of me. Not that there was much to tell. There was just the before and the after. He showed me what awaited and I emerged from Hell reborn. I'm not a danger, Patricia, I swear. The things I did – I disgust myself. But I didn't take those girls. I didn't. John knows that.'

I bet he does, she thinks, chewing her lip. She sees him now. Knows him. Knows how far his self-loathing took him. How far he would go to make amends. Fuck. *Fuck!*

'Dr Durrant was giving you psychedelics?' asks Pharaoh, calmer than she feels, stepping down from the bench.

'Making us re-enact our crimes. Role-playing. He'd have a serial rapist lay on his back while a nonce put their hand over his mouth and pounded them into the floor.'

'Jesus,' mutters Pharaoh. 'I'm guessing it went wrong?'

Parfitt shrugs. 'One of the lads – they had a heart attack in front of us. Right there in front of us, play-acting the role of a male rapist. I think he was dead before he hit the floor. Went rock-hard, though . . . you could see through his trousers. Sessions came to an end after that. All shushed up but Dr Durrant spat his dummy out. Said he was making progress, pushing boundaries. Came to say goodbye to us after he told them to shove it. Said we hadn't seen the last of him – that together we were making a difference. What do you say to that? I tell you, there are some bad men in this place, but Dr Durrant – there's something hungry in him; something that—'

Pharaoh closes her eyes, cuts him off. 'Some of them started getting off on it,' she says. 'Started liking it?'

'Dr Durrant most of all,' says Parfitt.

'And you?'

'My conscience is clear,' he says. 'Virgil showed me far more than any hallucination ever could. My disability meant I couldn't really partake in the role-play so during the sessions I would just sit and talk to John. He took the notes for Dr Durrant.'

'You told him about everything you'd done?'

Parfitt nods. 'The drink he gave us – it felt like we were all having one shared experience. It was as if we could see inside one another's souls. It was like being back in the darkness. With him. With you . . .'

Pharaoh pushes past Parfitt to where the rotten log is turning to mulch. At the mushrooms and toadstools and milky spores that cling to the bark. 'Nobody asks questions about this?' asks Pharaoh, disbelieving.

'Prison does nicely out of our holistic health parcels,' he says, moving the snail to the back of his palm. Pharaoh shudders. Remembers seeing him in her living room, lizard on his shoulder, wiping away Ruby's snot and tears with his thumb. It was OK, he was saying. Just a mistake. You stood up for me and that means so much. You're safe. You'll always be safe with me . . .

She turns back to Parfitt.

'When did you know?' she asks, squatting down. 'How long had she been with you before you saw what she was?'

A look of fear ripples across the ruined meat of Parfitt's face. His pupils shrink. He gulps, spit pooling at the corner of his mouth. He gulps again, painfully. His hands rise to his face. He starts tugging at the eye-patch, fingers slipping in the yellowy goop he's smeared on to his wounds.

'Parfitt? Decland, you don't look . . .'

He jerks in his seat as if strapped to an electric chair. Every tendon in his body seems to suddenly stretch out in a rictus of agony; fingers stiff, neck grotesquely extended, teeth mashing together around the pulp of his tongue.

Pharaoh jerks back, horrified. He's going into spasm. Fitting. There's blood running down his mouth.

There's a clatter as the vial of ointment drops to the stone floor. A crack as the snail hits the far wall.

Pharaoh watches as the eye patch flops forward. She looks directly into the ruined socket: a lamprey mouth smeared with yellow goop.

She's going to go for help, she tells herself. She's going to try and stabilize him, and then she'll shout for help.

There's a crack as Parfitt twists himself in his seat: a rib dislocating as he bucks in agony. Spit froths at his mouth. His skin tears as his mouth opens in a desperate screech of prayer.

'He's not there,' says Pharaoh, as Parfitt's eye swivels madly in the socket. 'Virgil. The one who holds your hand on the journey through Hell. He's not there, Parfitt. He's in a drawer at the mortuary. Daddy's girl opened his throat.'

She hauls herself up. Shakes her head.

'You want to live? Or should I let you go to whatever's waiting?'

Parfitt can't communicate. His throat seems clogged. There's a greenish tinge to his skin. Blood in his eye.

'He came here to finish the job, Parfitt,' says Pharaoh, and a gentler tone enters her voice. 'You poor bastard. Your best friend is the same vigilante who did this to you. The same man who's just given you one great big fuck-you of a goodbye.'

She doesn't wait for a response. Walks to the door and yanks it open.

She shouts for help.

She doesn't shout it loud.

THIRTY-TWO

M cAvoy forces himself to replay each word in his head, poring over every syllable. Tries to replicate the sound. Had it been a child? It had been less a cry than a screech. Not a screech . . . No. A squawk. The squawk of a seabird.

And then he's barging through the doors, sprinting across the car park towards the silly little car. He feels a sudden surge of adrenaline. Bempton Cliffs is maybe an hour away. But Pharaoh's car is fast.

He's already screeching away from the parking space before he's properly closed the door and phoned the rudderless incident room. It's Sophie Kirkland who answers, sounding pissed off.

'Sarge, we've had a call from the prison, and . . .'

'Possible lead on the missing child,' he shouts, over the roar of the engine, not quite making her out and wincing as the Mercedes hits a speed bump on two wheels. 'We need a location trace on the mobile phone of Gemma Tang. I'll ping you the digits over. Andy's taking a statement from a friend of Ruby's . . . she's been having a fling with the ex-prison psychologist . . .'

'Sarge, it's the Boss,' says Kirkland, teeth locked. 'Right in front of her. She said it was like he broke himself in half. Like something was trying to get out of him . . .'

He puts his foot down. Won't let up until he's close enough to hear the scream of the gulls.

THIRTY-THREE

Neilsen is sifting through the drawers in the master bedroom at Beresford's place. They'll do it properly, according to Wolsingham. Any minute now he'll call it in. He knows time is getting away from them. Beresford's dead. Stiffening.

Neilsen feels like he's underwater. His skull feels two sizes thicker; his thoughts all muffled and faint. Twenty years he's been decent; twenty years without ever crossing the line between not just what's lawful and unlawful, but what's right and wrong. A day in Wolsingham's company and he's ready to put his signature to a false narrative. He can't even understand what's in it for Wolsingham. The guy doesn't seem so ambitious that he would risk being fired over a quick result. No, he has no fear of consequences, thinks Neilsen. So that means he's got pull with somebody.

Neilsen sits down on the bed. It's low and Scandinavian-looking. Stripped pine. It neatly compliments the pale-blue walls and the dainty little watercolour prints that hang in oval frames around the room. He wants to lie down. Would love to kick his shoes off and fall to sleep and wake having made different decisions.

'You can answer your phone if it rings,' shouts Wolsingham, cheerily, up the stairs. 'Called it in.'

Neilsen doesn't reply. Closes his eyes. Licks his lips. He fishes out his phone and looks at the screen through blurry eyes. Missed calls. Missed notifications.

He listens to a voicemail from Pharaoh. His mouth goes dry. He clamps his jaw shut. Forces himself to listen to the next. It's Dr Vergette, urging him to call back. He manages to work some spit into his mouth. Swallows. Calls straight back.

'Ben, finally,' says Dr Vergette, excitedly. 'Things do move quickly around here, don't they? Quiet as church mice around here this morning and now look at us, all feverishly beavering away, which is better than fevering beaverishly away, if you'll forgive my saying so.'

Neilsen hasn't got the energy to be polite. He feels himself lying down on the bed. Thinks of Mem Ricci's little boy, whereabouts unknown. Thinks of Decland Parfitt, dead in the potting shed at HMP Ovenden. Thinks of Dr Munroe Durrant and the man called Roscoe. Wonders how much of this investigation is still his, and just when it all got so fucking unwieldy. Christ, he thinks – wait until they all learn about Beresford. Realizes, pulse racing, that they're going to have to change the story now that every other bugger seems to have their own interpretation of who's doing what to whom. God, his head's spinning. For the first time in two decades, he imagines jacking it all in. Not being a copper. Doing something else. He'd like to repair bicycles. Maybe lawnmowers. He doesn't know how to do either job, but he fancies he could get on board with the ripped jeans and oily-rag aesthetic.

'Fascinating tox reports on our Mr Dennic, and I shall continue to use him by that name for the purposes of our conversation, just so we both know where we're at. Now, as I explained . . .'

Neilsen returns to himself with a jolt. What had Vergette said? Something significant. Something more important than the whirl of intangibles in his head. 'He has a different name?'

'I'm getting to that,' says Dr Vergette, a little petulantly. 'It's the tox report that I need to tell you about. The bloods we took this morning show a man whose entire system was literally awash with every manner of chemical trace. Atropine. Belladonna. Wolfsbane. Evidence of many years spent ingesting trace amounts of poison. Physicians used to do the same in ancient times – inure themselves against murder by building up a tolerance. That's interesting, natur-ally. But it's the other traces that have really got the lab-coats flying. Ibogaine. I doubt you're familiar with it, but . . .'

Neilsen lets the words wash over him. Thinks upon Pharaoh. How pleased she's going to be with him. How little he'll deserve her esteem. Christ, one moment of weakness, just one, and the Devil slid in like night. He lets Vergette explain Ibogaine. Ayahuasca. All the tiny traces of toxins that riddled John Dennic's corpse.

'Enough to kill him?' asks Neilsen, at last.

'A miracle he was alive in the first place,' says Vergette. 'But he could certainly have continued to do so, were it not for the knife that opened his throat.'

'Ok,' says Neilsen, finding himself reluctant to move. He imagines himself replaying this conversation at a hearing. Wonders how the hell he'll explain himself.

'Now, as requested, we've conducted the full familial DNA sweep. You'll recall how I said there were no relatives or known associates on the system – nobody with a connection to a John Dennic, with that date of birth and National Insurance number, as entered when he was arrested over the incident in 2012?'

Neilsen grunts. He'd give anything to be with somebody right now. One of the people he trusts. One of the old guards who'd take a bullet for him. He begins to wonder if he deserves this. Feels self-pity begging to creep in and shakes it away. He refuses to change his narrative to make himself feel better.

'Rustled up some medical records. Blood type O, apparently.'

'And?'

'And our Dennic is B positive.'

'And that doesn't happen, I presume,' says Neilsen, swinging his legs off the bed and sitting down. 'Our man isn't John Dennic?'

'The John Dennic lying in the mortuary – he's not the same man for whom we have medical records, date of birth and complete medical history.'

'So who's John Dennic?' asks Neilsen, and pauses as he hears a creak outside the door.

'It's more of a job for your people than for mine, but Darling Denise has already managed to do the kind of job that one rather wishes the desk sergeant had performed when he was first booked in. Found mention of him on an alumnus forum. University of Exeter. "Anybody heard from old Denno? Last we heard, still getting barefoot and shamanistic in the malaria hotspots of the world. Never met a herb or a shroom that he didn't want to become friends with . . ."'

'Sounds like our guy.'

'Our guy, but with the wrong blood type, Ben. What I'm saying is that post, made in 2008, is the last mention anywhere of the John Dennic we have records for. And the man in our mortuary – he's not him. But he's travelled as him. He's got his papers. Got his passport.'

'His passport?'

'Frequent flyer into the UK – trips back and forth. Gabon. Patagonia. Colombia. Then nothing for the past years. We now know why – he's been inside, doing time for somebody else's crime.'

'No, that doesn't fit,' says Neilsen. 'No, he really did attack Beresford. Beresford said it came out of nowhere – a deliberate attack, targeted, right for the eyes. All he said was he had a feeling he'd seen him somewhere before.'

Wolsingham steps into the room. He looks disgusted. Looks as though he'd like to tie Ben's tongue in a knot and wear it at his throat.

'Oh, you've been to see the victim, have you?' asks Dr Vergette, sounding pleased. 'Excellent, well – as I said at the start, we do at least have another name for our gentleman on the slab. We've run the familial DNA trace. Amazing what you can achieve if you ask nicely. Suffice to say, we've got a hit on the father's side. Our man is father to a young woman who took her own life. Father Unknown – that's what's listed on the child's birth certificate. Pitifully little else on the death certificate. Found dead at the Hot House, in Pearson Park. I've crossed the t's and dotted the i's. Imagine my surprise, Ben. Foster daughter of . . .'

'Decland Parfitt,' says Neilsen, forcing himself to look up. To meet Wolsingham's gaze. 'Beresford just died. Poisoned.'

'Good lord!' barks Vergette, and covers the speaker long enough to relay the information to whoever's sitting near him. 'Good lord, that's – is Trish OK? Gosh, dropping like flies. Sorry, what's that?' There's another muffled conversation, then Vergette is back, excitement in his voice. 'There were two of them, yes? Two sisters.'

'Ruby is being sought in connection with our murder. This man.'

'Her father, one presumes. The man who isn't John Dennic. What shall we call him, henceforth?'

Neilsen watches Wolsingham turn. Sees him shake his head. Sees him walk away.

'I'll tell the Boss,' says Neilsen, quietly. He can hear sirens. For the first time since he was a young man, they don't sound reassuring.

'The Mighty McAvoy – sitting this one out, is he?' asks Dr Vergette, trying to sound charming. 'Bit close to home, I'd imagine. All that hedgerow magic. Fascinating woman, that creature of his. We could all learn a thing or two from her, eh?'

Neilsen ends the call. Thinks of Aector. His boss. His friend.

Knows, instinctively, where the big man will be.

'Go get him, Sarge,' he whispers, as he makes his way down the stairs and towards the flashing blue lights. He glimpses the glossy magazine. Dr Munroe Durrant – pioneer of alternative therapies; the man who can rewire a monster.

'Put the bastard down.'

THIRTY-FOUR

A ramis is frightened. He's been frightened for a long time now. He thought it might stop after a little while, but bad things just keep happening and every time he thinks he's as frightened as he's ever been, badness and darkness and nastiness descend on him like angry birds and he discovers that he can still feel more afraid.

He huddles against the bare brick wall. He's got a blanket, but he dropped it in one of the puddles of black, greasy water and now it's sopping wet. He knows that it's better to be nude than to wear wet clothes. Dad told him that.

He sucks in dirt as he sniffles. Sobs. He presses his head against the brick. It makes a funny noise as he does so; the wall grinding into powder.

'Stop it. Stop.'

He looks up. It's the nice lady. She's Chinese, he thinks. It's hard to tell. There's hardly any light down here. There's a torch dangling somewhere nearby, but it just gives off a big white glare and then peters out before it reaches the floor. He can't see much of the small room, with its loose pipes and spurs of rusty scaffold. There are cages mounted on the wall; the one that's scarred black. He'd thought he could see a picture beneath it, when Roscoe shone the torch around the room and told him there was nothing to be scared of. It had been like a brass rubbing: weird pictures of goblins and demons, eating each other and pooping each other out. He'd done brass rubbing with Dad, at a church in London where his grandad used to be somebody important. He's never met that grandad. Never will, according to Dad.

He sniffs again, wrapping his arms around himself. Pushes his head back against the brick.

'Don't,' says the nice lady, and her voice breaks. 'Don't hurt yourself. Somebody will be here. I promise, somebody will be here.'

Her voice breaks again. She tries to wipe her face but her hands are tie-wrapped around a length of metal pipe. She smudges her face against her shoulder.

'Let me give him my coat, at least. He's shivering. Let me do that!'

From the darkness, a single voice. 'No.'

Aramis drops his head to his arms. Shivers. He makes fists with his feet inside his trainers. He knows his trainers were expensive. The whole outfit was expensive: designer jogging bottoms and matching hoodie, gold chain like Dad's and a flat cap on top of a neat buzz-cut. He likes the way Dad takes pride in dressing him up. Likes it when people joke that they're twins.

He thought Dad would be here by now. He knows he's in a bad place with a man who isn't his friend any more, and he's always known that life can be full of mean and hurtful things. But he's always known that Dad will be there. Knows that if he's ever in trouble, Dad will be there to take the bad guy down with one punch. Dad's knocked out lots of people 'with one punch'. That's his thing. Aramis sometimes wonders if that's why Dad's friends are so nice to him – that they're frightened he will knock them out with one punch if they don't. He wonders whether he'd like to have that power. How he'd use it. He knows he wouldn't still be sitting here now, cold and snot-streaked in a room beneath the ground, risking another shove if he tries to get up from where Roscoe has told him to stay.

Roscoe, he thinks, and his little hands make fists. He doesn't even think it's his real name. Ruby calls him Munroe, sometimes, when she thinks nobody's listening. She's not as good at hiding things as she thinks she is. He's seen her talking with him in corners when Dad hasn't been around. Saw them both coming out of the store cupboard in the café when he was looking for somewhere to plug in his iPad. Saw what happened yesterday. Saw what happened to the man who tried to tell her he was her father.

He screws up his eyes. Remembers the man in the raincoat, poking around outside the café. Ruby had seen him on her phone on her camera and had told him, crossly, to get in the car. They'd driven straight to her place on Wincolmlee and got right in the man's face. He'd asked him who he was and what he wanted. He stood silently for what seemed like forever. Eventually, he told her he needed to talk to her. That he had things he needed to say. So she'd led him inside and left Aramis in the car. He'd had nothing to play with. No tablet. He wondered if she might lend him her phone, the way she sometimes did when he was getting bored in the back seat and she couldn't be bothered to talk to him any more. He'd gone into the café and couldn't see her. Gone up the stairs, in case they were in the room where the meetings used to take place.

He'd walked in just as the old man fell to his knees, hands at his neck as if throttling himself, blood spraying between his fingers.

It was Roscoe who noticed him first. Roscoe who nudged Ruby and told her to look at the little boy, piss-legged, open-mouthed, screaming mutely in the doorway. Roscoe who took over. Roscoe who shut him in the little closet. He watched him through the keyhole, like somebody in a story. Saw him strip the dead man. Re-dress him. Saw him take his possessions from his pocket and stuff them in his bag. Ruby had just sat there, rocking back and forth, blood on her hands. Roscoe kept stopping what he was doing to stroke her. To kiss her. To tell her she did the right thing.

'Please, he's shivering!'

'I said no.'

Aramis feels a little sick. He hasn't had very much to eat. Roscoe was still being nice to him when they left the café. Apologizing for being rough with him, telling him this was all going to be OK – that he was taking him somewhere safe until they could figure out what to do. Mummy would be joining them, he said, and it had taken Aramis to realize who he'd meant. He's never called Ruby 'Mummy'. Never will. She's Dad's girlfriend and she can be funny sometimes but she's mean to him when Dad isn't there and he doesn't think she really likes him. Sometimes he feels like he's just a sort of talking doll for her as she tries to set up a life that she likes better than the one she's got. He's not sure Dad sees it.

There's a clank from somewhere outside the little chamber; the sound of something sloshing into water. He hears the nice lady suck in a gasp of breath.

'Move and I'll hit you again. You understand? Make a sound and I'll put this through your fucking windpipe.'

Aramis wonders if Dad's here. He wonders what he'll say to him. What he'll do to Roscoe, for bringing him here, to this stinking, scary place. For shoving him and pushing him and getting rough with him when he tried to get out of the car. He'd been scared, that was all. There were birds screaming and waves smashing down on the beach and Roscoe was going mad, shouting and screaming and looking in the back of the pick-up over and over, his eyes frothing like they were spitty lips.

From outside, a low voice. It's gentle. Scottish-sounding.

'My name's Aector. If there's anybody in there, I want you to know, I don't mean anybody any harm. I just want to talk. I'm not armed.'

The nice lady can't help herself. She shouts his name, wild, head thrown back like a wolf howling at the moon. Aramis covers his ears. Screws up his eyes. He doesn't want to see.

Even with his hands over his ears, Aramis hears the door bursting open. Hears the muffled shouts and the thuds and the bangs. He feels a vibration in the wall behind him. Feels brick dust pitter-patter down his neck. There's a cry from the nice lady. Another sudden thud.

Then there's just silence.

THIRTY-FIVE

'It's OK, Aramis. I've got you. Nobody's going to hurt you. It's OK.'

McAvoy's panting, but he does his damnedest to keep his voice gentle. He licks his lip. Tastes blood. Spits, discreetly, into the black water.

'I've got a pulse. I think she's alive. Aector, you do this, I'll talk to the boy.'

McAvoy staggers back, bumping his head on something hard and metallic. He reaches up and grabs the torch that hangs from a hook in the ceiling. Points it into the darkness. Thinks of Blitz lights over London. Surveys the wreckage. Lets the light linger on Gemma Tang as she helps put her friend into a sitting position, smearing the blood from her cheek. She's weeping, but she's not letting it stop her.

He swings the light back to Dr Durrant. He's starfished on the bare floor: Vitruvian Man. He's bleeding from the nose. He'd come at McAvoy like something from an action movie, all kicks and twists and Ultimate Fighter take downs. McAvoy had been forced to hit him harder than he wanted to.

'Jesus, Aector . . .'

Gemma is at his side, looking at his hand. He notices how badly he's bleeding. Rummages in a pocket for a handkerchief and almost drops the phone.

'Butterfingers,' he says, automatically.

Gemma squats down in front of Aramis. Gently, she helps him uncover his eyes.

McAvoy, in exchange, crosses to where Halle is propped up against the brick. He confirms her pulse, pumping faintly below the skin at her neck.

'If you carry Halle, I'm sure Aramis and I can make it out behind you . . .'

McAvoy looks back at the outline of Dr Munroe Durrant. He'd like to leave him there. Knows that he won't.

There's a sudden gasp from the doorway, an intake of breath that seems to suck the air from the room.

McAvoy turns, sharply. Sees the outline. Ruby. Here, in the place where her real father carved bits off the man who raised her; the man who corrupted her; who taught her how to stalk, to capture and to kill. And she, his willing apprentice. Ruby, here with the man who poked around inside Parfitt's head and pulled out confessions he'd sought to conceal. Here with Dr Munroe Durrant, who dosed Parfitt with drugs and made him spill his guts about everything that happened down in the dark with the creature called Virgil. He'd got more than he bargained for. Parfitt had told him about his accomplice; about the girl who helped him doctor the drinks and arrange the girls and take the photographs of their grotesquely arranged bodies as they slept. Ruby, who Parfitt never touched – not because he was afraid she would tell, but because as soon as he'd looked in her eyes he'd known she had a taste for blood stronger than his own. Ruby, here with Dr Durrant. The man who befriended her. Joined her little therapy group. Seduced her. Raped her fucking brain. Who said he knew what she was and would help her slay her demons. He could rewire her, he said. Could make her well. Could let her feel safe to be around people. He had a new technique, he said. He could take her into the abyss, and whatever came back, they could mould it into a person together. She'd let him in. Fallen for him. Given herself to him. And now he was unconscious, on his back, in the dark. And Mem was going to kill them both.

McAvoy sees her take it all in. Watches as she falls to her knees. He can't help himself. He's at her side in two strides, whipping

off his bloodied, muddied coat and wrapping it around her. She sobs
against him.

'I didn't know,' she whispers. 'I didn't know. . .'

In McAvoy's mind, Pharaoh's voice.

Oh yes you fucking did.

THIRTY-SIX

Twenty-seven hours later . . .

Pharaoh's using every ounce of will to stop herself from
shaking. She feels her body trying to tremble, the adrenaline
leaving her system; that familiar sick sensation climbing up
her throat. She refuses to permit it. This is what it's all been for.
This is the moment when she proves who she is, and why she came
back. She takes a swig of black coffee. Tastes the burn of Scotch.

'You're ready?'

Pharaoh glances at her reflection. McAvoy's standing in the
doorway of the ladies' toilets, red-faced and awkward. He's got a
fat lip and a bandage on his hand and looks ready for whatever she
wants from him. He always does, poor sod. Always looks like a
boy scout eager for a chance to earn a new badge.

'As I'll ever be,' she says, opening her mouth and checking the
line of her lipstick. She's changed into a simple white blouse and
a navy suit. Her biker jacket is crumpled on the floor at her feet.
Her biker boots are sitting on the sink. Every time she looks at
them she feels the maddening urge to giggle, imagining coils of
smoke emerging from the tops, as if the owner has exploded,
cartoon-like.

'You knew, I take it,' says McAvoy, with the closest he ever gets
to reproach marbling his voice. 'Had your suspicions, at least.'

'I knew she had a taste for it,' she says, holding his reflection in
the mirror. 'Knew she helped Daddy. It took me a while to flip the
script – to wonder whether, maybe, Daddy helped her.'

'She'd been through hell before she was placed with him,' says
McAvoy, quietly. 'Her sister too.'

'And Parfitt saw that in her. Groomed her. Got himself an apprentice.'

'Do you think she stopped? Or has she been hurting people all this time?'

Pharaoh sighs. Turns around and leans against the sink. 'I think it would have started again as soon as Daddy came home.'

'And Dr Durrant?'

Pharaoh disentangles her hair from her earrings. Rummages in her bag and finds her cigarettes and an empty plastic bottle. Lights up, and blows the smoke, purse-lipped, into the receptacle. It swirls and settles. 'There's a perfect example of an arrogant sod biting off more than he can chew. The second he heard about Virgil – about this man who could drug his victims and convince them to repent – it chimed with his own pet project. Chimed with what he'd been secretly getting obsessed with – the idea of rewiring monsters, of being the man who could cure sex offenders. A pipe dream, you know that. But then John Dennic was posted to the wing. Quiet John Dennic, who everybody liked and who knew so much about plants and potions. I doubt they started them off on Ibogaine. Probably worked up to it. Treated the sex offenders at Ovenden worse than lab rats. Forced them to face not just their crimes, but to relive the trauma that twisted them in the first place. Three suicides, since.' She shakes her head. 'Dennic went to prison because he hadn't finished with Parfitt. Had himself bumped around the prison system until their paths finally crossed. And slowly, he started to finish what he started. Dosed him, until he went back to that place below the ground – the place I saved him from. He confessed to things even we didn't know about. And eventually, he admitted what Ruby had done. How excited she'd got the first time they decided to do it for real.'

McAvoy closes his eyes. Looks down at the floor.

'Dennic has been using his time on day release to visit the families of people hurt by Parfitt and his ilk. Criss-crossing the country best he could. A leap of faith, every time. Paulene phoned. Told me as much. A quiet man had come to her door. Told her he knew where Carmel's body was. He could tell her, but if she told the police, the man who was bringing peace to people like her would have to stop his work. He'd have to stop punishing paedophiles and sex offenders. She needed answers more than she needed to do what was right. He told her what Parfitt had confessed. There's nothing left of Carmel to find. Kaylani neither. Parfitt saw to that. Oil drum and a brazier.'

McAvoy rubs his hand across his mouth. 'So how did Dr Durrant end up running a talking therapy group in Wincolmlee?'

Pharaoh gives a tired smile. 'He's had the sense to be honest. When the authorities at Ovenden found out what he'd been up to with the SOTP group, they hushed it up and let him leave. He went straight into business with Dick Beresford. Big plans, styling himself as the man who could cure monsters. Jesus, that phrase disgusts me. But it was Dennic who'd been in charge of the doses. Dennic who helped steer their way through the minds of all these damaged people. He couldn't do it without Dennic. And at some point, he realized that Dennic was Virgil.'

'Did he know he was her father?'

Pharaoh gives him a hard stare. 'That depends on what you believe about instinct. About primal energies. About recognizing vibrations. But he knew what he was. Left the girls' mother with nothing because he knew his own nature. Went to the four corners of the earth looking for ways to stop himself being what he was. I think he drove himself insane along the way. Every drug, every type of therapy, every act of self-abuse. In the end, all he could do was begin his campaign of atonement. Castrated himself. Stole another man's life and came home. Started targeting bad, bad people. Showing them what awaited if they didn't change their ways. With Parfitt it was more personal.'

'And he told her? Before he was stabbed – he told her who he was.'

'She knew as soon as she looked at him. Remembers his eyes from when she wasn't much more than a toddler. It was instinct, I think. All those feelings just became one moment of violence.'

'I presume Dr Durrant is claiming he did it?'

'Oh yes,' smiles Pharaoh. 'He didn't, though. He may have taken over and told her that he'd take care of everything – that all she needed to do was pretend everything was normal and he'd find a way to make it all right. Even told her to make sure I saw her at the Hot House. He'd take care of everything. God knows if she believed him. They were in a fantasy-land, playing make-believe. Aramis saw all of it. I think they might have talked themselves into killing him, given time. You saved the boy's life. Gemma and Halle's too.'

McAvoy looks down at the floor. 'It's all just so ugly.'

Pharaoh doesn't speak until he raises his head and meets her gaze. 'The lies we tell ourselves, Aector – the narratives we come up with to make ourselves feel better . . . look at Dennic, or whoever he turns out to be. He rejects his kids because he knows he's got a predilection for young girls. Finds a way to come back as a hero – to punish those like himself. Even has himself sent to jail so he can carry on with his mission – all the theatricality, the sounds and smells and the circles of hell – the desperate urge to sign his work, to leave little hints of who he was and what he was . . . just another man getting his kicks.'

'Richard Beresford,' says McAvoy, mobbing to her side. 'Ben says he dropped dead mid-interview.'

'He knew what was coming, would be my guess,' sighs Pharaoh, puffing another lungful of smoke into the plastic bottle. 'Perhaps Dennic had given him a get-out if anybody ever came asking. Dr Vergette's very excited about the tox reports.'

Pharaoh watches him digest it all. She knows he has more questions. Knows he won't ask them, and loves him for it. She's told so many lies. Can't face telling any more.

There's a knock at the door. DC Sophie Kirkland pokes her head around the door. Gives a wide-eyed smile as she sees McAvoy and Pharaoh, her head on his shoulder, his hand patting her back.

'Press are ready, Boss. Lots of excitement.'

'And Gemma gets first question. You tell the press office that, or I'll tell them in a way they won't like.'

'Received and understood, Boss. She's operating on Red Bull and Monster Munch so I reckon she'll come up with a goodie. Halle's going to be grand, apparently, though there'll be scarring. I shudder to think how this will all play out in the documentary.'

Pharaoh gives McAvoy a tired smile. Lets Kirkland leave before she speaks. 'I don't want to do this any more, Aector. None of it.'

McAvoy holds her hand. Squeezes it. 'You're too good at it to stop. And if not you, whom?'

Pharaoh gives a giggle and immediately bites it back. She feels her eyes start to fill with tears and physically forces herself not to be such a big girl's blouse. 'You don't need to stay for the press conference. Get on home. She'll be waiting.'

For a moment, he seems about to protest. Then he squeezes her forearm. Whispers in her ear. Pharaoh feels his beard tickle her cheek. Fights down her every impulse. Lets him walk away.

She pictures him walking in his own front door. Sees Roisin waiting, open arms, soul glowing like fire. Sees his kids wrapping their arms and legs around him, making him blush, making him laugh, telling him they're proud of him and fighting among themselves who can take care of him the best. Can see him blushing. Fighting back tears. Can see him sitting awake in the dark, letting his tears flow in silence so he doesn't upset the people who need him to be strong.

She closes her eyes. Pictures her own empty flat. The empty bottles. The full ashtray.

She opens the bottle of smoke. Lets it rise and coil and wriggle, wraith-like, towards the ceiling.

For a moment, she's back in that place. She's watching John Dennic carve pieces of Decland Parfitt. It had been instinct alone that made her stop him. Given time, she'd have let Dennic finish his work. But she'd seen a person in distress and had reacted like a good person should. It had taken thirteen years to make amends.

She opens the door to the bathroom. There are half a dozen police officers waiting – a haphazard guard of honour. Ben Neilsen is among them. He can't meet her gaze.

This is what it's for, she tells herself. *This is why you do what you do.*

In her bra, her phone rings. It's Sophia. She glances up at the clock on the wall. Decides she's earned this.

'Tell them I'll be there when I'm ready,' she snaps. Answers the call, and looks into the smiling, gummy face of her granddaughter. Melts a little. Heads back into the bathroom, pulling silly faces. For a moment, she knows what's important. Knows how to keep going. Knows who to be.

'Who's Scary Granny's little treasure . . .?'

EPILOGUE

Evidence log HP000036

S i vales bene est, ego valeo.
I do not permit myself to pause in the composition of this note. If I stop, I think perhaps I shall die. I have read that sharks perish when they stop swimming. So I shall be like a shark. I shall flick my tail. I shall bare my teeth. I shall let you stare into my ink-black eyes.

There will be questions, when all is said and done. I do not believe I am so very many steps ahead as I had hoped. I am not suspected directly, but I fear that something of my nature has bled out into the air around me. Those with a sensitivity for such things would detect the wrong hue to my aura.

Do you know of Kintsugi? It is the Japanese art of repairing broken things. Kintsugi rejoices in the break: honoring the story of the object, its ruin and repair. Mistakes and accidents, perhaps, are simply a part of the experience of living. Rather than trying to restore a broken object to its original glory, Kintsugi focuses on creating a newly imagined, distinctive vessel. So does Virgil. So do I.

I ramble. Forgive me.

There will be talk of an entity known as Virgil. It is a name whispered among those whose souls hide terrible secrets. Virgil is whom the malefactors fear. He is tutor and guide to those whose desires offend decency. He is the figure who shows what lies beyond.

Virgil has come for many souls, child. Countless deviants; wave upon wave of twisted wraiths and shades; all have woken at the very mouth of Hell. I have ushered them into chasm and circle of malignancy. Strange languages, and frightful forms of speech, words caused by pain, accents of anger, voices both loud and faint, and smiting hands withal, a mighty tumult made, which sweeps around forever in that timelessly dark air, as sand is wont, whene'er a whirlwind blows.

Those who have seen, have been forever changed. Few have sinned again. Of those who broke their covenant with righteousness, the punishment has been swift. Their journey to an afterlife of agony and suffering has been hastened. In this, I took only small pleasure.

I am sick with it, child. I feel saturated: black-biled and rancid. Darkness swims within me, sloshing from my lips, my eyes and ears, my nostrils. I am brined in their salt-tear depravity. I repel myself. Revolt myself. And yet, there is pride, child. A sense of satisfaction. Of a job well done.

Declan Parfitt took four children as they slept. They were dead when he enacted the worst of his fantasies. I do not know if that brings you peace. It is scant comfort to me. Their terror was fleeting. Their death was not his primary purpose. Nor was his confession the reason for my journey through the circles of Hell. The confession was proffered under duress, but I saw truth in what remained of his eyes. The ledger of his sins is written in red. It reads:

Carmel Barry.

Kaylani Shah.

Aisha Hart.

Dora Creighton.

I hope it brings you peace to know that Parfitt, like so many others, has glimpsed what awaits him in eternity. He has the brand of Hades upon his flesh. Should he sin again, it is in the knowledge that he damns himself. Damns himself as never before.

There are bad people in this world, child. I count myself among them. But the gates to Heaven are barred to none. Even the worst sinner can be redeemed.

Open your heart to me, child. I shall be your guide and you my pilgrim. And together we shall journey into a place beyond endurance. And I will hold your heart in my palm as you look upon your misdeeds, and weep.

You are not too far down this path, child. I have been a worse man than you.

And if you will not . . . seek me when you wake. I shall be thy guide, and lead thee hence through an eternal place, where thou shalt hear the shrieks of hopelessness of those tormented spirits of old times, each one of whom bewails the second death; then those shalt thou behold who, though in fire, contented are, because they hope to come, whene'er it be, unto the blessed folk; to whom, thereafter, if thou wouldst ascend, there'll be for that a worthier soul than I.

Ever,
XX